GODS AND HEROES

CIRCLE OF SHADOWS

GODS AND HEROES BOOK 3: CIRCLE OF SHADOWS

Hardcover Edition

ISBN: 978-0-6484294-5-6

Brendan is not currently represented by any publishers or literary agents. He can be contacted at:
enquiries@brendanwrightauthor.com

Connect with Brendan:
Instagram: @brendanwrightauthor
Facebook: /brendanwrightauthor
Website: brendanwrightauthor.com

Cover art by Brendan Wright
Map illustrated by Renflowergrapx via Fiverr

Acknowledgements

I would firstly like to thank my amazing supporters on Patreon; Ali Styles, Dominic Riemenschneider, Toby Van der Zwart, and Damien Wright. You've been supporting me for a while now and I cannot thank you enough. It truly means the world to me. I would also like to thank the artists who created the cover art and maps of the Gods and Heroes series, Ren and Rebeca. You helped turn Pandeia into a reality for me and my books would be nowhere near as impressive without you! I'd also like to thank my mother and step-father for continuing to support me and for believing in my writing. And of course, my brother and sister-in-law, Damien and Emily, for making sure my books are as good as they can be before they go out into the world.

THEARA
THEARA
OROMUS
OLYMUS
OMAS
TARSIUS
Sitharkos
AKRILLUS
AROS
ANTEIOS
DYMEA
MARA
AMASEIA
AETHOS

ERMOOR

ERMOOR

SHANAKEN

SARNIA

AZAR

OMATUS

CARMERTH

TARSIUM

N

PANDEIA

Prologue

1773

Amalus was dead. Zanela's tears flowed down her cheeks, down her neck, first warm and then cold. The forest inside the Eternal Mountain was silent, as though life itself mourned for the fallen God. Zanela sat on the soft grass. She laid her hand on Amalus' body. Though an eternity had passed as she was shown the universe and beyond, only moments ago the God had been alive. She remembered feeling absolutely terrified by the gigantic snake, though now she couldn't think why. All she felt, staring at its corpse, was love and sadness.

Magic flowed through her mortal body. She felt it, a deep and complex well of energy. She had become the new God of Life and Shadow, of that she was certain. She felt almost all of the life on Pandeia, connected in some subtle way to her. A slight twinge of emotional connection reached her from each living creature. The animals and plants simply radiated survival, in whatever instinctive form that took; killing, eating, mating, fleeing. They were all growing and changing, and she felt it all.

The people were another matter. Zanela felt all of their emotional energy at the same time, in one writhing mass of unstoppable feeling. There was so much hate. So much love. So many powerful emotions at the same time. It was more complex than she ever would have realised. As well as acquiring the magic of a God, her mind had changed too. She understood Pandeia, all of Pandeia. Everything beyond it. Much was still a mystery, but her mind could see things now that would have sent mortals insane.

She knew two things now from her visions, the last gift of a dying God; firstly, there was a war brewing between the Gods themselves... and secondly, they could be killed. Far from being a relief, however, the knowledge terrified her in a deep, indefinable way. She knew she was Amalus. She didn't want to be a God, but what she wanted didn't matter anymore. Zanela had stopped existing; there was only the Eternal Mountain, and the life she felt flowing through Pandeia.

As Amalus had shown her, she could release her spirit at will and see anything, anywhere. But she could no longer interact with the world physically. She'd never before been so free and so trapped at the same time. Many things were clear now, where once there had been questions. But much was still unknown.

She spent a lot of her time in spirit form, exploring the universe and learning as much as possible. Learning about herself, her new self, was the most difficult. But she was learning. And she was learning about the others, too.

There are five. Five Gods. They are all awake again. And the war is coming.

Zeera

1745

Darkness surrounded her. The cave was vast, stretching in every direction, swallowed by the deep black that could only be found underwater. Zeera hovered in front of the sealed box in the centre of the cave, gently waving her hands and feet so she wouldn't drift away. It was held in place by eight thick chains, one attached to each corner, stretching off into the distance. She liked being in the chamber of Asheilos; the water-filled cave looked like all the others underneath Tarsium, but no other cave in Pandeia felt like it. Guards, stationed at every entrance into the chamber, continued their watch as they hung suspended in the water, staring out into the tunnels that connected every cave underneath Tarsium.

Zeera visited the chamber most days, staring at the ancient box and wishing she would be chosen. Dozens of other Tarsi visited too, but Zeera was one of the few who could get this close without a guard escorting her. She placed her hand on the sealed box, praying to Asheilos that she might be the one. It wasn't large, only just big enough to fit the book it contained; but the power it held would change the world. Her gills, a well-kept secret of the Tarsi, drew in the cave's water as she prayed. The water had a different quality; like the difference between breathing the air of a city and the air of a quiet forest.

It was only a matter of time before Tarsium's Hero was chosen. Sithares was captured and shut away thousands of years ago, and the magic that held it at bay wasn't permanent. Being chosen was once every Tarsi's dream; to be a Hero of the Gods. But Water Magic, and the Gods, were ancient history, and most barely worshipped Asheilos any more. Besides, out of all the Tarsi, only members of the Circle of Shadows really had any chance of being chosen. Zeera devoted herself to Asheilos ever since she was a child, over a hundred years ago. She studied magic, prayed every day, and joined the Circle as soon as she was old enough.

There was no way of knowing when or even if the Gods would awaken ever again, but Zeera felt something deep within herself; a strange certainty that she was important. She was meant for more than information gathering for the Circle. Every time she visited the box underneath the Circle headquarters in Azar, the feeling grew stronger. She felt Asheilos within the sealed box; a deep sense of power, calm but utterly immense. Like the ocean itself. Tarsi hadn't seen real magic for a long time, but remnants remained. Small spells that one could cast by tracing ancient symbols, nothing like the magic that filled the world when the Gods were active. Zeera longed for Water Magic to return to Tarsium.

A light touch to her shoulder ripped her from her wandering thoughts, and she jumped. Talas smiled, gentle and sad but full of love. She smiled back, and he gestured back to the Circle's headquarters. Pulling herself away, Zeera swam with him back down the tunnels and up to the surface.

"We've been given a mission," Talas said after they emerged from the water, "the Jewel was seen in Omas."

For a moment, all she could do was stare at her husband. He said it casually, but the Jewel of Tarsium was one of its most prized and important artefacts. He knew exactly how important the mission was for both of them.

"When was it last seen?"

"A few days ago, in Aros."

She smiled, thinking about the dangerous, rocky mountain city.

"Well, you did say you wanted a vacation in the mountains."

Talas laughed, shaking his head and walking into the corridor towards the headquarters proper.

"Not exactly what I had in mind, dear."

Zeera caught up, and they headed for the meeting room together. Each mission for the Circle was carefully planned beforehand, and most were completed by solo agents. Sending Talas and Zeera together was a sign of just how important the mission was. Tarra waited for them in the meeting room, and started talking before they'd even reached her.

"Zeera, Talas. A smuggler was seen with the Jewel two days ago. They're trying to sell it, and as you can imagine, there is a lot of interest. They're being very careful to avoid the notice of any Tarsi, but luckily we had an agent there on an unrelated mission who saw it."

Zeera nodded, and she saw Talas nod from the corner of her eye. They'd never been on a mission together, but in their every day life they were perfectly in sync.

"The smuggler is Omati, fairly tall but slim, and has been staying at an inn called the Elos. That's all the information we have, but you need to move quickly in case the Jewel is sold."

Tarra gestured to the two travel bags at her feet.

"These have been prepared for you, they should contain everything you need. Good luck, and may Asheilos guide you."

The journey to Aros took just over a month, but was surprisingly pleasant. Talas and Zeera took a barge from the port in Azar across the ocean and all the way down the Alpheus. Farming villages dotted the riverside on the north bank, and forested mountains covered the south. The waters of the Alpheus were calm, the river wider than any other in Pandeia, and Zeera simply enjoyed the time with her husband.

At the end of the Alpheus was a small port, with an inn, a tavern, and a stable. Zeera and Talas paid for a camel-drawn cart to take them to the base of the mountains near Aros. Though expensive, it was fast and easy, and they had the cart to themselves but for the driver. Already in disguise as Omati nobles, they talked of Aros and the beautiful views to be found there. They never spoke of their mission within earshot of another person, no matter who it was; a Tarsi knew better than anyone that there were spies everywhere. They were dropped off at another tiny village at the base of the mountains, and warned about Thearan tribes.

"Not just in the desert proper," their driver said, "there's tribes in the mountains, too."

From the village, they trekked up into the mountains alone; there was a marked path, but no guides sold their services to help travellers to Aros. Despite knowing a lot about the mountain city, Zeera hadn't been there, and didn't know the path well enough to know what to expect. They came across no other travellers, and thankfully no Thearan tribes, and after a few days of hiking through the mountains, they arrived at Aros.

Zailen

1774

Elana was a legend. Zailen watched her train a handful of times, and he'd been shocked by her skill. And then she was killed. By a traitor, and a fire worshipper. Word spread through Shanaken soon after the traitor returned and was buried alive by the *Duulshen*. Zailen, who'd been *Kaizeluun* for five years by then, was summoned a few days later.

"Zailen, do you know why you have been summoned?" One of the elders said.

"No, great *Duulshen*, I'm afraid I don't."

"Elana fulfilled a mission for Shanaken before she died. She returned with information about Ermoor. Her mission was a great success, but we have much more to do. You must take her place, and travel to Ermoor."

It was more of an honour than he deserved, far more. He had no idea why they summoned him, but to go on such an important mission for the *Duulshen* was something he couldn't have expected. Zailen completed missions for them all the time, but none on the same level as Elana herself.

"There is a network of tunnels underneath Ermoor, where thousands of slaves are forced to work to provide power for the city. Elana showed them the world above, but they were recaptured shortly after."

Zailen listened, his eyes wide. He couldn't hide his shock and excitement at hearing details of Elana's mission to Ermoor.

"You are to teach these slaves more about the world outside of Ermoor. Train them, and provide them with weapons, and they will rise up from below to fight against their oppressors."

Zailen's lungs stopped pulling in air for a moment. He didn't know what Ermoor looked like, but his mind was hard at work imagining a city being overrun by slaves, taking over and being free. *Only if I succeed.* It was a monumental task, one he wasn't sure he could even accomplish.

"Yes, great *Duulshen*. When must I leave?"

"Immediately."

Elana's mission was barely a year ago now. In that time, the most exciting missions Zailen had been on were to bring top secret messages to and from a mysterious Tarsi contact. He didn't know what the messages said, but the missions still felt important to him. He left the chamber of the *Duulshen* feeling a huge weight on his shoulders. Knowing he was now being sent on a mission similar to what Elana had done was unbelievable. It was like being a part of the old war between Ermoor and Shanaken; this was a mission important enough that he might be remembered for it.

"Ermoor? You're going to Ermoor?"

Laila couldn't keep the excitement out of her voice. She'd been Zailen's best friend for years, and she idolised Elana just as much as he did.

"Yeah! The *Duulshen* just told me."

"No way! You'll be doing the same thing Elana did... Do you think you'll meet any of the people she met while she was there?"

It hadn't occurred to him, but the thought made him strangely dizzy.

"Maybe, I guess it could happen. It's not like I'll be out there making friends, you know."

She rolled her eyes and punched his arm.

"Come on, you know what I mean."

"Sure. Just don't expect me to come back with stories about how I'm friends with friends of Elana's."

Laila put her hand gently on the place she punched a few seconds earlier.

"No, well... Zailen, you will come back, won't you?"

"Of course I will!"

Her eyes lowered, her lip trembling slightly.

"She almost didn't."

"Elana?"

"Yeah. I saw her when she first got back, you know. I was in one of the bed chambers, and she walked in there looking like a corpse. I've never seen anyone look like that before."

Zailen stopped, his skin cold. He'd been too excited to be scared before, but the idea that Elana barely survived terrified him. She was the best of all of the *Kaizeluun*. Still, he couldn't let Laila wallow in fear.

"Wow Laila, thanks for the inspiring speech. Now I'm really prepared."

A tiny giggle escaped her, but he could see the promise of tears welling in the corners of her eyes.

"I'll be fine, Laila," he said, drawing her into a tight embrace, "I promise."

The Shenza shared almost everything; food, living space, and resources were controlled by the *Duulshen* and shared equally between all the people of Shanaken. When a *Kaizeluun* was sent on a mission, they were allowed whatever provisions they might need for the journey. Zailen packed some potions, some food, and some coin into a knapsack and threw it over his shoulder. His *Kaizuun*, perhaps the only possession that belonged only to him, hung at his belt.

He would be taking the same steps to get to Ermoor that Elana took before him; reliving the most famous mission of his biggest hero. Before he left for Tarsium, he hugged his parents and friends goodbye. On one of the many training platforms scattered through the forest canopy, he performed one final *Zuunshai*. Laila sat on the edge of the platform, looking out at the trees while he danced with his blade. When he was done, she hugged him, and made him promise again that he would come back.

Zeera

1745

Aros was built into the peak of a particularly tall mountain and connected by bridges to two other smaller mountains, each with similar structures. The path that led from the Omasi desert went straight to the main gates of the smallest mountain. The smallest of the three mountains was mostly a military barracks and guard post; there were no homes or shops there, and only one inn. Zeera and Talas passed through the military post without much hassle, having their bags checked and being herded through the few narrow streets as quickly as possible. The soldiers of Aros were efficient and serious, taking no chances and watching the path constantly for threats.

All three mountains were connected to each other, but the largest was the main city, and where the vast majority of the homes and inns were located. Zeera and Talas crossed the bridge into the mountain and looked for a cheap inn. Half of the city was inside the mountain itself, fire-lit tunnels connecting buildings both inside and on the surface. After an hour or so walking around, Zeera spotted a small inn called the Acus, and they entered together.

"Greetings," the Omasi behind the counter said, "a room for two?"

"Yes," Zeera turned to Talas, "what do you think, dear? Four nights? Five?"

"Better make it five, just in case," Talas said to the man.

"Of course. Three coppers per night makes it fifteen."

Zeera didn't know or care if haggling was accepted in Aros; the price was easily affordable, so they paid. The room was small, but clean and cosy, and Zeera stayed behind to rest a while as Talas went to explore a little more. By the time he returned, she'd fallen asleep, and the door opening jolted her awake.

"I haven't found him yet," Talas said, "but I found the inn where he's staying."

"That's perfect," Zeera said, "well done. Any trace of an underground market for smuggled goods?"

"Whispers. Nothing worth looking into just yet; better to follow the smuggler."

Zeera left shortly after, following Talas' directions to the Elos; it was Talas' turn to rest while she gathered more information. They wouldn't need both of them until it was time to act. As she approached the inn, she shifted into another body; still Omati, but with noticeably different features. Disguise spells were helpful. Tarsi could look like anyone, at any time. As well as disguise magic, however, the Tarsi could also naturally shift their form to mimic others; one of their best kept secrets. But without a specific spell, they could only take generic forms. She strolled slowly around the building, circling up the mountain and back down again. Most of the windows were closed, but she peered into any that weren't; no trace of the man.

Settling on a rooftop above the inn with a good view of the entrance, Zeera watched a while. The smuggler didn't show up, but the Tarsi were nothing if not patient. She traced a disguise spell onto her palm, and when it took effect she threw the disguise over herself; she would look like a pile of rocks to anyone who glanced up at the rooftop. Then she settled in, and waited.

In the hours just before dawn, the Omati smuggler appeared at the bottom of the street, hiking up towards the inn. Zeera dissolved the disguise spell and climbed down into the street. When he entered the inn, Zeera sprinted across the street and entered after him, as silently and casually as she could. She overtook him, rushing past him up the stairs towards the rooms. Near the top of the stairs, she shifted into an exotic Shenza female form, and began walking slowly back down. When they crossed paths, she glanced at him and smiled. He smiled back, and they stared at each other as they passed. She turned back to face down the stairs, still walking slowly, and then felt his hand gently grasp her shoulder.

"Hello," he said, "I'm Antonis. You don't seem to be in a rush; I don't suppose you'd like to watch the sun rise with me?"

"I-yes, I'd like that," she said, trying to act flustered and shy.

He took her hand and they walked up towards the roof. They stopped partway up the stairs, and he turned to her again.

"I'm sorry, I just need to drop something off in my room first, do you mind?"

She shook her head and he dashed to the door marked 32. *Too easy,* she thought. When he came out again, they walked together in comfortable silence, and he opened the door to the roof for her. Under her cloak, her dagger sat sheathed against her lower back. She touched the hilt lightly as she walked onto the rooftop. He strolled to the roof's edge, staring up at the twilit sky. The stars had disappeared, and the black was gradually fading into blue already. On the horizon, a cascade of vibrant pink, red and orange slowly erupted from beyond the Omasi desert. Despite her present company, and the situation, watching the sun rise over the desert took her breath away. The districts of Tarsium were low to the ground, and full of buildings nestled against each other; but here there was a clear view as the sun slowly crept into the sky.

For a brief moment, she forgot the mission. Heat waves swept over the desert far below them, and the sky around the sun became an explosion of colour. A vibrant blue finally settled over their heads, and the desert appeared in full. Sand dunes rippled in the morning breeze, like an immense grey ocean before her, and mountains stood tall in the distance, shimmering behind the desert's heat waves. She thought she could just make out Omatus to the east, but it was too far off to be sure. They stood together a while longer, simply staring, until he took her hand.

"Isn't it beautiful?" he said, holding her eyes with his own, "I always come up here when I visit Aros, the view is too grand to miss."

"It is beautiful. How often are you here?"

"At least once a month. This inn is expensive, but the view makes it worth any price. As well as the company." he winked at her, and it took all of her effort not to laugh.

"You're too kind," she said, "but I don't see how anyone could afford to stay at a place like this so often. I've never been here before, but if I ever come back, it would have to be to a cheaper inn."

He scoffed and waved a hand, smiling. She looked at him, keeping her eyes wide and her mouth slightly open; men loved to feel superior, and it was easy to make them think they were impressive. If they had money, all they wanted was for everyone to know it. If they had a great skill, all they wanted was an audience to watch them prove it. She knew he was so eager to impress her that the thought she was manipulating him wouldn't enter his mind.

"When you have the gold I do, you can choose whatever inn you like. You know, you could always stay with me next time you're here."

He winked again, and Zeera covered her mouth with her hand, trying to appear shy again while stifling the laugh bubbling beneath the surface.

"But I don't even know you!"

"Well how about we get to know each other then?"

It was too early in the mission for her to attempt to steal the Jewel; she had no idea how dangerous he was or if he had other people staying with him. The information they'd received from Tarra was minimal and gave them almost nothing to work with; so Zeera and Talas needed to wait and watch until they were sure they could steal the Jewel.

"I'm-I don't know about that," she said, turning for the door, "I really should be going now."

Stepping in front of her, he grabbed her shoulder, hard this time. A deadly spark lit up deep within his eyes, and there was no trace of the gracious, wealthy traveller in the look he gave her.

"Come to my room," he said, "I'd like to get to know you."

A bird called somewhere above the city, and Zeera's thudding heart quieted almost immediately; she knew that call. She stopped struggling and followed the smuggler, trying to ready herself for the violence to come.

"I think you'll enjoy getting to know me," the smuggler said as he dragged her down the stairs towards his room, "and my friends."

Zailen

1774

A Tarsi woman sat in front of him, unblinking and unreadable. He recognised her, or at least he thought he did; Tarsi all looked too similar for him to tell for sure. But she looked like one of the contacts he'd been giving messages to for the *Duulshen*. Her name was Zeera. They sat facing each other in a pub in Azar. Zailen didn't drink much, but the woman ordered a shiny bright blue drink for him, and it tasted nothing like the eye-watering rice wine in Shanaken. It tasted almost like fruit juice, sweet and refreshing.

She stared at him as he sipped his drink. He coughed politely. Zailen would happily leap into battle against heavily armoured Emoori, but conversations with strangers were uncomfortable at the best of times. This wasn't even a conversation; he had no idea what to do. She ordered the same drink for herself when they'd sat down. Her glass was empty now; she simply sat and watched him. Finally, when he thought he was about to scream and run away, she spoke.

"We weren't aware of your first mission until your colleague left Ermoor. We would have helped if we'd known. I was quite sad to hear of her passing."

"You were sad? You met Elana?"

"Oh yes. I brought her back to Tarsium."

I haven't even arrived in Ermoor and I've already met someone who knew Elana, he thought, *wait until Laila hears this!* The barest hint of a smile touched the Tarsi woman's face, as though she could hear his thoughts.

"How would you have helped?"

"The Tarsi have many secrets, Zailen. I'm sure you're aware of this."

He hadn't told her his name. It must have been the *Duulshen.*

"Yes. I mean, I've heard rumours. Does that mean you'll help me?"

The *Duulshen* hadn't told him what the meeting was about. It was about the mission, but he assumed it would simply be organising his transport to Ermoor.

"Oh yes. Tarsium and Shanaken are on the same side in this war. We have to be."

War. Shanaken and Ermoor had been battling off and on for thousands of years; but he wouldn't have called it a war. And what stakes did Tarsium have in the battles of the Shenza?

Her stare somehow became even more intense. Zailen sipped his drink again, trying to look anywhere but her giant eyes and failing.

"The *Duulshen* didn't tell you. I see. They love their secrets, your elders. Even more than the Tarsi do, I think."

"The *Duulshen* tell us what we need to know."

"Of course," she said, "I meant no offence. Well, let us discuss this mission of yours then."

Zeera oversaw a huge chunk of the transport and trade between Ermoor and Tarsium. Zailen would come aboard as one of the apprentices, lay low during the trip, then bail in a small row boat and make his own way to the southern edge of the city.

Zeera helped him smuggle barrels full of weapons, books and food onto her ship, and had them stowed on the row boat. She gave him a separate bag full of dried meats and fruits for himself which would last however long he needed. The row boat had a set of wheels that could be lowered, so Zailen would be able to wheel the barrels into the city. Zeera gave him the information he needed to get to Tyra unseen.

Almost a month after leaving Tarsium, Ermoor appeared on the horizon. From afar it was beautiful. By the time the ship drew close enough for Zailen to get into the row boat and lower himself onto the ocean, night had fallen. As he rowed towards his most dangerous mission yet, Zailen suddenly felt like a fraud. *I'm nothing like Elana,* he thought, *how will I survive this?* No answer came to him, but he rowed on nonetheless.

Zeera

1745

The room was much larger than the one Zeera and Talas stayed in; there were four more Omati men waiting when she was dragged in by the smuggler.

"Well done, Antonis," one of them said, "I ain’t had a Shenza before. Livin’ in trees and all that, I thought they'd look like monkeys."

The others laughed, and Antonis threw her onto the nearest bed.

"Lucky you didn't grab one o' the ones with a sword," another man said, laughing.

Zeera sat up and stared. She took in the room as quickly as she could, and saw a small but heavily padlocked chest on the table in the corner. *There*. Distantly, she heard the bird call again, and readied a defensive spell.

"What are you doin' with your hands, monkey?"

"Yeah, there's only one thing you should be using those hands for."

Their laughter was cut short as she unleashed the magical flash, a thundering bang shaking the room at the same time. She snatched her dagger from its sheath and leapt off the bed just as one of the windows shattered. Talas shifted from the bird to his real form and rolled to his feet, drawing his own dagger too. Zeera buried her blade in the nearest man's throat, wrenching it out and kicking him away as he choked for breath. Talas hadn't quite reached his enemy's neck; his real Tarsi body was too short. They struggled, and by the time Talas managed to kill him, the remaining three had regained their sight.

Talas shifted into an Omati form, and used the smugglers' surprise and fear against them, sprinting at them before they could regroup. He shoved one of them hard enough to send them sprawling, then stabbed another in the gut. Zeera ran past him to the table, grabbed the chest, and made for the smashed window.

"Talas," she shouted as she reached the window, "I've got it, let's go!"

The Omati who'd been stabbed was doubled over on the floor, but the other two were fighting, and Talas only had a dagger. Their swords gave them far more reach, and they attacked from different directions. Zeera dropped the chest, traced the defensive spell again, and directed the blast of light and sound at the fighting men. It hit all of them, Talas included. As the Omati blinked and waved their swords in blind arcs around them, Talas lowered his dagger. Before she could do anything but scream, one of the swords swung into Talas' head. A wet crunch sounded from her husband as the blade lodged itself in his skull. The Omati men were still blinded, and though her mind was reeling, and her heart burning, she pushed herself to get out of the room.

Snatching the small but heavy chest from the floor, she shifted into a large Omati man and leapt out the window. *It's your fault,* her mind screamed at her as she ran, *it's your fault Talas is dead. He could have fought, could have won, if you hadn't blinded him*. She tried to focus on getting away, turning down alleys and into the tunnels cut into the mountain. Each time she turned into a new alley she shifted again, becoming different people every few minutes.

By the time she arrived at the inn, she was walking normally and focusing on anything but Talas. Her arm ached from carrying the chest, and she dropped it on the bed and picked the lock. The Jewel of Tarsium was bright blue, sparkling and flawless, like an entire ocean trapped in a perfect diamond. It rested in an ancient silver necklace with ornate chain links. One look and Zeera knew it was real. Relief passed through her mind, but it was brief and hollow.

Shifting back to an Omati woman's form, Zeera slipped the Jewel over her neck, making sure it was covered by her cloak. Immediately, a cold, soothing calm settled into her body. It felt the way she'd always felt hovering before the box that held Asheilos' book. She felt almost painfully aware of her entire body; felt every hair on her Omati skin, even every organ in her body working at keeping her alive. The blood flowing through her veins, pumped by her heart, spreading through her body; every inch of her form became a tuned signal in her mind.

Packing the empty chest into her bag, she threw it over her shoulder and picked up Talas' bag too. His body would be found and the smuggler's would know the Tarsi had gotten involved; but Tarsium had the Jewel back. She left Aros trying to keep her racing mind as empty as possible.

Karak

1747

He sat in a small tavern in Tarsius, the Tarsi trading settlement in Omas. It was dusty, untidy, and hot. Because Tarsius was a lot smaller than any of the three districts in Tarsium, it was even more crowded. *Kicked out of the Circle,* he thought, his mind a swirl of bitter thoughts and fury, *over some stupid misunderstanding.* He wasn't even given time to gather his things; all he had was the small pack he always carried over his shoulder, and the Tarsi cloak that had belonged to his father before him. It also meant he had almost no coin. He was exiled until he could prove he was worthy again. It was left to him to figure out what would prove his worth to the Circle, and he had no idea what that could be.

Throwing another coin on the bar, Karak ordered his fourth drink. The Omati made good wines, despite the majority of their continent being harsh desert. He drank quickly; today was a day best forgotten. After he'd spent too many coins in the tavern, he stumbled out, jostled by the crowd. He walked past a few inns, checking the prices and glancing at the coin left in his bag. *Not enough.*

Most of the streets of Tarsius contained food stalls. Some of them sold hot food, with vats of boiling oil or the fireless ovens of Shanaken built into the stall. Karak walked until he found one that sold his favourite, grilled luduk, and bought a small portion. He sat against the side of the food stall to eat. When he was done he cast a simple disguise spell, making himself look like a pile of garbage. Curling up against the warmth of the food stall, Karak fell into a restless, uncomfortable sleep.

He awoke in pain, his head pounding and his back and neck aching. The stall owner shrieked as he stood, the noise splitting his head open and forcing a groan from him.

"Do you mind?" he said, "I'm not feeling great right now."

The Shenza woman shrieked again and started yelling at him. He walked away as quickly as he could, but his hip and ankle throbbed in pain too. *Almost no coin, nowhere to live, and exiled from the Circle,* he thought, *what am I supposed to do now?* If he were still in Tarsium, there were places he could go and people he knew that would give him a job. But the Circle was adamant about his exile not just from the organisation, but from the country. Tarsius was very similar to the districts though; there would be places where people like him could pick up work.

The only problem was, he'd spent almost no time in Tarsius and had no contacts within the settlement. Taverns were always the places to go, so Karak moved from tavern to tavern, street to street, and he was already out of money. He'd spoken with countless barkeeps and travellers, none of whom had any work going. Stretching in the cold morning air, Karak walked into the next tavern. His hopes were low and his patience even lower, but he had to do something.

Inside the tavern, barely a dozen people sat around. A few low conversations were being had, the hushed voices creating a steady murmur that hissed at his pounding head. The tavern sat in an alley that branched off the main street he'd come from; a good sign. He sat at a small table meant for two and put his head in his hands. Looking for work was exhausting; looking for work with a pounding head from over drinking was torture. Looking up from his hands, he searched the room properly.

A few Thearans sat together, the shiny weapons they'd obviously just bought laying on the table. They admired each other's purchases, giddy smiles on their faces as they talked of bloodshed and murder. *Typical Thearans,* he thought. Two Tarsi discussed what sounded like a real estate purchase in Sarnia; Karak ignored them. He had no coin, let alone the kind of fortune it took to buy property in Sarnia. A small group of Omati merchants sat together in a booth. Karak couldn't quite make out what they were saying, but he knew he wouldn't find any work there either. Omati merchants were slave owners; they wouldn't pay anyone for work they could get for free.

An Omati man spoke with a cloaked, hooded figure, his face serious. A pouch of gold sat on the table next to his hand. Clearly searching for someone to hire. Karak sat upright, his headache almost forgotten. The cloaked figure intrigued Karak; what kind of work was this Omati looking for? The figure looked tall, and the cloak was mottled grey, with folded layers. Karak recognised it as a Tarsi design. The figure said something Karak couldn't hear, then left; as he moved away, Karak caught a glimpse of pale skin and bright blue eyes. The Omati man sighed, finished his drink, and was about to leave when his eyes caught Karak's.

"You look like you're looking for work, friend," the man said as he sat opposite Karak at the small table.

"Very observant," Karak said, "what sort of work are you offering?"

"Education. Training a very promising young student in Omatus."

"What are you teaching him?"

"Whatever you know well enough to teach."

Karak stared at the man, not bothering to disguise his puzzlement.

"I'm hardly a qualified teacher," he said, "and I don't know the child, or you for that matter."

"Forgive me," the man said, chuckling, "my name is Amphidas. I'm a mercenary. The boy is learning to fight, and he has a thirst for knowledge I've never seen before."

"So I would be teaching him to fight?"

"As I said, you'll be teaching him whatever you know well enough to teach. He wants to know everything, it seems. But yes, at the moment he has a particular... focus, shall we say, on combat."

"A man as well travelled as yourself must know how secretive the Tarsi are," Karak said, "we don't just go around offering our secrets to the highest bidder."

"I also know you haven't spent a single coin in here, and you jumped out of your skin when you saw my gold here," Amphidas said, "which means you're not doing so great. I can also see your clothes are filthy and you haven't bathed. I happen to know the Tarsi take care of their own, which means if you're on the street it's for a reason."

Too smart for his own good, this one, Karak thought, suddenly self conscious about his haggard appearance. *He has me though, I do need this job.*

"Fine," he said, "very observant, once again. I'm not in the best position right now."

"The pay will be substantial, more than enough to put you in a better position."

"I said fine. I'll teach the boy."

When Karak arrived in Omatus, Amphidas had a tailor make perfectly fitted clothing for him and washed the clothing he'd come in. He was given a private room in an inn nearby, and shown the way to the courtyard where the training would take place. Atillus, his student, intimidated Karak in a way he hadn't experienced before. The boy was young, but intelligence radiated from him in quiet waves; he learned everything almost instantly.

The only thing he struggled with was the basics of Tarsi magic, and Karak was glad. He believed Atillus when he said he didn't want anyone knowing about their training, but the idea that an outsider knew Tarsi magic because of him still weighed heavy on his mind. *I can afford to live comfortably for a while now, at least,* he thought. Long enough to hopefully find some way back into the Circle's good graces. Until then, this Atillus boy wanted to learn everything, and was willing to spend a fortune to do so. Karak taught Atillus everything he could bare to teach, but he kept the vast majority of the techniques he knew hidden. He taught only the most basic versions of the spells.

Out of curiosity, and caution, Karak followed Atillus after one of their lessons. Months had passed since the training began, and Karak's mind would not rest on the topic; he had to know what the boy's goal was. Children didn't simply decide to learn how to fight and kill on a whim; and if they did they certainly didn't approach it with the tireless dedication Atillus showed every day.

Karak had stolen a slaves chiton before the lesson, and put it on as soon as Atillus left the courtyard. His body grew with a series of faint clicks and cracks, filling the chiton as though it were made for him. A face with Omati features appeared in place of his own, the courtyard disappearing briefly as his eyes dissolved and remade themselves. Striding quickly into the corridor, he followed Atillus. The boy knew how to move; he walked casually down public corridors and quickly through private spaces. He kept his eyes focused on his destination, and adjusted his posture to be as inconspicuous as possible.

After leaving the Argyris palace and walking through a small side alley, Atillus slipped into a slaves chiton which matched the one

Karak wore. Winding through alleys and smaller streets, he eventually ended up around the back of the royal palace. Karak watched him disappear into a slave entrance, and quickly caught up. Dozens of other slaves rushed around them; they may as well have been invisible. A few corridors down, Karak had to ditch the slave chiton and shrink his body down into a cat; no easy feat, even for an accomplished Tarsi mage. He caught up to Atillus again, and the boy glanced back down the corridor, his eyes dismissing Karak.

He followed Atillus through a secret entrance into a gigantic library that rivalled the ones in Tarsium. Atillus walked through the aisles as comfortably as he moved through the corridors of his family's palace, eventually arriving at a bookshelf against a wall. Atillus slid the bookshelf to the side, revealing a pitch black corridor with a warmly lit room beyond. Karak ran up to the corridor, next to Atillus' feet, and peered into the room.

"Now now, little thing," Atillus said, picking him up and throwing him gently back down the aisle, "I'm sure you would make great company, but I think Fire Magic might be a little much for a cat to handle."

Karak sat staring at Atillus as he walked through the corridor and slid the bookshelf back into place behind him. *Fire Magic,* he thought in wonder, *it can't be. That means Sithares has risen again.* Heart thundering in his chest, Karak tried to decide if he was excited or terrified. On the one hand, the Circle of Shadows would gladly accept him back with news like this; but on the other, if the Circle didn't defeat the God of Fire again, it would mean the fall of Pandeia.

Zeera

1747

Two years after recovering the Jewel of Tarsium, Zeera still hadn't forgiven herself for Talas' death. She refused missions and stayed in her underwater chambers most of the time. The pod she used to share with Talas, where they slept huddled up against each other under the water, felt empty and wrong. After she returned from the mission, the Jewel was placed in a sub-cave, which branched off the cave of Asheilos. Heavily guarded and secret, it was almost impossible to steal now. Zeera missed the feeling that came over her when she'd put it on; not so much power as awareness, pure and enlightening. The magic stored within the Jewel was ancient and powerful, and it was one of the most rare and unique artefacts in Pandeia. Wearing it even once was an honour, but Zeera found herself longing to wear it again.

What she longed for most was Talas. His absence tore at her every day, every moment. They'd been married almost a hundred years, and she couldn't bare to live without him. No mission seemed important any more, nothing mattered but the space where Talas used to be. She felt it wherever she went, no matter what she was doing; that horrible empty space around her.

When word arrived from Omatus that Sithares had awoken, Zeera finally had something else to focus on; something important. If the Gods were coming back, it meant Asheilos would need to be awoken too. *And a Hero will be chosen,* she thought. The moment she'd prayed for since she was a child. *You won't be chosen,* she thought, *why would Asheilos want someone like you?* But she had to at least try to hope.

Asheilos would be woken in a ceremony, involving as many members of the Circle of Shadows as could be spared. Some were out on missions, and some had to stay above the surface to guard the headquarters. Zeera swam into the chamber, her heart racing as she saw how many people had turned up; she'd been alone since Talas' death. The Tarsi spoke their own language only underwater; it was a series of clicks, pops, and squeals that could be heard well through water, but sounded harsh and grating on the surface. But Tarsi music was slow and graceful. A choir hovered behind the box of Asheilos, each humming a different pitch that merged together to form a beautiful crescendo.

The Circle had no leaders, and neither did the Tarsi in general, but there were specific roles within the organisation that granted power and authority. Hovering near the box that held the book of Asheilos was the Speaker. It was the Speaker's duty to open the box and make sure a Hero was chosen. Asheilos could only be woken by opening the box and reading the prayer within the book. Along with their duty, the Speaker also had the privilege of reading the prayer aloud, therefore gaining the ability to wield Water Magic. Zeera watched the Speaker take an ornate and complex key from a chain around her neck and place it slowly into the lock. Before turning it, she addressed the waiting crowd.

"Sithares has risen again," she said, "and it is the duty of the Circle of Shadows to prevent Pandeia's destruction. Once the box is opened and the prayer is read, one of you will hear the voice of Asheilos. You will approach me, and I will hear Asheilos' voice also. When it is confirmed, the new Hero will be named."

She let the choir carry on for a moment, then finally turned the key in the lock. Zeera's heart stopped in her chest, a burning fear blended with fierce, painful longing. She hadn't wanted anything since Talas' death, except to have him back. Each day was long, and numb, and draining. But the one thing she'd always wanted when Talas was still alive was to be the Hero of Asheilos.

Silence filled the chamber as the last of the choir's voices faded. The Speaker held Asheilos' book in her hands. A certainty made from faith and desire filled Zeera's body with tingling cold. She felt doubt gnawing away at the edges, but she forced herself to ignore it and keep watching the Speaker. When the prayer started, Zeera was shaking; even her lower lip trembled.

"Oh great God of Water. I, your lowly servant, pledge to you my life and soul. I give to you all that I have, and pray that you see fit to bestow upon me but one small gift."

Zeera stared as the words filled the chamber, her heart utterly still. The time approached so quickly; the Hero would be named in a matter of moments. The Speaker kept talking, and Zeera tried to calm herself enough to listen.

"I beg of you, Asheilos, God of Water, grant me the power of Water Magic, that I might greater serve you. I swear on my life and soul, with the power you give me I will help to build life in Pandeia, and douse the Fires of destruction from the world."

A vortex appeared around the Speaker, the water twisting and roiling until she was obscured. When it cleared, she was utterly still for a moment, her eyes closed. The moment stretched on, and Zeera's twisting stomach couldn't handle it; she felt as though she might pass out. Would she hear the voice? Were they waiting for the Speaker to say more before Asheilos spoke? Someone swam towards the Speaker. Slowly, Zeera's panic and hope cooled, fading into a cold, calm certainty; *I am not the one. I never was.* The Speaker's eyes opened, and took in the approaching Hero. The crowd cheered their appreciation, and Zeera swam slowly back down the tunnel to her chambers.

Do not leave yet.

Zeera glanced around her, but the tunnel was empty. Confusion filled her mind, and her panic returned. *What's happening?* she thought, turning in every direction, *I can't possibly be hearing Asheilos.*

But you are.

"What about the Hero you just chose?"

They were not chosen. They only believed they heard me.

It felt unreal. Like a dream. She couldn't remember the last time she'd left her chambers except to get food, and even then she barely ate. *It must be a dream. I've gone too long without food, or grief is playing tricks on my mind.*

No, Zeera Sol. You are my chosen. You are my Hero.

She remained in the tunnel, her mind whirling. Shaking again, she looked back at the chamber, where the ceremony was still happening and the Tarsi still gathered. *It must be a dream,* she thought again, *but even if it is, it's the only good dream I've had in a long time.* Terrified, doubting everything, Zeera swam back to the chamber of Asheilos.

Zailen

1774

Cold darkness enveloped him. Constant drips echoed through the tunnels, and the occasional scuttling of some rodent or insect. The urge to draw his *Kaizuun* was almost overwhelming. He used as little Shadow Magic as he could; according to the *Duulshen*, Elana warned them that recouping Shadow Magic was next to impossible in Ermoor. Even without using it, just being there drained the magic out of him slowly.

Zailen had been to all three districts of Tarsium. He'd been to Omatus and even a few of the other cities scattered around the giant continent of Omas. But Ermoor was unlike all of them. It was strange and terrifying, and he hated every moment of it. Based on the report the *Duulshen* received from Elana, they knew how to enter the slave city of Tyra. Apparently it took Elana a while to find it. But with the knowledge she'd gained, as well as advice from Zeera, Zailen was able to locate an entrance and sneak down there the day he arrived.

Underneath Ermoor, the network of tunnels was endless. They disappeared in every direction, pitch black and cold as death. Zailen walked slowly, ears and eyes straining for any hint of sight or sound. His hand rested on his *Kaizuun*. When Elana found Tyra, they were unaware that they were slaves. Barely any guards patrolled outside their sealed city. Now that a Shenza warrior had penetrated Ermoor's defences once, and now that the Tyrans knew what lay outside their city, there would be far more security.

At Zeera's advice, Zailen entered the underground tunnels at the south west edge of the city. It was easy to sneak into the tunnels from this side; the entire south west of Ermoor was crumbling slums, built halfway into the swamps that covered the eastern side of the continent. Open sewers gaped at the city's edge, bare metres from houses full of poor families. Towards the end of the slums, the ground became solid and sat higher up. From there on into the city proper, the buildings became steadily more shiny and rich, the people cleaner and better dressed. But Zailen didn't care about the people; at least not the ones above ground.

He'd arrived at night, and though it was far from easy, he managed to haul the row boat onto the shore and drag it through the swamps to the city's edge. Once there, he'd simply walked right into one of the open sewer tunnels, wheeling the row boat behind him.

Hours after he entered the tunnels, cold and exhaustion began to set in. Steady dripping, both near and in the distance, became more and more maddening. The row boat's wheels made a grinding sound against the stone floor, almost but not quite squealing as he dragged. There was no way to tell if he was going in the right direction. He tried to keep track; tried to remember which way he'd been facing when he first entered the tunnels, but it was so dark and there were so many of them.

Eventually it became too much, and he stopped walking for a moment. Leaving his left hand on the handle of the row boat, he drew his *Kaizuun* with the other. A bright cloud of auras bloomed in the distance, directly in front of him. It was all he could do not to cheer out loud; he was going in the right direction after all. Nervous about using Shadow Magic, he sheathed his blade again. After a few steadying breaths, he kept walking through the darkness.

He drew his sword a few more times, checking his direction and proximity to Tyra. When he was close, he started heading west, as Zeera told him to. There was apparently a network of tunnels which connected Tyra to the sewer tunnels that the Ermoori had forgotten about. Since he knew what to look for, Zailen found the tunnels after a few hours of wandering. Each of the few tunnels that connected to Tyra were covered by cave-ins. Or at least, they *looked* like cave-ins. It took Zailen what felt like an entire day to clear away the debris enough to make a path that the row boat could be wheeled through. By the time he was done, he collapsed to the tunnel floor.

Some time later, he awoke with a start. For a few seconds he forgot where he was and what he was doing. Shivering, he sat up, greeted by nothing but cold and dark. Then he remembered the mission, and Ermoor. Groping in the darkness, he found the row boat handle, stood carefully, and started moving again. Beyond the cave-in, the tunnel changed. The walls and floor became rough, and the temperature dropped noticeably. After a while, the tunnel began to materialise in front of him.

He couldn't tell at first where the light came from; it was far too gentle to find a source. Then he realised it was coming from everywhere. Small clumps of glowing mushrooms sprouted from the floor, walls and ceiling. Each gave off just a tiny glow, but collectively the tunnel was just visible in their light. He walked further in, trying to stay silent as faint sounds drifted down the tunnel to him. The row boat's wheels kept grinding against the rough stone floor. There was no way he'd be able to stay silent. He just hoped the Ermoori guards didn't patrol this area.

Finally, the faint sounds he'd heard became clearer, and closer. Footsteps; hundreds of them. Rhythmic and terrifying. Zailen had been told about the gigantic wheels turned by the Tyrans, but hearing that many people marching in unison was still intimidating. The closer he came, the more his own walking and the row boat's wheels started synchronising with the Tyrans. He had no idea what to do when he reached them. He could speak their language basically; they spoke a primitive version of Ermoori. But he had no idea what to say, or how to present himself.

Eventually, he reached a point where he heard the Tyrans clearly. The tunnel he walked down ended in a corner; they were metres from him. He stopped, trying to gather his courage and energy. It was unlikely they'd try to fight him, but at this point he didn't know what to expect. Elana's report to the *Duulshen* had been a little vague on how her encounter with the Tyrans went. All Zailen knew was that they hadn't killed her, and that she'd been able to lead them out of Tyra until the Ermoori took control again.

His mission was simply to arm them, train them, and get them out again, but without getting caught this time. He had a rough plan, and Zeera's advice helped him develop a good strategy, but the mission was still terrifying. Taking one last deep breath, he turned the corner into Tyra.

Karak

1747

Contacting the Circle as an exiled Tarsi was surprisingly easy; although they didn't want him back in the country, they were happy to communicate with him, if only to allow him to prove his worth again. Karak had a message sent to one of his contacts in Azar as soon as he was able after what he'd seen in the royal library. She agreed to meet him in Omatus.

Just like most cities in Pandeia, Omatus was full of inns and taverns. Tarra didn't like them, but she didn't like any place where people gathered; she'd agreed to meet him there only on the off chance he had information valuable enough to welcome him back into the Circle. It meant she would be in a foul mood, and he wasn't looking forward to the conversation. Tarra was the mission leader in Azar, the Circle agent responsible for assigning missions. She had the authority to lift his exile; or to make it permanent.

The tavern where Karak sat now was cramped, stuffy, and full of thick smoke. He'd arrived early, sitting in one of the few empty booths along the wall and wishing he hadn't suggested the meeting place. He should have suggested somewhere that would put her at ease. Finally, Tarra walked in, scanned the room, and walked over to him.

"Karak. It's been a while," she said.

"Hopefully long enough for some things to be forgotten."

"Tarsium never forgets. You know that."

"Of course, just a joke. Forgive me."

"You've spent too long around Omati peasants. What do you have to report that's worth you bringing me to this horrible city?"

"Sithares. The God of Fire has awoken."

"You're certain? You've made mistakes before."

"I am certain. A young nobleman wields Fire Magic, I saw it with my own eyes."

"Did you see the book?"

"No."

"So you can't be certain. It could have been a trick, or an artefact. Do you really think this is worth revoking your exile?"

"That's up to you. All I'm trying to do is help Tarsium, and the Circle."

Tarra sat back in the booth, staring at Karak. If she believed him, not only would it mean his return to Tarsium, his information could be the difference between Pandeia's destruction or its salvation. It was the entire purpose of the Circle.

"Give me the name of the child. I'll look into it myself."

He hesitated for a moment, and Tarra watched closely. He wouldn't have lied at this point, but putting Atillus in Tarra's path might mean she would find out Karak shared Tarsi secrets with outsiders. His exile would be permanent if she found out.

"Atillus Argyris."

"We will watch him. In the meantime, you are to search Omatus for the book. If you find it, bring it to the Circle's headquarters and you will be accepted back into the organisation."

Zeera

1747

When she returned to the chamber, the Speaker waited patiently, staring at the faces in the crowd.

"Who has heard the voice of Asheilos?" she asked.

Zeera swam past her fellow Circle agents, trying to control the hope building in her chest. *If it's a dream,* she thought, *or if I'm wrong like that first person was... I'll never move on from it.* The people around her moved away when they noticed her approach, clearing a path to the Speaker. Her eyes, previously focused on the shadowy depths below the crowd's feet, finally settled on the Speaker as she drew near.

"Zeera," the Speaker said, "You heard the voice?"

"Yes."

The Speaker's eyes closed, and after a terrifying, eternal moment, opened again. She nodded, and handed the book to Zeera. Cheers erupted throughout the chamber, and Zeera stared at the book of Asheilos. She flipped open the cover, and the pages inside moved freely and lightly, as though they were above water. All of Tarsium's libraries were on the surface, and the Tarsi hadn't developed waterproof methods of keeping records.

The Speaker turned through the pages until the prayer, and pointed to the beginning of the paragraph. Zeera's feeling of unreality grew to a point where the words in front of her blurred and moved on the page. She remembered how many people were watching, and blinked at the painful thump in her chest as her heart beat again. *Please be real,* she thought, *please. I can't stand it any more. If this is just a dream, I don't want to wake up.*

She started reading, quiet at first and louder when the Speaker nudged her. In her mind, she saw the vortex engulf the Speaker the instant she stopped reading. *What if I'm not really chosen, and the magic kills me?* She faltered, and the Speaker nudged her again. As she approached the end of the prayer, her heart sped up. Her mouth felt thick and useless, and the words started blurring in her mouth. The

Speaker placed her hand gently on Zeera's shoulder, and she forced herself to finish speaking.

Cold swept through her body and around her skin; the same sensation she'd felt emanate from within the box so many times, but far more powerful. It tingled and filled her with strength. She saw the crowd staring at her, and wondered when the vortex that obscured the Speaker would cover her vision too. But the crowd didn't disappear, and after the tingling waves of cold faded, they cheered again.

"Zeera Sol," the Speaker announced, "you are hereby named the Hero of Asheilos. You answer only to the God of Water, and the sole duty Tarsium can impose on you is to find and gather Pandeia's other Heroes."

Another cheer filled the chamber, and Zeera still felt an unreal dizziness in the back of her mind. *I'll wake up any moment now,* she thought. *This can't be real. I'll wake up in my pod and Talas will be there and this whole thing will be a dream.*

This is real, Zeera. You are finally the Hero, just as you always wanted.

When the cheers died down, the book was returned to the box and locked again by the Speaker. The crowd dissolved, and before too long Zeera and the Speaker were alone together.

"Did you ever think this would happen in our lifetime?" she asked Zeera.

"No. I always hoped. I dreamed about being chosen for so long. It didn't feel real. It still doesn't."

"I know exactly what you mean. There were at least ten Speakers before me who went their whole lives without fulfilling their roles. Almost three thousand years, with no need for a Speaker."

Zeera hadn't even thought about how the Speaker would feel. She looked at her, and saw a deep spark of passion and excitement in the Speaker's eyes. No doubt she'd felt just as unreal as Zeera had when it was announced that Asheilos would be awoken again.

"You were perfect during the ceremony, Speaker," Zeera said, "thank you for helping me through it."

"Call me Zalla," she said, her smile as warm as the spark in her eyes.

"Well thank you, Zalla."

They hovered in silence for a while, next to the sealed book. Its power flowed through both of them now, and Zeera felt Zalla's presence just as clearly as she felt Asheilos. Something felt different. A gap had been filled; something that she always knew was missing was finally present. Talas' absence was still there, still aching, but a different part of her was whole now. For the first time in a long time, she felt at peace.

"Is Asheilos talking to you right now?" Zalla asked.

"No. I heard its voice during the ceremony, but not since."

"It's so strange, isn't it? Hearing a voice in your head?"

"I thought I was going crazy," Zeera said as she nodded, "especially since I thought a Hero had already been chosen."

"The previous Speaker told me to expect it if Asheilos was awoken on my watch," Zalla said, "people build up their hope so much that they take any sound to be the voice of Asheilos. It's why the Speaker must pray first, so they can hear Asheilos confirm the Hero's identity."

"What did Asheilos say to you?"

"Just that you are the Hero, and that you will find the others eventually."

"Any hints about where I should start searching?"

Zalla laughed, and put her hand on Zeera's shoulder again.

"I'll let you know when I hear anything from our scouts," Zalla said, "but I've done all I can as Speaker, Zeera. The rest is up to you, and Asheilos."

Zailen

1774

The room was huge. A giant wheel, matching the *Duulshen's* description, sat in the centre. At least a hundred people turned it, pushing large handlebars. Around the walls, another group of people sat or stood. Some together, some alone. A few of them spoke in hushed voices, but most were silent. Turning the corner wasn't as climactic as Zailen thought it would be. At first no one saw him. When someone did, there was no shock or alarm; not even a raised voice.

A Tyran happened to be facing the corner Zailen entered from, but they were distracted by a conversation. Zailen saw him first, then a few moments later their eyes met. He stopped talking, but instead of his eyes widening in surprise, they slightly narrowed. As though he was merely curious. More eyes turned to him gradually, and after a few minutes all the Tyrans who weren't pushing the wheel were looking at him. There was no animosity; there was almost no reaction other than staring.

He tried speaking and his voice caught in his throat. The Tyrans simply stared, as though it didn't matter if he spoke or not. Then, as he was trying to work up the courage to address them all, almost every Tyran turned away again, going back to their business. Standing alone, ignored, Zailen froze. *Was it like this for Elana?* He thought, *did she show up and just get blank looks?* He shook his head, blinking in the flickering light of the cavernous room. Surely an entire city unaware of the outside world would have had a bigger reaction to a stranger appearing from nowhere?

Zailen wouldn't have thought he'd be uncomfortable being ignored; usually he hated attention. But the Tyrans acted as though he wasn't there, and he felt stranger than he ever had before as he dragged the row boat into the room. Ermoori guards patrolled outside of Tyra, through corridors that ran parallel to Tyra's outer tunnels. Zailen wouldn't have to deal with them unless something tipped them off. Training could be done further into the underground city, as far from the outer tunnels as possible. Careful to avoid scaring the Tyrans,

Zailen approached a small group. When he was close enough to touch them, and they still ignored him, he finally built up the courage to speak.

"My name is Zailen," he said, his voice sounding thin and small even to his own ears. "I've come from Shanaken."

The Tyrans didn't look at him. Didn't acknowledge him. *What is happening?* As gently as he could, he placed his hand on the closest Tyran's arm. There was a gasp, and the man shrank back from him.

"I'm sorry," Zailen said, "I didn't mean to hurt you. I'm just trying to help."

The group took a few steps away from him without talking. He'd never been utterly ignored before. It felt like he was a forest spirit; present but invisible.

"Can you understand me?" He asked, loud enough that most of the room could hear.

Rhythmic footsteps and the deep grinding of the wheel continued.

"Hello?"

Of all the things that might have happened, being ignored was not a problem Zailen expected to face. What had Elana done to get the Tyrans to listen to her? He knew she freed them; but according to the *Duulshen* her report had simply said she'd led them out into the sewer tunnels. *It can't be that simple. There must be some way to get through to them.* Maybe he wasn't speaking their language properly. Maybe he needed to make more of an impression on them. Or maybe their experience with Elana, and their failed uprising, taught them to simply ignore outsiders.

Stone benches lined the wheel room, and Zailen sat on one near where he'd come in from. The row boat sat near his feet, as useless as one of the boulders blocking the tunnels outside Tyra. He felt as though he'd already failed. Glancing at the people standing around the room, he noticed some of them nibbling at mushrooms. Not the large, vibrant mushrooms that grew all through Shanaken; tiny, shrivelled, grey mushrooms. They looked as though they'd taste of nothing but dirt.

An idea came to him, and he opened one of the barrels. It didn't take much searching for him to find some food; dried luduk meat. Zailen, like almost every other Shenza, only ate luduk fresh; but he was sure that to the Tyrans, the dried meat would taste better than anything they'd ever eaten before. It was wrapped in kalnad leaf, a kind of large leafed plant which kept food from spoiling for a long time. The meat wouldn't spoil, as it was dried, but kalnad was used to transport most foods from Shanaken regardless of their shelf life.

Zailen brought the wrapped food to the small group that had moved away from him, unwrapped it and offered the meat without speaking. It was spiced, and even though it wasn't hot, the smell drifted through the group. It got their attention. Zailen watched as they all stared at the food in his hands, shuffling a little closer to him. They glanced furtively at one another, as though each was waiting for the other to take some food first. He held it out closer to them, and finally one of them took a tiny piece. The others took equally tiny pieces, then stared at him as though he'd only just appeared. To encourage them, he took a piece for himself and ate it.

The spices made it tolerable, but he much preferred fresh luduk. He smiled as he ate, to let them know it was okay. In one unified movement, all of the group stuffed the luduk into their mouths. Eyes wide in wonder, the Tyrans stared at each other as they ate. Zailen had to stop himself from laughing; they looked as though they'd never eaten food before. But they didn't take more than the first tiny pieces they'd eaten. Instead, they turned to their fellow Tyrans and waved them over.

It didn't take long for the luduk to be shared among the Tyrans in the room. There was a barrel full of food, so Zailen grabbed another wrapped kalnad leaf parcel and handed it over. The second batch of luduk got devoured even faster. Finally, the Tyrans opened up a little, at least acknowledging his presence. A larger group gathered around him, some of them even looking directly at him. He introduced himself, and a few of them nodded. None of them gave their own names.

He opened the other barrel, and pulled out a few swords. Rushing into things might scare them a little, but Zailen had no idea how much time there'd be to train the Tyrans. When they saw the blades in Zailen's hands, they went right back to ignoring him.

Zeera

1748

A year after becoming the Hero of Asheilos, Zeera still trained every day. Training started the day of the ceremony, and it filled Zeera with an exhilarating sense of purpose. She'd studied Tarsi history, just like every other member of the Circle, but using Water Magic was drastically different to reading about it. Zalla trained with her; she'd studied the specifics of magic far more than Zeera. They learned together, following the information Zalla had been studying her entire life. She seemed to have an easy affinity with Water Magic; it was inspiring and infuriating at the same time. Zeera had to push herself almost beyond her limits to keep up with the Speaker.

The things she could do after a year of training stunned her. Control of the water around her, the ability to travel through water incredibly quickly without even using her arms or legs, and she was beginning to learn to change the properties of liquids. Just by focusing, she could change a cup of water into poison. It still looked and smelled exactly like water, but it was so lethal it would kill in seconds.

The poison scared her; the idea that she could create something so dangerous from thought alone. *What if I do it accidentally,* she'd thought, *and kill an innocent person?* But Zalla assured her it was just an example. They had to practice every skill that Water Magic could give them. They could also change it into a healing potion just as potent as the poison had been.

Halfway between Azar and Sarnia, an immense lake branched off the Nimriene river. The river itself was connected to the network of underwater caves and tunnels beneath Tarsium in several places. Each day, Zeera and Zalla sped through the water to the lake, faster than she ever would have believed possible. They spent their time submerged in the centre of the lake, training and experimenting with Water Magic.

Zeera fashioned a sphere of condensed water and launched it at Zalla, who met it head on with a slicing motion. The sphere split, and both halves veered away from her, carried by their own momentum before dissipating. Zalla pulled her hand towards herself and Zeera felt a wall slam into her back, forcing her through the water towards Zalla. She brought her hands and feet up against the wall behind her and kicked off, launching straight at Zalla. They connected, twisting through the water as each tried to use their magic against the other. Zeera couldn't get any attacks through to Zalla, but she managed to block Zalla's magic too. Eventually they broke apart, staring at each other, before Zalla laughed.

"I knew the Hero would be powerful," she said, "but for someone who struggles to use Water Magic, you're certainly very talented."

"I'm not powerful, though. Water Magic seems as easy to you as breathing, but for me it's just... out of reach."

Zalla swam close, shaking her head softly.

"Zeera, I've been training for this my entire life. Even without Water Magic, the Speaker's training involves learning how it works. You can learn a lot about magic without using it."

She placed her hand on Zeera's arm, her voice gentle and soft under the water of the lake.

"This is what I was born for, Zeera. So yes, after the training I've been through, Water Magic is something I can get used to easily. But you've only been training for a year and you're beginning to hold your own against me already."

It was true; for the last few weeks, their mock fights had been ending without a clear winner. But the struggle of training stuck in her mind, blurring her progress. The year of training somehow felt like a decade and a month at the same time; but no matter how long it seemed, it was always difficult. And because her progress was gradual, she hadn't really noticed how much she'd improved.

"Zeera," Zalla said, "Water Magic hasn't been around for thousands of years. Learning a new type of magic will always be difficult."

She nodded, knowing it was true but still frustrated at her slow progress. They hung suspended together in the water, looking up at the rippling surface, their training temporarily forgotten.

"How long do you think it will take the other Heroes to surface?" Zeera asked.

"Years. Decades, maybe. Who knows?"

Zalla's voice was still gentle, calm, as though finding the Heroes was no more important than deciding what outfit to wear each day.

"What if Sithares destroys Pandeia before we've even found them?"

"That's very unlikely, Zeera," she said, "after being dormant so long, Sithares will be weak. It can do nothing but whisper and grant magic to a select few until it gains strength, same as Asheilos and the other Gods."

"Isn't it still better to find the Heroes and fix this before the enemy is too strong?"

"You need to be fully trained first. We have scouts in every country, as you know. They will alert us when a likely Hero is identified."

Zeera nodded again, but her chest felt constricted, as though she was being crushed.

"Speaking of which," Zalla said, "our scout in Ermoor has stopped communicating with us. We've sent a new scout, but they'll be even better hidden than the last one. No more of that Spectre nonsense the Ermoori love so much, it's too public."

"Do you know what happened to Krana?"

"Not yet, our new scout is looking into it. There are still rumours of the Spectre, so he hasn't been killed as far as we know."

"No scout has ever dropped contact, have they?"

"No, they haven't. It is... concerning. But you should be focused on finding the Heroes, let me deal with the scouts."

With the thought dismissed, they fought again, to another draw. Afterwards they travelled down the Nimriene together, then through the underground caves until they reached home.

Zailen

1774

It took almost a week of living with the Tyrans before they warmed to him enough to let him train them. By the time they started training, Zailen felt Shadow Magic dissipating from his body like sweat on a hot day. He'd barely even used any magic. Inside Tyra, there were several types of rooms, connected by the network of tunnels. The most important were the wheel rooms. Then there were the sleeping quarters, which worked the same way in Shanaken; large shared rooms full of beds where everyone slept together. Other than the sleeping quarters, there were harvesting rooms full of mushrooms, and rooms set aside for candle making and crafting other resources. The last rooms, which the Tyrans showed Zailen after he explained what the training would be, were simply large empty rooms that the Tyrans used to hold meetings.

Once they started listening to him, they picked the basics of combat up surprisingly quickly. None of them would win a real fight against any Shenza warrior; but if they could gain some skill quickly enough it could make all the difference. Especially if they had surprise on their side.

The beautiful thing about the *Zuunshai*, the blade dance of the Shenza, was its simplicity. It was designed to follow the body's natural flow, activating every muscle and allowing the body and spirit to harmonise. It could be broken down into a series of slow, simple movements. Zailen taught the Tyrans one movement at a time, as slowly as he could bear, making them do it over and over until their movement was perfect. Then he moved on to the next move in the dance. He didn't allow them to use blades; it was simply too dangerous to attempt until they knew the *Zuunshai* properly.

Another week passed, and the group he was training could complete the first half of the *Zuunshai* with almost no mistakes. Dancing the entire thing at full speed with a sword was a long way off; but Zailen was pleased all the same.

He was beginning to learn some of their names; and they learned his. The familiarity helped him gain a little comfort, and he soon settled in to life in Tyra. Larger groups were showing up to his training, and things were going well.

Mana was a forager, one of the Tyrans whose job was to find and prepare food for everyone. As soon as Zailen was accepted, Mana approached with a seemingly endless list of questions about the food outside of Tyra. Where they found it, how it was prepared, how many different types of mushroom there were. It was endearing, and Zailen found himself enjoying Mana's conversation.

Sope was a worker, one of the hundreds if not thousands of Tyrans who moved the wheels of life. She picked up the *Zuunshai* faster than anyone else. Zailen only ever had to show her once, and she replicated each movement perfectly. She instantly fell in love with the blade dance of the Shenza, and Zailen loved her passion.

After training, the Tyrans sat together either at the sides of the wheel rooms or in the meeting rooms and talked. They made a strong drink out of mushrooms, and even a few sips made Zailen dizzy. They sat and laughed, telling stories and jokes, enjoying their drink and Zailen's food. Despite the cold, dark, and lack of magic, Tyra was quite a nice place.

Zeera

1752

"We might have found a Hero for you, Zeera," Zalla said, "in Shanaken. Very powerful."

Five years had passed since she was named Hero, and her training with Zalla had reached a plateau; she was beginning to feel like a real Hero. It was the first mission for Zeera since Aros. Since Talas.

"His name is Shaiden, a *Kaizeluun* who's becoming something of a legend among the Shenza."

"How do I find him?"

The Shenza lived in a network of walkways and buildings in the canopy of the Shanaken forests, moving between five major hubs. At any given time, all of the hubs were home to at least some of the population. They didn't move as often as the Thearans did, but finding one Shenza in a giant forest would still be difficult.

"Our scout, Teelo, will find you when you arrive. He'll take it from there."

The scouts in each country shifted into forms to blend with the locals; they were so convincing that they remained in their roles for a lifetime without being detected. Zeera believed the scout would be able to find her, especially if Zalla warned him that Zeera was coming. Tarsi could see active magic, and could see through shifts to the true identity underneath. If she saw the scout, she would recognise him as a Tarsi too, but his speciality was remaining undetected; if he didn't want her to see him, she wouldn't.

"All you need to do is get there," Zalla said, "our scout will find you, and then you can check Shaiden directly. Have a conversation with him, see if you feel any strange magic. I believe Asheilos will tell you if we've found our Hero."

"Okay," she said, "I'm ready."

Everything was planned. A room had been booked in a barge from Carmerth to the south west shore of Shanaken, where their biggest port was located. A bag was packed containing everything she might need for the mission. Zeera shifted into a Shenza form before approaching the barge, and all she had to do was wait to arrive in Shanaken. The journey didn't take long, and Teelo was waiting at the port for her. So far it was the easiest mission she'd ever been on; but it hadn't really started yet.

"Greetings, Daishen," Teelo said as Zeera stepped onto the lush grass of Shanaken, "I've been waiting for you."

"So I was told. Is there somewhere we can talk?"

"I've been spending a lot of time in the south most parts of the forest," Teelo said, "it's peaceful down there."

They walked south together, along the coast. To their right, the ocean stretched out as far as she could see. The view was beautiful, but Zeera had seen the ocean plenty of times; what captured her gaze most was the forest itself. Trees so tall they made the mountains of Tarsium look like small, rolling hills, their trunks wider than most of the buildings in Azar.

As they walked, they made idle conversation, nothing to do with the mission. The south dock was the main port of trade in Shanaken, and it was constantly busy; thousands of people milled around them, close enough to overhear even when they walked right up against the ocean. Teelo spoke of the weather in the forests lately, and of the animals he'd spotted in the trees to the south. He spoke of his friends; Kaishan, Daila, and Shaiden. Zeera's pulse quickened at the last name; Teelo had made contact already. After a long walk, they reached the forest's edge. The crowd had thinned, and Teelo smiled as he looked up at the giant trees.

"I know it's just a mission," he said, "but it really is beautiful here."

"Lucky you have to stay here a while then."

He laughed, genuine and warm, and Zeera decided she liked him.

"I am very lucky. This is a great mission to be assigned."

After a moment's pause, he strode into the forest without another word. Though the Shenza lived in the canopy, no climbing aids were built around the edges of the forest, even near the trading port. One had to brave the forests until far enough in to begin climbing. Zeera knew that subtle signs pointed towards the black metal climbing structures; but she didn't know what they looked like or how to find them.

Teelo guided her through the forest almost effortlessly; he'd been the Shanaken scout for decades already. When they reached one of the climbing trees, Teelo gestured, and Zeera went first. The handholds were easy to grip, and comfortable, but the climb itself was still exhausting; she lost count of how long it took by the time she reached the top.

"How..." Zeera said, panting as her lungs roared, "how do the Shenza do this?"

Teelo laughed again, and she noticed he was barely sweating.

"They grow up climbing, Zeera. They learn to climb at the same age they learn to walk. Besides," he added, "every Shenza has a connection to Shadow Magic, even the ones who aren't *Kaizeluun*. It helps a lot with climbing, even for the ones who can't actively use it."

"Well, I could definitely use some Shadow Magic right now," she said, "but at least we're finally at the top."

"True," Teelo said, "but we still have a long way to travel."

Teelo had been keeping a close eye on Shaiden, under the guise of friendship. Shaiden was staying in the southern hub, and Zeera finally met him after a long journey through endless trees. They stood together in one of the common areas, a walkway right next to a group of training platforms.

"Shaiden," Teelo said gesturing to Zeera, "this is Kaila. Kaila, meet Shaiden."

All Tarsi agents needed cover names; Tarsi names were recognisable and Shenza names were just as unique. Teelo's was Shelak. Shaiden nodded to her.

"I've heard a lot about you, Kaila."

Shaiden was the most well known *Kaizeluun* of his generation. The Shenza idolised the *Kaizeluun*, and Zeera knew any real Shenza would be thrilled if someone like Shaiden had heard of them. She tried feigning delighted surprise; but she had no idea what that looked like on her face.

"Oh wow, you're too kind," she said, then realised how stupid it sounded, "I mean, I hope you've heard good things!"

He laughed, but there was an ego behind it that told her everything she needed to know about him. She focused on him, looking through the physical body and reaching for the magic within. He was powerful; she felt that immediately. *But is he a Hero?* she thought.

Not this one. Amalus has not chosen yet. It will be some time before the Hero of Shanaken is named.

Shaiden stopped talking as Zeera jumped at the voice in her head; she hadn't been listening to him, but the sudden absence of his voice was jarring. She hadn't heard Asheilos speak in her mind since the day she was chosen. *It would have been quite helpful if I'd known that before coming here,* she thought.

I could not tell until you were in Shanaken. I can only see so much, child. I need your eyes and other senses until my strength returns.

Shaiden had begun talking again, this time about the people he was training. A young girl walked up to them, standing beside Shaiden. He smiled and put his arm around her.

"I'll be training my daughter too, of course," he said, "she was just made *Daishen*, so her *Kaizeluun* training will begin very soon."

The girl beamed at Zeera, the sword in her belt as new and fresh as her young face.

"Kaila, meet my daughter, Elana. Elana, this is Shelak's friend, Kaila."

"Hi Kaila," Elana said.

"Hello," Zeera said, smiling at the young girl.

Elana was powerful, just like her father. In fact, Zeera felt an even stronger magic coming from the girl. Even better, one look at Elana told Zeera that the girl had no trace of her father's ego. *I hope she's the Hero,* Zeera thought, *even if I have to wait a decade for her to be chosen.* Although she wanted to find the Heroes as soon as possible, she couldn't help but be relieved that Shaiden hadn't been chosen. An ego like his had no place in the Circle of Shadows.

You will know when you meet a Hero. You will feel it straight away.

Zeera knew she couldn't answer out loud, but Asheilos responded to her thoughts anyway, so she focused a thought as Shaiden, Elana and Teelo spoke; *I really hope so.*

Zailen

1774

He woke, his mind filled with fog. Something was wrong. He'd woken up with a terrible headache each time after drinking, but this was different. Panic set in when he realised he was already upright, and unable to move. The room was dark, even darker than what he'd become used to. As his head slowly cleared, he felt the smooth cold of metal gripping his body. He tried to move, but there was no give.

"Hello?" he said, quietly at first; when no one responded he shouted "What's happening? Where am I?"

There was no response, no movement. No sounds in the room but his own breathing. His feet didn't touch the ground, and the echoes from his shouts told him the room was huge. But other than that, there was nothing else he could find out. After a moment, he realised his hands were throbbing with a deep, hot pain. He couldn't see what was wrong, but he couldn't move them either. Trying to stop his panic from overwhelming him, he breathed as slowly as he could.

He had to think. Someone put him here for a reason. They wouldn't just leave him here; they'd have to come back eventually, whether that was to get information, kill him, or punish him. He just had to wait, and stay calm. With his hands injured or trapped, he couldn't use Shadow Magic. He couldn't draw his *Kaizuun*, or see anything. As his heart thudded in his chest and his lungs burned, Zailen tried to picture the forests of Shanaken. Anything but the pitch black nothingness in front of him now.

He must have dozed off again. When he woke, the room was still too dark to see, but it felt different. Like there was someone there with him. He tried not to make any sounds, listening for anything he might be able to hear. Silence pounded his ears, and his hands began throbbing again, a kind of pain he hadn't felt before. It felt as though his entire hand had been smashed or crushed; every single part of both his hands throbbed and ached. His mind was still foggy, as though it sat in the middle of a dense swamp. Other than the pain, his senses felt dim. *What is this?* He thought.

"Who's there?" He said, forgetting about trying to stay silent.

A slight shuffle came from somewhere in front of him.

"Who's that? I can hear you!"

But there was no response, and no other sounds. He kept listening intently, his heart pounding. After a while, his heart calmed back to its normal rhythm. He tried to wait for more sounds, but he felt himself slipping away again.

The darkness was starting to get to him. Tyra had been dark, but there was light to be found, and the Tyrans were always there for company even when the darkness was complete. But wherever Zailen was now, he knew it wasn't Tyra. *Ermoor,* he thought, his mind churning slowly through thoughts like boots through thick mud; *it must be Ermoor.* But there was simply no knowing. Whatever or whoever made the shuffling sound was gone, and there was complete silence again.

He passed the time by imagining what Elana's mission was like, picturing the parts he'd heard about and inventing new parts to fill in the gaps. Eventually, even that wasn't enough to keep his mind occupied. *Why am I here? How can I get out?* But he knew even as the thought surfaced there was no way out. He might find out why he was here, if he didn't die of starvation before his captor revealed himself; but if whoever put him here wanted to talk, they would have started talking by now.

Dying of starvation was a real possibility; Zailen tried to accept that. Even if the cause wasn't starvation, he was almost certain he would die here. Wherever *here* actually was. Still, *Kaizeluun* never gave up, and Zailen was determined to live up to his title. His hands continued throbbing, the ache only seeming to grow worse as time went on. The darkness was so complete that his eyes didn't adjust to it. He was used to casting the simple spell that allowed any *Kaizeluun* to see perfectly through any shadows; being blinded by darkness was more terrifying than he would have thought. His mind became more and more desperate with every moment that passed. Still foggy, his thoughts simply became more chaotic, his heartbeat irregular. When it seemed he'd reached the height of panic, a cold voice spoke from the darkness.

Karak

1754

He trained Atillus for a total of five years, up until Thorinos Argyris publicly beheaded the boy's lover and then exiled his son from the city. In the years that passed since his conversation with Tarra, Karak still hadn't found the book. He knew it should be in the little hidden room Atillus kept visiting, but he couldn't enter the room itself. Whenever he tried, the door on the far side of the corridor slammed shut with an eerie silence and Karak was forced to head back into the library.

When Atillus first fled Omatus, Karak thought his time in the city was done. The boy had left quickly, unexpectedly, and vanished without a trace. It was impressive, really; even to a Tarsi. Perhaps he'd taught the Omati boy too much. Not enough to stand against a fully trained Tarsi, but more than any outsider had a right to know. Teaching him so much had been necessary; Atillus was a clever boy, and would have suspected him had he kept too many secrets.

But Karak couldn't leave Omatus until he was absolutely certain the book was in the royal library's hidden room. Nothing he did got him through the pitch black corridor. Without the book of Sithares, he wouldn’t see Tarsium again. Tarra had stopped responding to the messages he sent. There were no Tarsi in Omatus that he could find; he was alone. But at least he had coin; and a lot of it. The private room he'd been living in was too risky to return to after Atillus' exile, so instead Karak hired a cheap room on the commoner's side of the city. Far less luxurious, but much safer.

After the assassination of the king of Omatus, the city broke down. The next in line to the throne, a young man by the name of Dassius Megalos, was crowned a few days later. Atillus' father and brother were imprisoned, and his youngest brother and mother were confined to the Argyris palace. Karak watched everything unfold from the shadows.

Almost two years after Atillus fled the city, Dassius released Thorinos and Alliphis. Citizens and nobles alike campaigned and protested until the king had no choice but to let them free. The day of their release, the king brought them out from their cell into the public courtyard where all announcements were made.

"Citizens," King Dassius said over the crowd's murmuring, "true to my word, I present to you Thorinos and Alliphis Argyris."

A cheer swept through the people gathered, and Dassius' face darkened.

"But," he said, "as Atillus has still not been found, and I still have reason to believe the Argyris family were conspiring together to murder my father, I will give Thorinos one last chance to prove his loyalty to the king."

Angry whispers spread from person to person, gaining momentum until the whispers turned to shouts.

"Just release them!"

"They've been locked up so long!"

"Why should they be loyal?"

Dassius had to be a similar age to Atillus; but the similarities ended there. Atillus was quiet, calculated, driven, and more mature than most adults Karak knew. Dassius was an emotional, overgrown child with an ego bigger than the royal palace. Karak found himself instantly disliking the boy.

"Silence!" the king screamed.

"Thorinos Argyris, this is your last chance. Tell me where Atillus is, or die."

The crowd's shouts and jeers grew louder. A piece of fruit splattered on the king's shoulder, and he drew his sword. His face was blotched and red, his eyes wide, his teeth bared like an animal. The crowd quieted; Dassius looked insane.

"I don't know, I swear," Thorinos said, "I disowned him before he killed the king, he fled from the city, I didn't know what he would do, I swear."

In the seven years Karak had lived in Omatus, he'd never seen Thorinos Argyris look the way he did now. He wouldn't have believed the head of the Argyris family would beg, even for his life. He wanted to stop Dassius; Omatus deserved a much better king. Normally he couldn't have cared less about who ruled Omatus, but it was his home now, and he liked the city.

The crowd began shouting again, and after a while the shouts converged into a single chant; *let them go! Let them go! Let them go!* Karak didn't join, his eyes and mind taken by watching the young king grow more and more furious.

"Shut up!" he screamed at the crowd, "SHUT UP!"

When the chant only grew louder, Dassius turned to Thorinos, an animalistic grin plastered on his face.

"I told you it was your last chance," he said, and swept his sword through the man's neck.

The crowd reacted as one, screaming and throwing whatever was at hand. Dassius gestured, and his royal guards descended on the citizens, forcing them back out of the courtyard. Karak left as quickly as he could. Instead of crossing the bridge into the commoner's side, he doubled back towards the royal palace. Disguised as a slave again, he entered the palace through the doorways he first saw Atillus use.

He wasn't sure what drove him; he had no right to be so invested in Omati politics. But living there so long had given him a soft spot for the city. The fact that he was living far more comfortably in Omatus now than he ever had since being exiled certainly helped too. He couldn't return to Tarsium anyway, without news of the book. Omatus had become his home; and he wanted to protect his home from the awful child who sat in the throne.

Killing Dassius Megalos was one of the easiest things he'd ever done. He stole a set of the royal guard's armour from the armoury in the barracks, the building next to the royal palace itself. Shifting his body into an Omati, he simply walked into the palace. Once inside, he made his way to the king's chambers, nodding to the two guards at the door, and stepped inside.

"What?" the king said, without even looking up, "this is clearly not a good time."

"I'm sorry, my king," Karak said, "there's just a very important message for you."

"Well what is it? Tell me and leave, I don't pay you for your company."

He got as close as he could, and finally the king glanced at him. Karak moved in the blink of an eye, and Dassius died with his face twisted into a grimace of confusion and condescending frustration.

"Wha-" he started saying, before his throat opened and his lungs filled with blood. He tried to shout for the guards outside his door, but he couldn't make a sound other than choking and grunting. Finally, he lay back, his convulsing body drenched in blood. There hadn't been enough sound to alert the guards, and Karak walked out the way he'd come in, nodding again to the two guards. He left the palace still wearing the royal guard armour.

Zailen

1774

"Shenza. I expected you sooner."

Zailen panicked; his heart thudded painfully in his chest, so hard his head pulsed with it.

"Who are you?"

"My name won't mean anything to you."

The voice was so cold. As though the person speaking had absolutely no heart, no emotion. He tried struggling again, but he was just as stuck as when he first woke up.

"How did I get here?"

"Ah, a good question. You're thinking. This might be fun after all."

A pause filled the darkness for a moment. Zailen thought the question would go unanswered, but then the voice spoke again; this time much closer to him.

"I simply walked into Tyra and took you. Never drink in enemy territory, Shenza. Your second mistake."

"Second..." he couldn't help but say, "what was my first?"

Footsteps moved away from him, echoing slightly in the huge space. He tried to count the steps. *Fifteen? Sixteen?* But he couldn't focus enough. Then a dazzling light exploded in his eyes, blinding him.

"Your first mistake was coming to Ermoor."

Zailen forced his eyes open, blinking through the pain, trying to see something, anything. His captor walked over again, each footstep forcing Zailen's panic to rise.

"I let your friend live," the man said, "I hope she's grateful for her life."

It was all moving too fast for him; his mind was still foggy and his eyes still hadn't adjusted. *Elana...*

"She's-she died."

"One less of you to worry about, then. She was rather troublesome."

Zailen screamed, struggling as much as he could and not moving an inch. A sharp slap to the face cut off his scream. Stunned and flinching from the sting in his cheek, Zailen settled into stillness again. Finally, his eyes adjusted, and the room appeared in front of him. His gaze fell on the man who'd captured him. He looked just as evil as his voice sounded; pale, thin, with cold blue eyes that held no compassion whatsoever. His thin lips curled into a subtle, cruel smile.

"There now, does the light help?"

Kind words; but the tone was dripping with lethal intent. Zailen had always been uncomfortable around people, but this man terrified him.

"What do you want?"

"I want to learn about you. Your people. Your magic."

The man's eyes glanced down at Zailen's hands as he said the last word. Suddenly, Zailen was certain he didn't want to know what happened to his hands.

"I'll tell you anything you want to know about the Shenza," he said.

Surely it won't make any difference as long as I don't tell him about the mission. But even as he thought it, he knew it wasn't true. This man struck him as the type who didn't ask useless questions or make idle small talk. Any information he gave would be used against Shanaken.

"I know you will. I look forward to it. But first, I'm going to learn some things for myself."

The man walked to a nearby table that Zailen hadn't noticed. Facing away from Zailen, his captor started picking things up and looking at them, as though choosing what spices to use on some roasting meat.

"The nature of my work is experimentation," he said casually, "I learn the most not by asking, but by doing."

A cold weight dropped into the pit of Zailen's stomach. *Experimentation.* It was an odd word, one that Zailen almost didn't understand, but he caught the meaning easily enough. In his foggy, panic riddled mind, it translated to *torture*.

Karak

1754

In the days following the king's death, Alliphis Argyris was crowned the new king, with the full support of Omatus' citizens and Nobles. The atmosphere in the city changed overnight. Karak watched the Argyris family closely from that day on, looking for any signs they may turn out like Dassius.

Alliphis was a little headstrong, but was genuinely doing his best to rule Omatus fairly and well. Eirene, Alliphis' mother, was a perfect diplomat; reasonable and logical, well spoken and able to resolve even heated arguments. The youngest son, Anamas, was silent, bookish, and perpetually nervous. He only spoke if he had to and even then only a few words at a time. Karak thought Omatus couldn't be in better hands; except maybe for Atillus himself.

He stayed close to the family, watching and making sure nothing happened; but they were loved by almost everyone, and he needn't have worried about any more assassination. The family didn't spend too much time together; Alliphis was busy as king, Eirene took over running the businesses, and Anamas preferred solitude and silence.

Watching Anamas was always interesting; the young boy was clearly very intelligent, possibly even more so than Atillus. But he seemed to have no social skills or situational awareness. He also lacked the ambition possessed by his brothers and father. He was perfectly content to simply read and learn until he died; disappearing into anonymity while his family ruled Omatus. It was a little sad, but Karak admired the boy for it; most people yearned for the crown simply for the power it afforded them, without thinking about the responsibilities.

Karak was following Anamas the day he died. Omatus had calmed so much that he forgot about Arrus Megalos; Dassius' younger brother. Five years younger than Dassius, and the sole surviving member of the Megalos family. He was waiting in an alley between the Argyris palace and the Omati library, a jewelled dagger in his hand.

Anamas didn't look up from the book he read as he walked, and before Karak could intervene, Anamas' throat was opened.

Arrus went pale as soon as he saw the blood, then vomited and crumpled to the ground. Karak ran to Anamas' side, but the boy was far too gone to save. He grabbed the dagger and slammed it into Arrus' neck, snarling as the boy woke and tried to fight him off. Arrus grew weaker by the second, until both boys lay still and silent.

He sat in the alley for a moment, trying to think past the panic. There would be no family war; the Megalos' were dead. But Anamas' death might cause enough distress in the Argyris family that it could upset the balance of power. He didn't know the other noble families enough to be sure that they would leave the Argyris family to the crown. Some of the support Alliphis received might have been false, the other families simply biding their time until a weakness presented itself.

The Argyris family had to be strong, united. Whole. With half a plan swirling through his mind, Karak heaved Anamas' dead body to a nearby sewer grate, stripped his clothes as quickly as possible, and shoved the body down through the hole. His stomach twisted as he heard thuds and splashes echo up from the sewer. Karak pulled on Anamas' blood drenched clothing, assembled a disguise spell that copied his face, and became the youngest son of the Argyris family.

Zailen

1774

His captor turned from the table, holding a thin, long blade. Zailen knew he couldn't move, but he struggled against his bonds. The blade approached, and nothing else in the room existed as it came closer and closer.

"You're going to scream," the man said, "and that's fine. But don't beg. I hate begging."

Pain ripped through his left bicep as the blade slid into his muscle easily. It kept going deeper, then Zailen felt a thud and the pain exploded as the blade hit his bone. He screamed, just as the man said he would. Leaving the blade in his arm, the Ermoori returned to his table, picking up another tool. When he turned, showing the thick mallet in his hand, Zailen almost drifted back into unconsciousness. He could do nothing, not even watch, as the man held the blade steady with his free hand and slammed the mallet into it.

He thought he'd been in pain before; he was wrong. Everything disappeared, and all that existed was the blade smashing into his bone. He felt it; not just the pain, but the blade itself, embedded in his arm, pushing further into solid bone, cold and unstoppable. Tears streamed down his face, mingling with sweat as cold as the blade inside him. Blood flowed down his arm, hot at first and then cold. He kept his eyes shut, though he wouldn't have been able to turn his head enough to see his arm.

His breaths were ragged, painful; his lungs stinging, his throat dry. After a few more hits with the mallet, the man carelessly slid the blade side to side. Zailen felt it grinding against his bone, could have sworn he heard it scraping. White light erupted through his vision, even with his eyes closed. Then the blade was pulled free, and he screamed again. A deep stinging emanated from the wound. The man came back with a tool Zailen hadn’t seen before; two long stems, even thinner than the blade had been, with tiny cup-shaped blades on the ends.

"Doctors and scientists in Pandeia don't know this yet," the man said, "but a lot of information can be obtained from the marrow inside bones."

Without hesitating, he pushed the tool into the wound in Zailen's arm. The odd shape made it difficult to slide in, but the man simply shoved it, twisting, until it reached the cut in his bone. Zailen screamed again, thrashing, willing himself out of the metal that bound him. Nothing made a difference. There was no escape. Sharp, grating pain seared his arm, emptied his mind. His captor pushed the tool into his bone. He felt it pinch and cut, and his vision failed. The room faded into blinding nothingness, and Zailen finally escaped.

Pain brought him back. The man hadn't stopped after he passed out. Two more wounds, just as deep as the first, pierced his other arm and one of his legs. Just as the room was coming into focus again, he felt the blade slide into his other leg and screamed.

"Awake again, I see," the man said, "I'm glad-"

Thud.

He grunted each time he bashed the mallet.

"-you haven't-"

Thud.

Zailen screamed again, barely hearing the man's words, "-begged me yet."

Thud.

He put the mallet down and jagged the knife from side to side. Then he went back to the table and brought the tool over. Crouching by Zailen's leg again, he pushed the tool into the wound. Pure, mind numbing pain flashed through his body as it scraped and cut into his bone. Time began to escape him; he couldn't tell how long he endured for. All he knew was the pain.

"Good." The man rose, put the tool into a glass holder of some type, and brought a needle and thread over, "that should be enough for now."

He started stitching the wound closed, but the pain in his bones was so far beyond a simple needle that he barely felt it. After the stitching was done, he took the glass container over to a machine and busied himself pressing buttons and twisting dials.

Shanaken was beautiful. So many shades of green that the eye could barely comprehend them, so much life that Shadow Magic pulsed from every direction. Zailen sat on the forest floor, hearing the insects and animals around him. The deep cuts in his arms and legs throbbed, stronger than any dream he could have, but he held to the forest with all his will. It was the only thing he could do to survive; the healing spells and potions usually at his disposal were no longer an option.

Being in Shanaken, even only in his mind, helped to calm his spirit. Though it did nothing to help him regain any Shadow Magic. The man left him alone for a while after cutting into his bones, and Zailen was determined to keep his spirit strong. He tried to focus enough to feel soft sunlight on his skin. To smell the life, decay, and rich earth of the undergrowth. Every element of the flow of life present in an ever moving cycle. Footsteps interrupted the vision, and Zailen opened his eyes to see his captor approach with yet another tool. This one looked like the peeling knives used by Shenza cooks to remove the skin of fish and birds.

"Your bone marrow is very interesting," he said, drawing the tool close to Zailen's skin, "now I'm intrigued by these tattoos of yours."

Karak

1754

He walked back to the Argyris palace, shaking and cold. *Blood and shock,* he thought, *the blood is cold but I'm definitely in shock.* When Eirene—*no, mother*—saw him, she screamed and ran to him, pulling his arms up and looking over his body, turning him around until the room spun in front of his eyes.

"What happened?" she said, her voice carrying across the palace.

"Nothing, mother," he said, his voice croaking and then adjusting to the spell, "Arrus..."

"That horrible child attacked you? Guards, guards!"

"No, mother, it's all... well, he attacked me, but he's-I killed him."

Eirene drew back, staring at the blood with wide eyes. It *was* Anamas' blood, but for his story to make sense everyone had to believe it was Arrus'. They stared into each other's eyes for a moment, Anamas trying to appear as innocent and truthful as possible. He was a talented deceiver, as most Tarsi were, but this was a new face and he hadn't had much time to practice Anamas' behaviours and body language.

"Arrus is dead?"

A group of royal guards burst through the doors, weapons ready. When they saw Eirene and Anamas, they slowed and scanned the room.

"How can we assist, my lady?" one of them asked.

"Do you need a doctor, master Anamas?" another asked.

He went quiet; Anamas spoke very rarely, especially to the guards. Eirene took over, speaking for her son as usual; ordering them around and sending for a doctor. He simply stared at the floor, hoping all the chaos would end soon so he could relax and settle into Anamas' life. It was an awful thought; he'd taken someone's life and identity, and all he wanted to do was relax and live comfortably. But he was sick of feeling like he didn't belong. Even if he had to be someone else to belong, he would do it.

His mother ushered him to his chambers and sat him on the bed. The doctor came in shortly after, looked him over and announced there were no wounds. After that, Eirene sat with him a while, until he asked to be alone. After she left, he took off the soaked red clothing and put on a simple robe. He called a slave over and ordered a hot bath. While he waited, he thought about Atillus. He wondered what the boy would do now; he was intelligent and talented, and more ambitious than anyone Karak knew. Without the Argyris name behind him, things may be a little more complicated; but he was sure it wouldn't stop a young man like Atillus.

Slaves entered his chambers with a tub and buckets of hot water. They set up the bath in silence, dutifully avoiding the pile of blood soaked clothing on the floor. As soon as they were done, they left the room as quickly as they could, their eyes down. Karak slipped out of the robe, locked the door to his chambers, and stepped into the tub. Tarsi magic held through almost anything, but he dropped the spells that made him Anamas, sighing as the hot water eased his sore body.

Alliphis ruled well, and for a long time. There were no assassinations, no unrest, and Omatus lived on. But the king was too intent on maintaining the status quo; slavery, poverty and petty infighting amongst the nobles continued unabated. It was no worse than it had been before Alliphis' rule; but it was also no better. Though Atillus had wielded Fire Magic, Karak couldn't help but wonder whether he would have made a better king; something told him it was so. But without the eldest Argyris in the city, Alliphis was its only choice. Karak certainly couldn't think of anyone who would improve Omatus other than Atillus.

He lived a comfortable life as Anamas. Eirene was pleasant, Alliphis left him alone, and he had almost no responsibilities. As far as Karak was concerned, the Tarsi could exile him permanently. One detail still bothered him though, usually at night, in the moments before he drifted off to sleep; *Sithares has woken. If the Circle doesn't act, Pandeia will fall.* He wanted to do something about it, he truly did. But being exiled from the Circle, and being unable to get to the book, meant that his hands were tied. If they wanted or needed his help, they wouldn't have exiled him in the first place. *Empty words to soothe a guilty conscience,* he thought, *you could help if you really wanted.* But could he? Would he? He finally belonged somewhere; Anamas' life was perfect for him.

"The Circle is full of people more powerful than me," he said, breaking the silence of his chambers, "with or without me, they will succeed. Why should I have to help them save the world if they don't even want me in it?"

There was no easy answer, and Karak had no one to talk to about his problems. But the doubts and fears consumed less of him as time passed, and eventually he forgot about Sithares. Anamas Argyris was a quiet boy, who no one paid much attention to, and who always had his nose in a book. He showed up to feasts and public events when required, but he rarely spoke to anyone, and nobody in Omatus seemed to notice that he wasn't Anamas Argyris.

Zeera

1756

She'd spent the last four years travelling; spending a while in each country with the local scout before moving on. It would be her life from now until the Heroes were located. Her current mission was to Ermoor; perhaps her least favourite place in Pandeia. Cold, heavy rain splashed over the rooftops. Zeera huddled into her cloak, grasping for any warmth and finding none. *Korol is supposed to be here by now,* she thought. The Ermoor scout had been in place for ten years, ever since the original scout stopped communicating with the Circle. Previously, the Ermoor scout had gone under the name of the Spectre of Ermoor, and was the subject of rumours and urban legend. Since Krana, the previous scout and the last Spectre, stopped speaking with them, Zalla had decided to put a scout in Ermoor who would be utterly invisible. Her name was Korol, and at the moment she was a little too good at being invisible.

"Come on, where are you?" Zeera said, shivering in the icy rain.

She'd met Korol before, but the scout had never been late to meet her.

"The Spectre is dead."

Korol's voice came from behind her, barely audible over the pouring rain. Zeera turned, questions already forming in her mind as she took in the Ermoori form standing on the rooftop.

"Krana? How? When?"

"Let's go somewhere private."

Korol had blocked off a small section of tunnel in the underground network underneath Ermoor. There were quite a few cave ins throughout the tunnels, and when she was first assigned to Ermoor she'd moved debris around to create her own very modest home. There was no door, and Korol made an entryway at the top of the rubble that was too small for a person; they both shifted into smaller animals to crawl through. Inside the makeshift home was a small fire pit, a ratty mattress, a pile of firewood, a large container, and a bag of supplies. Zeera recognised the bag; the same type of bag was given to every Circle agent embarking on a mission. Korol set to work building a fire, and Zeera sat close.

"So," she said, watching as Korol worked on the fire, "Krana is dead?"

"Yes. He died ten years ago, when he stopped speaking with us."

"But the Spectre has been seen since then," Zeera said, "stories continue of his presence in Ermoor."

"Up until a few months ago, yes."

"So who is the new Spectre?"

Korol sat back as the fire caught properly. She stared into the flickering light for a moment, a slight frown creasing her brow.

"I don't know. Not Tarsi, but he definitely has all the gear and training of the Spectre, so whoever it is he knew Krana somehow."

"You haven't discovered anything about him in ten years?"

"The Spectre was designed to be just that, Zeera; a spectre. A ghost. The Tarsi are brilliant at remaining undetected, but the Spectre was created to be something more. Ermoor has always been violent and corrupt, and hiding here has always been difficult, even for the Tarsi. By Asheilos, just look where I'm living."

"But why create the Spectre if there are other ways of hiding?" Zeera gestured to the space around them, as if to say *it's not that bad.*

"Because one thing the Ermoori have always been, other than corrupt and violent, is superstitious. My predecessors knew that to truly be able to remain in Ermoor for any length of time, they had to be feared, like the monster in a camp fire story."

It seemed absurd to Zeera, but she didn't know Ermoor's history the way Korol did. She sighed, moving a little closer to the fire; it was finally roaring, and her clothes were gradually drying as they spoke. This far underground, they couldn't hear the rain; but echoing drips carried down the tunnels from every direction as water drained down from the streets.

"There's no trace of Krana? At all?"

"No. I only know he's dead because I've scoured the entire city and there's no sign of him. No Tarsi scout would abandon their post like that."

"Do you think the current Spectre killed him?"

Korol shook her head, brow furrowed as she stared intently into the fire.

"No. Whoever the latest Spectre was, he was trained by Krana. It's the only explanation for the skills he has."

"Could he be the Hero?"

Crackling fire and dripping water were the only sounds for a moment, as Korol frowned at the flickering light. Zeera's breath caught, and she watched Korol's face carefully; there was doubt there, and hidden even deeper, buried in her eyes under layers of focus, there was fear. She'd seen the new Spectre, even if she didn't know anything about him. She had hunted him, sought him out for a decade, and found nothing.

"It's possible," Korol finally said.

"Is there any way we can draw him out?" Zeera asked, "for me to know if he's the Hero, I need to get close."

"Well, that's the thing," Korol said, "a few months ago, this new Spectre disappeared."

"Two of them have disappeared in a row?"

"Apparently," Korol said, "though this time it seems different. There's no replacement, for one thing."

"Maybe whatever killed Krana got his replacement too."

Korol shook her head slightly, her frown deepening in the low light.

"No. The last Spectre was different. He had all the training, but he used the Spectre to fight Ermoor's crime and corruption, instead of being a scout for Tarsium. Now, other than the corruption of their government, there is very little crime left in Ermoor. It seems the new Spectre chose to stop, instead of being killed or vanishing like Krana."

"Are you saying you don't think the last Spectre is dead?"

Korol looked up from the fire, staring directly into Zeera's eyes for the first time that night.

"That's exactly what I'm saying. And he might know what happened to Krana."

Zailen

1774

It felt like fire and ice at the same time. The blade pulled through his skin, tearing and slicing as the man sawed it back and forth. Zailen threw up. Unable to turn his head, the contents of his stomach cascaded over his chest, sticky and hot.

"If any of that got on me, you'd be in a lot of trouble," the Ermoori man said.

"Am I not... al... ready?"

Zailen couldn't speak in clear sentences any more. He wasn't sure why he'd spoken at all. Angering this man was the worst possible thing he could think of. The knife kept sawing at him, but he was beyond screaming now. Pain streaked through his body every waking moment. He couldn't remember what it felt like to not be hurting. For the first time in his life, Zailen wanted to die.

A final tug at his arm pulled the chunk of skin free. Zailen saw his tattoo in the man's hands as it was carried back to the table. The room was grey, his mind was grey. His body screamed. Footsteps echoed through the room, and through his mind, but it was too difficult to focus. Another blast of pain lit up his arm where the tattoo had been cut out, but Zailen was already fading again.

When he woke up, the lights were still on. The man was at another one of his machines, his back to Zailen. Through the pain, he finally began to take in the room around him. Most of it meant nothing; complex machines and tools he didn't understand. One thing he recognised immediately; his *Kaizuun*, sitting on a table without its sheath. His heart stopped for a moment. Every Shadow Blade was forged by its owner, a process which took months of careful, precise work. *Kaizuun* were then intricately carved with ancient Shenza runes, which had to be done using a tool only the *Duulshen* possessed. The carving took weeks, and once finished, the *Kaizeluun* reheated their blade in the forge and dipped it in specially prepared oil which contained the same magical properties as the ink of their tattoos.

Zailen still remembered forging his own blade vividly. The connection he shared with his blade was sacred; he could feel its presence, and it reacted to his touch instantly. Wielding another warrior's *Kaizuun* was one of the worst crimes for a Shenza to commit. His captor had removed the blade from its sheath. For just a moment, Zailen's rage overcame his pain and exhaustion. He screamed and thrashed, ignoring the pain. The man turned to watch him, no emotion in his eyes, and Zailen stopped trying to move again.

"What got you so excited?"

Zailen said nothing, but his eyes gave him away; he couldn't stop staring at his *Kaizuun.*

"Ah, the sword. Yes, the other Shenza was quite attached to hers, too."

He walked up to it, picked it up off the table, and stared at Zailen. After a cruel, smug smile, he looked down at the blade, turning it over in his hands.

"It is beautiful. Obviously contains magical properties."

He was talking to himself, Zailen realised. *It's like I'm not even here any more.*

"The other one cut clean through one of my sentinels. Metal cutting metal that easily..."

He trailed off, still ignoring Zailen. Then, abruptly, he looked straight at him again.

"I've been thinking about these swords ever since your little friend showed up. I wanted one for myself, and now I have one."

He took it over to another machine, and slid it into a tray that seemed built for just that purpose. The machine began humming and clunking, the occasional spark shooting from the sword. Twinges of pain began, somewhere deep inside Zailen. At first he couldn't figure out what it was. But as his *Kaizuun* sat in the machine for longer, and the sounds grew more violent, he realised; the blade was being attacked.

"Stop," he said, "stop doing whatever you're doing, that's my *Kaizuun.* You have no right to touch it."

The Ermoori turned to him, a touch of lethal threat in his cold, deep eyes.

"I can touch whatever I want, Shenza."

But he did shut off the machine, and walked over to Zailen.

"Unless you think you can stop me?"

As if to illustrate his point, the man placed his hand gently on Zailen's shoulder. A jolt flashed through his entire body, burning and crackling. The smell of smoke filled his nose. His thoughts scattered again, and all he could do was blink and try to drag air back into his spasming lungs.

"Hmm. A more violent reaction than non magic wielders. Interesting."

Without another word he turned back to the machine and turned it on again. The twinges of pain came back, and Zailen screamed. The Ermoori watched him closely as the machine continued damaging his sword. Then, his eyes still on Zailen, he raised his hand to the blade, smiling.

"No!"

Crackling yellow lightning jumped from the Ermoori's fingers to the *Kaizuun's* razor sharp tip. The machine itself was hammering away at the blade, but barely doing anything. The lightning tore something within him as a loud crack filled the room. As Zailen screamed again, the machine holding his *Kaizuun* exploded. Pieces of the machine flew out in every direction, and his captor was thrown violently against a table. His *Kaizuun* streaked across the room and clattered to the floor next to his bonds. The lights faltered, and the metal holding him in place gave way, dropping him to the floor.

Rising to his knees as quickly as he could, trying to ignore the pain ripping through his body, Zailen grabbed at his Shadow Blade. Finally, he saw what had happened to his hands. He drew them closer to his eyes, not wanting to believe the horror in front of him. Forgetting about his sword, his captor, his mission; he screamed.

Zeera

1758

Zeera stayed in Ermoor for just over two years, hiding with Korol and scouting the city for any signs of either the Hero or the Spectre. They found neither. She did feel a strange energy throughout the city; a kind of muted, restless fury which left her physically uncomfortable. In the time she was there, she couldn't find the source. She did have a theory however, and near the end of her stay in Ermoor, it was confirmed.

She was wandering through the districts, searching and stretching out for any sense of magic, when she reached the district known as Darkpoint. A heavy, suffocating dread filled her chest, as cold and thick as the fog in the night sky. The feeling rose up from the very ground itself, as though the city was rotting under her feet.

Taranos stirrs.

"Has it awoken?"

She still felt strange talking out loud to Asheilos, but it was easier than trying to focus specific thoughts towards the God.

No. But something is happening. Not enough for me to see clearly.

"I can't tell where it's coming from."

It felt as though it rose from the ground itself. The Tarsi knew of Tyra, but Tyra didn't extend this far underneath Darkpoint; so it was nothing to do with the underground city of slaves. There was an extensive network of tunnels separate to Tyra, but they were either sewers or just empty. Besides, Darkpoint was only home to a few bureaucrats and scientific laboratories; there was nothing there of note, and certainly nothing that would cause Taranos to wake.

She kept moving, until she saw a new building, not quite built yet still impressive in its silhouette. For the last few months, Korol and Zeera had focused on the southern districts, the slums of Ermoor; there were still rumours of the Spectre among the poor citizens, and they were desperately chasing any lead they could find. She'd missed the announcement of whatever was being built here; but whatever it was, it certainly wasn't a home.

Creeping closer on the nearest rooftop, Zeera stared at the monstrous building. Its design was aggressive, and she found herself hoping she wouldn't have to sneak inside. As she reached the very edge of the rooftop, three people walked out the front door; a young boy, a nervous looking man, and an older, serious man with a dangerous presence. Something about the older man unnerved her.

"I am very happy, Henry, thank you." the boy said.

"I'm glad to hear that, Master Hayne," the nervous man said, "of course, there is still a ways to go, but we will spare no expense to have it fully operational by your deadline. I just wanted to show you our progress so far. I knew you'd be as excited as I am."

"I am quite excited. And I see you are following my blueprints to the letter. Very impressive. What do you think, Lord Commander Symond?"

"If it allows you to design better and more powerful technology for Ermoor, I'm satisfied."

"We are all in agreement, then. Thank you again, Henry. I will see you when the lab is finished."

The man named Henry stepped into a cart and drove away, and the boy and the older man entered a cart together, driving towards

Ironhaven. *A laboratory,* she thought, *only much larger than any I've seen before.* The feeling of dread still emanated from the ground around her, and with the building now empty, Zeera decided to see if she could find the source.

No. You have a different path to take. Taranos will rise in time, and a Hero will be chosen. If you die before that happens, all is lost.

Her resolution melted, and was replaced with a painful, hot vice around her heart; *if you die... By Asheilos,* she thought, *what is down there?* But she wasn't answered, and she pulled herself away from the building and returned to Korol.

When she told Korol about the laboratory later that night, she shook her head slowly, the corners of her mouth drawn down.

"It's beginning. That child will be the downfall of Pandeia."

The words made no sense; Zeera thought they'd be discussing the intense feeling she sensed from the ground around Darkpoint, not a child scientist.

"What do you mean?"

"His name is Riffolk Hayne. He's already made huge leaps in technology out of nowhere, and that older man you saw was the Lord

Commander of Ermoor's military. It's only a matter of time before Hayne starts designing weapons."

"What should we do about it?"

Korol glanced at her, eyes wide, then resumed staring at the fire.

"I'm a scout, Zeera. My only role is to watch. I have no authorisation to act unless the Speaker demands it."

"Surely this is important enough to contact her?" Zeera said, "if you're right, stopping him now makes more sense than waiting until he arms all of Ermoor."

"He's contributing far more than weapons for the moment, and not just to Ermoor. I'll update Zalla as soon as I can, but I've worked with her long enough to know she won't act on it."

They settled into silence again, but it was tense, and Zeera found herself feeling too restless to stay there.

"I need to move," she said, "I'm going out for a while."

Korol nodded, and Zeera went back to the surface. She had to keep clear of Darkpoint, and she had nothing else to do; she just needed to move. It started raining again, and Zeera's mood darkened as she sprinted over rooftops in the freezing cold. Asheilos wouldn't allow her to investigate Darkpoint, and a potential threat to Pandeia was being ignored; she couldn't remember ever feeling so powerless. She was supposed to be the Hero of Tarsium, and yet all she could do was watch events unfold and follow orders.

After an hour or so running through the rain, her restlessness gave way to cold and exhaustion. Shifting into a cat body, she leapt down into the street and sprinted along the pavement. Most of the walkways beside the roads were covered, so she managed to avoid a lot of the rain on the way back to Korol's makeshift home. Not that it did much good; she was already soaked to the bone and shivering. By the time she crawled through the tiny entrance and shifted back into her own form next to the fire, Korol was asleep.

Zailen

1774

There was almost nothing left of his hands. They looked as though they'd been chewed on by some horrible, giant monster. He couldn't even see the tattoos on his palms any more. Staring, horrified, his mind refusing to accept the mess of bone and flesh that used to be his hands, Zailen groaned. He couldn't use the *Kaizuun*; he wouldn't even be able to pick it up. The Ermoori hadn't just injured his hands, they were utterly destroyed.

Dizziness overwhelmed him, and he threw up again. He stopped looking at his hands; his mind simply couldn't take it any longer. His *Kaizuun* was so close. It lay on the floor right in front of him, a jagged chunk missing from the tip of the blade. Zailen stared at it, numb and empty.

Behind him, he heard the Ermoori stir and get up. He didn't bother looking as footsteps approached him. His captor was breathing heavily, but sounded unharmed. He stopped just behind Zailen. Something smashed into the back of Zailen's head, and a cascade of white stars exploded in his vision before everything slipped away.

When he woke again, he was back in the familiar metal binds that held him still. He didn't struggle. He didn't argue. The Ermoori stood before him, smiling.

"I should have known the machine couldn't take that kind of magical attack. Still, I consider it a successful experiment."

Zailen stayed silent. There was nothing more to say. He just wanted his *Kaizuun* back. He wanted to talk to Laila again, tell her how much he missed her. Over his career, he'd been close to death several times, but he always fought back, never gave up. Until now.

"You've helped me a lot, Shenza. Far more than your little friend. With your sword, and your tattoos, I'll be able to upgrade our weapons and armour; Ermoor will be unstoppable."

"Why?"

The man blinked. His face became the picture of confusion. Somewhere deep inside Zailen, a tiny flash of victory lit up the darkness.

"Because Ermoor must rule Pandeia," the man said, in a tone that suggested he was speaking to a child, "Shanaken, Tarsium, Omas... they are all so uncivilised. They need to be shown order."

"And... who will show them?" Zailen said, his voice weak, "you?"

The Ermoori laughed; but the sound was utterly devoid of humour and warmth.

"Of course, Shenza. Who else has the intelligence? The power? The resources? No one from Shanaken, I assure you. The Tarsi are sneaks and cowards. The Thearans are scattered to the deserts, fighting among themselves, and the Omati have no ambition beyond their own walls. No, I will rule Pandeia."

Zailen lowered his eyes. He believed every word the man was saying; his captor wouldn't stop until he ruled the world. Even worse, Zailen believed he could do it. He'd looked into this man's eyes up close, and he'd seen absolutely nothing. No wonder the *Duulshen* had been communicating with the Tarsi for the first time in centuries; Elana must have discovered this man's plan. Zailen couldn't escape, and he was done being defiant. But an oddly urgent feeling of curiosity had started driving his thoughts, as though suddenly all the smallest details mattered more than his certain death.

"Where did your magic come from?"

Again, a look of confusion passed over the man's face, but this time it disappeared much faster.

"Where all magic comes from. I'm surprised you of all people don't know that."

"You mean... your magic came from Amalus?"

"Not your God, no. But... one of the Gods."

"One of..." *there are others?* he thought, "What God is there other than Amalus?"

The man shook his head, an infuriating look of disgust curling his lips. It didn't reach his eyes though; nothing did.

"You see? Ignorance is rife throughout Pandeia. It's repulsive. There is so much information available, if only people would seek it out. But instead, you wallow aimlessly, waiting for someone to lead you."

He strolled to a table and picked up a gun. It looked a little different to the ones he'd faced on the north shore of Shanaken, but the shape was still instantly recognisable. *This is it. I'm about to die.* There was no fear any more. He was still in so much pain; he just wanted it to end.

"Do you have any last words, Shenza?"

The gun's barrel pointed directly at his face. It was as deep, dark and cold as the eyes of the man holding it. In that moment, before death took him, the only thing that entered his mind was the dappled sunlight of the forests in Shanaken.

"None that would mean anything to you, Ermoori."

The man nodded.

"You're braver than I thought you would be."

Coming from his evil, emotionless captor, the compliment meant nothing. He simply stared into the gun's barrel, waiting for death. His body was broken; if not for the binds holding him up, he wouldn't have been able to stand. Pain, bright and pulsing, wracked his entire body. His mission didn't matter any more, though he felt a pang of regret. All that remained was the forest, beautiful and peaceful and far too far away. A bright flash and a crashing boom erupted in his face, and then the forest appeared before him again.

Zeera

1763

Omatus hadn't changed a lot. A different family ruled, but other than that it was more or less the same. Not quite as corrupt and oppressive as Ermoor, but certainly not a place Zeera would want to live. She'd been in the city once or twice since being named Hero, but like Ermoor, she only stayed as long as she had to before moving on. Searching for the other Heroes took a lot of time, and a lot of waiting. Usually she ignored the politics of the places she scouted, blending into the shadows and the general population instead.

But one discovery about the royal family shocked her more than she thought possible.

She was near the royal palace, in a generic Omati form, when she saw him. Something about the royal palace was off; she had a very similar feeling to being near the lab in Ermoor five years earlier. Asheilos hadn't spoken with her, so she was wandering around and scanning the streets on the noble side of the city just in case. She almost didn't recognise him at first, but it came rushing into her mind all at once.

Anamas Argyris walked through the street, quiet and shy. Zeera had seen him before, and recognised him on sight. But after a second or two, her Tarsi senses kicked in and the form shifted to show the real face underneath; Karak Toor. *I wonder if he knows his father is dead,* she thought. He'd been exiled around the same time that Zeera was named as Asheilos' Hero; around sixteen years ago. Before he could see her, she turned down a nearby alley.

Karak had been an enforcer in the Circle; an assassin, more or less. Zeera didn't like the enforcers. There was an art to what they did, but she'd always felt that it directly contradicted Tarsium's no violence stance. Besides, they were often so focused on combat and killing that none of them bothered to learn the history of Pandeia, and knowledge was the most noble trait a Tarsi could pursue.

There was nothing to gain from confronting him; he was exiled, and had obviously found a way to live in Omatus without causing too much trouble. On top of that, his placement in the royal family could prove useful in the future; if she ever needed something done in Omatus badly enough, she could offer Karak a place back in the Circle in return. Her main concern was why the scout in Omatus, Tarat, hadn't spotted him. Granted, it was pure luck that she found him in the first place, but Tarat had been in Omatus for fifty years; he had to have noticed something. She left for the Omati safe house on the commoner's side, trying to put her uneasy feeling around the royal palace aside. Unless a Hero was nearby, Asheilos would most likely warn her away. When she arrived at the safe house, Tarat was cooking a midday meal.

"Zeera," he said, "hungry? There's enough for us both."

She nodded and sat at the small table behind him. When he was done cooking, he brought two bowls over and handed one to her.

"Any news?"

"Not about my mission," she said, "no Heroes have been spotted since I was chosen."

Tarat shrugged and started eating. He was always a little too casual for Zeera's taste; she hadn’t seen him during a mission, but he spoke about everything as though it didn't matter.

"I did see something surprising, though."

"Oh, fun. What could possibly surprise the great Hero of Asheilos?"

"Karak Toor."

"That enforcer who got exiled? What's he doing in Omatus?"

"He's posing as Anamas Argyris. No idea why. I was hoping you could tell me."

"And why would I know what's going through his mind?"

"I just figured, since you're the scout, that you would have seen him by now."

The slightest frown passed over Tarat's face, his eyes darkening briefly. The expression passed as quickly as it appeared, and Tarat was smiling and shrugging again.

"I watched the royal drama happen when the crown changed heads, but I don't pay much attention to the individual noble family members. As odd as it sounds, most of them lead pretty boring lives."

"You need to take this seriously, Tarat," she said, "Sithares is risen, and every day that passes brings Pandeia closer to destruction."

Tarat shook his head, and laughed. He brought his hands up and out, palms up, as if to say *what did I do?*

"He's an exile, Zeera. He's not out there killing people or taking the crown for himself. Who cares what he gets up to, if he's quiet about it?"

"If you didn't see an exiled Tarsi right under your nose, what else have you missed?"

He shook his head again, a sardonic half smile pulling his lips up. Zeera saw the shade of disappointment dull his eyes underneath the smile though, and she knew some part of the message had gotten through to him.

"I haven't missed anything important, Zeera. I've been here a while. If I wasn't good at being a scout, the Circle would replace me, you know that."

His words were earnest, but his tone was still slightly mocking. Zeera tried to breathe through the fury that radiated through her chest. *It's just his nature,* she told herself, *he's not being disrespectful, he just speaks like that.* She'd never been so close to hitting someone who wasn't threatening her life.

"I need to be able to trust that you'll see anything important, Tarat," she said, "I'm not here often, so the Circle relies on you."

"Of course."

She left the safe house again after she was done eating, but this time wandered through the commoner's side of the city. It was almost time to move to the next city; she'd already been in Omatus a little while. The importance of her mission stayed strong in her mind, but sometimes it was difficult to keep her hopes up. It had been sixteen years since she was chosen, and she was still no closer to finding the other Heroes. For all she knew, they hadn't even been chosen yet themselves.

Lashek

1772

His blade swept around him in tight arcs, controlled and precise. A good Shenza didn't go a day without performing the *Zuunshai*. In Carmerth, as well as the other two districts of Tarsium, Shenza had set up training platforms specifically to be able to practice their blade dance daily. It was a tradition the Tarsi supported. There were walls around each platform; the Shenza, although happy to live in Tarsium, were still very secretive. Lashek was glad for the privacy, as well as the company; dozens of Shenza practised the *Zuunshai* each day at the platform he visited.

Shenza were a fairly large proportion of the population in Tarsium. Trade between the two countries was booming. It meant the Tarsi understood the Shenza culture better than any other outsiders. Lashek enjoyed Tarsium a great deal more than most Shenza. He didn't fit in in the forests; they didn't seem to give him the same sense of peace every other Shenza felt. He left Shanaken a long time ago, and had felt at home in Tarsium ever since.

After he finished his *Zuunshai*, he walked to a nearby tavern. He was making good coin these days, and he could afford good drinks. The tavern he frequented, The Shining Sceptre, was a hot spot for fellow mercenaries and assassins. Lashek had many friends who frequented the tavern too. He sat at the bar, next to a couple of regulars he knew by sight but not by name. They nodded; Lashek nodded back. He dropped a few coins onto the bench and gestured to his favourite drink. A small glass of fortified wine slid over the bar, passing from the barman's hand to his own.

The Sceptre wasn't just a tavern, or a hangout for mercenaries; it was a job market. Those who knew Koros, the barman, could pay a few extra coins to see any open contracts posted by the Tarsi Peacekeepers. After enough jobs had been done, the barman offered closed contracts. Lashek had worked through the Sceptre for most of the time he'd lived in Tarsium. After he finished his first drink, Koros handed him a menu.

"We have a few new things for you, Lashek. Exclusive, if you want them."

The tavern's menu was on a small clipboard, and there was one on every table and scattered along the bar. But the one Koros handed him was different. Behind the bar was the pile of menus that contained all active contracts in Tarsium; assassinations, bodyguard jobs, armies for hire. Tarsium held a strict no violence policy, but the one exception was the people the Tarsi deemed worthy to work directly for them. They were only hired to work against those who broke the Tarsi's rules in the first place. Lashek was a talented *Kaizeluun*, and familiar to the Tarsi.

At the front were always the biggest jobs; the most risk for the most coin. Lashek flipped past the first page; he very rarely took the biggest jobs. It was for the assassination of a woman who'd begun poisoning her husbands. Lashek had no desire to get involved in that kind of game.

The next page was a small group of explorers who wanted to search for an ancient treasure in the Shanaken forests. Lashek chuckled and flipped to the next job; the idiots would die within an hour of entering the forest. The only people who could realistically keep them alive were Shenza, and no Shenza would take that job in the first place. After that there was a job he liked the look of. Local, good money, within his skills, and best of all quick. He tore the page out of the menu and handed it to Koros.

Local thieves need a lesson in manners, the job said. *Mercenary needed to teach them to stop stealing from travelling merchants.* Killing not necessary, as long as the message got through; thieves weren't welcome in Tarsium. There was a group of seven thieves; two Shenza, three Thearans, and two Omati. A few more and it might have even been a challenge for Lashek. He crouched on a tree branch near the main road, wrapped in Shadow. The thieves would be along shortly.

As thieves often did, they showed up after sundown. Lashek watched them approach, his *Kaizuun* ready in his hand. Trees hugged the road on both sides most of the way between Carmerth and Azar. The thieves had no reason to look up. Laughter rang through the wood as the group walked past him.

"I still can't believe that old lady had two hundred silvers on her," one said, "easiest pay day I've ever had."

"You didn't have to kill her though, Leo," said another.

"You know I don't like loose ends. Besides, we haven't seen a good fight in ages."

Lashek took the chance, and leapt silently to the ground behind them.

"Somebody order a fight?" He said.

The group turned, though not as one unit and not as quickly as *Kaizeluun* would have. He let them scramble to draw their swords. In the time it took them, he could have killed them all.

"What the-"

"Who's that?"

"Lenai, Haris, get him!"

By the time they were ready to fight, Lashek was almost laughing. He didn't bother hiding the throwing blades he'd conjured in his left hand; these thieves didn't have the reflexes to defend themselves. Two of the thieves rushed at him, their weapons raised. Lashek would have preferred to get through it without killing, out of respect for the Tarsi; but this group was violent and aggressive. He threw two blades, and guided by Shadow Magic, they both slammed home into their targets. The two thieves died choking on their own blood.

Lashek sheathed his *Kaizuun*. He had to at least give the rest of the group a chance to quit their crimes and start anew.

"I'm here to persuade you to stop stealing from the people of Tarsium," he said, "by any means necessary. I don't want to kill you, but if any of you attack me again I will."

The remaining five thieves fanned out along the path. The Omati man standing in the middle of the group spoke; he was clearly the leader.

“Give us any valuable possessions you have, and you can walk from here unharmed.”

The others stared at Lashek, stony faced and menacing. Lashek didn't move. The leader raised his sword, his fury overriding his sense.

"Did you hear me, Shenza?"

"I heard you," Lashek said.

"Then make your choice."

"How about this one: Do as I said. Stop stealing and murdering, and you won't die screaming in agony."

The thieves were taken aback, and Lashek smiled. "Did you hear me, Omati?"

He glared and bared his teeth.

"Quiet yourself, scum! The man who seeks to fight five men at once deserves his fate."

Lashek couldn't help but roll his eyes; the man's blustering bravado was obscene. The group proceeded towards him. Instead of backing away, Lashek shook his head.

"And the group of thieves who seek to attack one man deserve much worse."

They reached him, and two of them attacked at once. Dropping to his knee, Lashek ducked under the first sword and unsheathed his *Kaizuun* just in time to parry the second. He rose to his feet again, his blade rushing up to meet with the soft skin of the first man's throat. The blade went deep, straight up into his head, and he died without a sound.

As Lashek pulled his weapon clear, the second man attacked again, this time swinging at his legs. Lashek side-stepped and scooped the man’s sword away with his own, following his attacker’s strike to use the momentum against him. It worked, and the attacker stumbled sideways, falling onto Lashek’s waiting blade. The sword sank into his side, between two plates of cheap armour, and the bandit screamed as he died.

The leader of the gang looked surprised at Lashek's skill, but rallied quickly.

“So you beat two men. They were clumsy and stupid in any case. Now the real battle begins.”

Lashek laughed openly, with genuine good humour.

“You think you know battle? You don’t leave the sides of your brutes, and you only fight those you know you will defeat. That's not battle, it's murder. You're no match for a *Kaizeluun*, and before you die you'll realise your mistake.”

The leader gave a somewhat unconvincing smile and raised his sword. The remaining bandits rushed at him, swords raised. But when they reached him, the two men behind the leader faltered and slowed. The leader kept running, and threw a reckless attack at Lashek's side, which he blocked without difficulty.

Before the group's leader could stop running, Lashek pointed his blade at the man’s unprotected side, and his own speed forced the blade to sink deep. He fell, and Lashek let his *Kaizuun* slide out of the man as he did so. He then turned from the gasping leader and faced the last two men, who promptly turned and sprinted in the opposite direction.

Lashek watched the men as they fled, and sighed.

“Wise move,” he said to himself, “I didn't wish to kill today. But you,” he snarled, turning toward the leader, “I most certainly wish to kill you.”

He descended upon the wounded thief, and as he saw Lashek's figure looming toward him, the man shrieked in utter terror, wide eyed and flailing. He had no doubt the two running thieves heard the screaming as they ran; hopefully it would be enough to deter them from breaking Tarsi law again.

Koros burst into laughter, spilling some fortified wine as he handed it to Lashek.

"I always love hearing your tales, Lashek," he said, "you're as good a storyteller as you are a fighter."

"My stories would be boring if my targets weren't all such idiots," Lashek said.

"True, true," Koros replied, "but you're still the most entertaining of our... patrons here."

Koros put a bag of coin on the bar. It made a satisfying thud on the thick wood. An easy job for a bag of coin; Lashek didn't even break a sweat.

"Thank you, Koros."

He took the bag and tied it to his belt, then finished his drink. Just as he ordered another, the door to the Sceptre opened and Delan walked in. He waved to Lashek, but there was something odd about his movements.

They'd been friends for years; Delan left Shanaken far later than Lashek had, but they both ended up at the Sceptre by chance, and became fast friends. They'd even done a few jobs together.

"Delan, what's wrong?"

"I've just heard word from Shanaken," he said, "Elana Zadan was killed. They're saying it was that Shenza who was smitten with her... Dakesh Zakiil."

Kerberos

1773

He watched Aella leap off the bridge, her figure tiny from such a distance. The Soul Blade was still in his hand; Athan's blood had wicked off it the second it slid out of his body, but it still looked filthy to him. *I'm sorry, Athan*, he thought, *I really thought you were with me*. Omatus was his, but the victory felt hollow next to the loss of Athan. Despite everything, Kerberos had loved him.

A small part of him was expecting to rule with Athan by his side. *Fool*, he told himself, *it was never going to work out that way. You knew Athan wouldn't go along with the invasion and occupation of a city. Especially after you threatened Aella. It was always going to end with him dead.* Sheathing the sword, he turned his back on the view of Omatus and strode back into the throne room.

His warriors stood waiting, disciplined and silent. The majority of his army, the group he'd sent against Aella, were given orders to patrol the city and stamp out any resistance. His gradual infiltration of the Omati Royal Guard over the last decade meant that there was far less of a fight than there should have been. After waiting so long for his victory, the ease of it felt like a disappointment.

At least there was more work to be done; Sithares wasn't satisfied with ruling a city. Omatus was simply a prize given to Kerberos for his loyalty. For Sithares to prosper, death, violence and pain had to be spread as far and wide as possible. And fire; everything must burn.

Shoving his brother's remains off the throne, he took his place and sat on the blackened wood. The crown was half melted, fused to Alliphis' head; he didn't bother with it. Kerberos didn't need a crown, his army was loyal to the core. For a while, he simply sat in silence, savouring the feeling of the throne and the smell of his brother's burnt corpse. Then he called his commanders in, and their planning started.

A purge, he thought, *Sithares wants me to purge the entire city. It wants me to destroy the one prize I was given for being its faithful servant.* He was tasked with killing all those who wouldn't worship the Fire God. But there was a better way, a way that would create much more conflict, negative emotion and violence, while at the same time bringing any remaining civilians into order. It had been his idea, one he was particularly proud of when Sithares reacted with emphatic support; round them up, force them to fight each other. Not only would it mean Sithares' satisfaction, but it meant Kerberos would still have a city to rule.

An arena sat within the walls of the Noble side of Omatus. Underneath it were hundreds of small stone cells that could each hold a few people. Those cells were now full, and more people who'd refused to worship Sithares were being held in the Royal dungeons. The purge was going to be glorious; so many people fighting for his entertainment, and for the glory of Sithares. They would make an excellent example to the rest of the city; a large group of the resisters might even be convinced to convert after seeing their loved ones slaughter each other.

Then there was the rest of the Argyris family. His father died during the years Kerberos was wandering Omas, building his army. His mother and younger brother Anamas still lived. They'd been captured during the battle at Kerberos' orders. He didn't know what to expect from them.

Kerberos held no ill will towards the surviving members of his family; if they could display their loyalty and worship Sithares, he would let them live. He wanted to let them live, but killing them would be easier than killing Athan, if they made it necessary. He deeply regretted not being able to kill Thorinos himself; he couldn't imagine anything more satisfying, but the chance had been taken from him. He would make do with the rest of Omatus.

"Anamas."

The youngest Argyris child was a man grown now, though still far smaller than either of his brothers. He sat slumped on the small stone bench, staring straight ahead at the wall in front of him. Two tiny dots of bright torch flame danced in his eyes, but the dungeon's shadows threatened to swallow them. Kerberos stood outside the bars, watching his brother. For a while, nothing moved but the fire on the wall, and the ones in Amanas' eyes. He couldn't read the young man; he'd been away too long. The mannerisms he'd memorised all those years ago were gone.

"Anamas. Look at me."

The two tiny fires shifted, and Kerberos felt the dark eyes of his brother fall on him again for the first time in decades.

"Welcome home, Atillus."

"What happened to Thorinos?"

"Thorinos? You won't even call him father?"

"That man was no father to me." Kerberos could barely keep the rage out of his voice. "I want to know only so I can better understand where the Argyris family stand. So I know how best to take over."

Anamas lowered his head and sighed. In that moment he truly looked like a prisoner; powerless, weak and resigned to his fate. It only spurred Kerberos' fury.

"Who killed him? How many wanted him dead?"

His brother's head snapped up, and now the torch's reflection wasn't the only fire in his eyes.

"Why do you assume he was killed, Atillus? You always hated him. It doesn't mean anybody else did."

"You were always the naive one. Thorinos was hated by most of Omatus even when the Megalos family ruled. You should have seen the way his workers looked at him when his back was turned. Any one of them would have gladly stabbed him in the back if it did not mean their own death."

"Father was a great man. He only wanted what was best for our family, and for Omatus. I wish you could have seen-"

Kerberos slammed his fist against the thick metal bars of his brother's cell. Fire curled over his fist from within, lighting the cell as brightly as if the sun itself had been conjured. Anamas stared at the flame, mouth open and eyes wide.

"Thorinos Argyris was a fool and a weakling. My only regret at him dying is I did not get to kill him myself."

"Atillus..."

"My name is Kerberos."

Anamas paused, the reflected fires in his eyes growing as he stared back at Kerberos in shock.

"I'm sorry, *Kerberos*, that father was such a disappointment to you. But is that really worth attacking all of Omatus? He's dead. You'll have no closure by killing others."

Kerberos stared hard at his brother. Anamas had read almost as much as Kerberos himself when they were younger; he'd expected a much sharper mind. Instead, Anamas seemed to have taken after Thorinos after all.

"I do not care about closure. He deserved whatever he got, that is not why I am here. I simply want to know how and when he died so I understand where our family stand. Tell me what I want to know."

Anamas shook his head faintly, still staring at the fire licking Kerberos' skin. In that moment, he looked old beyond his years.

"You're really not Atillus any more, are you?"

"Atillus died the day Thorinos cast him out of this city. I am who I was always meant to be."

"I don't know you, Kerberos."

"Tell me what I want to know."

A few moments of silence stretched out between them, and Anamas' eyes returned to the wall in front of him. Kerberos contemplated torture for a few seconds until finally his younger brother started speaking.

"Father was planning it for decades. He was undermining the Megalos reputation ever since we were children; paying workers and servants to spread rumours among the lower class and nobles alike."

Kerberos nodded; he knew all of that.

"I want to know what happened after I left."

Anamas continued on as though Kerberos hadn't spoken.

"After Andron was assassinated, Dassius took over and imprisoned father and Alliphis. Mother and I were forced to stay within the family palace, with guards watching our every move. He was every bit the horrible person father's rumours warned he would be. Cruel and arrogant, with no understanding of what it took to be king. He kept them locked up for far longer than was legal, convinced they knew where you were and that our entire family had conspired to kill his father.

"Eventually a coup began, from the bottom up. People began protesting Dassius' rule, and supporting our release and return to the throne. He agreed to release us, but he gave father one last ultimatum; hand you over, or die."

A swell of triumphant satisfaction burned in Kerberos' chest; his father had been killed because of him after all. He'd said he didn't want closure, but the fact brought a smile to his face nonetheless. Anamas kept talking, unaware of his brother's happiness.

"He swore he didn't know, and the public believed him. In front of thousands, Dassius cut off father's head himself."

Anamas turned to him then, noted his smile, and lowered his eyes to the ground.

"It didn't take long after that for someone to assassinate Dassius. No matter how powerful someone becomes, there is always a way to have him killed. No one knew who the killer was, or who paid him, but by then no one cared."

The way Anamas said it gave Kerberos pause; it sounded almost like he'd been involved. But he kept talking, and Kerberos let him continue.

"The Megalos family didn't dispute our claim after that, and Alliphis stepped up as king. He ruled well. You might even have been impressed. Tell me, Kerberos, did you plan on releasing Mother and I?"

He thought about it. Although they were technically family, and the public were obviously on their side, releasing them this early could be risky. Especially if Kerberos' suspicion that Anamas was the one to organise Dassius' assassination was correct.

"I was, yes. Eventually."

"I see. I'm assuming we'll need to prove our loyalty somehow?"

He hadn't thought about it, but historically there was only one way to join Kerberos' tribe. He was a king now, not the leader of a mere tribe, but the concept was the same.

"Do you know much about the Thearans, Anamas?"

"Enough to know where you might be going with this."

He walked away, not bothering to raise his voice as he left his brother behind.

"Good. Tomorrow then. Be ready."

Karak

1773

When Omatus was invaded, Karak was in his chambers in the royal palace. He didn't know what was happening until loud footsteps thudded down the hallway outside his door, and he barely shifted into Anamas in time before half a dozen royal guards burst into his room, weapons up and eyes searching.

"Master Anamas," one of them said, "you need to come with us."

He followed, terrified and wondering whether it would be safer to disappear. They brought him down through the palace, further and further until he realised where they were leading him.

"Are we going to the dungeons?" he asked.

"Yes, it's the safest place for you. There's been an attack, and the king ordered us to bring you there to keep you safe."

Curious, he thought, *since when were members of the royal family brought down to the dungeons?*

"Is there not a safe room near the throne room?"

"Master Anamas, please," one of the guards said as they marched him through the lower corridors, "there's no time for a discussion."

Karak let himself be led into a cell; any half decent Tarsi magician could escape a dungeon cell, if it came to that. His curiosity overtook his fear for the moment, and he wanted to see what might happen. *Besides*, he thought, *it probably will be much safer in a cell; if no one can reach me, who could harm me?*

The guards closed the cell door, and all but two of them left the dungeon. The two who stayed behind stood facing away from him, down the corridor they came from. *So they are protecting me after all. If they were imprisoning me, they'd be watching me instead of looking out for people approaching.* It was a comforting thought, but he wasn't convinced it was true. His question about a safe room was a test; he already knew a safe room was hidden behind the throne for situations exactly like this one.

He waited in silence, though a hundred questions burned in his mind. Anamas wouldn't ask questions, even under stress, and he'd already spoken to the guards far more than the real Anamas would have. Instead, he tried to puzzle out who would dare attack Omatus. Other than Theara, it was perhaps the most easily defended city in all of Pandeia.

Ermoor wouldn't attack Omatus without first conquering Shanaken, and they were no closer to that than they were to building machines that could fly. Shanaken had no interest in invading or conquering anyone, and neither did Tarsium. Thearans were divided into small tribes, and though they did have a reputation for attacking smaller cities, they hadn't attempted an attack on Omatus in thousands of years. Not since the ancient Thearans first left their home city and began wandering the deserts of Omas. They had no motivation to take Omatus.

Karak bolted upright in the dark cell, startling the guards into drawing their weapons and turning on him. *Sithares,* he thought, his heart racing, *Sithares has gathered the Thearans together somehow, chosen a Hero and started its quest to destroy Pandeia.*

"Who is attacking?" he asked the guards.

"Master Anamas, we've only been told to keep you safe," one of them said, "nothing more."

Karak sat on the stone bench again, his heart still thumping far too quickly. If his theory was correct, it didn't matter if he was Anamas Argyris or Karak Toor; all of Omatus would burn.

He recognised Atillus walk up to his cell, even out of the corner of his eye. The eldest Argyris boy had been big even as a child; as a grown man he was gigantic. As Atillus approached, the royal guards walked away, leaving the dark corridor empty but for the two brothers. Keeping his eyes firmly on the wall in front of him, Karak affected an expression of resigned disappointment on Anamas' face. He wasn't sure of the exact nature of their dynamic before Atillus was exiled, but he knew it wouldn't be good under the current circumstances.

"Anamas."

How did he gain the loyalty of the royal guard so quickly? he thought, *he hasn't been in Omatus for so many years.* He wouldn't have put it past Atillus to install corrupt guards over the time he was gone; a lot of the guards were hired from Thearan tribes and mercenaries in Tarsium or Tarsius.

"Anamas. Look at me."

Karak turned to him, seeing him directly for the first time. He hadn't just grown up, he'd changed. His skin was dark, his eyes gold. A full beard framed his face, dazzling white against his dark skin. He was bald, which served to make him look even older; it felt like such a long time since he'd seen Atillus. The change wasn't just skin deep, either; Karak felt power and lethal intent pour from the man like smoke from a fire.

They spoke a little, and Atillus asked him about Thorinos. He seemed pleased to learn his father was dead; not surprising considering the circumstances of his exile. What surprised Karak almost as much as the change in his appearance was his new name; he'd shed his old identity as Atillus, and would only accept being called Kerberos. The name sent a shiver down his spine, and a cold weight into his gut.

Karak was once an enforcer for the Circle; his role was to remove enemies and threats to Pandeia. He knew a little about the war of the Gods, but not nearly as much as the scouts and agents of Tarsium; Tarra and her peers. Despite his lack of knowledge, everyone in the Circle knew about Sithares and its army. Thousands upon thousands of burning souls formed the ranks of soldiers, with a Demon at the head of each legion. Above the Demons were the Phenixes, Arch-Demons and Royal Guard of Sithares. Above them, and second only to Sithares itself, was the Demigod Kerberos, son of Sithares and second in command of the Army of Fire.

Their conversation revealed a few more things about the man Kerberos had become. None of them were reassuring in the slightest. He was utterly devoted not just to Sithares, but to the Thearan way of life. Despite the fact that he'd shed his previous identity as Atillus Argyris, he was adamant on claiming the crown as his birthright. Before he left Karak in darkness again, Kerberos gave him one last shock, though he didn't say it out loud; to win his freedom, he would have to fight for it. To the death.

Aella

1773

She'd been walking through the desert for two weeks, alone and lost, when a sliver of memory came flooding back. A greysnake slithered out of the sand in front of her as she walked, shocking her into stillness. By instinct alone she conjured a fireball into her waiting hand and launched it at the venomous snake as it streaked towards her with its fangs bared. The fireball hit the snake square in the face in mid air, and the explosion knocked Aella off her feet.

She stood, shaking, and when she saw the remains of the snake burning in the sand, her eyes locked onto the flames. She heard the crackle and saw fiery tongues lick the air in a chaotic but beautiful dance; the smoke that was her memory solidified into a handful of jagged pieces, and she collapsed to her knees under their sudden weight.

Kerberos. Kerberos took everything and everyone. He took my very soul. He took Omatus. He will pay.

The thought ran through her mind on a loop, over and over. She was helpless to stop it, and she didn't want to. She remembered the burning farmland, the slaughtered innocents, Erasmus' execution, Kerberos stabbing Athan through the heart, and her leap off the great bridge of Omatus. She remembered being swept away in the Alpheus, spun around endlessly underwater until she was taken into darkness. And then the fire.

It was exactly as Athan had described it; feeling, hearing and seeing nothing but fire for an eternity. She had gone mad in that place; even now, with memories crashing through her head, she still felt the fracture her death left behind. Some thoughts were disconnected, out of her control. What memories she had were just pieces, fragments. She tried to hold on to the memories that made sense, the ones that were vivid and real; Kerberos was evil. Erasmus and Athanasius were dead. Omatus was conquered. She was powerful.

Powerful enough to kill Kerberos.

You must be careful, little warrior.

O great God of Fire! I, your lowly servant, pledge to you my life and soul!

Had she said that? Were those her thoughts? Her memories? Or something else?

"I get the feeling you're a much better fighter than I am, Roxane."

Athan's face, saying those words to her. But was that her name? Roxane? Her name was still lost in the smoke of her mind. It sounded wrong, but she remembered... *I fought an entire army, all of Omatus came to face me in the desert. I left one survivor to tell the tale.* She remembered the army on the bridge. But had she killed them? She couldn't remember. She fought, and many had died; she remembered that. But the entire city? Surely not.

The Omasi stone hides the blood and ashes and scorch marks. But the bodies are everywhere; the stone cannot hide them. She saw the city then. It was ruined, lifeless and empty. Only corpses lived there now.

It is your time to burn.

Kerberos' face now, saying those words and grinning like a lion in her mind. He gestured to the side and she looked over to see Athan, Erasmus and her mother burning alive, screaming and writhing in agony.

Help! Save us! Only you can stop him!

They screamed for her help, and she started towards them but saw herself burning next to them too, and suddenly she couldn't move.

You will be so powerful.

Her mother's face appeared. Her mother... What happened to her? She wasn't dead, was she? No. She hadn't seen a body. There had been no bodies left behind after Kerberos moved on.

No bodies.

She didn't actually see Athan die either, she realised. Not at Mara, and not in Omatus.

It was so far away... was that really Athan I saw?

He walked to our camp. He tried to tell me not to kill Kerberos. Has Athan been Kerberos' this entire time?

Her mother's face became stretched and monstrous. Fire blazed from what had been gentle eyes only seconds before.

YOU MUST CHOOSE YOUR BATTLES!

YOU WILL KILL ANYONE WHO CHALLENGES YOU!

The screams hammered her mind, deafening her. The terrible face slowly faded. When it was gone, she felt utterly alone.

My mother... Did she join him too?

Was no one loyal to me?

North. That was all she could think as she trudged through the unforgiving desert. *North is home.* Her memories were still shifting, changing. Nothing was clear. She knew she was Aella, daughter of

Helene. But she was equally certain that she was Roxane, the most powerful Fire Mage in history.

You are the most powerful Fire Mage your father and I have ever seen.

I get the feeling you're a much better fighter than I am, Roxane.

I am Aella.

No. I am Roxane.

The desert stretched on forever as she walked. The gigantic mountain in the distance grew, slowly eclipsing the sky. There was something eerily familiar about it. It seemed to pull her inexorably forwards, drawing her on. The sun beat down on her, and although the heat was intense, it seemed to give her energy.

She remembered Kerberos. He needed to be stopped; he needed to be killed. But she needed to go home first, she had to go north. The mountain, slowly growing larger in front of her as she walked; that was home. It had to be. There was magic in that mountain, she felt it even from so far away; and what better place for the world's greatest Fire Mage to call home than a mountain filled with fire tall enough to reach the sun?

Roxane pushed on through the desert. She was on her way home.

Sitharkos. The name leapt into her mind as she sat on the sand in the twilight just before sundown, eating a burnt greysnake and staring at the hulking mountain. She knew it, had been there before. Its pull was unmistakable now; it was where she belonged, where she was destined to go. It was home. She tried to remember more about where she had come from. The memories were so vivid only days before. She'd been certain. But now the solid visions had evaporated into smoke again. Each day, she felt herself slipping. Sitharkos took up more and more of her horizon, and as it grew closer her memories fled further away. But still, she knew it was her destiny, and she couldn't stop herself from walking towards it each day.

She remembered walking up the mountain; how alive she'd felt. How free. And she remembered someone walking beside her, taking her hand and calming her soul when she feared she'd started going mad.

Erasmus.

His beautiful face rose from the smoke of her broken mind and smiled. A tear glided down her cheek, and she remembered again. He made her feel whole. He had simply walked next to her up the mountain, silent and patient and steady. She remembered; it was the mountain itself that made her feel so awful -

She screamed as a sword swept through his neck and those loving eyes emptied. She fell, and the ground below her suddenly felt as smooth as stone, and the sunshine wasn't beating down on her because -

The corridor was dark. There were no windows to let the sunlight in. It was underground. Erasmus' corpse lay on the cold stone floor, and Aella couldn't scream. She was paralysed as Kerberos' warriors dragged her back the way she had come. Nomiki was walking away, and though she couldn't see her face, she knew the warrior was still wearing that evil grin she had shown when she took Erasmus' head off.

The warriors suddenly disappeared and she was alone, laying on the cold stone floor. The light in the distance on either side of the corridor disappeared with the warriors, and then there was nothing but her mind and her heartbeat and the cold black stone.

Kerberos

1773

He watched Anamas fight, his certainty dissolving more every moment. Kerberos had always been discarded by Thorinos, but he'd at least had size. Even when he was young, he had the body of a warrior; the muscles and skill had only come after training, but the potential was there. Anamas, on the other hand, was small enough that he'd even been picked on by children several years younger. It always felt strange to Kerberos that he inspired more anger and disappointment in his father than the youngest Argyris boy. Anamas was everything his father hated, even more so than Atillus had been.

But now, Anamas moved like a snake. He fought against one of Kerberos' warriors, and it seemed he might win. Kerberos watched intently, following every movement. His younger brother wielded a short sword and a half shield; light and fast, but vulnerable. He wore ill fitting armour and moved as though he'd never worn it before. His opponent, a man named Stathis, was larger and fought with a traditional Thearan full length spear. His armour fit well and he moved like a true Thearan warrior.

Anamas swayed beneath the spear as it swept at his throat. He leapt in and lashed at Stathis, opening a long but shallow cut over his chest before diving back out of reach. Stathis roared, out of fury rather than pain, and attacked again. Kerberos was certain of the outcome by the time it happened. Stathis bled from several shallow cuts. He was overexerted, and furious enough to make mistakes. Anamas knew exactly what he was doing. He touched his blade to Stathis' right forearm in a light arc.

Stathis dropped his spear, and Anamas stepped in, smashing his shield into the man's face. Dazed and blinking, he barely reacted as Anamas cut his throat. Bleeding and choking, Stathis dropped to his knees, grasping for Anamas. He died twitching in the arena's grey sand, his arm still outstretched to his killer.

After the fight, Kerberos kept his word; Anamas was released from the dungeons. Eirene too; normally each individual had to fight, but Anamas made a point of challenging on behalf of both of them. He had to admit a brief flash of relief; his mother certainly would have died in combat. As much as he hated Thorinos and Alliphis, Eirene Argyris had always been warm towards him. She was ever the diplomat, and most of her time endeavoured to keep the family from fighting. If Alliphis was as decent a ruler as Anamas said, Kerberos was certain it was only because he was smart enough to listen to his mother's council. One of the many mistakes Thorinos made as king was to push Eirene's words aside.

Once free of the dungeons, Anamas and his mother disappeared quickly, without looking back. Kerberos knew without needing to ask that they would live in the Argyris family palace from now on, instead of the royal palace. He was glad to have them out of the way. But he made a note to himself; Anamas had to be watched.

Omatus looked beautiful under the setting sun. Kerberos stood on the balcony of the king's chamber, looking over the city as the light faded. He ignored the slave boy, who snuck out of the bed and closed the door quietly behind him. The city was his, but there was still much to be done. Too much of the population was resistant to a new ruler.

He understood it, but it had to change. He knew they would eventually see things the way he did, but as long as people rebelled, control would be difficult to maintain.

The arena was set up and running; it wouldn't be long before the fights began to have an effect on the survivors. Once those not loyal to Kerberos and Sithares started dying in greater numbers, fear would do most of his work for him; but with fear came conspiracies, assassination attempts, and treason.

Ruling a city would not be the same as taking over a Thearan tribe; the people of Omatus weren't superstitious, nor was their culture based around a Fire God. But if Thorinos could do it, Kerberos could do it far better. He'd planned for it his entire life. Standing over the city now felt right. It took far too long to get here, but it had been his one goal since the moment Thorinos disowned him. Since before that, even. Sithares delivered on its promise, as Kerberos knew it would.

Patches of smoke still littered Omatus; though the fighting during his invasion had been relatively contained, there was still damage. He'd ordered his warriors to clean as much as possible, but Fire Magic was designed for destruction. Omatus would forever be stained by the battles of Kerberos' invasion. The damage didn't detract from the city's beauty, and Kerberos took one last look at Omatus shining under the setting sun.

He moved back into his chamber, relieved that the slave boy was gone. The only person he wanted to spend time with outside of carnal pleasure was Athan. Sighing, he slipped back onto the bed.

Without Athan, he felt a sensation he hadn't experienced before. Not even after his father beheaded Amares. For the first time in his life, he felt truly lonely.

Mathys

1773

Walking quickly through the crowd, Mathys cast his eyes over the street. Though busy and chaotic, he still spotted several Ermoori soldiers. They wouldn't be allowed to start a fight in the middle of Azar, but they had ways of capturing people without violence that would be within the laws of the Tarsi. Mara followed him, eyes wide and face pale. He held her hand so they wouldn't lose each other, and tried to clear a space so she could move without being shoved or knocked. Her belly was becoming larger, and he had to keep her safe not just for her own sake, but for the baby's.

He pushed a trolley ahead of them, loaded up with all their belongings. Constant noise battered his ears; talking and shouting, thousands of footsteps, and the clanking and clatter of trading in the open markets. The air was full of the smells of cooking food, sweat, and drying rain on the cobblestones. He glanced around again; there was no time to waste. If they were spotted, it would be over. He headed for the eastern side of the city; there had to be places outside the districts that the Ermoori wouldn't bother looking.

Thanks to Isobel at the Copper Dragon, Mara and Mathys managed to disappear for two months in the swamplands of Ermoor outside the city. It was long enough for the Ermoori presence in Tarsium to dwindle, but not quite long enough for them to stop looking entirely. Mathys suspected they wouldn't stop looking.

"Hey!"

Mathys didn't see the person shouting, but the accent was Ermoori. He pulled Mara along faster.

"We need to leave, now."

"But we just got here!"

They rushed through the streets and alleys of Azar, shoving their way through the crowd as shouts echoed after them. Azar wasn't as big as Ermoor, but there were far more people; so going even a short distance within the district took longer than Mathys was used to.

With the soldiers behind him, the trolley full of their things, and Mara to take care of, he wasn't sure they'd make it.

More shouts rang out behind them, closer now. He couldn't believe there were still so many Ermoori searching for them; from what Isobel said, the search had died down. *They must have been swarming the streets two months ago,* he thought, *why are the Tarsi allowing this?* But he knew even as he thought it; the Ermoori knew Tarsium's no violence law as well as any others. As long as they didn't harm anyone, they would be allowed to stay and patrol the streets.

He hoped there were Tarsi watching now. If the Ermoori attacked in the streets, and the Tarsi intervened, Mathys and Mara had a good chance. The people ahead of them stepped out of the way, staring at them as they pushed past. Some didn't move fast enough, and the trolley was jostled as it bumped them. Mathys didn't bother apologising; there was barely time to breathe, let alone stop for conversation.

"Stop!" another soldier shouted.

He pushed on, faster. Mara barely kept up, and he found himself half dragging her through the crowd. Steering the trolley as best he could past thousands of people, Mathys finally caught sight of the east gate out of Azar. It was at least five metres tall, several metres wide, and the doors stood open. *Almost there,* he thought, *not much further...*

Right in front of him, an Ermoori soldier appeared in the crowd. It was too late to try to change direction; the soldier spotted them almost as soon as Mathys spotted him. Mara screamed, and he rushed at them. He grabbed the trolley, grinning at Mara.

"I've got them!"

The soldier pulled a baton from his belt; not necessarily fatal, but violent enough that the Tarsi wouldn't stand for it. All he could do was hope the Ermoori would be stopped before they hurt Mara. If they were anywhere else, he would have simply killed the man, and anyone else who got in their way; but the no-violence law in Tarsium meant that as well as relying on the Tarsi for safety, he was unable to take matters into his own hands. Desperate, Mathys rammed the trolley into the soldier, knocking him to the ground. He grabbed Mara again and steered past the Ermoori, pushing as fast as he could.

"They're here," the soldier shouted from the ground, "they're getting away!"

Another Ermoori appeared ahead, shoving through the crowd towards them. He unholstered his gun and raised it, straight at Mara.

"No!" Mathys screamed.

For a second that stretched into what felt like hours, Mathys watched the Ermoori soldier grinning, his finger tense against the gun's trigger. When the explosion shattered through the noise of the street, his heart plummeted into his stomach. Screams and chaos followed as everyone nearby tried to escape the man with the gun. Mathys stopped, too terrified to look at Mara. *If she's dead,* he thought, *I can't handle it. I can't see that.*

But she screamed again, and his eyes dragged towards her even as his heart screamed at him to look away; and she stood next to him, terrified but unscathed. He looked again towards the soldier who fired his gun, but there was nothing there. *The Tarsi?* he thought wildly, *can they do that?* But it was too late to stand around wandering, and he shoved the trolley forward again.

He guided Mara to the gate, not daring to look behind them. Beyond it, green valleys and gently rolling hills stretched into the distance. Shouting followed them, but Mathys managed to haul the trolley into a cart and jump in after Mara before anyone caught up to them. Another sharp explosion boomed somewhere close, but the cart remained whole. It carried them almost silently along the smooth pathway, and Mathys finally allowed himself to breathe.

Out of Azar, he thought, *but it's not over yet. They've caught our scent, and we're being hunted.* As Azar gradually shrank behind them, Mathys found himself thinking about what came next. There was no relief about having escaped Azar; all he felt in that moment was exhaustion. They'd be living in hiding for the rest of their lives. Riffolk wouldn’t stop until Mara and Mathys were both buried under his feet.

Zeera

1773

Another ten years passed. Ten years of searching all of Pandeia, responding to rumours. Zeera was in Ermoor again, after another rumour surfaced; *I believe Taranos has been summoned into the physical realm,* the note from Korol read, *this could very well mean a Hero will be chosen.* Now she was back in the makeshift safe house Korol lived in, and even there she felt the presence of Taranos. It was subtle and weak, but everywhere.

A God hadn't been summoned in thousands of years, and even then Zeera was almost certain it was merely a rumour. She had no idea what the consequences might be. Even more concerning was how difficult it was in the first place; who in Ermoor had the knowledge and power to summon a God? The population of Ermoor believed in a deity they simply called God, and in a strict and nonsensical scripture full of contradicting rules.

It took her a while to remember the last time she was in Ermoor, and the feeling that swept over her in Darkpoint. *What was that boy's name?* she thought. He would be older now; maybe old enough to understand how to summon Taranos. She remembered hearing about his accomplishments, even in Tarsium. His inventions were being used all over Pandeia. But she still couldn't remember his name.

Korol was out, scouting for information. Zeera decided to head to the lab in Darkpoint again, if only to get a better sense of Taranos' energy. *Just watch,* she reminded herself, *don't interfere unless the safety of Pandeia is at stake.* It was far easier to say it to herself than to do. The night was cold and foggy, and Zeera approached on a rooftop without bothering to hide. The Tarsi were skilled with stealth, but the fog meant anyone could have been invisible; she couldn't see the road below her, and barely saw the lab itself.

Zeera didn't think there would be any activity this late at night, so she settled in place, closed her eyes and simply stretched out with her senses. *At least it's not raining,* she thought, *though it's certainly cold enough.* A pulse of magic tugged at her mind; *that's not Taranos.* Her eyes flew open. *There's a* Kaizeluun *in there.* She had no idea what was happening; what was this scientist boy getting himself into? The Shenza hadn't set foot in Ermoor that she was aware of.

Heart racing, Zeera leapt down onto the street and raced to the lab's entrance. The front door was locked; but with technology instead of physical locks. She wouldn't be able to figure out a coded security lock in time, so she began climbing instead. Every building had windows, vents, pipes; any number of entry points that were easy for a Tarsi to access. Shifting into a cat's body, she slithered into a small vent after prying it loose.

The magic she felt led her down, underneath the lab. Zeera followed powerful waves of magic through vents in the ceiling until she saw the cause; a secret lab, with a captured and now unconscious *Kaizeluun*. Just as she reached a small vent in the wall, the *Kaizeluun* woke and the young Ermoori scientist spoke with her. The binds holding her were thick metal, but Zeera knew what Shadow Magic was capable of; she wasn't surprised in the slightest when the *Kaizeluun* broke out of them.

Zeera watched as the young warrior destroyed a huge deadly machine. She made it look easy, as though the machine were made of paper and harmless. The scientist fired at her over and over, missing her but for one spray of blood from her arm. The *Kaizeluun* knocked him to the ground, and he tried to fire one more time; but he was out of ammunition. They stared at each other for a moment, and Zeera felt the scientist's rage even from her hiding spot.

"What you do here today will make no real difference," he said, "Shanaken will fall. All of Pandeia will fall."

The *Kaizeluun* smashed her shield into his face, and he collapsed to the ground. She immediately leapt up to the roof, turning into a blurred shadow and disappearing into one of the larger vents in the ceiling. Zeera left the lab as fast as the small form let her. Seeing the *Kaizeluun* fight was breathtaking, but seeing her mercy towards the Ermoori scientist left her conflicted. *Why did she let him live? He's clearly a danger to her entire country, and to all of Pandeia besides.* His words before she knocked him unconscious rang through her mind, chilling in his flat, careless voice; *all of Pandeia will fall.* It was a direct threat. Surely the Circle would act on it now.

After the confrontation, Zeera followed the *Kaizeluun* to a small but high rooftop where she had built a camp site. She watched as the young warrior performed her *Zuunshai* and dressed her wounds. Once she was finished, the girl went to sleep, and Zeera crept as close as she could. *Is this Shanaken's Hero?* She thought, focusing the words so that Asheilos might hear them. But no answer came, and Zeera couldn't feel anything different about the girl other than a huge amount of power.

The girl turned in her sleep, and Zeera finally saw her face properly. Her mouth fell open; it was the daughter of the man she'd thought was Shanaken's Hero just over twenty years earlier. *She's even more powerful than her father,* Zeera thought, *even in a place as dead as Ermoor and wounded, she's so powerful!* She almost didn't believe it. *Elana.* Zeera remembered her name. Surely someone this powerful had to be the Hero. But without an answer from Asheilos, she couldn't do much but keep watch from a distance.

Zeera watched as the girl visited the Lord Commander. She didn't see what was done or said inside the building; the girl simply disappeared during her visit. *Kaizeluun* were talented with stealth; not quite as talented as Tarsi, but they were infamous for their Shadow Magic. It meant Zeera couldn't get closer without potentially being spotted by Elana. As she watched, Elana left the Lord Commander's home and ran back towards her camp.

The next few days, Zeera lost track of her, until she felt another pulse of intense magic. She knew it was Elana immediately; there was no other person in Ermoor as powerful as the young *Kaizeluun.* Leaving Korol to her scouting, Zeera sprinted for Dreadhold; the military district. By the time she got there, Elana was sneaking through alleys and over rooftops, strategically killing Ermoori soldiers one at a time. Even watching for her, and stretching out to sense her magic, Zeera barely saw her with eyes alone. Only her sensitivity to magic allowed her to know where Elana was with any certainty.

It took Zeera a while to figure out what she was doing, and by the time she realised, it was too late; she was going down into Tyra. She followed Elana's progress from above, but didn't dare to enter the sewers after her. Now that she was attuned to Elana's specific magical trace, Zeera could feel her moving through the tunnels. It felt like pulses, or vibrations, but in her mind instead of physical. After a while, Elana found Tyra, and all Zeera could do was wait and hope she would survive whatever mission she was on.

Aella

1773

Sunlight pierced her eyelids and she woke on the soft sand, taking ragged breaths and clawing the ground. The desert stretched out forever in every direction, broken only by distant blurry mountains and the massive, ominous silhouette of Sitharkos to the north. Her memory had fractured again. She found it odd that she knew, even though she had no idea what her real memories were. Sitharkos was close now. Another two days walk at most.

She survived by using her Fire Magic to kill and cook any animals she came across. She slept on the sand, with no protection or shelter. And she walked. All day, every day, until she couldn't walk any further and collapsed on the sand to sleep. There were days when she didn't find any food. Even when she did, it was more often than not a greysnake or small diamondback; and she'd still be hungry after eating. Every day was a new eternity. She woke, walked, and starved.

Her mind went blank, and there was a numb sort of comfort in the nothingness she felt. Days bled into each other as the sun mercilessly baked her shrinking body. She was close to death; she could feel it. From somewhere in the detached haze that was her mind, the idea of death terrified her. She'd been there before, hadn't she? She saw the fires for herself. An eternity of burning awaited her, and even the half missing memory of it was torture. But still she kept walking; she could do nothing to stop death now.

She held on until she reached the southern base of Sitharkos; the sheer wall of black stone. A few metres from the wall, she collapsed and let the fires take her again.

The fires within Sitharkos rumbled and roiled, far below the peak. There was so much magic. She sat on the precipice of the volcano, staring wide-eyed into its fiery depths. Nothing else existed for her now. It spoke to her when the sun was high, whispers echoing incoherently from the fires so far below. Every day she sat on the edge, trying to understand the words. They never seemed to become any clearer.

She could almost remember someone making the whispers disappear, a long time ago. A partial face swam into her mind, the features not quite settling. *My beloved,* she thought. But the name would not appear, and the face didn't become clear, and the whispers took hold of her again. She listened, rapt, as they formed words she almost understood. So close, and then they would fall back into meaningless noise. Distantly, she wondered if she'd already gone insane.

Aella. Your name is Aella.

The thought entered her mind without warning. She was sitting on the edge of the volcano's peak again, staring down and lost in the incoherent whispers of the fire below. She jumped and gasped; the thought hadn't come from her own mind.

Remember, Aella.

A flash of light blinded her and a roaring assaulted her ears; for a moment she thought the volcano itself was erupting. Then her mind flooded with memories. A stream of images, sounds and sensations rushed through her, tearing at her mind the way a strong enough wind can topple a building. It happened so fast, but felt like forever; within her mind, as vivid as the black rock of Sitharkos beneath her feet, she relived her entire life. Tears rushed down her cheeks as she struggled to keep up with the memories.

When she jumped off the great bridge of Omatus, she started moaning "no, no, no..." but there was nothing she could do to prevent what had already happened. The dark grey water sped towards her and she screamed as she smashed into the unforgiving surface for the second time, her body as utterly destroyed as if she'd dived onto stone.

This time, however, she didn't lose consciousness; she felt the Alpheus sweep her away, tossing her like ashes caught in the hot air above a fire. She was swept through the current for hours, dead and alone, as the Fire Magic within her put the pieces of her body back together. It took a long time; the water of the Alpheus worked against the magic. Finally, she came to rest on the beach where she had awakened.

She wandered into the desert again, losing her mind and herself gradually until she came to Sitharkos, where she died once again at its feet. Then came the fire. She rose, made of fire instead of flesh, her body already repaired, and sprinted up the mountain. Not along the winding, gently sloping path as the Thearans did; up the sheer wall that faced her. She ran easily, as if the laws of nature no longer applied to her. She was unchained and unburdened, and she felt more herself than she ever had before.

She reached the plateau of the mountain, and kept running until she reached the volcano's peak. There, on the edge, she collapsed as the Fire dissipated. As soon as it left her, she lost consciousness.

Kerberos

1773

Kerberos watched as a man and woman fought viciously. They were siblings, that much was clear at a glance; but they fought like the bitterest of enemies. The emotion, and the passion, were entertaining; the skill of the fighters, however, left much to be desired. He had to remind himself that they weren't trained. Shouts and screams came from the crowd watching, both on the seats above and from the cages below. Chanting, from those loyal to Kerberos and Sithares, overpowered the crowd's screaming; the prayer he'd taught them. It served to channel Fire Magic into the chanters, and to heighten the emotions of unbelievers; fear, anxiety, hopelessness, rage. All were valuable to Sithares.

Only half a year had passed since his rule of Omatus began, and already the vast majority of his subjects were converted. He was brutal, and fear played a huge part in his control over the city, but the people would see him as a true ruler soon enough. Screaming with rage and grief, one of the siblings swung her sword with both hands, squeezing her eyes shut. Against a trained opponent, it would have meant her own death; but her brother was as inexperienced as she was. He didn't see the attack, couldn't move away in time, and the sword planted itself in the side of his head with a wet cracking sound.

Her brother dropped his weapon immediately, stood on his feet for a moment longer, then crashed to the ground, convulsing silently. The victor continued screaming, but her voice was one among thousands, as the crowd cheered. She'd won her life. If she stayed loyal to Sithares and Kerberos, she would keep it.

He didn’t just watch the fights; he joined in every day. There were two reasons, other than for the glory of Sithares; he wanted to show the people that he wasn't some pompous king who wouldn’t get his hands dirty, and he just loved the violence. Whenever he delved into the arena, he let at least a dozen civilians in, usually more.

Without fail, they cooperated to try to bring him down. The hope and determination in their eyes would have been touching, if they had any hope of victory. Seeing his subjects work together so readily certainly made him fall in love with Omatus again, and it didn't take long before he remembered why he'd wanted to rule so badly in the first place; it truly was the greatest city in the world.

Back when his family ruled, and the Megalos family after that, Omatus was struggling on, led by cowards and corruption. Finally, Kerberos had his chance to make Omatus what it should have been; what it was in ancient times, when Sithares ruled Pandeia. The Age of Heroes, Kerberos heard it called; Sithares called it the Age of Gods. Whatever the name, the time was coming again.

Returning his attention to the resisters, he casually threw a fireball at one of them, smiling as the others flinched at the man's screams. He could have made short work of all them with his favourite weapon, the Demon's Tail, but he wanted to drag the fight out. Longer fights meant more rage, more pain, more fear. Besides, Kerberos found a particular pleasure came from giving false hope and then snatching it away; when he just used his old steel sword, and some Fire Magic every now and then, the resisters seemed to get the idea they might be able to win. It didn't matter if he fought every day, and always won; they held out hope.

A small group of the civilians in the arena shied away, and Kerberos focused on the ones who didn't. Three of them launched at him simultaneously, enthusiastic but unskilled. He grabbed a spear by the wooden shaft; it was thrust at him wildly, missing his head entirely but close enough to snatch out of the air. Yanking on it, he pulled the attacker off their balance and swept his sword through the man's neck. The other two lunged at the same time, and Kerberos dodged one spear and blocked a sword.

Several more of the arena fighters moved in, clearly under the impression he was overwhelmed. He let them get close, playing with the two attacking him as the rest closed in. He threw another fire ball, this one engulfing three opponents at once. As the fire spread, Kerberos kicked a woman in the chest, sending her flying into the grey dirt. Two more unbelievers rushed him, but he sidestepped and cut them both down.

Kerberos stared down the remaining arena combatants, judging them each by their stance, movements and choice of weapon. *There are no real warriors here*, he thought, *just victims*. They all stormed him at once, and within moments all of them were dead. Cheers rang through the arena, echoing and clashing until the sound was all that existed. Screams and boos from below were almost unrecognisable, merging with the cheering and laughing from his loyal followers.

Karak

1773

I *had no choice,* he thought, *it was either pretend I can't fight like Anamas and die, or win and attract Kerberos' suspicions.* He didn't teach Atillus any combat when he'd trained the boy all those years ago; he learned how to fight from the other trainers and certainly didn't need any tips from Karak. Besides, even though the Tarsi fighting style didn't use any magic, it was still a Tarsi secret, and he'd promised himself that he would only share a few small techniques. Karak had watched the other warriors training Atillus; he knew what he could expect if it ever came to a fight between Kerberos and himself, and he was certain he couldn't win. Especially now that Kerberos had watched him fight in the arena.

After the fight, Kerberos let him and Eirene free from the dungeons, and they went straight to the Argyris palace. Karak would send for their things later. Eirene went straight to her old chambers, where she'd slept before Alliphis was king, and stayed behind locked doors without so much as a word to Karak. He went to Anamas' chambers, knowing Kerberos would be watching him but not knowing how. *The guards will be loyal to him,* he thought, *but how much further does it go? Has he hired spies?*

Paranoia was a natural side effect of working in the shadows, and Karak couldn't help but think Kerberos was the kind of man who understood spying and secrets better than most. The time Atillus had been away would work to Karak's advantage, at least; any differences in the way Anamas behaved could be blamed on his natural growth, and would be less suspicious. Still, Karak had to be careful. Kerberos was clearly not the forgiving type.

One thing he'd felt when Kerberos approached him the first time stuck in his mind; the sheer depth of magic within the giant man. Karak knew he wielded Fire Magic, but there was something more to what Karak felt, something truly terrifying about the power emanating from him. As if he really was Kerberos, the Demigod son of the God of Fire.

Forcing Karak to fight for his life wasn't the only violence Kerberos brought to Omatus. An arena was opened, and all citizens who didn't openly accept Sithares as their God were made to fight to the death. Kerberos himself joined in the fighting most days, and Karak found himself hoping the new king would die in battle.

As a boy, Atillus had been driven and ambitious, and took to combat like no one else he'd ever seen, but Karak hadn't picked up on the merciless cruelty Kerberos now displayed in the arena. He was well and truly taken by Sithares. Atillus would have made a good ruler, but Kerberos was a danger not just to Omatus, but to all of Pandeia. He left the arena before the battles were done, shutting himself in his chambers to think. *Even if it's too late to rejoin the Circle,* he thought, *I have to do something.*

Sundown brought an uneasy stillness to Omatus. Karak stayed within the Argyris palace after dark, and Eirene stayed in her chambers even during the day. The guards in charge of protecting the Argyris family were clearly loyal to Kerberos, and watched Karak whenever he left his chambers. He took to leaving out the window, shifting into a cat to escape. He'd kept the royal guard outfit he stole to assassinate Dassius, stowing it in a locked chest on top of an archway over one of the alley ways near the Argyris palace. Even then, he only left the palace when he was certain it was safe.

A week or so after Karak won his freedom by combat, Kerberos showed up at his chambers. No guards announced him, and no entourage followed him. A quiet knock on the door gently broke the silence of Karak's chambers, and he opened the door to find the giant ruler of Omatus staring down at him.

"Anamas," he said, his voice strangely gentle, "I want to talk with you."

"Of course, come in."

A small table with two chairs stood on Anamas' modest balcony. Karak sat down and gestured for Kerberos to do the same. The sun was down, and the sense of frightened stillness Karak had grown used to settled over the city below.

"You have seen the arena fighting?" Kerberos said.

"Yes."

"You know why we fight?"

"Sithares demands death."

Kerberos leaned back, his eyes boring deep into Karak's own.

"You are different, brother."

"As are you. What do you want from me?"

"The same thing I want from all of Omatus. Worship Sithares, accept the Fire God as your own. Live as one of us."

"And if I don't? You'll throw me back in the arena?"

He didn't answer at first. They stared at one another, and the longer they did, the more Karak was certain Kerberos knew he was an imposter.

"I will," Kerberos said, "if I have to. But I do not want to."

"I'll think about it, Kerberos. Give me another day."

"What is there to think about?" Kerberos said, his voice even, "you worship Sithares, or you die."

Zeera

1773

Elana's magic and strength pulsed from underneath the city, powerful but flagging. Zeera had no idea what was happening. After a while, Ermoori soldiers began flooding towards the manholes above Tyra. *She's set off alarms,* Zeera thought, *even someone as powerful as her may not survive an entire Ermoori battalion.* Zeera had even less chance, so all she could do was wait and watch.

Ermoori soldiers milled around a few entrances, but Elana branched off and went back to Tyra. *What is she doing?* Zeera thought, perched on a rooftop above one of the manholes. Even from so high, sounds of intense battle carried up from under the city. *She freed the Tyrans,* Zeera thought, *and they're fighting!* As far as Zeera was aware, it had never happened before.

She felt Elana move from Tyra again, heading west. Zeera followed, and they crossed into Ironhaven. As Zeera rushed over the rooftops, Elana exploded out from one of the manholes in the middle of the street. She carried a Tyran over her shoulder, and glanced in a few directions before pausing. Then she sprinted away from Zeera, into the fog. Zeera followed as far back as she could; with Elana above ground again, she had to avoid being seen.

Elana dropped the Tyran at the feet of an Ermoori girl, and then leapt straight up to the light poles running over the streets. She sprinted along the light poles, and Zeera followed along the rooftops. When they were most of the way through Dawnton, Elana's magical trace disappeared and she fell suddenly, crashing to the ground. Zeera skidded to a halt so quickly that she almost fell to the ground as well.

From her vantage point, she watched Elana slowly get to her feet and limp down the street. Five Ermoori soldiers turned onto the same street, heading towards Elana. As Zeera watched the *Kaizeluun* kill them, two more soldiers approached from the street below her. She glanced down, cursing as the two soldiers snuck towards Elana. Zeera dropped to the street behind the guards without a sound.

She had a dagger; they had guns and armour. But Elana was badly injured and already facing five soldiers, and she had to do something. As Zeera caught up to the two soldiers, an explosion lit up the street ahead, and Zeera threw a hastily conjured defensive spell while the echoes still rang. The soldiers in front of her covered their eyes and stopped running, and Zeera sliced the throat of one of them and rammed her dagger into the other's side. He grunted, but didn't fall.

Zeera felt a hand clamp down on her arm. The Ermoori pulled her close and punched her side, hard. They grappled, the Ermoori's strength not fading as fast as it should have. She wrenched the blade side to side, still buried to the hilt in between his ribs. His breath caught, but Zeera's arm was still crushed in his grip. She heard a gunshot further down the street, and distantly hoped Elana hadn't been killed. Desperate, Zeera wrenched her dagger out of the man's side, shifted into a taller figure, and used the height to shove the blade into his neck before he could react.

Elana looked even worse than she had before; but the five Ermoori soldiers were dead, and after she was done with them she kept moving towards the docks. *How is she not dead?* Zeera thought. Elana kept fighting, through injuries and setbacks, and despite having no magic left. It was truly remarkable; Zeera hadn't seen anything like it. *She must be the Hero. She has to be.* Following along the rooftops, Zeera watched the girl limp towards the docks, shedding her costume as she approached. *She won't get out of there alive,* she thought.

Ignoring the voice of reason in her mind, she sprinted past the *Kaizeluun*, leapt to the ground on the other side of a building, and made her way to the docks.

The Tarsi managed all of the importing and exporting of goods between Ermoor and Tarsium. They were good with numbers, incorruptible, and respected. Luckily for Zeera, Ermoori couldn't tell Tarsi apart from each other, so Zeera snatched a cargo manifest from the nearest Ermoori dock worker and affected an authoritative posture. It was the first time she'd ever pretended to be something she wasn't without an actual disguise in place; she felt exposed, as though anyone might recognise her.

Before too long, Elana showed up, stumbling toward Zeera. She was barely conscious. Zeera herded her onto the ship and made sure she was well hidden in the cargo hold. After that, she stayed with her; if she truly was the Hero, it was Zeera's responsibility to bring her to Tarsium. If she wasn't, it wouldn't take much to travel back to Ermoor. Zeera took care of her, pouring water gently into her mouth and trying to feed her.

By the time they reached Tarsium, the girl was well enough that Zeera left her alone until they left the ship for solid land. They spoke, briefly, but the girl seemed utterly unaware of the danger Pandeia was in. She'd obviously not been spoken to by Amalus. *She's not the Hero.* A deep, profound sadness filled her at the realisation. Zeera liked the girl a lot; she would have made a great Hero for the

Circle. Instead, she gave her a message to send to the *Duulshen*, the elders of Shanaken, and sent her on her way.

Lashek

1773

As soon as he heard of Elana's fate, he packed his things and left for Shanaken. He'd known her since she was a child. Her death at the hands of a traitor was the biggest shock he could have imagined; her skill with both blade and magic was unparalleled. In her relatively short life, Elana had become a legend of the Shenza, even among her fellow *Kaizeluun*. The word spread rapidly through Shanaken and then through Tarsium; many Shenza travelled through, and lived in, the beautiful country with the blessing of the *Duulshen.*

Lashek had been living there for over a decade. He'd occasionally seen Elana, whenever she travelled for a mission, and kept in contact with several other Shenza. But he'd grown used to the Tarsi way of life, and had no plans to live in the great forests again; until word came that Elana had been murdered. The funeral was held before he arrived, as was the execution of the traitor, Dakesh. Lashek was just as shocked to find out who killed her as he was at Elana's death; Dakesh was a good friend of Elana's, and by all accounts had been in love with her. It made no sense.

Tarsium was a beautiful country, with gently rolling hills, sprawling districts and a bustling population full of people from every culture in Pandeia. Lashek loved it. But even he had to admit it was nothing compared to the majestic forests of Shanaken. Lashek was *Kaizeluun.* The forest filled him with magic and energy; he felt it building even as the ship approached, before he'd set foot on land. As soon as he arrived, it felt as though Tarsium had simply been a dream; pleasant, but ultimately meaningless. He was home again.

Though the magic and energy of the forest revitalised him, there was a noticeably sombre mood as he walked through the city. An odd quiet had fallen over the Shenza, as though Elana's death was a personal blow to each and every one of them. He supposed it was; she was a hero even to those who didn't know her. Besides that, no traitor had been executed in Shanaken for hundreds of years. The Shenza weren't just mourning a hero, they were deeply saddened by Dakesh's breach of the tenets.

A group of Shenza practiced their *Zuunshai* on a nearby training platform. Lashek watched as he passed by. He felt the magic coming from them even without his blade in hand. He wondered if he would have even noticed if he hadn't spent so much time away from the forest. Even after a few days in Shanaken he was growing used to the immense ocean of magic that filled the air.

"Lashek!"

His sister, Nalesha, cannoned into him, almost toppling both of them off the walkway.

"Hey Nal, How's things?"

"How's things? Really? I haven't seen you in years and that's all you have to say?"

He laughed and rolled his eyes; Nalesha hadn't changed a bit. Except for the sword in her belt. He nodded his head towards the newly forged blade.

"*Kaizeluun*, huh? Impressive... Only ten years after me!"

"Well I'm nine years younger than you, so take that," she shoved him, "and I beat your time on the tree too!"

That was a surprise; Lashek's time in defeating the Tree had come close to Elana's, and hers was the fastest in Shenza history.

"You beat my time? I don't believe you."

"Ask Father, he was there!"

"Maybe I don't want to."

They walked into the city proper together, arguing and shoving as though the years that separated them were only a day.

Kerberos

1773

After the arena, Kerberos returned to his chambers. The sun had sunk low on the horizon, and despite the combatants putting up almost no worthy fight, Kerberos was tired. He found himself thinking about what would happen when he finally had control of Omatus, and the favour of the people. Sithares wouldn't be content with stopping at one city. Even if Kerberos kept the arena battles going, Sithares would want more; demand more. He'd allied himself with the God of Fire, and it was a commitment he couldn't change or get out of. Even thinking about it was dangerous; Sithares had access to his thoughts, his emotions. There was no knowing when he was being listened to.

Pushing the thoughts away, Kerberos busied himself by stripping his armour and cleaning the blood off. Thearan steel was durable, but Kerberos liked to maintain it every chance he got. He laid his Demon's Tail and sword on the bed; he would clean and sharpen them after his armour. As he worked on the second gauntlet, a tiny sound broke the silence in his chambers. A Tarsi crept along next to the wall, towards the balcony.

Silently, Kerberos placed the gauntlet down and grabbed the Demon's Tail. He threw the spiked ball as hard as he could, aiming just ahead of the intruder. It smashed into the stone wall, embedding itself and stopping the Tarsi cold. He wrenched it out of the wall, taking pleasure in the Tarsi flinching. Pure terror lit up the intruder's eyes, a grimace splashed across its tiny mouth.

"I do not know who you are," he said to the tiny figure, "but today is your last day."

The Tarsi bolted, and a flash of light blinded Kerberos from nowhere. Blinking for a brief moment, Kerberos thought the intruder would escape. But the light faded almost as quickly as it appeared, and Kerberos saw it almost at the balcony. He threw the spiked ball again, this time hitting the wall inches from the Tarsi's legs. The intruder tripped on the chain and crashed to the floor, and Kerberos leapt across the room, landing square on the tiny figure.

He hit the Tarsi in the face over and over, then rained punches on the rest of its body. Bones cracked under his fists, and he felt the flesh becoming soft and ruined as he kept hitting. Grabbing the tiny intruder by the throat, he threw it against the wall.

"I don't know what your purpose was in coming here, but if I see you again I will tear you apart and burn the pieces."

Kerberos grabbed it again, and hurled it out the door, over the balcony to the street below. It was very unlikely the Tarsi would survive, but if it did, it wouldn't go near Kerberos again. He returned to the bed, placing the Demon's Tail down and glancing around the room. As he searched, the intruder's presence bothered him more and more. *It wasn't an assassination attempt*, he thought, *or it would have attacked while I was unaware.* As far as Kerberos could tell, nothing had been stolen. No information could be gained from his chambers; he had no private conversations in his own room, and he kept no written records there either.

Kerberos hated mysteries. Or rather, he hated not being able to figure them out. *I should have kept it here*, he thought, *asked it directly what it was trying to achieve*. Omatus was a busy city, however, even this close to the royal palace; the Tarsi would be gone one way or another. It might have had help. Or it could have crawled away, or might already be dead.

One thought flashed through his mind and disappeared again before it had even fully formed: *Anamas hired the Tarsi*. His brother was most likely involved in Dassius' assassination. Kerberos had no proof, but the way he'd told Kerberos what had happened... He decided to pay Anamas a visit the next day. The youngest son of the Argyris family may have just committed treason. He could have sent his royal guard to question him, but Kerberos wanted to be the one to find out for sure.

Kerberos returned to cleaning his armour, frustrated at himself for throwing the intruder away. Fire Magic pulsed through his body in response to his anger, glowing and burning. It felt incredible; the strength of it, the energy it gave him. Emotions crashed together in his mind, indistinguishable from each other. Being angry or upset had almost become a pleasure. He tried to push the thoughts away, focusing on his armour and weapons. But the anger remained, and the odd pleasure that came with it.

"I'm sorry, my king, but master Anamas is far too ill to speak with you."

Kerberos stared at the guard outside Anamas' chambers. The young man shifted, fear sparkling in his brown eyes. He tried and failed to maintain eye contact with Kerberos.

"Are you saying no to your king?" Kerberos asked.

"I'm very sorry, your highness. It's not up to me, I follow master Anamas' orders. He's been ill since yesterday, and none of us have been allowed into his chambers."

As soon as the guard said it, Kerberos was certain; Anamas was involved with the Tarsi who'd appeared in his room. He moved past the guard, ignoring the man's weak complaints, and pushed Anamas' door open. Inside, all was still. He saw the open doorway into the bedchamber, and beyond it he could just see Anamas laying under a mound of sheets. Kerberos approached the bed. He watched, ready for an attack, but Anamas remained where he was.

"Anamas."

His brother groaned feebly, barely moving under the sheets. There was real pain in his voice, real suffering. *Maybe he really is just ill*, he thought. He left the room, ignoring the guard again on his way out. Anamas was either talented at deception, or very ill. Either way, Kerberos decided to wait until Anamas showed his face again to question him. *I will find out what Anamas is up to*, he thought, *sooner or later.*

Karak

1773

Kerberos, as the new king of Omatus, was utterly ruthless. Countless battles raged all day in the arena he'd set up, all fought by the terrified citizens who'd refused to worship Sithares. Kerberos continued to fight in the battles himself, slaughtering dozens every day. Every single man, woman and child was given the option of praying to the God of Fire, or fighting for their life in the arena. Karak would have thought most would just give in and pray to whatever God Kerberos told them to, as he'd done himself;

but a large number of Omatus' citizens resented being told what to do enough that they were willing to fight for it.

There was so much death. After a while, the grey sand in the arena was stained to a deep, sickening purple from all the blood. There were whispers of an uprising; the commoners and nobles alike, trapped in the cells below the arena together, spoke in hushed tones of attacking Kerberos as a group. It wouldn’t work; Kerberos proved that every day by walking into the arena by himself. He barely wore any armour, and even refrained from using Fire Magic, and was still unscathed.

If Kerberos kept slaughtering the people of Omatus at the rate he was, there wouldn't be a city left to rule before long. He couldn't be beaten in battle. But every man could be killed somehow. Karak loved living in Omatus, and didn't want to give up now, but something had to be done. Even if it meant risking his life or his identity as Anamas, and the home he now lived in. He'd long since given up on the idea of rejoining the Circle, or even ever living in Tarsium again. Omatus was truly his home now, and seeing it ripped apart by the one man he'd thought could rule it best... *I have to do something*, he thought, *nobody else will.*

It had been a long time since he'd had to kill someone; Arrus was the last death by his hands, and that had been eighteen years ago. He still used magic all the time; he wouldn't be able to hide as Anamas without it. But assassination was a different game, and someone as powerful as Kerberos would be difficult to kill even if taken by surprise. He prepared himself, ready for a death; either Kerberos' or his own. When he was ready, he headed for the royal palace.

The king's bedchamber was empty when Karak arrived. He thought it would quiet his fears at least a little, but he was wrong. Waiting in the silent chambers of the most dangerous man in Omatus was nothing short of terrifying. Hours passed in complete silence, as the sun slowly sank into the horizon. In a corner of the room lay a locked chest made from Shenza steel and old thick wood. Karak knew exactly what it contained without needing to investigate; the book of Sithares.

If I can steal it, he thought, *maybe I can kill him with its magic.* But he knew it wouldn't be enough even as the thought occurred to him. Instead, he simply sat and waited for Kerberos. He had no plan, other than surprise, and even then it didn't feel like enough. Just as the last hints of sunlight faded from the room, the door swung open and Kerberos strolled in. He moved like a predator; fast yet calm, purposeful even when he wasn't hunting.

He'd felt magic when Kerberos visited him in the cell on the day Omatus was taken, but the power he felt now was suffocating. Karak had no idea how Kerberos lived with so much power coursing through his body. Crouching in a corner of the room, dagger in hand, he watched Kerberos take off the minimal armour he wore and begin wiping the blood off it. *What am I doing?* He thought, *even in such a vulnerable position he'll kill me easily.*

The Tarsi had been silently assassinating threats to Pandeia for thousands of years, but never one of the Heroes of the Gods. Looking at Kerberos, feeling his power pulse throughout the room, Karak was struck with the certainty that he wouldn't survive if he attacked. *I need to get out of here.* As silently as he could, he crept towards the wide open balcony doors.

Kerberos' spiked metal ball slammed into the wall right in front of Karak's face. Before he could turn to face the king, it was ripped out again in an explosion of shattered stone.

"I do not know who you are," Kerberos said, "but today is your last day."

Karak sprinted for the doors, panic flooding his mind like a sudden storm. He ignited the defensive spell as quickly as he could; but in his rush it was only half as strong as it should have been. Kerberos snarled, and Karak was given a moment of freedom, but before he reached the doors the spiked ball smashed into the wall in front of his legs. He tripped, and Kerberos was on him in an instant.

Something slammed into his face, and for a second he thought it was the spiked ball. He was hit twice more before he realised dimly that it was Kerberos' fist. All he could see was the ceiling of the room, covered in bright white spots that pulsed in his vision, and Kerberos. The king of Omatus punched him again and again, and each hit felt like a war hammer crushing his body.

There was no air in his lungs. He couldn't speak or breathe, couldn't even lift his arms to try to stop the attacks. Kerberos grabbed him by the throat with one hand and threw him against the wall. The room disappeared under a blanket of blinding, burning white as pain overtook him. Somewhere, distantly, he heard Kerberos' voice, but the words were swept away by waves of agony. He felt air whooshing past him, cool and strangely comforting, as he realised that Kerberos must have thrown him again. His body fell far, too far, and he crashed into solid stone.

Tarsi magic could do amazing things. Healing spells and potions were common, and Karak knew most of them. But laying on the street, shattered and broken, he could do nothing but hope Kerberos wouldn't show up again. He couldn't use magic in his current state; even moving was beyond him.

The street was empty; sundown in the noble district was always quiet, except for the feast halls inside each palace. Laying in the darkness, pain throbbing through his entire body, Karak drifted away again. When he woke, the sun was breaching the sky's edge and shop keeps were beginning to set up ready for nobles to purchase their goods. Karak dragged himself to his feet, limped into the closest alley and collapsed again. *At least I'm out of sight now,* he thought.

Slowly, Karak dragged himself towards the Argyris palace. The road in front of his eyes faded in and out, replaced with exploding pinpoints of sharp light. The pain tearing through his body was constant; he didn't want to think about how much damage had been done, and he could barely think even if he'd wanted to. Underneath him, the ground was cold and rough, dragging against his skin and jarring his already broken body. *Just need to get home.*

The Argyris palace may as well have been in a different country. He pulled himself along the ground, trying not to scream as his wounds caught on the rough stone pavement. Time stretched out before him, as endless and painful as the road between him and the palace. He faded into unconsciousness more than once, the pain overwhelming. Each time he woke again, the sun had barely moved in the sky.

Zeera

1773

She was relieved to be out of Ermoor. Returning to Tarsium always put her at peace. But by the time she arrived in Azar, Zalla pulled her aside desperately.

"What are you doing back here?" she said.

"I came across a *Kaizeluun* I thought was Amalus' Hero," Zeera said, "What's happening?"

Zalla stared at her, an unreadable intensity filling her eyes as her mouth almost disappeared in a thin white line.

"Taranos awoke and destroyed a chunk of Ermoor, two weeks ago. We're almost certain a Hero has been chosen, but it's chaos there right now."

Taranos is in the physical realm, Zeera thought, *just as Korol said.* The idea of the God of Power roaming through a city left her mouth dry and her lungs empty. After Korol's last note had summoned her to Ermoor, Zeera got used to the idea in theory; but knowing a God was truly out there right now was something else. *I should be there.* She'd decided to board the ship that carried Elana to make sure she was okay, but the journey by boat was almost a month; with her new speed in the water, Zeera could have made that trip in a handful of days.

"I'll go back," Zeera said.

"You shouldn't have left."

Disappointing Zalla left a sharp sting in Zeera's chest, and looking at the Speaker was suddenly difficult.

"I know," she said, "I was doing what I thought was best for Tarsium, and Pandeia."

"Zeera, I understand how frustrating it is to wait around until your purpose presents itself, believe me. But we have a mission. Our focus needs to be on that, and nothing else."

She was right. Zeera knew it, but a part of her also knew that Elana was special. If she wasn't already chosen as Hero, Zeera was almost certain she would be soon.

"Of course," she said instead, "I'll go back to Ermoor now."

Zalla looked pleased, but Zeera couldn't stop thinking about the fact that she might not notice a Hero because she was too busy following orders. It made her feel even more helpless than just sitting around in each city, waiting for pulses of magic or Asheilos' voice. Still, she knew that leaving Ermoor when she did wasn't good enough; now there was something to look for. She left Zalla, heading straight for the tunnels under Tarsium.

Speeding through the ocean felt different to going through the tunnels and rivers of Tarsium; as soon as she emerged from the underground cave system and into the ocean proper, there was a daunting sense of scale. She was suddenly tiny, surrounded by endless depths in every direction. Living beings were everywhere, and though she couldn't see them, she knew they were there. The endless, featureless ocean ahead of her served to distort her sense of speed and time. She had no idea how fast she was going, but she pushed her hardest. Being surrounded by ocean had one advantage; Zeera felt an unstoppable well of Water Magic within her. She felt more alive than she ever had in her life. Her energy was as limitless as her magic, and she kept pushing until she saw the land ahead of her. *How long have I been swimming?* she thought, *surely not days?* But it had to be at least a few days; the distance between Tarsium and Ermoor was immense.

Zeera climbed onto the shore at the south side of the city. The military had a much smaller presence in the poor districts, and Zeera was able to sneak in and out without being seen. She went straight to Korol, slipping through the fog over rooftops until she reached a manhole close to the safe house. Korol waited for her by the fire. She didn't raise her head when Zeera crept through the tiny entrance.

"Zeera. You chose an interesting time to leave Ermoor."

Her tone was cold, distant. Zeera looked at her as closely as she could in the low light. She hadn't seen Korol angry at her before; it felt strange and uncomfortable. All she had done was her duty; locate a possible Hero and escort them safely to Tarsium. It wasn't her fault Elana turned out not to be the Hero.

"How was I supposed to know Taranos would wake?"

"You were meant to be in Ermoor. The Circle didn't approve you leaving like that."

"I'm the Hero of Asheilos!"

Zeera didn't mean to shout, but her voice echoed down the tunnels regardless.

"I should be allowed to make some decisions."

"The Circle is in charge, you know that."

Korol's tone was still cold, but somehow gentle at the same time. All it did was confuse Zeera. She'd disappointed the Circle, and Korol, and Zalla. Korol spoke to her with some distance, but there was no real anger underneath her words.

"I know, but don't you wish sometimes you could have a little more freedom? You're stuck in Ermoor a lot longer than I am... Don't you get sick of it?"

Korol turned to stare at her so quickly that Zeera didn't even see the movement.

"We work for the safety of all of Pandeia."

Her voice was quiet. There was still no anger, but her tone had shifted; it now felt dangerous.

"This is bigger than freedom," Korol said, "I chose to be a Circle scout. I knew what I was getting into. I've never wished for anything else."

Zeera's mind filled with more fog than the streets above them.

"I thought you wanted this too," Korol said, "haven't you dreamed of being the Hero for most of your life?"

"Of course," Zeera said, "but wandering from city to city, waiting and watching... it's so much more difficult than I thought it would be."

"Zeera, you need to focus. The Heroes aren't free agents, living as they please. They're servants of the Gods. This is your mission, and we need you."

Hours later, Zeera perched on the corner of a rooftop facing the laboratory in Darkpoint. It was utterly destroyed. The feeling she'd first sensed here before Taranos' awakening was gone, but there was a trace of magic in the air. A magic she hadn't felt before; *Power Magic,* she thought, *it has to be.* It was barely there, but so unique that it tingled on her skin.

Being near magic set off her senses, but magic didn't usually remain after the user disappeared; whoever had been here was powerful. She knew there had been a Hero in the area, but she had no way of knowing where they were now. Every Tarsi could sense magic, but direction and distance were very difficult to discern. Being near the lab was already helpful enough though; she knew there was a Hero, and now it was just a matter of finding them.

Aella

1773

The rushing, roaring flood of memories finally stopped as she caught up with the present. She still sat at the edge of the volcano's peak, and she heard the rumbling fires at its heart. Exhausted, but feeling more whole than she'd felt in a long time, Aella simply stared into the fires of Sitharkos while her mind stopped reeling. She remembered everything now.

Good. We must speak properly. Start a bonfire, child.

The words formed from the constant flow of whispers that emanated from Sitharkos itself; finally, she understood what they were saying. And they were talking directly to her. Still shaking from the intensity of reliving her entire life over again, she stood, tenderly, and did as she was bid.

The plateau was large enough to accommodate thousands, and Kerberos' tribe had visited many times. There was a stockpile of wood left behind, collected but rarely used; the Thearans didn't need much for their fires after Fire Magic returned to the world. She built a tower from all of it, and when it was complete she threw a few fireballs into it. The fire caught quickly, boosted not only by Aella's powerful magic but by how dead and dry the wood itself was. When the fire was raging, the voice came again.

I need your blood.

She took one of the arrows from her quiver and slashed her hand with the blade. She didn't hesitate; even as she wondered why she was following orders from this mysterious voice, she did as it told her. She cupped her hand under the wound and watched it fill with blood. When it was full enough to start overflowing, she threw the blood at the fire. It hissed and crackled, and the voice moaned as it spoke:

More!

She threw two more handfuls into the fire, and then stopped as it turned from bright orange to deep red. A whistling started piercing the low roar of the flames. A powerful rumbling came through the hard packed sand, growing and growing until it hurt. Just as it became too much to bear, it stopped. A figure emerged from the fire, slowly and tentatively. It formed from the thin, burning logs Aella piled together. It moved like an elderly person, weak and shaking. As it stepped out, it turned and reached back into the burning wood, pulling out a cloak of red fire which it swept onto its shoulders.

"Aella."

The demon took another step towards her, close enough now to reach out and touch. As it stood in front of her, a cold feeling rushed through her body as she realised what it was. She stared into its eyes; faint red embers glowing deep within two whorls on the misshapen wooden head.

"Yes." It regarded her coldly, despite the powerful heat emanating from its body. *"You know what I am."*

She dropped to her knees, bowing her head in silent shock. Sithares itself had visited her; had given her back her memories.

"You are a powerful being. I want to help you achieve your mission."

"My – my mission?"

"Revenge. A powerful emotion. My favourite."

"You would help me kill Kerberos? Is he not your son?"

The God laughed; a rasping, grating, terrible sound.

"I am not only the God of Fire, child, but the God of Destruction. There is nothing so sacred to me that it cannot be destroyed. Besides, there is a greater war coming, and I want you in Omatus when it starts."

Sudden hope burned within her, and the image of Kerberos dead at her feet turned in her mind from fantasy to reality. She looked up at Sithares, directly into its eyes.

"What do you want of me in return?"

"You know what I want of you. Death, destruction. Fire. Pandeia must burn."

Still on her knees, Aella nodded. Though her memories had returned, her mind still felt fractured. Having her God lead the way, give her a clear path, gave her some peace from the swirling chaos in her head. Images of her life before passed through her mind, but the feeling was missing; the memories meant nothing to her now, they were just facts and pictures. Sithares was real. Her mission was real. The Fire within her was real.

The only thing she felt when she focused on her memories was rage. *Kerberos.*

"Yes, Kerberos. He must die. His loyalty fled as soon as he was given what he wanted."

"He took everything from me."

"Yes. We both want him dead. You are powerful enough to kill him. Once he dies, the fall of Pandeia will begin."

After Sithares walked back into the fire and disappeared, Aella left Sitharkos. There was work to be done, and she wanted to start immediately. Sithares' voice remained in her mind even after the fire. It was a comfort as she marched through the northern deserts; a guiding presence in the chaos of her thoughts. It told her where to go, what to do, and she could just let her thoughts whirl as she followed the voice.

It didn't take long for her to come across a travelling Thearan tribe in the desert. A modest tribe; no more than a hundred warriors. Aella greeted them with open arms. They unsheathed their weapons; whether she was prey, a threat, or wished to join them, it meant battle. She had no weapons of her own other than arrows, but she felt endless raging Fire within her body. If she had to, she could kill every last one of them without a weapon.

"Greetings, warrior," one of the Thearans said, "do you wish to join our tribe?"

Challenge their leader. Take the tribe as your own.

"I wish to challenge your leader," she said.

They stared at her, their eyes sweeping over the empty sword sheaths on her belt, the quiver of arrows without a bow. Laughter rang out from every Thearan close enough to hear her challenge. No weapons, no tribe; she would have laughed too. But the tribes who hadn't joined Kerberos still couldn't use Fire Magic, and even if they could they would be no match for her. When their laughter died down, she continued staring them down, waiting for the tribe's leader to present themselves.

Eventually, he did. He walked through the crowd, holding a steel axe that looked as though it weighed more than she did. The circle of death formed around them, and the silence slowly transformed into chanting and cheers.

"You wish to challenge me?" the leader said, "with no weapons?"

He hefted his axe, ready to swipe it through her waist. Aella smiled.

"I *am* a weapon," she said.

His axe flew towards her, but Fire leapt over her skin and engulfed her before it struck. When the blade passed through her body, she felt it shearing through flesh and bone; but there was no pain, and the Fire kept burning. Gasps and shouts of alarm rang through the crowd, and Aella lunged at the tribe's leader as his people watched.

Her fingers wrapped around his head as her thumbs found his eyes. She squeezed, focusing her Fire into her hands as she did. The tribe leader barely had time to scream before his head caught fire, melting and burning faster than any normal fire could have worked. Letting go of his ruined head, she picked up the axe with one hand and raised it high. The Thearans around her dropped to their knees, eyes wide as they stared up at her.

"Into the desert," she said to her tribe. "I want an army."

Lashek

1773

L*ashek.*

He stopped in the middle of one of the metal walkways between the trees. He could have sworn he heard someone whisper his name. The usual chatter of the forest seemed somehow more dense, more urgent. Like the forest was trying to tell him something. After a moment listening intently, he shook his head and walked on.

Lashek.

Again. Louder this time. *That was definitely my name,* he thought.

Can you hear me?

"Yes?"

He didn't know what was happening, but replying out loud to a disembodied voice made him feel like a lunatic.

It worked! Lashek, we have much to discuss.

"Who is this? Where are you?"

You wouldn't believe the answer to either question. Find somewhere quiet to sit down... We're going to have a long talk.

He sat on the forest floor, near the edge of the city. Cool air stirred gently, carrying the smell of water, earth and life. The somehow both pleasant and rotten smell of decaying leaves and other things sat heavy this low in the forest. Lashek felt life all around him, vibrant and intense even without his *Kaizuun* drawn. When he did finally draw his sword, everything around him came into sharp focus; the sounds clearer and closer, the auras of countless animals painting his vision in glowing colours. He wasn't sure what to do. The voice wanted him to find a quiet spot, but now that he'd sat down, he didn't know how to contact it again. He felt like a madman, sitting on the ground waiting for a voice to speak from the forest.

After almost an hour, he stood, his legs cramping. Partly to alleviate boredom, and partly to get his mind off the voice, he settled into the *Zuunshai*. He cycled through the dance twice, and on the third time, he almost dropped his *Kaizuun*.

Lashek.

"Yes!" he shouted into the forest, "yes, I'm here."

You may want to sit down for this.

Lashek sat on the cool, damp ground, laying his sword across his lap as he did.

You knew the traitor, Dakesh?

"Yes."

And you knew his sister, Zanela?

"Yes, though not as well."

Good. What do you know of Amalus?

"The same as everyone else; Amalus is the God of Life and Shadow, the creator of the Shenza and all life on Pandeia. What I don't know is who you are, or why you're talking to me."

There was a pause, and to Lashek it felt like the forest itself held its breath.

I forgot how impatient you are, Lashek. It's been a long time since we spoke.

There was a lightness in the voice's tone, as though it was playing with him. But Lashek's chest had gone cold, his stomach squirming.

"Since we - who are you?"

It's a little complicated. I used to be Zanela. I think... I think she died. Now I am Amalus.

"Well, I'm clearly insane," he said, "but just to humour you, how exactly did Zanela become Amalus?"

Amalus is dead. Zanela travelled alone into the forests after Dakesh's exile, and was led to the Eternal Mountain. I don't understand what exactly happened, but I do understand that I am Amalus now.

"Amalus... died? How is that possible? Amalus is a God."

Gods are living beings. The only difference is they live in another realm, a spiritual realm. They live far longer than mortals, but they do age. And they die just like everything else.

"I really thought if Amalus ever spoke to me, it'd be a little more inspirational," he said, "but I guess if you're really Zanela you haven't mastered the art of speaking like a God yet, huh?"

Another pause filled the forest. Lashek felt the trees around him loom closer; it felt like they were staring at him. The idea of talking with Amalus felt decidedly less ridiculous as a Zuzuk landed a few metres in front of him.

There are other things I've mastered, Lashek. But we have more important things to discuss.

The Zuzuk lowered itself to the ground gracefully, its eyes locked on his own.

"You've, uh, got control over this thing, right?"

He is my friend, as are all of the animals of the forests. You have nothing to fear. But I suggest treating them with more respect, Lashek; the Zuzuk can understand the Shenza.

"They... you can understand me?" he said, turning to the huge predator.

It nodded its head. A chill flashed down his spine, his skin breaking out in a cold sweat. The Shenza had maintained a healthy fear of the Zuzuk since ancient times, but knowing they were intelligent enough to understand the words he said made them terrifying in a new way.

Lashek, listen to me. There is a war coming. The other Gods are rising, and Pandeia will not survive if Sithares prevails. I need your help.

"How am I supposed to help in a war of the Gods?"

It's complicated. But I need a talented Kaizeluun, *and with Elana dead, you're perhaps the most talented in Shanaken.*

"Nice to know I was first pick. And 'perhaps' the most talented. You're really good at enlisting soldiers, Zanela."

The Zuzuk's snarling face filled his vision before he could blink, its black fangs bared inches from his face.

I told you, I am Amalus. Zanela is dead. Will you fight for me, Lashek? For your people and your country?

The weight of it pressed on him, and for once he couldn't think of a joke. The Zuzuk backed away and lay down again, staring at him as it did. He looked down at the *Kaizuun* in his lap, at the tenets carved into it, and sighed.

"Yes," he said, "of course I'll fight."

Thank you, Lashek. Now be still, and I will bless you with the strength of Heroes.

Another Zuzuk landed silently in front of him, and padded over the forest floor to where he sat. Something sat in its huge mouth, held gently by fangs that could rip through him as easily as a *Kaizuun* through Ermoori flesh. As it neared, Lashek felt his heart begin beating erratically. Zuzuk were terrifying; there was a reason most Shenza didn't venture down to the forest floor. When it drew close enough for him to feel its breath on his face, its giant mouth opened, and the thing it held fell onto his lap. It let out a slight growl and padded away, and Lashek stared down at the thing in his lap; a book, bound in what looked like pure darkness. He opened it, confused, and started to read.

Kerberos

1773

In the months after the Tarsi showed up in his chambers, Kerberos gradually turned all of Omatus to his side. Anamas hadn't left the Argyris palace, and Kerberos was happy to let him stay there while he improved the city. There were no more intruders in his chambers, or anywhere else for that matter; he hoped the last attempt would serve as a warning for any other people who felt the need to sneak into the royal palace.

The rebellion was done. Unbelievers were more or less extinct, and Sithares reigned in Omatus. Kerberos kept the arena open, but now the fights were voluntary competitions for the glory of Sithares, the champions celebrated as heroes. He even offered money to the winners. Even in the span of two months, the atmosphere of the arena battles went from tense and terrified to thrilling. People previously kept in the cells and forced to fight were now allowed to sit freely in the audience, and the fighters were now devout followers of Sithares who chose to be there.

He'd built a new peace from the ground up, abolishing the petty squabbles of the noble families over the crown and firmly establishing himself as the only ruler. He publicly killed any members of the noble families who disagreed with his rule; it didn't take long for the rest to fall in line. Omatus had previously thrived on the slave trade, but Kerberos freed them all and let them either fight in the Arena or continue in the farms and orchards outside the city as paid workers. His generosity pulled every lower class citizen to support him, and allowed the Arena to thrive, with battles held every day. Sithares gained power and support, while Omatus remained one of the most powerful cities in Pandeia.

He knew it wouldn't be enough for Sithares, but for now the God of Fire didn't seem desperate to push him further. The day would come when he would be required to spread Sithares' fire to the rest of Pandeia, but for now Sithares was not speaking to him at all. He enjoyed the peace, though he was careful to control his thoughts in case Sithares lurked in his mind. Just in case, he focused on a plan of attack for when Sithares inevitably gave the order. A large map of Pandeia lay flat on a table before him; he would normally invite his commanders in for this kind of work, but he stood alone in the command room.

Now that Omatus was his, the next logical step would be the rest of Omas. If it was up to Kerberos, he'd sweep south west first, down the Alpheus to Aethos. The Omati of Aethos were peaceful, according to the history books he'd read as a child. Aethos was the original home of the Austris Arans, the mythical winged people who ruled over Omas in ancient times, before Sithares turned it into a brutal desert. According to legend, they abandoned Aethos in favour of a magical floating city that drifted south on the clouds. Kerberos had had a difficult enough time believing in Gods back then, let alone floating cities and people with wings.

From Aethos, he would turn north to the mountain city of Aros. Even for Kerberos, Aros would be almost impossible to take. Aros was built into the mountains themselves, and the entrance flowed directly into their military barracks; it was a funnel, guiding would-be invaders into what the ancient Thearans used to call a killbox. Aros was the only city built in honour of Theara after the Thearans left their home country. It meant the city was built to be utterly impregnable. As far as Kerberos could tell, they lived up to the reputation. Gangs of roaming Thearans lived in the mountains; they were far more brutal than the desert travelling Thearans Kerberos was used to. Aros was constantly under attack, and had not once been penetrated.

Travelling through the mountains wasn't easy at the best of times, but the mountains west of Aros were particularly harsh. For Kerberos' hypothetical plan, he would journey south again from Aros, and cross the mountains at the very south end of the range. From there he could conduct a swift and effective attack of every western city; Amaseia, Anteios, Akrillus, and Olymus. The four western cities of Omas were much like Omatus, though smaller and with far less resources; the west coast didn't have the fertile soil and farmland that covered most of south eastern Omas. Oromus to the north, as well as Theara, were abandoned. Not worth even a visit. From the west, Kerberos would head east straight to Tarsius. After the trading settlement he would journey over the sea to Tarsium itself, then Shanaken, and lastly Ermoor.

Kerberos would put it off for as long as possible. But if he absolutely had to attack the other cities in Pandeia, he would do it properly; even if he didn't want to, Kerberos didn't do anything by half measures. Looking at the map, Kerberos couldn't help but imagine the entire world in flames. Again, the strange feeling of pleasure mixing with anger and sadness overtook him, and for a while he couldn't stop himself from picturing the hundreds of thousands of people who would die by his hand.

He already grieved for them. So many people would die for Sithares. And where would it end? When it burned itself out, as any fire eventually did. Then there would be nothing; no people, no cities, no Sithares. Kerberos found himself terrified of Sithares, and of his own role in what was to come. But a small part of him, a powerful part, longed for the destruction. The chaos. The fire.

Zeera

1773

Almost a month after Zeera arrived in Ermoor again, she still hadn't found any trace of the Hero. Korol gradually warmed to her again, and they sat in her safe house after another unsuccessful day of scouting.

"I would have thought someone with magic would stand out in Ermoor," Zeera said, "no one else here can wield it, and they don't even believe it exists."

"They may not know they've been chosen yet," Korol said, "or maybe they're in hiding because they know they'll be killed if anyone else finds out."

It was true; anyone displaying magical ability would be rounded up and killed in a place like Ermoor. Zeera didn't believe that the Hero hadn't been chosen yet, but Korol's second point rang true.

"I'm sweeping the city every day, and I've found nothing," Zeera said, "if I'd come near them I would have felt their magic."

"Ermoor is a big city. All we can do is keep looking."

The next day, a public announcement in Rookfell Square stopped Zeera's search entirely. She stood in the crowd next to Korol, both of them shifted into generic Ermoori forms, and listened to the Lord Commander's speech.

"Mathys Corby is hereby stripped of his rank and title, exiled from the great city of Ermoor, and sentenced to death on sight. He is guilty of treason, conspiracy, murder, sabotage, and blasphemy."

The crowd exploded, shouting and screaming for the man's blood. Korol and Zeera glanced at each other; there was no way to be certain, but Mathys Corby was very likely Taranos' Hero. She looked back at the stage as the Lord Commander kept speaking.

"A reward of one hundred thousand crowns will be granted to whomever provides information leading to his capture, and five hundred thousand crowns to anyone who brings him to me, dead or alive."

"He won't stay in Ermoor," Korol said, "we'll check in with the Circle, of course, but the obvious destination for him is Tarsium. Looks like you'll be going home after all."

Zeera nodded; no sane person would stay in Ermoor with such an excessive reward placed on their head. They couldn't prove that Corby was the Hero until Zeera got close, but it was likely enough that she thought the Circle would approve of finding him. It was certainly the strongest lead she'd had in a while.

"Tarsium is even bigger than Ermoor, and the three districts are absolute chaos when it comes to finding someone."

Korol smiled, a little sadly, but with genuine warmth.

"So you'll be home for a while, I suppose."

Zeera smiled back.

"I suppose so."

She was relieved to be going home; but with Korol's demeanour becoming positive again, and with a fresh lead to a new Hero, her motivation for the Circle returned. They spoke some more, mostly about the possible Hero, and settled in for the night. Before she drifted to sleep, Zeera found herself thinking about how terrifying it must be to live in a city like Ermoor and discover magic in one's self.

She certainly didn't envy Mathys Corby, even if he wasn't the Hero of Taranos.

Karak

1773

Anamas' bed was small, but soft and comfortable. Karak didn't remember most of the trip between the royal palace and his chambers. Soft sunlight fell through the windows and pooled on the stone floor. He was healing slowly, and his magic was returning along with his strength; soon he would be able to heal himself with spells.

Shut up in his chambers, Karak had no idea what was happening in the city, but he knew it was bad. Every day that he took to heal, dozens more people died in the arena. *Even when I'm healed, I can't face him again,* he thought. Kerberos was simply too powerful. Even if Karak had taken him fully by surprise, he knew the outcome wouldn't have been any different.

He had some Tarsi potions he'd picked up from travelling merchants who visited Omatus every now and then. They helped, but the process was still slow. Every day stretched into an eternity, his body aching and throbbing constantly. The fear that Kerberos may have recognised him plagued him just as much as the pain. Karak lay in Anamas' bed, waiting and healing, until he was finally able to walk again.

He wasn't sure how long it took, but when he was finally well enough to leave the palace, he went straight to the arena. He had to see if the people were still fighting, or if Kerberos had slaughtered or converted every last person. Seeing more death and violence was not what he wanted, but he needed to know what had happened in the time he'd been healing.

The arena was full of people when he arrived. It could only mean more death. He made his way into the noble section of the seats, under a roof and placed higher up than the commoners. On the opposite side of the arena, the king's viewing section loomed over the battlefield. Kerberos sat watching the fight, a satisfied smile visible even from the distance between them.

Karak watched the fight for a moment as well. The two fighters were Thearan, not Omati, and certainly not nobles or commoners.

Those are Kerberos' warriors, Karak thought, *why would they be forced to fight?* Off to the side, the cages which usually held all the unbelievers and criminals Kerberos forced into fighting were empty. Frowning, Karak glanced over the crowd in the seats; they weren't shouting in anger or sitting in fearful silence; they were cheering.

One of the Thearans beheaded the other and a wave of screams swept over the crowd; disturbingly gleeful screams. Karak shook his head, the noise and chaos suddenly overwhelming; *how long was I stuck in my chambers for?* he thought, trying to remember how many days or weeks had passed since Kerberos' attack. The slaves had brought him food each day at the regular times, but even their visits blended into repetitive, meaningless patterns. *Certainly weeks*, he thought, *but months? Possibly.*

In whatever time he'd taken to heal, the arena somehow changed from an oppressive and horrifying method of execution to a form of entertainment where people could watch instead of being forced to participate. The shift in tone was jarring to Karak. Kerberos couldn't possibly have won over the citizens of Omatus so quickly; he must have slaughtered thousands by now.

Another fight was announced as he was about to leave, and Karak watched as Kerberos leapt down from the king's viewing chamber into the arena. Two Thearans strode out to face him, and Karak couldn't help but sit back down and stare as the fight began. If not for Kerberos, Karak would have thought the two Thearan warriors tall; but Kerberos towered over them. They had strength, possibly even comparable to the king himself. But they moved slower, and Kerberos had strength as well as speed.

Watching the battle, Karak knew without a doubt that he wouldn't be able to assassinate Kerberos. The first attempt, botched though it was, almost killed him. If he tried again, even in the best conditions, his chances of survival were slim to none; let alone his chances of success. Besides, whatever change had come over the people of Omatus under Kerberos' rule was far better than the slaughter he'd witnessed before he tried assassinating the king.

If the change in the arena was permanent, and no other innocents would be killed, perhaps Kerberos wasn't such a terrible king after all. *I have to be sure*, he thought, *if Kerberos can rule well and fairly then maybe Omatus can prosper again.*

Eventually, he discovered he was bed-ridden for close to two months. In that time, Kerberos managed to convert most of the citizens to worshipping Sithares; though there were still many deaths. Karak didn't agree with forcing people to worship any God, but historically the Omati worshipped Sithares. It could be said that Kerberos was simply restoring the city's religious beliefs.

Besides, the arena had turned into a space for warriors to display their skills and fight, by choice, to the death. The warriors who chose to participate were doing so to please Sithares. The crowds had begun enjoying the battles, if only because they knew they wouldn't have to fight themselves. It was an interesting balance between peace and combat, and a very intriguing compromise for a man such a Kerberos; no one *had* to fight, but those who did honoured their God.

Arena battles were held daily, and Kerberos ordered that the word be spread even outside of Omatus; the best warriors would be rewarded with gold. He encouraged gambling on the warriors, and put outlandish odds on the people he fought himself. The city began receiving visitors from every city in Omas as well as Tarsius, Tarsium, and even Shanaken; all keen to either bet or fight.

Kerberos at first spent all the money made from the arena on fixing any damage caused by his invasion of Omatus, and then on paying allowances to the poorest of the commoners. The slaves were paid wages, and granted better living conditions. He repaired and improved the buildings on the commoner's side of the city. Within a year of taking the city, he'd gone from a feared and hated invader to a beloved and benevolent king. Karak watched it all happen, and still barely believed it.

Mara

1773

Riffolk stared at her, a small smile twisting his lips. She felt the cold metal binds against her skin, harsh and unmoving. The lights of his lab were too bright.

"You can't hide from me, Mara. I will always find you."

Even though she knew it was pointless, she struggled against the device holding her in place. Her heart pounded so hard she heard it thumping in her ears. *He found me,* her mind screamed at her, *he got me, I'm dead, he's going to kill me!* Lining the walls of the lab were countless horrifying tools and weapons. *Torture.* Riffolk saw her eyes taking in the tools; his smile grew wider.

"We're going to have some fun, you and I. You're going to wish you'd behaved, as a wife should."

She couldn't speak. She tried, but her mouth wouldn't move. Riffolk grew, swelled, in front of her until he took up her entire vision.

"I'm going to kill you," he said, his eyes glowing bright blue, "you cannot stop me and you'll never escape. I'm going to kill you, Mara, *I'm going to kill you!"*

Terror chased her into the morning, as it often did, and she woke screaming, cold and sweating. Every night, her dreams were chaos; all cold blue eyes, crackling yellow lightning, and explosions of blood. Pera's death haunted her, seared into her mind. The soldiers she'd killed when they attempted to arrest her weighed heavily on her soul too; she hadn't meant for anyone to die.

Mathys appeared, sweeping into the room and pulling Mara into a tight but gentle embrace. He often had to talk her down from pure panic, at the slightest provocation. It seemed everything set her off. Sleep was the worst though; she hadn't slept a full night since Pera died. The only thing that kept her calm was Mathys, and her daughter Eliza. Without them, she would be lost. Eliza was so small, so fragile, and having a child who needed her helped her to push the nightmares away.

Tarsium was an interesting place, to say the least. Though they'd been living there for barely a year now, she felt like she was still getting used to it. They'd moved to a lazy little village to the east of Azar, beyond the hills. Mathys took a job at the inn, and they had a modest house built nearby. Before Riffolk revealed himself as still being alive, Mara had taken as much money as she could from the bank. It was Mathys' idea, and at his insistence she hid it in a sack with their things in the Copper Dragon's cellar before they left Ermoor. Now, it sat beneath the floor under the basement. They'd used a large chunk to have their house built, but there was so much of it that it still didn't look like they'd spent any.

Pulling gently away from Mathys' embrace, she moved close to Eliza, putting her arms around her. She insisted her daughter sleep in the same bed as her, and Eliza seemed to not be bothered by her mother's night terrors. Which was good; Mara had them every single night. Mathys slept in a different room. But he was always ready to appear when her screams started, and he never once complained. He was so strong, so steady, and Mara couldn't imagine living without him.

Mara still felt Riffolk. His energy. His rage. No thoughts came through, thankfully, but the emotion burned as though it was her own. Taranos still spoke to her too, as it gained its memories. Thinking "it" about a creature she spoke to was an odd feeling. But she knew purely from feeling its energy that it wasn't male or female. Gods were a whole different form of life. Mara learned more since leaving Ermoor than she ever had in her life before.

It had taken a while for her to come to terms with Taranos being a God. One of the five. The idea had at first been terrifying, but being away from Ermoor helped her see the world a little more clearly. For one thing, she'd learned that religion throughout the rest of Pandeia was far less oppressive, and that people who worshipped other Gods lived happy, fulfilling lives. She'd seen people who didn't believe in any God do wonderful things to help their fellow people.

She'd also heard people actively cursing God's name, even taunting Him, and remain unscathed. The first time she saw a busker in Tarsium, he'd begun a song about God, and she'd stopped to listen. It sounded lovely at first, and put images in her head of the priests speaking passionately at church services. Then he'd winked at Mara, and launched into a new verse which went into detail about God's anatomy in a way that made her stomach cramp and her pulse speed up.

She'd reeled, expecting some horrible disaster to strike. But the song went on, and Mathys dragged her through the street until they were beyond earshot. The song stayed in her head for days, taunting her. She felt as though she may get punished just for accidentally humming the melody every now and then. Finally, Mathys sat with her and sighed heavily.

"Mara, before I met you, before everything that happened, my faith was absolute. I'm sure yours was too. But when you're presented with evidence, and good reason, faith becomes a little difficult."

She'd nodded, thinking of Taranos and her magic powers.

"I can see it's affecting you. It's affecting me too. But I wanted to tell you something: I still believe in *something*. I believe that there is something out there, more powerful than the Gods you told me about. I believe that whatever it is, it created everything, and gave us all life."

Mara stared, drawn in by the unshakeable certainty in Mathys' eyes. Without raising his voice, or pacing up and down a stage, he was infinitely more believable than the most devout of the Ermoori priests.

"But one thing I've learned after all this is that we believe what we choose to believe. I could go on believing in the Ermoori God if I wanted, although it's clear to me that it's not worthy of belief any more."

Not worthy. The idea was unlike anything she'd felt before. All her life, she'd been taught that God was all-knowing, all-seeing, all-powerful. That she should sacrifice to be worthy of Him. Not once had it ever occurred to her that He may not be worthy of her.

"He's... not worthy?"

"I don't believe so. Think about it. What kind of God treats people the way the Ermoori God does? We didn't see the Twelve, yet they dictated all of God's wishes. They enforced rules that kept the people down, miserable and poor, while the few in power became richer. Does that really sound like Godly behaviour?"

Tears streamed down her face as she thought about the rules she'd followed to please God. The way her parents treated her. The violent words of the priests. Her marriage to Riffolk. Praying, crying, desperately wishing to hear God's voice. None of it ever made her feel the way the priests said she should feel. Then she thought about Taranos. Though monstrous, the God of Power had lived up to its name, and its voice was the first thing that had ever made her feel truly connected to something. It felt real in a way that the Ermoori God simply didn't.

"No," she said, "I suppose it's not very Godly at all."

"Now Taranos, on the other hand, gave you power and magic and strength. That's a God I can believe in."

The conversation had been a few weeks ago, but it stuck in Mara's mind, and she found the Ermoori God fading from her mind ever since. Her habits remained, like making the protective circle around her heart any time someone spoke ill of God, but even they began fading too. Mara forced herself to focus on her magic whenever God did enter her mind. It reminded her that Taranos had given her far more than God, and that Taranos was worthy of her belief, like Mathys said.

Her nightmares didn't fade, however, and Riffolk's cold face continued haunting her whether she was awake or asleep. Being indoors terrified her; if she thought about it too long, it felt as though she was trapped, the way she'd been trapped in Riffolk's lab. But being outdoors was difficult too. It made her feel too vulnerable. The only time she felt even vaguely calm was with Eliza in her arms, or with Mathys by her side.

Mathys

1774

Nestled against the eastern edge of the mountains, on the banks of the Nimriene river, was a small trading town called Berda. Further east, closer to the forest, an even smaller village rested. The smaller village was called Saford, and it wasn't even on the map of Tarsium he'd bought when they first arrived a year ago. It was there he settled with Mara.

Now, he was in Berda, picking up supplies. Berda was two hours cart ride from Saford, and being away from Mara made him nervous; especially with her daughter being less than a year old. But Saford was so tiny that it couldn't be entirely self-sufficient; everyone who lived there had to make the journey to Berda or even into one of the districts for supplies every now and then.

Berda was almost as quiet as Saford, despite the larger population and trading activity. He bought a few small sweet cakes from a street stall, and put them gently in the bag he carried. He'd already picked up most of the necessary supplies, and was now strolling through the market stalls, looking out for treats for Mara and enjoying the quiet.

Market Street, where all the stalls were located, ran parallel and right next to the Nimriene. The western bank of the river was rocky and barren, sloping harshly up into mountains. Despite the lack of trees and bush on that side of the river, it was still a beautiful view. Calm and clean, the Nimriene gurgled quietly only a few metres from the market stalls.

He'd been to Berda many times by now, and always enjoyed the sense of quiet productivity, even if he was a little anxious at leaving Mara in Saford. Mara, her daughter and himself so far were the only Ermoori he'd seen since they escaped the soldiers in Azar. This far into the countryside, actual Tarsi were more common, but it was still mostly Omati and Shenza.

Mathys enjoyed making conversation with the Shenza who lived in the small towns; at first he'd been worried about being attacked or receiving nothing but hatred. But the Shenza truly were a peaceful people, and when they weren't directly threatened they were humble, gentle, and compassionate. Their way of life made far more sense to Mathys than the Ermoori attitudes. Now that he'd been away from Ermoor a while, he was beginning to see how horrifying it truly was.

Tarsium was a free country, open to all people and beliefs; and though Mathys felt lucky to be able to live there now, it made his entire life in Ermoor feel like a suffocating nightmare. He'd devoted his life to a God that might very well not exist, and a government that actively conspired against its people. The lessons taught in the name of the One True God were terrible; he was shocked at himself for not seeing it earlier. Mara was the same, he knew. And now an actual God had spoken to her.

Another stall further ahead sold fried dough, and Mathys walked straight to it; the dough was his favourite, and Mara loved it almost as much as he did. A few metres from the stall, he stopped. An Ermoori man stood in the street, staring at him with a slight frown. Mathys tried not to react, forcing his eyes to scan over the man without pausing too long. He bought some dough and kept walking, ignoring the Ermoori man.

As a Commander in the Ermoori military, Mathys was well known. He'd changed his appearance as much as he could after leaving Ermoor, but with more than a cursory glance he would still be recognisable. Walking further down the street, Mathys pulled some of the fried dough from its bag and ate a mouthful. He had to focus on not looking back; every instinct told him to make sure the man wasn't still looking or following.

As he walked, he packed the dough back into his bag and slung it over his shoulder. He angled north up the street, towards the forest. Berda was small; there were only so many places he could go to get away from his follower. *Don't rush,* he thought, *nothing is more suspect than running*. He stopped at another stall, looking at dried fruits and nuts but not seeing them. After a moment, he turned and walked back the way he came. The Ermoori man was right there.

"Hello," he said, "I'm sure I know you."

Mathys walked back down the street, and the man followed next to him.

"I'm sure you don't."

"I'd just like to talk to you for a moment, if you have the time."

"I don't."

The man kept pace beside him. *This will only end badly,* he thought. If it were Ermoor, or even one of the districts, he'd be able to lose the man in the crowd. Berda was busy, but only as busy as small towns could get. Several small streets branched off Market Street, and there were enough buildings that visual cover could be found, but it was a matter of getting distance between him and the Ermoori. At the moment, that was impossible; he was half running to keep up with Mathys' stride, and still pestering him for conversation.

"I think we should go somewhere private," he said, "I think you'll be really interested in what I have to say."

"I'm not."

The man's voice stopped for a moment, and Mathys kept walking the way he'd first come from. Towards the southern edge of Berda was the road that lead to Carmerth. If he could give the man the impression he was staying in Carmerth, it would throw him off. Whoever he was reporting to would search Carmerth, and the southern district was big enough that it would take them a long time to realise he wasn't there.

"I'm a friend of Isobel's."

Mathys stopped walking. In one fluid motion he turned and grabbed the man by his shirt, rushing up against a wall to hold him in place.

"How did you find me?" he asked.

"It was a coincidence, I swear!"

The man's eyes were wide, his hands up and open. Genuine fear; he was telling the truth, as far as Mathys could tell. No one in Ermoor knew of his connection to Isobel and the Copper Dragon, not even Arthor. He was always careful about speaking with her, always covered his tracks. It couldn't possibly have been discovered by a spy.

"So Isobel doesn't know where I am?"

"No. She's worried about you though. The Ermoori presence in Tarsium hasn't lifted much lately."

"They still haven't left the districts, though." Mathys said. It wasn't really a question, but the man shook his head.

"No, they haven't. They're still in Azar, though when you escaped they assumed you were going to Carmerth, so now there's a much larger presence there."

"So what are you doing in Berda?"

"I help run the tavern in Azar that Isobel's uncle owns. The freshest produce can be found in Berda, and Alden demands the best."

It made sense. But it also left Mathys feeling uneasy; after being a Commander in Ermoor and dealing with organised crime for so long, he'd stopped believing in coincidence. Still, the man seemed genuine, and as long as it couldn't lead anyone back to Mara and the baby, he decided to believe the story.

"Well," he said, "you can tell Isobel that I'm okay, and that I'm staying in Carmerth. The Ermoori haven't found me, and they won't."

Even if he believed the man, he couldn't tell the truth. It wouldn't help Isobel to know where they were, and she would know that. At the moment, the fewer people who knew where they were, the safer they would be. And Mathys believing the man's story wasn't enough to make him trust the stranger.

"I'll let her know."

"What's your name?"

"Of course, please excuse my manners. Jacob Rayburn, at your service."

They shook hands, and Mathys watched his face closely. There was still no trace of a lie.

"Glad to meet you, Jacob," he said.

"And you. I should probably get going, but before I do, Isobel gave all of her contacts in Tarsium a message for you in case one of us found you."

"What message?"

"She said no matter what news you hear from Ermoor, don't go back. Never go back."

Mara

1774

She sat in the garden, holding Eliza to her chest. She was less than a year old still, and Mara was unable to let her go for more than an hour. She stared at her daughter's tiny face, lit up by the sunlight despite the shade she sat in. Mathys had travelled to Berda for supplies, and Mara needed Eliza in her arms even more with him gone. Even then, whenever a man from the village walked past their garden, Mara's heart sped up and her breathing became ragged and painful. Riffolk's puffing breaths echoed in her mind, right next to her ear as he took his pleasure. The sound wouldn't leave her, nor the memory. But whenever it got bad, she held Eliza tighter, and her mind cleared just enough to breathe.

As Eliza babbled away, oblivious to Mara's struggle, she kissed her daughter's forehead. Eliza was the best thing to have ever happened to her, despite coming from her marriage to Riffolk. Mathys was a close second, but at least Eliza didn't leave her by herself for entire days. She wanted to see Berda, but the idea of travel terrified her as much as anything else, especially after their narrow escape from the Ermoori soldiers when they first arrived a year ago.

Saford was quiet. It was perhaps the best place she could have lived, though there was still plenty that set her heart beating too fast. Feeling her heart speed up just thinking about it, she sang to Eliza. Keeping her voice even and gentle, she watched her daughter's eyes widen a little at first, and then flutter closed. Her heartbeat raged for a moment longer before settling into a normal rhythm again. She was getting used to soothing herself, though she still needed either Eliza or Mathys around to do it. Something told her she always would.

It's not fair on them, she thought, *that I need them like this*. Mathys worked so hard. He seemed to be able to fix everything. But no matter how hard he worked to help her, Mara somehow always needed more support. *He deserves an easier life*. Before she realised it was happening, tears slipped down her cheeks. Drops appeared on Eliza's face, and Mara pulled away, wiping her daughter dry and sobbing as she did. She brushed her thumb gently over Eliza's cheek, staring at her pure face.

"I hope your life is better than mine, my love."

She had no idea what the future held, but she was determined to keep Eliza safe and happy. Even if it killed her, she would make sure her daughter lived a life free from the oppression and corruption of Ermoor. And Riffolk. *He's coming for me*. She knew it was true. His rage was the fuel that created her nightmares; she felt it constantly, lurking in the back of her mind like a monster in the shadows. She was more frightened of Riffolk than of anything else in Pandeia. If the hell of the Ermoori God was real, she would have preferred to go there for eternity than be anywhere near Riffolk again.

Mara had no idea if they could avoid Riffolk forever. Mathys had done a brilliant job of keeping them hidden so far; but Riffolk was the most powerful man in Pandeia, and if anyone could find them, it would be him. *If he finds us,* she thought, *he can never know about Eliza.* The idea of being separated from her daughter was physically painful; a burning in her heart and stomach that threatened to overwhelm her. But if it came to it, Eliza's safety was the most important thing. Riffolk could have Mara, as long as Eliza remained unknown to him.

Eliza's eyes were green. Mara thanked whatever God had seen to that every day; if her eyes had been blue like her father's, Mara wouldn't have been able to look at her without panic turning her insides to chaos. Riffolk's cold blue eyes flashed in her mind's eye every day and every night in her dreams. If her daughter's eyes looked the same, she wouldn't have been able to accept it.

As she stared at Eliza's eyes, a loud bang nearby shattered the afternoon quiet. Mara screamed, and Pera appeared before her, the Tyran woman's face exploding as the bang echoed through her memories. Mara's heart thudded so loud in her chest that for a moment she couldn't breathe. Shaking, she held Eliza close and ran from the garden chair. Her foot slipped on the soft ground and she crashed to her knees, almost dropping Eliza.

Kneeling on the ground, Mara tried to control her breathing. Her entire body shook, her lungs pushing out the air she tried to breathe, her heart slamming into her chest as though someone was viciously hitting her. She groaned, and everything disappeared but the tears flooding her cheeks and the tiny, warm life in her arms. In her mind, Pera crashed to the cold ground again, what had been her head now merely a jagged stump of bone and flesh. Blood spurted rhythmically from the horrible wound, splashing the lab's floor and spreading until it covered everything. Everything but Riffolk's horrible face.

Mara screamed, and Eliza woke up and screamed as well. She felt someone grab her arm, and she scrambled away, pushing and kicking until she was free. Glancing up at whoever had touched her, she saw a concerned face. A man's face. *No,* she thought, *no, no!* For a moment he looked like Riffolk, and she screamed again.

"Are you okay?" he said, "sorry about the noise, there was a snake in my yard. Had to use the gun I bought in Azar. From Ermoor y'know, like you."

"Get away from me! Get away!"

She ran inside, slamming the door behind her and sprinting up the stairs to her room. She held Eliza close as her daughter screamed and cried. After what felt like an entire day, Mara's heart finally calmed, and she could take a full breath. The shaking didn't stop for hours afterwards. Mathys arrived just after sundown. Eliza was asleep, but Mara ran to him, grabbing him and sobbing into his chest. He didn't say anything, but he didn't need to. He simply held her as she cried, steady and calm against the raging horrors in her mind.

Zeera

1774

She hadn't found a Hero. No leads appeared, and no matter where she went, she picked up no traces of Power Magic in any of the districts. A year passed, and she remained in Tarsium, searching and finding nothing. Zalla appeared to her one day after she'd returned to her home; she spent the day strolling through Azar just like she had the last few months.

"Zeera. You sent a message to the *Duulshen* through the *Kaizeluun* you met last year, yes?"

"Yes," Zeera said, "I told her to tell them that the Circle is rising again."

"She told them. They're sending another *Kaizeluun* to Ermoor. You are to smuggle him in."

It was the first mission she'd been given since the Ermoori was exiled. She was still searching for him. *Why are they ordering me away from a potential Hero?* she thought.

"I see. With all due respect, Speaker, is there a reason I'm being sent on this mission? We know the Hero of Taranos is exiled, and Tarsium is the most logical place for him to be. Shouldn't I be here?"

"The Shenza are working towards removing Ermoor as a threat. Our duty is to protect Pandeia, and Sithares isn't the only threat to the world. All you need to do is help him get there, and then you can return."

Zalla told her about the *Kaizeluun's* mission. It was a continuation of Elana's previous mission, as she left without properly sabotaging Ermoor.

"Why wouldn't they send Elana again?" Zeera said, "she's so powerful. Even more powerful than her father, and he was one of our potential Heroes."

"Elana was killed, Zeera. A Shenza traitor murdered her when she was sent to hunt him down."

Zeera's mind was wiped blank. *She's dead?* Elana was one of the most powerful people Zeera had ever seen. The Shenza who killed her must have been truly talented. She drifted under the water for a moment in her chambers, unable to think of anything to say.

"We need you, Zeera. Help smuggle the *Kaizeluun* to Ermoor, then you can resume your mission."

They met in a pub in Azar. His name was Zailen, and Zeera felt barely any power in him compared to Elana. He was shocked when she mentioned she knew Elana. They planned for his mission; she told him she was in charge of most of the trade between Ermoor and Tarsium. It was an easy cover to keep; the Circle was in charge of all of it, so Zeera could commandeer a ship with no trouble.

She told him about the sewer tunnels on the southern edges of Ermoor, in the poor districts. His mission was to sneak into Tyra and train the slaves to prepare for a revolt. Zeera doubted it would work; the Ermoori had kept the Tyrans under their control for thousands of years, and their military power and technology were growing every year. Still, the success of his mission wasn't her responsibility, and she wanted to focus on finding the exiled Ermoori man.

Zeera stayed on the ship until they got close enough for Zailen to lower the row boat with his supplies to the water and begin rowing for Ermoor. Once the tiny boat began growing smaller, Zeera jumped off the opposite side of the ship and sped towards Tarsium again. Another Tarsi had been on board, and Zeera convinced him to take over the actual unloading and trading that would occur when the ship docked. Speeding through the water again filled her with a rush of energy. For the entire time she swam, her mind settled into a sort of focused peace. All the things that worried her faded into the black depths of the ocean. She felt as though nothing mattered; only the magic coursing through her. Only the Gods, and their Heroes. Only the war looming on the horizon. Even though her focus was turned to the coming war, she felt no fear; just magic, and power, and a new confidence.

Mathys

1774

A few months after meeting Jacob Rayburn, Mathys couldn't help but visit Azar for news. He knew it was a bad idea, and he hated leaving Mara so vulnerable, but he had to know what was happening. Several taverns in Azar were hotspots for news and gossip, and Mathys sat in one of them, the thick smell of spilled alcohol and old smoke cloying. He smoked as well, his cigar resting in an ashtray on the bar for a moment as he sipped his drink and listened for news.

Bartenders in Tarsium were repositories of endless information; they seemed to know everything that happened in Pandeia. Even the non Tarsi bartenders had a vast knowledge of current events. Mathys sat at the bar, waiting for Ermoor to come up in conversation. If something big had happened, which Isobel's message hinted, it would come up eventually.

Most of the news was focused on Omatus; a new king was in place, and had started forcing the citizens to worship the Fire God of the Thearans. A lot of the conversation meant nothing to him. The bartender and two Thearan customers were in a heated debate about the new king of Omatus.

"He's never going to keep the city if he kills his own citizens," the bartender said, "it won't be long before he's assassinated and someone better takes his place."

"Oh please, Omatus is almost as corrupt as Ermoor," a customer said, "if anything, they deserve a purge."

The bartender—who was Omati—stared, speechless for a moment, before turning red in the face and shouting at the customer.

"How dare you? Take it back, or you're banned."

"Fuck that, Omatus deserves what they're getting," the customer said with a smirk, "Kerberos is the son of Sithares, Omatus belongs to him."

"Out! Get out of here. If I see you again I'll get the Tarsi Peacekeepers on you."

The Thearan men left, and the bartender shook his head as he watched them go.

"Fucking savages," he said, "they fight so often they have no respect for life."

Mathys nodded, picking his cigar back up and taking a few gentle puffs.

"He was right about both cities being corrupt, though," Mathys said.

"Sure he was. Doesn't mean people in Omatus deserve to die just because they don't want to believe in Sithares."

"True."

"How long have you been out of Ermoor?"

"A year or so. Any news?"

"It's a mess. Some high ranking military man tried to kill an Overseer, and he has a price on his head that would humble most of the people living in Sarnia."

"Yeah, I knew that part," Mathys said, "that happened last year. Heard anything lately?"

"The military can't find the guy, and they're *still* roaming the Tarsi districts with sketches of the man. He looks a little like you, if I'm honest."

The bartender raised his eyebrows, and a tiny smile curled the corner of his lip up. His expression said *I know it's you, I just don't care,* and Mathys smiled back. He couldn't come back to Azar again.

Even if the bartender didn't tell anyone, it would only be a matter of time before someone recognised him from the sketches.

"Anyway," the bartender went on, "they've apparently also started raiding the poor districts of Ermoor, taking and interrogating people for information on his whereabouts. There's talk of a revolt among the lower classes, but there has always been that kind of talk."

Mathys stared at his drink. Because of him, Ermoori soldiers were detaining and torturing innocent people. Now he understood why Isobel urged him not to go back to Ermoor; the drive to take the next available ship to his home city was almost overwhelming.

"Sorry, friend," the bartender said, "I do hate giving bad news. How about a drink on the house?"

"Appreciate it."

He puffed his cigar and drank what he'd already ordered while the bartender poured another for him. Another customer sat at the bar and the conversation turned to a festival in Sarnia. When his cigar and drink were finished, he nodded to the bartender and left.

The journey back to Saford took some time; a cart took him south east, over a bridge on the Nimriene, and further towards Carmerth. In a small town in the crook of the forest called Tawic, Mathys was dropped off and the cart kept on to Carmerth. At the Tawic carthouse, he rented another cart to take him north through the forest to Saford. This far out from the districts, he was less worried about being recognised; but he wore a travel cloak and kept his hood up just the same.

Mara

1774

The Spectre leapt over her head, a cloud of smoke exploding at her feet. Heart pounding, she dived into a roll towards where the Spectre had been seconds earlier. She heard a light thump as he landed where she'd been, and rolled to her feet just in time to block an attack. Despite the Spectre's fearsome appearance, Mara was no longer scared of it. Because she knew it was Mathys, and she knew Mathys was the one person who wouldn’t hurt her, the Spectre had become a very welcome image.

Mathys had resumed her training as soon as she was healed enough from Eliza's birth. Being in a combat situation, even a pretend one, still panicked Mara; but it was a distraction from the horrifying memories that usually plagued her mind. If she trained hard, she could sometimes fall asleep fast enough that she didn't have time to remember anything from Ermoor. And when she was truly exhausted, sometimes she didn't even dream. Those were the best nights of her life.

He swiped at her with both fists. Mara ducked under the first and swatted the other away. Mathys twirled and kicked her legs out from under her. She hit the ground, all the air forced from her lungs. Mathys stopped. His posture changed instantly, and he reached a hand down to help Mara up. She took it, and they stood together for a moment as Mara's breathing slowly returned to normal.

"You're doing well, Mara," Mathys said.

She beamed; any time Mathys complimented her skills it sent a bright warmth through her heart.

"How do you feel?" he asked.

The warmth she felt flared into a hot wave that left her mouth dry. She tried to hide most of her panic from Mathys; there was no need for him to worry over her more than he already did. Mara felt guilty enough as it was.

"I'm fine. Do you want to keep training?"

His hand fell on her shoulder. A deep sadness echoed from his eyes as he looked at her.

"Mara..."

"I'm fine, Mathys. Don't worry about me."

He shuffled from foot to foot, his awkwardness comical in the Spectre's armour and demonic mask.

"Okay," he said, "well... maybe you should have a rest then?"

Mathys walked back to the house. The back of the house was fairly private, and they trained there when they knew there was no one around. With Eliza so young, they couldn't both be too far from the house. As Mathys walked away, a cold, sharp weight appeared in her stomach. *I either push him away, or overburden him,* she thought. *How do I fix this?* But nothing came to mind, and despite the hour they'd spent training, her mind returned to visions of Riffolk and Pera.

Cold, sterile walls surrounded her. She knew them too well; the underground lab. But instead of scientific equipment and the giant tank, the room was empty. Mara stood in the centre, glancing around at the walls. Slowly, Riffolk's laugh rang from somewhere in the silence, echoing over and over until the sound could have driven her insane. Pera appeared in front of her, and Mara looked at the gun in her own hands. She didn't know how it came to be there, and she couldn't stop herself from pointing it at Pera's head.

"No," she said, as her heart sped up, "no, please, Pera, get out of the way, run!"

But she pulled the trigger, and Pera exploded in a shower of bright blood. Riffolk's laugh grew louder until it turned into a demented screech, and his cold eyes chased her into consciousness.

She woke screaming again, a sheen of sweat covering her entire body. Cold and shaking, she tried to control her breathing as Mathys rushed in to comfort her. Her screams gave way to sobs as tears flowed. Eliza remained silent; still fast asleep. Even through her terror, she felt a swell of relief that her daughter wasn't as terrified as she was. She cried into Mathys' shoulder, shaking and mumbling as the visions of her nightmare repeated in her head. All she wanted was peace; even just one day without nightmares and terror.

"You'll be okay," Mathys said, holding her close, "you're safe with me."

Mathys

1777

Dust swirled lazily through thin shafts of afternoon sunlight, and Mathys exhaled a cloud of smoke that merged with it, roiling like a silent storm. His cigar was close to the end, but he kept smoking. They were only sold in the districts, and he couldn't visit just to buy them whenever he wanted. Below the smoke and dust, near the floor where the air was relatively clear, Eliza Watson giggled as she drew on a sheaf of paper with colourful wax crayons.

Four years old now, she took after her mother; innocent and beautiful, and with a deceptive intelligence that continued to shock him.

In a sleepy little village in Tarsium, their modest home blended in with the rest, though it was built far more recently. When they first arrived in Saford four years ago, he'd selected a plot of land a little off the main road leading into the village. He made sure their home was built small and inconspicuous. There would be people still after them. Assassins, soldiers, spies. Mathys had used everything he knew to try to keep them safe. They didn't use their real names, they never ventured into the major districts. Mara cut her hair and died it darker, and Mathys had done the same to his own; he looked younger now, a closer fit to be her husband. Not that they'd ever have that kind of relationship; but the appearance helped to hide their identities.

He'd thrown out anything related to the Ermoori military. Except his gun. He couldn't get rid of it; it was far too valuable to him. It sat in a locked chest in the basement. He wouldn't use it; he'd even bought a more standard weapon on one of his few trips to Azar, but knowing it was there calmed him. It brought back memories of training at the barracks with Arthor. Back before he'd started withdrawing and acting strange. Before the invasion was planned, before Riffolk started his evil project.

Their life in Tarsium was simple. Quiet. For the first time, Mathys felt no pressure to be anyone other than himself. No one knew them, and the anonymity was the most freeing thing he'd ever experienced. The irony of being able to be himself while in hiding was not lost on Mathys. But it had been four years, and the Ermoori presence in Tarsium was far smaller now than it had been. Sketches of his face were nowhere to be seen in the districts, except on the occasional noticeboard. He was certain a price remained on his head, and would remain in hiding; but the constant fear and suspicion he'd felt when they first arrived was now merely a dull uneasiness.

Eliza giggled as she scrawled on the paper. Mathys smiled straight away; he couldn't help it. She lit up his heart more than he would have believed. Her innocence, her joy, her eagerness to learn and explore; it was the most perfect gift he could have imagined, and knowing that she wouldn't have to grow up in Ermoor made it all the sweeter.

"It's all yellow!" she said, her eyes not leaving the paper.

"That sounds perfect, little one."

"The other bits are green." She studied the drawing with a tiny frown. "And grey."

"Well, that sounds great too."

She giggled again, dropping the yellow crayon and reaching for a blue one.

"And the eyes are blue!"

"Oh good, that sounds lovely."

Mara came down the stairs, and Eliza spun around and ran to her, giggling and squealing. She was the happiest child Mathys had ever seen. Mara laughed as well, her face glowing. She was perpetually frowning lately, except when she was close to her daughter.

"Hey sweetie," Mara said as Eliza jumped into her arms, "what are you up to?"

"Drawing! With Maffs!"

Mathys smiled. She still couldn't quite pronounce his name, but he found the nickname endearing and didn't bother correcting her any more.

"What has Eliza drawn for you today, Maffs?"

He laughed, shaking his head. It was endearing coming from Mara, too. He stood and wandered over to the messy pile of papers in the middle of the room, talking as he went.

"Well, it's yellow and green and grey, with blue..." the drawing screamed at his mind, blurring out the rest of the room.

"Mathys? What's wrong?"

He stood slowly, holding the picture in both hands, staring as though it might change at any moment.

"It's... Mara, I don't know how to describe this."

When Mara first saw the drawing, she screamed. She almost dropped Eliza, backing away from the paper in Mathys' hands as though it was a wild animal. Eliza started crying, and Mara sat heavily in one of the chairs at their small table. She held her daughter close, her eyes wide and her face pale as she her hand ran up and down Eliza's back.

"Mara," he said as gently as he could, "is it what I think it is?"

Silence filled the room, Mara's eyes staring at nothing as she mindlessly rubbed Eliza's back.

"Yes."

He had to strain to hear her voice. In the years they'd known each other, even after everything she'd been through, Mathys hadn't seen her look the way she did now.

"It's him."

Zigzagged yellow lightning covered the page, almost obscuring the face. Riffolk smiled up at Mara and Mathys, bright blue eyes glaring through from underneath the chaotic yellow lines. Mara hadn't described him to Eliza; she'd made a point of never mentioning him. She'd never talked about the magic she could wield, or Taranos, or anything that happened in Ermoor.

Eliza was in her bed, soothed and fast asleep after the drawing incident. Mara managed to get herself under control enough to calm Eliza down, and sat with her a while, singing softly until she fell asleep. Now she sat across from Mathys, and he saw how shaken she still was. Her eyes didn't rise from the table, her pale skin even paler than usual, and her hands shook as though she was freezing to death.

"How could she know his face?" She said.

"I... don't know, Mara."

"I can feel him, you know. His presence. His emotions. He still wants to kill me. I've never felt so much rage in my life."

"Maybe Eliza shares the same connection with him."

As soon as he spoke, he regretted the words. Tears spilled down Mara's cheeks, and her shoulders began rocking back and forth as she tried to hold back sobs.

"Oh God, please no," she said, her voice catching at each word, "I can't let her feel what I feel, I need to protect her from him."

Mathys was always in control, always had a plan; except for that moment, sitting across from Mara. He had no idea what she was going through, no idea how to fix it. He couldn't protect her from a magical connection that stretched over oceans and countries.

"If he comes here, will you know?"

"I don't think so. I can't feel where he is, just that he's there. That he hates me."

They both fell silent, thinking about Riffolk. He was perhaps the most dangerous man in the world, and he wanted Mara dead. Mathys too, most likely. There had to be a way to use the connection between Riffolk and Mara against him.

"You and Eliza will be okay, Mara," he said, placing his hand on hers, "I promise."

Mara

1777

It had been months since the drawing of Riffolk. Mara's nightmares grew worse; Eliza appeared in them most nights, snatched by Riffolk and taken back to Ermoor. She was four years old now. Mathys was beginning to take care of her more since the drawing, and Mara struggled to deal with things while the two of them were busy. Riffolk's face was certainly familiar enough to her; she saw it every night and most days, lurking in her mind and terrorising her with his horrible, cold eyes. But seeing it in a drawing, especially a drawing by her own daughter, was a whole new horror.

Does he know about her already? Her stomach cramped, a cold emptiness squashing it in painful twists. If he was connected to his daughter the same way he was connected to Mara, she wouldn't forgive herself. She could barely handle Riffolk in her mind; it must be hell for a four year old. But there was no escape from it. She couldn't kill Riffolk, or cut him off. They couldn't let him find them. All they could do was run, and hide, and hope for the best.

One night, as she lay awake trying not to fall into nightmares again, Mathys told her that Eliza could use magic. The same magic Mara used. He wanted Mara to train her daughter. Her heart exploded into jagged, painful rhythms; her own magic terrified her enough, but knowing her daughter had to be trained to use magic at such a young age tore at her. She knew it was necessary. If Mara knew how to use it back in Ermoor, perhaps the Ermoori soldiers arresting her wouldn't have died. A child with this kind of magic could be dangerous. But at the same time, Mara knew she wasn't fit to train anyone. Even gentle combat training with Mathys sometimes ended in panic attacks. There was no other option; she agreed to train Eliza.

They sat together, in the woods north of their house. Mathys remained at home; Mara told him she wanted to be alone with Eliza when they trained, at least at first. When she showed the lightning to Eliza the first time, she giggled and squealed. Her eyes shined as brightly as the lightning itself, and Mara had never seen her smile so wide. Mara tried to explain how to focus the lightning into the hands, how to visualise it and then make it appear. She hadn't described it out loud before, and it was hard enough without simplifying it for a child.

But Eliza simply listened and nodded. A tiny spark flew from her finger, and she giggled and squealed again. The moment the spark appeared, Mara's heart stopped. It lingered in the air just above Eliza's hand, and Mara blinked, holding her breath without realising. Then it faded into nothing, and Mara could breathe again. *How does she have so much control?* She thought, *she's so young!* But Eliza just sat happily on the grass, looking at Mara the same way she always did. There was no hint of her powerful, deadly magic in her daughter's eyes.

After a little while playing with sparks and getting used to magic, Mara walked them back to the house. Before they reached the door, she stopped Eliza and put her hands on her shoulders.

"Remember, Eliza, no using magic in the house, and you're only allowed to use it when I say it's okay."

"Okay Mumma."

They sat down together in the main room. Eliza picked up some toys and started playing like nothing had happened, and the training suddenly felt like a dream. Eliza was so unaffected by everything. Mara had no idea how it was possible, but she was more grateful than she could say. Mathys came in from the kitchen, glanced at Eliza and smiled. He sat next to Mara, and they both watched Eliza play and mumble to herself.

"How did the training go?" he said, his voice low enough that Eliza couldn't hear.

"Very well," Mara said, "a little too well, actually. She's already got control. It's... scary."

He didn't react, merely continued watching Eliza play. Mathys was always difficult to read. She trusted him entirely, but not knowing what he was thinking could be scary.

"Control is a good thing," he said, "I don't think she will be much of a danger. Keep up the training though, Mara. She needs to understand this magic as well as you do. Besides, it's a way for you two to bond."

She hadn't thought of that. Thinking about it now, sitting with her daughter on the grass together in the afternoon sun had been so peaceful. Other than her reaction to seeing Eliza cast magic so easily; that had given her a shock. But the magic was one thing they had in common that no one else could share with them. She smiled, looking at Mathys. A deep, bright swell of love filled her heart. No matter the situation, he always knew how to help her.

"You're right," she said, "we did bond."

"I'll keep an eye on her drawings," he said, "but I haven't seen any more... troubling ones. You just focus on magic, and being with Eliza."

The love in her heart spilled over, and tears fell before she could stop them. Concern splashed over Mathys' face instantly, but Mara gestured and shook her head with a small laugh.

"It's fine, Mathys, I'm just... Thank you. For everything. I couldn't survive without you."

"I'm sure that's not true," he said, shuffling uncomfortably in his chair.

He hadn’t taken any of her compliments or her thanks well. It hurt, but mostly it just left her feeling low. She really meant it; without him, she would be dead. Maybe Eliza, too. Riffolk would have found her, or even just some criminal on the streets of Ermoor or Azar. She just wished she could show him how much he meant to her, how much he had saved her and helped her. Before she could say anything more, he left the room, mumbling about getting more fire wood. Her tears continued, but now they were born of sadness instead of love. She just wanted Mathys to understand how much he meant to her and Eliza, but something told her he never would.

Mathys

1777

No more drawings of Riffolk surfaced after the first. Mathys wasn't sure if Eliza had just forgotten about it, or if she purposefully avoided drawing him again because of Mara's reaction. She was certainly a smart enough kid. Still, a sense of uneasiness settled over the house, remaining in the air like a fog. It felt to Mathys as though Mara was simply waiting to see his roughly drawn face again. As though she couldn't relax until she saw it.

Eliza, other than being deeply upset at Mara's reaction, seemed unaffected by whatever had made her draw Riffolk's face. It could have simply been a dream as far as she was concerned, an unassuming image she drew like all the others. Mathys kept a close eye on her behaviour, especially after she woke and while she was drawing. Nothing was out of the ordinary. All he could do was take care of Eliza and Mara, and hope that her vision didn't mean anything sinister. Neither Mara nor Mathys were comfortable with mysteries, especially after Ermoor, but there was simply no way of knowing what had happened.

A few times, she drew yellow lightning, but it was formless and not as disturbing as the drawing of Riffolk. Mara glanced at the drawings and gave distant compliments to Eliza, but otherwise seemed to push them from her mind instantly. Mathys sat down with Eliza one day, while Mara was sleeping, to ask her about the drawings.

"Do you remember the man you drew?"

She nodded, and a painfully serious expression appeared on her face.

"Do you know anything about him?" he asked.

"He's very bad," Eliza said, "and he wants to hurt mumma." She thought for a while, her tiny brow furrowed. "And he doesn't know me. He's very angry all the time. I like drawing the yellow stuff better."

"That's called lightning," Mathys said.

He doesn't know her, he thought. He was grateful for that much, at least.

"Yeah, lining," she said, her frown disappearing in an instant, "it's so pretty. I made some on my hands."

His stomach suddenly felt cold and empty, like a midnight sky in the middle of winter.

"You made some lightning?"

"Yeah!" she giggled, imitating the sound of lightning with her mouth.

Born with the ability to wield magic, he thought, *I didn't realise that was possible*. Up until he first met Mara, he didn't think magic itself was possible either. He'd been almost convinced the Spectre was a being of magic when he first came into contact with it, but by the time he took the title for himself he knew better. Now, it seemed anything was possible, and if magic was real, who knew what else might be real too. Mathys was shocked enough to discover that there were other Gods. He was still coming to terms with it, even four years after Mara told him about Taranos.

"Can you show me the lightning, Eliza?"

"No. Let's go outside!"

Mathys had to stifle a laugh; Eliza was so bossy sometimes. It was as endearing as it was frustrating.

"Why can't you show me the lightning?"

"I want to go outside."

"We can go outside after. This is important, little one."

She frowned again, her tiny face far too serious as she stared at her hands. Mathys saw the adult she would one day become, and it scared him. She was already growing so quickly, and he wanted all the time he could get; eventually he would have to tell her about Ermoor and Riffolk, and it would break his heart to put her through that much fear.

"I don't know how."

Mathys glanced up at the stairs. As much as he didn't want to make Mara deal with her memories, she would need to be involved. A child as young as Eliza wielding magic without understanding it put everyone in danger. And the only person Mathys knew who could wield magic was Mara.

"Did you know that your mother can make lightning too, Eliza?"

Her eyes lit up, sparkling like emeralds. Thankfully, she had her mother's green eyes, instead of the cold blue of Riffolk's.

"Really?"

"Yes, really."

He picked her up and made for the door.

"How about we spend some time outside, and then I'll talk to your mother about the lightning."

"Mara."

He stood in the doorway to her bedroom. Her vague form was blurry in the low light, buried under blankets and unmoving. The last few years had been difficult for her; constant nightmares, panic attacks, and trying to take care of Eliza all added up to Mara being perpetually exhausted. She spent most of her time in the bed. A slight shuffle and a groan came from the bed, and Mara's head popped out from underneath the covers. She stared, but didn't say anything.

"We need to talk about Eliza."

She stirred further, sitting up and letting the blankets fall off her. Mathys averted his eyes, although she wore a modest nightgown. He knew that she was beautiful, but a big part of him couldn’t see her that way, and he didn’t want to.

"Is she okay?"

"She's fine, but something has come up that we need to talk about. I can't do it without you."

"What's happening?"

"I think Eliza has some magical abilities like yours. She said she made lightning with her hands."

For a moment, Mara didn't move, and the low light in her room engulfed her pale face in a blur of grey.

"And you want me to train her?"

Mathys had to strain to hear her.

"I think it's necessary. You know how dangerous this magic can be."

Another moment of silence filled the room, until finally Mara shuffled out of the bed. They walked down the stairs together, Mara's movements sluggish and hesitant. Though she didn't take care of herself very well, she was a great mother, and by the time she reached the bottom of the stairs she was smiling and walking far more confidently. Eliza sat on the floor, playing with a wooden doll Mathys bought her two years ago. She broke into a wide smile when she saw Mara.

"Mumma!" she said, running to her and almost dropping the doll.

She jumped into Mara's arms, and the two held each other a while before Eliza remembered Mathys' words.

"Mumma can you really make lining too?"

Mara glanced at Mathys, and the look on her face made him almost burst into laughter. She hadn't been prepared for Eliza's pronunciation of lightning, and she was utterly confused.

"Lightning? Yes sweetie, I can."

"Show me!"

Kerberos

1778

Five years after taking the city, Kerberos sat alone in his room, ignoring the chill from the open balcony. The sun had set hours ago, and the temperature dropped quickly. Aella was out there; he knew it. Waiting. Training. Raising an army, perhaps. The idea disturbed him more than it should have; but she was very talented. She could have beaten him in one-on-one combat. In all-out warfare, however, he had the upper hand in every way. Omatus was a fortress, and Kerberos had not only his original Thearan tribe, but the entire Omati Royal Guard and army at his disposal.

If she tried an attack, she was doomed. And yet, he found himself thinking about her often. Her determination was as fierce as her skill with swords and bows; she wouldn't give up until either he was dead, or she was. If she did manage to break through his army, through the city's defences... It would certainly be a challenge. Aella was the one person Kerberos felt threatened by.

Even so, he had a soul blade; she didn't. Even if she killed him, he would come back. But if he managed to kill her, she was gone forever. He also had Sithares on his side. He was the Fire God's most devoted servant. After taking the city, and the events leading up to it, the concept of death scared Kerberos more than it had when he wasn't immortal; Athan had been truly scarred by the experience, and the other warriors who'd been killed were shells of their former selves. For Kerberos, his mind was his most prized possession. After returning from the dead, each Thearan had forgotten who they were. If that happened to Kerberos, he would rather be dead for real.

Sithares still hadn't ordered him to burn any cities; or even spoken to him at all. Far from being a comfort, the total lack of contact deeply unsettled Kerberos. He hadn’t gone this long without hearing Sithares' voice. *Five years,* he thought, *has Sithares abandoned me?* An intense relief echoed through him at the thought that Sithares might be done with him. He pushed it away. *It must be a test. My loyalty to Sithares is what got me this far; I cannot let it waver now.*

Quiet footsteps scuffled outside his door. Kerberos didn't post royal guards at the door to his chambers. They hadn't done the royalty of Omatus any good; two guards wouldn't stop a skilled assassin, and Kerberos welcomed any attempt on his life with open arms. Not because he wanted to die, but because the challenge of combat had become his favourite thing. He still fought in the arena, and would be on the front lines of his army if and when Aella ever came back.

The footsteps drew closer, stopping at his door. If he'd been asleep, they may have succeeded in taking him by surprise. But he heard everything; there were about a dozen of them by the sound of their footsteps, working quickly but quietly to prepare for their attack. Kerberos pulled on the armour and weapons he wore in the few seconds before they opened the door. Once it had opened wide enough, he threw the spiked ball of his Demon's Tail through the gap, crushing a man's chest instantly and throwing several others to the ground.

Ermoori, he thought, *what are they doing here?* They held weapons he'd never seen before, and their armour was dark, matte and slim. He yanked the chain back, tearing the man who'd been hit open. One Ermoori approached with what looked like a narrow, lightweight baton; there was no way it would do any damage if he hit Kerberos with it. But instead of swinging, he simply jabbed the end of it at Kerberos' side. An explosion of jarring pain lit up his entire left side, and crackling filled his ears.

Another jab hit him and he grunted, grabbing blindly at the attacker. His hand fell on the man's face, and he squeezed as hard as he could. The man screamed, and Kerberos' vision returned just as his attacker's face imploded. One of the Ermoori shouted in disgust, but Kerberos didn't listen to the words. He turned to the next closest Ermoori and punched the man as hard as he could. His head snapped back, his nose flattened against his face, and he fell without a sound. Kerberos drew his sword, forgetting the Demon's Tail for the moment; the Ermoori had already come too close to use the long chain effectively. The remaining nine Ermoori fanned out through the room, trying to surround him.

"You made a mistake coming here," Kerberos said.

They rushed in all at once. Kerberos grabbed one by the throat and swept his blade through the head of another. He brought his left hand into a fist around the man's throat, ripping it out with his bare hand. Another pulse of pain hit him, in the thigh this time, and his muscles bunched uncontrollably. If he'd been mid step he would have fallen. Standing still instead, he let them come to him. Two of them grabbed him, and another jabbed him with their powerful weapons.

"Get it now!" one of them said, and the remaining Ermoori who weren't attacking him sprinted over to the chest in the corner.

They want the book, he thought, *interesting.* Laughing and screaming, Kerberos let flames engulf his body, and the men holding him screamed as well. Seconds later, they were nothing but ash and half-cooked flesh. The Ermoori with the baton weapon tried another jab, but Kerberos simply grabbed the weapon, ignoring the blast of pain in his hand as he pulled the man close. He died screaming as Kerberos hacked away at his body with the sword.

Four warriors were left, all trying to break open the chest. Kerberos laughed again, fire still lapping at his skin. They noticed him then, standing above the destroyed corpses of their fellows and laughing. One of them kept working at the chest, and the other three approached. Two of them lunged with their strange weapons, and Kerberos swayed from one and cut the other in half with his sword. He kicked the weapon out of the first man's hand. The third man jumped in, touching his weapon to Kerberos' stomach.

Through the pain and the blinding light, Kerberos pushed forward. He swept his sword through anything it could reach, until his vision returned again. When he could see, two of the men in front of him had been dismembered. One was dead on the floor, the other holding the jagged stump of what used to be his right arm. A deep cut went from the man's shoulder down through his stomach, but he ignored it, staring at his missing arm instead. Kerberos cut his throat just as the third Ermoori attacked again.

The man was nervous; he was well trained, they all were, but it was obvious they hadn’t been in a situation like this before. Now that he was the only one fighting, his movements were careful, almost timid. His fellow was still trying to break into the chest in the corner; he was no closer than when he started. Kerberos grinned at the man he faced, and saw the terror he knew would burn in the Ermoori's eyes.

For a moment, they simply faced each other. Kerberos let the tension grow, staring the man down until he glanced back at his fellow soldier working the chest. The second his eyes turned, Kerberos cut his head off.

Zeera

1778

Four years after she smuggled Zailen into Ermoor, Zeera was still in Tarsium. Normally she would have moved on to another country by now, but no news had come from any of the scouts, and she was still certain Mathys Corby lived in Tarsium somewhere. She searched Sarnia, the luxury district; constant parties and festivals filled the streets, and every house was a mansion. Zeera loved Tarsium, and was proud to be Tarsi, but Sarnia was everything she couldn't stand in one blustering, self-important district.

Sarnia contained the highest Ermoori population in Tarsium, and a huge number of wealthy Omati as well. Its focus was entirely on extravagance, excess, and decadence. She found it almost as oppressive as Ermoor, just in a different way. Each day, she wandered down the street, as close to the buildings as she could to avoid the festival goers.

Reaching out with her senses, she scanned the district one street at a time. She didn't find anything. *They wouldn't hide in Sarnia,* she thought, *who would? Only the wealthy can afford to stay even a week.* In her duty as Hero she had to search every possible place, even if it made no sense, so she resigned herself to searching the streets of Sarnia until it was done. When she could finally leave, she did so gladly.

Her home was becoming a rare pleasure; she felt as though she hadn't been there in years, and every time she returned the tension melted from her shoulders. After Talas died, her chambers felt empty and strange. But now that she was Hero, and barely spent her time there, the feeling of home returned to it. Seeing Zalla, on the other hand, was far less of a pleasure. Tension had been building between them ever since Zeera left Ermoor without approval. The Speaker swam into her chambers silently, a cold distance emanating from her stare.

"Zeera."

Another rumoured Hero, she thought, *that will lead to nothing. Again.* She smiled as politely as she could.

"Zalla, what brings you here?"

"A mission."

"Another Hero?"

"Spies. In Tarsium."

Who would be stupid enough to try to infiltrate Tarsium?

"Who are they? What are they looking for?"

"Ermoori. As far as we can tell, they're trying to find the book of Asheilos. Ten of them, well equipped and trained. They've been here for at least a few months already."

"Where?"

"Right here in Azar. I think they know exactly where to look."

Later that day, Zeera sat in a tavern known to be a haven for criminals. The spies had been seen here almost every night since first being identified. She took the form of an Omati, and sat at the bar, waiting. A skin full of water was tied to each side of her belt like daggers; she still had her dagger, but after her years of training, water was a far deadlier weapon for her to use. As a Circle agent and Tarsium's Hero, Zeera was known to most of the Tarsi. Generally, it was considered polite for Tarsi to ignore any other Tarsi who were shifted into another form in public; discretion and secrecy were a universal priority in their culture.

In Zeera's case, she was treated like any other shifted Tarsi, except she was also granted any assistance she may need at a moment's notice. Sitting at the bar for hours without ordering a drink would usually get a person kicked out. But the barman, a fellow Tarsi, let her be. He even occasionally handed her bright blue drinks that looked like the liquor Jewel of Tarsium, but contained no alcohol.

Four hours after Zeera arrived, six Ermoori strolled into the tavern together, talking and laughing. *The other four must be laying low,* she thought, *planning, or maybe just staying separated to avoid too much attention.* They wore the extravagant clothing that the Ermoori were known for; no armour or stealth gear. It made sense, and it showed at least a little restraint on their part. She'd been expecting to see people who at least looked like warriors; but then again, Zeera hadn't heard of a branch of the Ermoori military devoted to stealth, so she hadn't truly known what to expect.

They passed themselves off as rich tourists well enough, but Zeera saw their combat training in the way they moved. She watched their eyes scan the tavern's patrons, then flick to the corners and the exits; they were certainly well trained enough to be ready for unforeseen situations. All but one of them went to a large table and kept talking loudly. The last approached the bar and ordered drinks for the group. Zeera returned her eyes to the bar in front of her, and focused on their voices. They spoke about nothing important; she tried listening for odd patterns in their speech, or out of place words, but it seemed to be a normal conversation.

Two hours later, they left. Zeera waited a moment before following. Their inebriation wasn't faked; but there were still six of them, so Zeera was as careful as she could be. Azar was more or less always busy, so Zeera disappeared in the crowd behind the spies as she followed. They walked casually, talking and laughing the whole way. Snippets of their conversation floated through the noise of the street to her; it still sounded like every-day tourist chatter.

It didn't take long for them to turn down a smaller street. The crowd thinned almost immediately, and after only a few minutes Zeera found herself walking down the street alone but for the Ermoori spies ahead. She kept her distance, but it was only a matter of time before they realised they were being followed. Just as she thought it, they turned down an alley, and when Zeera turned in after them, they were waiting for her.

Kerberos

1778

Shortly after their attack, Kerberos sat in the secret room in the royal library, waiting for the only surviving Ermoori to wake. He'd tied the man to a chair, and brought several weapons and tools into the room with him; he'd made a mistake letting the Tarsi assassin go five years ago, and he wasn't going to make the same mistake again. This time, he would find out what the Ermoori were up to. As Kerberos watched, the man stirred. Kerberos pulled a bag over his head before carrying him down to the secret room; he had no idea where he was. The bag pulled against his face as he turned in different directions then hung his head low. After a moment of silence, the man started sobbing.

"I need to know what you were doing here." Kerberos said.

The man flinched at his voice, shoulders hunched up, head low. His sobbing stopped, but his breathing remained shaky and uneven. He'd spoken in Ermoori, though he wasn't fluent in the language. Kerberos yanked the bag off the man's head. Pure terror poured from his eyes as he looked at the king of Omatus.

"I will not ask again."

"We were just following orders."

Kerberos stood, taking a razor from the small table next to him. He kneeled in front of the Ermoori. Staring right into the man's eyes, Kerberos pulled his boot off and positioned the razor next to his smallest toe. He struggled, screaming and trying to kick, but Kerberos held him still. The razor was sharp; Kerberos had a few of them made shortly after taking Omatus, to better shave his head. He pushed it into the soft pale flesh of the Ermoori man's toe. When he started sawing at the tendons, the man screamed even louder.

"Stop! Stop!"

A small splat sounded as his toe hit the ground. He stopped screaming, his face as white as paper.

"You have nine more," Kerberos said, "and then I will move on to your fingers."

"Please, no! I'll tell you, I'm sorry, please!"

Kerberos watched him, eyebrows raised as he waited for the information. He'd never tortured someone before, but he'd read about the techniques involved. Like almost everything, there was an art to it; but Kerberos much preferred actual combat.

"Overseer Hayne—" the man's breathing came in ragged bursts, breaking up his words, "—has ordered some books, ancient books, retrieved for him."

"For what purpose?"

"I don't know, I swear!"

Kerberos cut into the next toe, holding the man's foot as still as possible. He ignored the screams, and the begging, and focused on nothing but cutting until the man spoke again.

"Wait, wait, I heard a rumour!" he screamed, and Kerberos paused, "I heard a rumour... that the books have magic in them. The Twelve Crowns hate magic, it goes against God. They probably want to destroy them."

"Do they have any of the books now?"

"I've heard that there is one in Ermoor. Teams were sent to every country, so it won't be long before they have them all."

"If no one returns from Omatus, another team will be sent eventually, yes?"

The man nodded, his skin sickly and pale. His eyes bored resolutely into the wall above Kerberos' head. Fear lit his features, but underneath that was a dull certainty; he knew he would die soon.

"The Twelve Crowns don't accept failure."

Kerberos nodded back. *There is a book for each God*, he thought, *it makes sense. And they won't stop until they have all of them.*

"Tell me everything else you know about the books."

"That's it, I swear. Please, please don't cut me again."

Kerberos rose, putting his razor down and staring at the Ermoori. He considered letting the man live, sending him back to Ermoor as a warning. But it wouldn't make any difference; they would send more men to take the book no matter what he did. Sighing, he conjured a handful of fire and threw it into the man's lap. It caught quickly, and Kerberos said a quick prayer to Sithares as it burned.

The next day, Kerberos stood once again in his command room, looking over the map of Pandeia he kept there. This time he'd brought Nomiki in with him. She stood opposite him, on the side of the table where Ermoor sat on the map. Nomiki was his favourite commander; logical, intelligent, ruthless and loyal.

"You want to go there?" she asked.

"Yes. I believe they already have at least one book, possibly more. They are trying to get the books for a reason, and I want them first."

When he read the prayer to Sithares all those years ago, it gave him Fire Magic. It stood to reason that if he read the prayers from every other book, he would gain the magic from them too. With that much power, it wouldn't matter if Sithares hated him for staying in Omatus. All he wanted was for Omatus to be the city he knew it could be. In the five years since he'd become king, Omatus had improved drastically; but if he left the city and fulfilled Sithares' demands by laying waste to Pandeia, it would fall to chaos. It would end up even worse than it was before he was a child.

"I understand," Nomiki said, "and you need someone in charge while you're gone."

It wasn't a question. He admired Nomiki for the way she spoke to him; there was respect, but none of the blind worship he heard in most of his followers.

"Yes. You."

Nomiki nodded, no trace of surprise in her features.

"Would it not make more sense to send me there instead?" she asked.

"No. I want to do this myself."

She nodded again, staring at Ermoor on the map. Kerberos looked at it too. Ermoor was a city unlike any other in Pandeia. They thrived on technology, and there was very little living there other than the people themselves. Kerberos had read about it; but he was interested in seeing it for himself. He wouldn’t have gone there if not for the books, but it would be a great experience for him. The most valuable lesson he'd ever learned was that one could only learn so much from books; at some point, real experience was necessary.

Seeing Ermoor in person was a secondary concern, and barely even that. The books of the other Gods were something he hadn't even thought about since becoming the son of Sithares. Now that the idea occurred to him, it made so much sense. Fire Magic on its own was incredibly powerful; if he had every other type of magic at his disposal as well, he would be unstoppable. Instead of just Omatus, he could rule the entire world the way it should be ruled. Instead of burning Pandeia down, he could raise it to a new level of peace and prosperity.

Zeera

1778

What took you so long?" One of the spies said.

Four of them were fanned out in the alley in front of her, and as she realised two were missing, they appeared behind her, cutting off her escape. *I still don't even know where the other four are,* she thought. The group continued laughing as they had while walking down the street, taunting her and brandishing weapons she didn't recognise.

"We've been waiting months for one of you frogs to follow."

Zeera said nothing, focusing her magic instead. No one had ever spotted her so quickly before; she wasn't prepared for a fight. Her plan had been to simply watch and try to find out their plan. Her breathing came in ragged hitches; but it was fury, not fear. The Ermoori looked at every race other than their own as subhuman. They called Shenza monkeys, they called Tarsi frogs, and they called Omati and Thearans sand eaters or camels. They weren't the most creative of insults, but the disdain and condescension with which the Ermoori said them made it sting.

"Speechless? I shouldn't have expected anything less from a sneaky little frog." The one who spoke was clearly the leader; none of the others spoke, just laughed at his every word.

"I have to say, the way you change to look like anything is remarkable. I almost believed you were just some sand eater."

After the laughter died down, the leader's expression slowly changed from smug to annoyed.

"Well, since you don't understand manners, I suppose we'll just have to teach you how rude it is to ignore your betters. Kill the frog."

She heard the footsteps behind her, and rushed at the four in the alley. Tearing one of the water skins from her belt, she loosened the cap, focused on the contents, and threw it at the leader. It hissed and steamed viciously the second it hit his face; she'd turned it into a powerful acid in mid-air. He screamed, clawing at his face, and fell to his knees. The other spies paused for a moment, and that moment was all she needed.

Water Magic allowed her to control liquid; not only change it, but move it with nothing but her thoughts. The acid that tore through the leader's face was still under her command. She formed it into a sphere and sent it flying into the stomach of another spy. As she did so, she focused on the blood pouring from the first spy's face; it formed into a sphere and turned to acid as well, and she launched that at a third Ermoori.

The two behind her caught up and grabbed her, but her focus was entirely on magic. She barely felt a pulse of lightning jab into her neck, though it forced her body to seize up and pain to lance through her muscles. Three were dead or dying, and with their blood spilling and the water she'd thrown, there was more than enough liquid in the alley for her to take care of the rest. Another jab to her side brought a fresh wave of bright pain through her entire body. Pushing past the pain, she formed a spear out of blood; it flew like an arrow straight through the head of one of the men grabbing her. He fell without a sound.

"What the fuck is happening?" one of the spies said.

"Overseer Hayne said they'd use magic, just keep hitting it with the prod 'til it's down!"

Three more jabs slammed into her body, one in the side, one in the head, and one in the back. Each one was followed by a wave of intense pain, a blinding light behind her eyelids, and every muscle in her body tensing up to the point that she couldn't move. She screamed, but no sound came from her spasming throat. Cold white nothing overtook her vision, and she almost slipped away. Another jab pushed her further; her body felt like a slab of metal hit by lightning.

"Is that enough? Do you think it's dead?"

They let her go, and she fell to the ground like a solid object.

"It's still seizing, but the Tyrans did that during testing even when they were already dead."

"Yeah, I remember." laughter echoed through the alley, distant and hollow.

"Wait until it stops flinching, then cut its head off to be sure."

Zeera focused with everything she had left; the alley was gone, the Ermoori a thousand miles away, and her body felt broken and dead. But she forced her mind to think, and she felt the liquid around her. She couldn't see, and didn't dare open her eyes. Instead, she focused on their voices as they spoke, and tried to pinpoint where they were. Though the voices sounded far away, they were standing close. Close enough to kill her quickly when she stopped seizing.

"It's almost dead. Kill it, we need to get to the others to help take the book."

One of them kicked her leg, and then she knew exactly where they were. Blood covered the alley floor. All she needed to use Water Magic was for any kind of liquid to be out in the open; blood was useless to her if it was still inside a person. As soon as it was out of their body, it became her weapon. She felt it all around her, waiting for her mind's touch. Without waiting, she sent a wave of it up at head height, throwing it around the alley until she heard the disgusted shouts of all three remaining Ermoori. A few seconds after the blood hit them, she turned it to acid. As their screams filled the alley, her spasms calmed, and by the time they were dead she could almost stand. Her mind was cloudy, her body weak. But now she knew where the other four spies were going to be.

Kerberos

1778

Ermoor was more or less the exact opposite of Omatus; cold, dark, and constantly raining. Its people were tense and suspicious, and its leaders were secretive, unknown to their subjects. Kerberos wore a travelling cloak, and the Tarsi disguise spell on his face that made him look like an Ermoori. He couldn't do anything about his height, so he still received pointed glances from the Ermoori on the street. The spy he'd questioned in Omatus had no knowledge that could help him find the books other than the name of Overseer Hayne, so he was starting with a blank slate.

An invention called the teleradio was stationed at even points down every street, as well as in carts, shops and homes. Announcements were made regularly throughout the day, echoing through the crowds. One name was mentioned almost constantly; the Overseer for Scientific Advancement, Riffolk Hayne. He was apparently responsible for the vast majority of Ermoor's technological advancement over the last twenty years. He was the wealthiest man in Ermoor, and the highest ranking public figure that Kerberos could determine.

Kerberos headed for the district known for scientific development, called Darkpoint. Though its government was buried underground, most of Ermoor was easy to understand; they hid the things that should have been public, and advertised the things that should have been secret. Kerberos noted everything, committing it all to memory as he explored Ermoor. If he ever had to attack, making a plan would be easy after seeing the entire city.

As advanced as Ermoor was, their military was confined to one district, and made up a relatively small proportion of their population. The population itself was massive, so it was still an intimidating army; but compared to the Thearans, the Ermoori were weak and would not survive an attack on their own soil. If a fight was ever necessary, Kerberos made a note to himself to pre-emptively invade. Ermoor opened onto the swamplands on the south west side, and although it should have focused some defences there, it was the least defended part of the entire city.

Battle plans were already fully formed in Kerberos' head by the time he reached Darkpoint. If he'd wanted to, he could have laid waste to a huge chunk of the city single-handedly before their military reacted. But his purpose was finding and retrieving the books, and he didn't want to start a war unless he had to. Still, serving Sithares for so long had affected his mind; the temptation to burn everything he saw was almost overwhelming.

Ermoor was a huge city. It dwarfed Omatus, and walking from one side to the other took a long time. *No wonder they all use carts here,* he thought. If everyone walked in Ermoor as they did in Omatus, they would be walking all day. By the time he reached Darkpoint, the sun was well and truly set, and a black sky pushed down on Kerberos. Lights twinkled everywhere above his head, but he saw almost no stars above them; just endless black. Stars were one of the only ways to navigate the deserts of Omas, and without them Ermoor felt so separate from the rest of Pandeia that for a moment his head whirled.

The closer to Darkpoint he came, the more military presence he found. He had to move carefully, but the night made things a little easier. He wasn't used to sneaking around; he hadn't needed to hide his face since escaping Omatus as a child. Still, Kerberos was a patient man; he had faith in Nomiki's leadership while he was gone. So he took his time sneaking through the city. After all, the potential benefits if he was successful were invaluable, and certainly worth the time it took.

Through his decades of reading and research, Kerberos hadn't heard of anyone being able to wield more than two magic types simultaneously; there was the ancient Thearan legend of Darkfire, but other than that magic seemed to be limited for most people, and rare even then. But if anyone could wield more than two types of magic, Kerberos knew it would be him. The only complication he could think of was how he would handle a confrontation with whoever currently had the books in Ermoor; if they already used magic, they may be quite formidable. Especially if they already had more than one book.

He knew a little about Shadow Magic; Shenza joined the Thearan tribes relatively often, and he'd become fairly familiar with Dakesh. And he knew enough about Tarsi magic from his training with Karak, although he wasn't sure what book or God it came from. Other than those, Kerberos had no idea what to expect. *What God do they worship in Ermoor?* he thought, *I have not heard of any magic type being attributed to the Ermoori.*

Kerberos hadn't gone somewhere like this without a plan before; except for fleeing Omatus and heading into the Omasi deserts, but then he had the voice of Sithares guiding him. It seemed Sithares was too busy to guide its son nowadays. He trusted himself, his own instincts, enough to believe he could handle things, but a deep cold still tightened his stomach as he ventured further into Darkpoint. Finally, he reached a huge building, its windows shining with light even in the late hour. Its placement and design made it clear to Kerberos the building was important.

Sneaking in would be almost impossible for him. There were certainly people inside the building, and his size made it difficult enough to sneak through the wide open streets. Deciding on a direct approach, Kerberos knocked on the thick metal door. A short, slim Ermoori man answered, staring up at Kerberos with undisguised shock.

"I have a message for Riffolk Hayne," Kerberos said.

"Overseer Hayne doesn't take unannounced visitors," the man replied.

"He will want to speak with me."

Kerberos stepped close, letting his presence wash over the tiny man before him. He'd lost count of the people he'd killed long ago; and this man had clearly not killed anyone, let alone even been in a fight. There was a desperate fear falling off him like sweat. He knew he couldn't stand up to Kerberos, even if he didn't know who Kerberos was.

"With all due respect, sir, he never wants to speak with anyone."

Kerberos stepped forward again, halfway through the door and inches from the Ermoori.

"I will speak with him. The only choice for you to make is whether or not you die before that happens."

They stared at each other, and to the man's credit he maintained eye contact far longer than some warriors Kerberos knew. But, as he knew would happen, the Ermoori lowered his gaze and stood aside to let Kerberos in.

Inside, the corridors were blank and clean, and as smooth as the glass in the windows in Tarsium. The small Ermoori man led him through corridors that each branched off the other endlessly. Every time Kerberos turned onto another corridor, a deeper sense of weight pressed on him, as though the building was drawing him into its depths. He didn't feel in danger, but the unsettling sensation of a trap enveloped him as he walked. Focusing on the turns and the number of steps he took between them, Kerberos committed the walk to memory. He knew it wouldn't be long until he would have to rely on knowing how to get out of the suffocating corridors without a guide.

Finally, he was brought to a large room full of Ermoori rushing around between benches covered in scientific equipment. Standing near the far wall, tall and imperious, was Riffolk Hayne. Kerberos recognised him simply by his body language; where every other person rushed with shoulders hunched and eyes down, Riffolk stood calm and collected. The man who led him there ran up to Riffolk, whispered something, and watched as Riffolk approached Kerberos.

"I've not been given your name, stranger."

"I want to talk with you privately."

Riffolk studied him intently, his eyes boring into Kerberos' without expression. Though the Overseer wasn't physically intimidating, Kerberos found himself slightly unnerved by the blank, deep cold in his eyes. It felt almost like looking into the eyes of a dead man; except Riffolk's eyes glowed with vicious intelligence.

"If that's the only way you'll talk, then so be it," he finally said, "you're already wasting my time as it is."

Riffolk gestured back out the door.

"Come. I have somewhere *very* private where we can talk."

Lashek

1778

Shanaken felt so vibrant now, so alive. Shadow Magic was everywhere in the forest, and Lashek was always naturally talented with it, but now... He couldn't believe the difference it made, after Amalus blessed him, even five years later. He seemed to be his own source of Shadow Magic, instead of drawing it from the forest around him. His favourite place was the southernmost point of the forest. A small clearing where the animals and plants felt particularly vibrant. He sat in the centre, meditating and feeling the life all around him, when Amalus' voice pierced the silence in his mind.

North. Now.

His eyes flew open, and he leapt to a sprint in less than a second, shooting north as fast as a Zuzuk.

"What's happening?" he asked as he ran.

Ermoori spies. Attempting to steal the book.

Lashek didn't need to ask which book. There was only one that mattered in Shanaken. He didn't know where exactly the book was; the only times he'd read from it, it was brought to him by a Zuzuk under Amalus' command. *Now I'll know where to get it myself,* he thought, *though only if I stop these spies first*. The forest opened itself to him, branches moving out of the way or pointing in the right direction. Predators ignored him, other animals scrambled to clear a path, and Lashek sped through Shanaken faster than he ever had before.

"Where?" he said as he sprinted.

In the mountains on the northern reaches. I will guide you when you get there.

"How do they know where to look," he puffed, "if you won't even tell your Hero?"

Now is not the time for jokes, Lashek.

He pushed himself faster, as fast as he could possibly go.

"I wasn't entirely joking."

But he didn't expect a response, and Amalus didn't give one. He ran underneath the city to avoid the other Shenza, along the forest floor.

Hurry. They are close.

"I can't go any faster," he said, "if I could, I'd be there by now."

I have set my Zuzuk on them.

"Tell them to leave some soldiers for me."

Veering west, Lashek got out from under the city and leapt from branch to branch back up to the canopy. He circled around the Eternal Mountain, leaping from giant tree to giant tree. From near the treetops, he saw the mountains drawing closer.

They have it.

"But they're still in the forests, aren't they?"

Yes. You can still catch them if you hurry.

"Have I not been hurrying this whole time?"

Lashek. Move.

The voice sounded further away somehow, as though it was being carried away. His legs burned with the effort, his lungs roaring as he pulled in gulps of air. He'd crossed the entirety of Shanaken in almost no time. Before today, if anyone had told him he would run so far in such a short time he would have burst into laughter.

Finally, the feet of the mountains loomed into sight. The trees stopped short and rough grass and rocks took their place. Without stopping, Lashek sped up the side of the nearest mountain. At the top, he felt a wordless nudge pulling his gaze towards a point in the distance. He sprinted towards it, pulling Shadow Magic from the life around him and pouring it into his muscles.

One Ermoori soldier stood his ground against a giant Zuzuk. They were surrounded by the corpses of other Ermoori, and two dead Zuzuk. The live Zuzuk was grievously wounded, growling and swiping as the Ermoori unloaded his hand cannon again and again. Lashek threw a Shadow throwing blade, guiding it with magic as he ran. By the time he reached the Zuzuk, the Ermoori was as dead as his fellow soldiers, a thin but deep hole slashing his neck. He put his hand on the Zuzuk's maw, letting some Shadow Magic flow into its body to help it heal.

Not now, Lashek. They still have the book.

"Is this not all of them?" he asked, glancing around at the group of bodies. There were almost a dozen of them.

No. There is one more. He has the book.

Lashek grunted in frustration and sprinted away from the Zuzuk. The nudges continued, pulling his vision in the direction of the last Ermoori. *He has to have some kind of vehicle,* he thought, *if I can't catch him this easily.*

He was already too far. The rest of them stayed behind to delay the Zuzuk.

He reached the far slope of the furthest mountain, and saw the Ermoori jump into a tiny boat.

"I can catch that!" he said, racing down the mountainside.

But as he drew closer, the boat suddenly zoomed across the water's surface, leaving a trail of churning foam in its wake. In moments, it was a dot on the horizon.

Kerberos

1778

He was led down even more corridors, then through a secret hidden entrance into a large room underneath the building. Riffolk didn't blindfold him or try to hide the entrance in any way; though he ordered his underlings to stay where they were. Once in the secret room, Riffolk turned to him and waited.

"I have heard about the Twelve Crowns of Ermoor," Kerberos said, "and I know they are looking for certain artefacts. Do you know anything about this?"

Riffolk's face remained absolutely still, his eyes burning.

"Yes."

"Do you know why they want these artefacts?"

"Yes."

Bright, vibrant rage tingled in Kerberos' chest. Riffolk wouldn't make this easy. There was something almost inhuman about the man; he wouldn't have been surprised if Riffolk wielded magic himself. Whatever it was, Kerberos could tell that Riffolk wasn't intimidated by him in the slightest.

"Tell me."

"I have a question for you, first; what is your name?"

He sighed.

"My name is Kerberos. I am the king of Omatus."

Lifting his hood off, Kerberos dropped the Tarsi spell and revealed his true face. *No point trying to deceive this man,* he thought, *I have a feeling he's smarter than anyone I have ever known.*

"Ah. I suspected as much. Not many men are as tall as you, your highness."

There was no hint of mocking in Riffolk's tone, but the way he said *your highness* still irked Kerberos.

"You know of me already."

"One must be aware of any and all potential threats if one is to rule effectively."

"I thought the Twelve Crowns ruled Ermoor?"

Riffolk hesitated for just a fraction of a second, but it was enough to show Kerberos his mistake.

"They do. I merely make it my business to know these things, and they benefit from my knowledge."

"I see."

"Now, onto the business at hand. You have the same interest in the books as Ermoor, correct?"

"I am trying to find out what interest that is," Kerberos said, "once I know that, I can answer your question."

"You know what the books are," Riffolk said, "the power they hold. You're a king now, but surely you've thought of being more."

Suddenly, Riffolk made sense to Kerberos. *He wants the books for himself,* he thought, *he's going to overthrow these secretive leaders of Ermoor, and try to take over all of Pandeia.* Though their military was a small proportion of their population, it was still big enough to be a real threat; especially considering the technological weapons at Ermoor's disposal.

"That is what the Twelve Crowns want, then? More than Ermoor?"

"Why wouldn't they?"

"And you?" Kerberos asked, "you are content with simply helping them achieve their goal?"

Riffolk smiled. A small, evil smile. If Sithares could have been given human form, it would have smiled exactly the way Riffolk smiled now. Kerberos was ready for an attack at any moment; he didn't trust Riffolk enough to even blink around him. But Riffolk didn't attack.

"My goals *are* the Twelve's goals. From one ruler to another, why don't we drop the pretence? You killed my spies, and you've come for the other books I may already have."

"That is correct. There are no Twelve Crowns, are there?"

"Correct. Now, I want to rule Pandeia with the power of the books, and so do you. How do we proceed from here?"

Kerberos had never been in a calm, respectful conversation with an enemy before; Thearans fought and killed even those who weren't their enemies. Riffolk kept him guessing, and he didn't like guessing. He would have preferred open hostility and battle to standing around talking as though they were friends.

"Surely you know enough about me to know how I would handle the situation," Kerberos said.

Riffolk laughed, though his eyes remained cold and empty.

"True enough. Well, I welcome a fight, if that's the only option you see. But Pandeia is a big place. I don't see the harm in two people sharing the rule, if you can accept it."

Shared rule? Surely he's lying. Kerberos couldn't trust the offer, not from a man like Riffolk. He would pretend they were working together until all the books were found, then try to eliminate Kerberos and take Pandeia for himself. It was what Kerberos would have done himself. The only thing that bothered Kerberos was Riffolk's casual attitude towards a fight between the two men. Riffolk was slim, and there was absolutely no combat training evident in his posture or movements. In the deserts of Omas, Riffolk wouldn't have lasted a day. But here, on his own territory, he clearly had some advantage Kerberos was unaware of.

"How could I trust you?"

"I will take Shanaken and Tarsium, and you can take all of Omas and Theara. Two continents each, and we rule them as we choose."

The concept made a lot of sense, and Kerberos found himself genuinely considering it. He would find himself constantly looking over his shoulder for assassins and spies sent by Riffolk; but if he refused, he would have to look over his shoulder.

"Except that I already rule the most powerful city in Omas," Kerberos said, "and Theara barely counts. Besides, you declined to mention Ermoor. You would be taking three and I would be taking two, one of which is abandoned."

Riffolk's small smile twitched his lips again.

"Do you have a more fair way to divide Pandeia between two rulers?"

"You take Ermoor and Shanaken. I take the rest. Two populated countries each, and we consider Theara as an extension of Omas."

"And if I disagree?"

"Then you die, and I take all of it."

"You really don't know who I am," Riffolk said, "do you?"

"It makes no difference. You will either join me and we will rule Pandeia together, or you will die."

"I see. You're quite determined to turn this into a fight, aren't you?"

"I am merely stating the likely outcomes. We cannot easily trust each other, and if one of us betrays the other, it will certainly end in death."

They faced each other in silence for a moment, both considering the likelihood of battle. Kerberos didn't assume victory, but unless Riffolk had a huge amount of technological fire power, Kerberos could win. *Or unless he has read one or more of the books already,* he thought.

"I agree. Trust will take a long time to build. But I wanted to at least offer to join forces. I'm assuming you haven't found any other books?"

"No," Kerberos said, "just one."

"And you clearly aren't willing to share its power," Riffolk said, "or my men would have brought it back with them."

"They tried to take it by force. No conversation was had, they simply attacked. But even if they had asked, I would not have shared it, no."

"I see."

"Have you succeeded in stealing any other books?"

Riffolk's smile finally spread to his eyes. Instead of giving him warmth, it served only to make him look even less human.

"Oh, yes. I have two."

Zeera

1778

Limping, still dizzy from the lightning weapons, Zeera made her way to the Circle headquarters. The six she'd followed were a distraction, it was so obvious now. *Visit a known criminal tavern every day, talk loudly and get yourself noticed... Meanwhile a smaller group stays hidden and goes for the book and soon as the larger group is followed.* It was a good plan, and one that she should have seen from the beginning; she knew there were supposed to be ten of them.

The book was guarded from within the underwater caves; Zeera had a lot of faith in the Tarsi guards, but even so, the Ermoori were clearly improving their weapons drastically. *Who knows what weapons they've got for underwater use,* she thought, *but I hope the guards can handle them.* She wasn't moving fast enough. If she'd been underwater she would be able to reach the cave of Asheilos within moments, but as it was she could only limp.

It took her almost an hour to get to the nearest underground tunnel entrance. Just like Ermoor, underneath Tarsium was a complex network of secret tunnels. The difference was that every tunnel under Tarsium was submerged under water. By the time she got there, her muscles were just beginning to get over the effects of the lightning, and her mind had cleared a little. She slipped down into the darkness, feeling the water cover her like a second skin. A surge of energy hit her, and for a moment she just hovered as Water Magic filled her entire body.

Zeera felt the way she imagined the Austris Arans did in ancient times; they wielded Air Magic, and being constantly surrounded by the element that gave them magic made them powerful. Whenever she was fully submerged in water, Zeera felt magic pulsing like a heartbeat in her body. She sped through the tunnels, hoping the Tarsi guards had beaten the four remaining Ermoori spies.

When she arrived in the cave of Asheilos, a dead silence greeted her. In the centre, where the box usually lay suspended by chains, was an empty expanse of water. *Where are you?* she thought, glancing at the tunnels that branched off.

The lake. Hurry.

The voice was weak, distant. Zeera sped for the tunnels that lead to the lake where her and Zalla trained. It didn't take her long, but when she reached the lake it was empty too. On a hunch, she sped to the far end and leapt out of the water, bringing a huge sphere of it with her, covering her as she hovered in its centre. In the distance, a small group of Ermoori ran towards the ocean.

They must have a ship waiting, she thought, *for a fast getaway.* How a ship large enough to make the journey approached and landed without being noticed she had no idea, but this was her best chance to stop them. Controlling water had finally become second nature to her after so many years. She could make water move through the air much faster than she could run. Suspended in the large sphere, she propelled it through the air towards her targets.

They reached the boat before she reached them, and she stopped for a moment, stunned. The boat was tiny. It would have only just fit the ten Ermoori, maybe a dozen if they sat close together. *How did something so small get from Ermoor to Tarsium?* she thought. There was no room for supplies, and the journey took almost a month.

How did they survive the journey? Her question was answered as soon as they'd all boarded. Using some kind of technology, the boat began moving without the Ermoori rowing, and with no sail.

It picked up speed quickly, and was soon headed out to the open ocean. Zeera dove into the water, speeding after them as fast as she could. *They haven't seen me,* she thought, *I should be able to take them by surprise.* She had no doubt she could move faster than the boat; at least at first. But as it sped on ahead, her certainty faded. She pushed as hard as she could, rocketing through the water faster than she ever had before. Diving deeper, she flipped to face the mottled sky as she sped towards the tiny boat. As she caught up, it drifted into her vision, floating in the sky with a trail of churning water behind it. Although she had trained underwater, she hadn't been in a combat situation like this before. She smiled; they thought they were free and clear, their mission successful. Zeera would take pleasure in proving them wrong.

Ermoor had a tense relationship with the rest of Pandeia, at best. Tarsium allowed trade between the two countries out of mutual benefit, despite their arrogance and racism. But stealing from them, especially an item beyond value, was an act of war. And as Asheilos' Hero, Zeera was perhaps the most dangerous Tarsi in Pandeia. Magic screamed through her very soul; she turned some of it towards the tiny boat above, and it exploded into two jagged pieces.

Splashes erupted on the surface; the spies were thrown clear of the boat. A cloud of blood spread from one of them as they slowly sank, but the other three began swimming. *They haven't seen me yet,* she thought, *perfect*. But just as she prepared another attack, one of them spotted her. He didn't hesitate; he levelled a gun of some kind at her and fired. A spear streaked towards her faster than she could react, slamming into her leg.

Screaming, Zeera focused on the water around the man, and it closed in on him, crushing him to death in an instant. When she let go, a burst of red mist exploded out into the water. The two remaining spies saw her and fired as well. She blocked one just in time with a wall of condensed water, but the other sliced her shoulder as it sped past. They reloaded quickly, but Zeera launched a blade made of water into one of them and threw up another shield between her and the last.

A spear appeared in the shield, suspended half a metre in front of her. The Ermoori she'd launched the blade at twitched, blood gently floating from the wound in his chest. He twitched again, and his gun fired. Zeera lurched to the side, but the spear moved far too quickly; she felt it thud into her stomach. A deep, sharp pain exploded in her gut, spreading through the rest of her body. The last Ermoori reloaded again, and she crushed him under the weight of the ocean around him.

Zeera woke in pain. Her stomach felt as though someone had cut her open and filled it with hot coals. For a moment, she didn't know where she was or what had happened. Her eyes flew open, and though her stomach and leg screamed in protest, she took a combat stance. Blinking, she looked around; she was in a healer's room.

"Glad to see you're still well enough to fight," Zalla said, "but you really should be resting."

She hovered in the corner of the room, watching Zeera with a wry smile. Zeera settled back into the resting pod, grunting as another wave of pain pulsed from her stomach.

"What happened? I don't remember anything after killing the spies."

"You brought Asheilos back to us, Zeera. Well done."

After the spear hit her stomach, everything was a dark, pain-filled blur. She didn't even remember seeing the book, let alone bringing it back to Azar. She tried to focus, but the memory was as hazy and black as the ocean depths. Groaning, she stopped trying to focus; all it did was hurt.

"As long as the book is safe and the spies are gone." She looked at Zalla, "There are no more spies, right?"

"They're dead, and we have no word of more. You can rest, Zeera. You've done your duty as Hero for now, and your missions can wait until you're well again. Focus on healing."

The water around her helped a lot, but she was still visited by healers. She took potions and food whenever they were offered, and gradually the pain faded and her strength returned. The encounter, or what she remembered of it, stuck with her for a long time; the Ermoori were becoming a serious threat. They'd never breached Tarsium, but as she drew closer to being healed, all she thought about was how Tarsium would react against Ermoor. She knew about Ermoor's planned invasion; but knowing about it didn't calm her fears. *War is coming,* she thought, *and I'm the Hero meant to fight it*.

Aella

1778

There were still far more tribes travelling the desert than Aella had expected. Sithares guided her, moving somehow from tribe to tribe in the vast wastelands of Omas. She gathered an army within five years, a population that could have filled a city. Something about the situation clashed in her mind, however; it felt too familiar. She knew she was Aella, but sometimes she felt as though she was remembering events from a different life. *Did Roxane gain followers travelling through the desert?* She thought. *Maybe.*

It occurred to her that she didn't remember her old tribe. *Or anything before Kerberos.* His presence echoed in her mind every waking moment, like a beacon of rage. He wiped out everything else, and though Sithares had granted her memories back to her on Sitharkos, they faded again under the weight of the fury she felt for Kerberos.

Every tribe she came across accepted her challenge for leadership. Every one of them became hers. Each time a tribe merged with her own, there was infighting amongst her old followers and the new. She watched, smiling, as blood stained the grey sand. Occasionally, she joined in. Sithares whispered constantly in those moments, reminding her of the glory of bloodshed and chaos. The desert took hundreds of corpses from Aella's tribe; a small price to pay to Sithares. She left them in the sand for the lions and the lizards.

After her tribe grew big enough, Sithares told her to go to Theara. Aella smiled, relief and yearning filling her heart. *Home,* she thought, *Theara is home*. A brief flutter of memory formed in her mind; *"We should go back to Theara,"* someone said, *"We can take our tribe, and any other tribe who wishes it, and live the way the ancient Thearans did."* Who said it? The memory disappeared before any more details surfaced, and Aella let out a strangled sob as it left her mind again. She couldn't even be sure it was real, but it felt as real as the desert in front of her. *Maybe once I get to Theara, it will become clear,* she thought. Either way, Sithares wanted her there, so that's where she would go.

Do not bother yourself with your past life. What matters now is the mission.

By then her tribe was east of Sitharkos, in the southern reaches below the mountain range. She ordered her warriors north, into the mountains. Small sparks of memory danced just out of her reach as she looked up at the mountains looming over them. Something happened there before Omatus, possibly even before Kerberos; something that filled her with as much yearning as the idea of coming home to Theara. But she couldn't place it, and the tribe marched north.

When they reached the feet of the mountains, her memory still hadn't become any clearer. They marched in through the lowest ground, and after a few hours the sand and rock gave way to the occasional gentle stream. Trees and even grass appeared, and Aella allowed her tribe to slow their pace a little. This low in the mountain ranges, predators were far more common; their prey was even more common, however, and the tribe enjoyed good hunting for the entire time they stayed in the mountains.

Smaller tribes usually climbed the mountains themselves, to avoid Thearan lions and Omasi sand panthers. But Aella's tribe was vast now, and she was powerful; they weren't threatened by wildlife in the slightest. Stopping in the centre of the range, Aella ordered a camp be set up. Her warriors busied themselves with the camp, and a group of them wandered away to hunt. Aella sat next to a small stream and thought about the mountains. As much as she trusted Sithares' guidance, she desperately wanted to remember what her mind was trying to tell her.

Sithares didn't want her to know. It felt strange, knowing her own memories were forbidden to her. But she would be nothing without Sithares; she would have no Fire Magic, and she would most likely still be wondering the desert with no memory if not for the Fire God. At least she had *some* memories. Burning farmland, the invasion of Omatus, and the murder of Erasmus. Athan's murder, too. Though she couldn't remember if he was really dead or if he'd just been stabbed. *We were made immortal after all*, she thought, *maybe Kerberos just hurt him to send a message*.

She drank from the stream, then walked to a nearby camp fire her warriors started. A small group sat together, talking about their life before joining Aella's tribe. Their voices stopped when she sat down, but she gestured for them to keep talking, and they did. Though each of the warriors speaking occasionally glanced at her nervously, it was a pleasant conversation, and the desperate sparks of memory faded without her realising. They stayed in the mountains for two weeks, and by the time they packed up the camp and marched on, Aella forgot about Sithares hiding her memories.

North of the mountains, the desert stretched endlessly into the horizon. It was a difficult journey even for a powerful fire mage, but the tribe marched on without complaint. They trusted her as much as she trusted Sithares. She taught her best warriors the prayer to

Sithares, and Fire Magic spread through the tribe. Wind snapped at their exposed skin, sand stinging them as they marched. Night was as cold as the day was hot, and they built huge fires in their camps and huddled together around them to sleep.

Weeks passed as they marched, and the hunting grew as hard and harsh as the desert itself. Each day, she sent warriors to hunt and bring back whatever they could find, and each day less food came back. After a while, less warriors came back each day. It was the life of the Thearans, and Aella knew she was used to it even though she didn't remember much of her life any more. The death of her warriors left no impact on her, and she kept pushing them on through the desert.

By the time they reached the giant bridge that joined Theara and Omas, Aella had lost hundreds from her tribe; but it was still thousands upon thousands strong. The bridge itself took an impressive amount of time to cross; Theara and Omas were actually separate continents. The span of ocean between them, though narrower than most, was still enough that Theara's mountains were small and hazy in the distance. Wind roared against them as they marched across the bridge; and with the ocean below, it was salt that stung their skin instead of sand. The closer they came to Theara, the more calm Aella grew.

Kerberos

1778

He has two books,* Kerberos thought, *hidden somewhere here.* All he needed to do was find out where they were. Even if he couldn't steal them, as long as he could read the prayers, he would gain the magic within them. *Riffolk can only stop me if he also has their magic*. Even then, he thought he had a good chance; Riffolk looked young, and Kerberos had been using Fire Magic for most of his life.

They faced each other in silence, tension building until it felt as though the slightest movement would trigger violence.

"Where are the books?"

"I keep them in secure chests, in a secret storage room attached to this lab."

His arrogance is unbelievable, Kerberos thought, *I expected anger or lies, but for him to tell me exactly where they are... he really thinks I cannot take them.*

"You have already read the prayers, yes?" Kerberos said.

Riffolk's reaction was a slight frown, his eyes narrowing as he stared at Kerberos. In that brief instant, Kerberos' stomach dropped; *he was not aware he needed to read the prayers to gain magic*, he thought. But Riffolk's frown disappeared as quickly as it showed up, and the cold certainty reappeared.

"You want to know if I've already gained the ability to wield magic? Oh, yes, I have."

Kerberos let his hands curl into fists.

"Careful, Kerberos," Riffolk said, "you're in far more danger here than I am."

"I have dealt with more danger than you since before you were born, boy."

"Don't be too sure. I guarantee, your highness, you've never met anyone like me."

Kerberos looked around the room, searching for any trace of a secret entrance. He knew it would be hidden well, but the tension between them was close to exploding into battle; there was no use for subtlety.

"You won't find the room," Riffolk said.

"Then tell me where it is."

He laughed, and pulled a weapon from a sheath on his belt.

"I've tried talking with you, Kerberos. Make your choice. We join forces, or we kill each other."

Kerberos walked around the room, ignoring Riffolk for as long as he could. To his credit, Riffolk remained calm, simply watching him.

"You want the power of the books I own for yourself," Riffolk said, "I understand. But if you won't agree to join me, why would I let you even see them?"

"Because if you do not, you will die."

A high pitched beep sounded from somewhere, and seconds later two complex-looking machines appeared from panels in the floor. They grabbed Kerberos' wrists with giant metal claws and lifted him off the ground. Riffolk kept his distance, his weapon pointed at Kerberos' face.

"How do you propose to accomplish that, your highness?"

Without hesitating, Kerberos unleashed the Fire within him, focusing it into his hands where the machines held him. Nothing happened. The metal didn't melt, or bend. He looked again at them; the metal was black. *Shenza steel,* he thought, *how is that possible?* He looked at Riffolk, and the man smirked.

"I knew from the rumours, and your reputation, that you were a warrior at heart," he said, "that no matter how intelligent you are, you would default to violence to get your way. It's a weakness, your highness. To be an effective ruler, you will need to learn some diplomacy."

"You think you are a better ruler than me? Ermoor is broken, its people suspicious and disgruntled. Your poor districts squabble over resources while the rich use them without care. Omatus, for the first time in history, is a paradise. I have gotten rid of slavery, I have improved the economy, brought peace and prosperity to the city. You look down on me for being a warrior, but it is war that turned Omatus into what it should have been."

He hadn't meant to speak so much, but Riffolk stoked his rage like no other person; except maybe Aella. Being trapped right in front of the man he wanted to kill only pushed him even further into rage. *If we faced each other without his technology, he would not stand a chance,* he thought.

"We'll see when I bring all of Pandeia to a new era of peace," Riffolk said, "without your help, apparently. In the meantime, you've helped me with something that had been bothering me. It's time to fix it."

Kerberos strained against the machines; with his Fire Magic active, he was far stronger, but they wouldn't budge. If he brought the Fire out to cover his skin, what the ancient Thearans called a Fire Wight, he would be strong enough to break the bonds. But he'd only get one chance, and he wanted to see what Riffolk was doing before he committed to it.

Riffolk disappeared from his view, and Kerberos heard a low metal sliding followed by a click behind him. *The hidden room.* He returned into view carrying a small black metal chest. It was twisted into an organic curved shape, like the buildings made from Shenza steel in Tarsium. *Shadow Magic.* Riffolk placed it on a bench, with its back to Kerberos. When he opened it, all Kerberos saw was the top of the chest's lid.

"I genuinely didn't know how to gain magic from these books," Riffolk said, "I've done as much research as I could, but I gained Power Magic by being touched directly by a God, and no information I found shed any light on how these books work."

Kerberos let him talk; as long as he was talking, his attention was at least partially diverted. Until Riffolk lifted the pure black book from the chest. Once he turned the first page, Kerberos let all the Fire inside him out, and tore himself from the machines' grip. He sent a wave of explosive energy in every direction, knocking the machines and Riffolk over. The chest stayed in place, as did the book; as though fire had no power over the magic they held. Riffolk was slammed into the wall behind him.

As quickly as he could, Kerberos flipped through the pages of the black book to the prayer. He read it several times in a row, committing it to memory, then sprinted to the hidden room. As he ran, the machines pushed themselves back to their feet. Among the benches and shelves covered in strange devices and written records was another chest, this one made of a more standard metal. The front of the chest was covered in complex locks; Kerberos brought his fire-covered fist down onto it as hard as he could. It crunched and bent under his hand, and he pulled it open.

Whirring emanated from the main room, and Kerberos saw the machines stomp over to the secret room's entrance. They both pointed their remaining clawed arms at him, weapons attached and ready. Kerberos flipped through the second book, flinching through the pain of the lightning which bound it. He remembered that pain; it was just as intense as his burns from first touching the book of Sithares. But he forced himself to ignore it and flipped through the pages, and came to the prayer. The prayers for each book were at roughly the same page, quite close to the book's beginning.

Reading as quickly as he could, Kerberos heard a groan from Riffolk as he woke. There was no time to recite the prayers now. And he couldn't sneak the books out with him when he left Ermoor; sneaking himself through the city had been hard enough. All he could do was read the prayers, remember them, and recite them when he was back in Omatus.

Footsteps echoed outside the doorway, and Kerberos left the book where it was, preparing to face Riffolk and his machines. They still guarded the entrance; there was nowhere to go but through them.

"Get out here, Kerberos," Riffolk said from behind his machines, "there's no way you can win. Your power and strength were surprising, I'll grant you that, but I have many more weapons at my disposal."

"There are a lot of very valuable things in here, Riffolk," he said, "you may have me trapped, but if you do not let me pass, I will destroy everything before you can kill me."

Riffolk does not know I am immortal, he thought, *though I do not want to die, the worst he can do is kill me, and I will just come back.* In his position, he could do far more damage to Riffolk than Riffolk could do to him. Silence drifted from the main room, as Riffolk thought about his threat. *I have him now,* Kerberos thought. Getting out of the lab, and Ermoor itself, would be difficult no matter what happened. But with his threat hanging over Riffolk's head, he may be able to escape unharmed.

"Surely you understand why I can't let you pass," Riffolk said, "come out here and we'll settle this properly."

Fire still coursed over Kerberos' body, filling him with energy and power. He balanced on the balls of his feet, ready for the violence to come. The whirring of Riffolk's machines sped up, and Kerberos heard a crackling beyond them. A pale yellow glow shone from the room where Riffolk stood. *Riffolk's magic,* he thought, *this is going to be interesting.*

Aella

1778

Theara was a beautiful place. Ancient power emanated from it, almost as much as Sitharkos. It was empty, except for an infestation of the large venomous lizards known as Deathclaws; but it felt like as much of a home as the desert. Her mission was to return Theara to glory, build it into a powerful city again, and then destroy Kerberos and Omatus with him. But timing was important to Sithares. She had to wait a long time before her attack; to her, that just meant more time to turn Theara into the fearsome city it once was.

Before any of that, however, she wanted to make Theara more than just a great city on its own; she wanted to turn it into a beacon for the Thearans still wandering the deserts, calling them home. Despite its beauty and power, it had become a desolate wasteland. Sithares would bring some to her, she knew. But in the meantime, she would do her part. Rumours took time to spread between tribes, since most tribes didn't talk directly to each other without a slaughter taking place. She sent a group of her warriors to the one place where rumour could take hold and spread; Tarsius. The Tarsi settlement on Omas' east coast was the one place where Thearans spoke to each other and traded without bloodshed.

Meanwhile, she worked her way through the city, cleaning and burning. Theara was almost entirely fireproof, designed to withstand the attacks of the most powerful mages of the ancient world. The more she conjured flames to burn the city clean, the stronger she felt. Outside of Sitharkos and Theara, using Fire Magic was draining. She had to recover. But inside places where Sithares' power was strong, it felt like there was no limit to her magic. As she grew stronger, so too did the warriors she gave Fire Magic to.

Deathclaws weren't too fond of fire, as it turned out. When she drew near to their nests, they fled the old buildings and rushed to safety. Gradually, she herded them to a small section of the city, and set up a perimeter of burning torches around it. That place became an easy source of food for her warriors, as well as a test of their bravery and skill; she sent warriors in alone, one at a time, with the instruction to bring back a Deathclaw for their fellow warriors to eat.

Months passed as they cleaned and restored the city. It was hard work, but Aella was determined to join in instead of simply giving orders. She wanted to show her warriors that she was more than a leader; she was one of them. After a few months, a tribe appeared at the city's entrance. Several dozen Thearans, a very small tribe; but more warriors nonetheless. By the time they reached the city square, Aella was waiting for them, perched on the silent dry fountain in the centre of the large space. Her warriors were busy on the northern side of the city, and she wanted to make an impression.

"Greetings, warriors," she said, "I've been waiting."

A hushed murmur swept through the tribe. Most of them looked at her as though she were one of the heroes of ancient Theara. *This must be how Kerberos feels,* she thought. *I could get used to this.*

"Is it true?" one of the warriors said, "You're the daughter of Sithares?"

A smile tugged at her lips; she felt it coming, and couldn't stop it.

"Yes."

Louder murmurs arose this time. She watched, as still as she could be. Although she couldn't remember most of her life, Kerberos himself stuck out like a jagged mountain piercing the cloud of her mind. She remembered the way he'd held himself, the sense of pure unquestioned authority he exuded. One of them spoke up, visibly shaking. It was all she could do to stop herself from laughing at the instant power she held over her new subjects.

"With respect, my lady... what do we call you?"

The question sat heavily in the air, as palpable as the smoke drifting above the city. In the years since leaving Sitharkos with her mission, she hadn't thought about a title. She realised as soon as the Thearan asked her that she hated being called *my lady. My lord* wouldn't work either.

If you want a title, you can be called queen of Theara.

Aella stood, smiling again, and looked down at the small group.

"I am Queen Aella. You may address me as *your highness,* or *my queen."*

They dropped to their knees, bowed their heads, and simply waited for her to speak again. No challenge of combat, no display of Fire Magic as Kerberos had done; just obedience. She leapt from the fountain, dusted herself off, and ordered the new warriors to the north with the rest of her subjects.

Kerberos

1778

Riffolk wouldn't reveal himself; his two machines stood at the doorway into the hidden room, and Kerberos knew Riffolk was the kind of man who wouldn't take unnecessary chances. Moments stretched out in silence, Kerberos' entire body burning from the tension as well as Fire Magic. In his Fire Wight form, he was more or less indestructible, but he'd never fought against machines made from Shenza steel before. He'd been able to rip free, tearing their arms from their sockets, but that was only because the joints themselves didn't contain any of the black metal.

His Fire Magic would do nothing. It should melt anything that wasn't made of Shenza steel, but he couldn't guarantee it would destroy them in time to escape. Kerberos, just like Riffolk, wouldn't take a chance unless it was necessary. There was no way to cause a distraction; Riffolk's attention, as well as the machines', was firmly focused on him. He had to make a decision soon. His Fire Wight form was temporary, and he wasn't sure how much longer it would last.

We'll settle this properly, Riffolk had said. Kerberos knew exactly what that meant. He would walk out of the room, and Riffolk would set both machines and whatever magic he had on Kerberos all at once. It may kill him; it may not. But Kerberos didn't mean to find out. Settling into a ready stance, he watched the machines adjust their own stance in response. *I really do not like those things,* he thought, as he prepared to fight, *or Riffolk, for that matter*.

"If we are going to settle this properly," Kerberos said, "how about you call off your machines? I do not think having your machines fighting for you is *settling things properly*."

In the brief silence that followed, Kerberos reached into the depths of his power and launched himself from the room. At the same time, he threw a fireball backwards into the hidden room, and a brutal explosion followed him into the main room, knocking one of the machines over and hurling Kerberos through the doorway. The other machine fired its weapons, and Kerberos felt metal projectiles ripping into his body; but he was made of fire, and they didn't so much as slow him down.

A bolt of yellow lightning filled the room, blinding him and slamming into his chest. He smashed into the wall behind him, and for a moment his Fire almost went out. The machine fired again, and this time there was pain; but it was faint, and he knew he was still protected by Fire. *Another bolt of lightning,* he thought, *and I will be in serious trouble*. But the machine stopped firing, and the second returned to its feet.

"I haven't seen magic used like that before," Riffolk said, staring at the fire coursing over Kerberos' entire body, "I wonder if Power Magic can be used in the same way."

His tone was casual, as though they were friends speaking about one of his experiments. Sighing, Kerberos got back to his feet. He couldn't hold his Fire Wight form much longer. Riffolk's hands glinted, small arcs of lightning dancing between his fingers. He watched Kerberos, eyes cold and unblinking. Kerberos stared back, and a moment of silence followed again before Kerberos heard the whirring of the machines' weapons.

Taking every bit of Fire within him, Kerberos screamed as he forced it out in an unstoppable wave. The wall behind him creaked under the force and heat, and the two machines buckled and flew backwards. Riffolk threw his hands up, a cascade of buzzing sparks wrapping around him as the Fire hit. Kerberos didn't stop to watch the damage. Sprinting, he ran back up the steps to the main lab, smashing the hidden door down and speeding down corridors.

Trying to remember the turns and steps in reverse order as he ran was more of a challenge than Kerberos had been prepared for. Soon enough, after he began to suspect he may be lost, he heard the bustling of the main room where he'd met Riffolk. Stomping footsteps boomed from behind him; the machines. He was running out of magic, and the machines would catch him if he continued down the corridors. *One way out,* he thought, and threw a fireball at the far wall of the main room.

The wall exploded, throwing Riffolk's underlings to the ground. As he'd thought, the wall faced the street, and he leapt out the huge hole, sprinting away from Riffolk's lab. Behind him, the machines fired their weapons. Projectiles hit the road and the buildings around Kerberos, and one or two slammed into him, but he ran on. The machines stopped at the hole in the wall, however, and didn't pursue him down the street. Now all he had to worry about was the Ermoori military.

Just out of Darkpoint, Kerberos' Fire went out. He still had a small amount of magic, but not enough to maintain the Fire Wight form. Magic formed quickly, at least for Kerberos, so it wouldn't be long before he could use the form again; but for now, he had to go back to sneaking. Tarsi body magic drew on natural forces that lay within every person, as well as the magic inherent within the ancient language they used to draw the spells; it was the only reason Kerberos was able to learn it. It also meant that he could use Tarsi spells even when he'd run out of Fire Magic. He fixed the disguise spell to his face again, and headed south for the docks.

His cloak was still fine, though it had looked better. Torn from the machines' weapons and singed from Riffolk's lightning, it didn't look as new as it had when Kerberos arrived. Still, it covered him and helped with the deep cold of Ermoor. As he walked, rain pattered gently on the smooth road. Within minutes, it pelted everything in sight, until all Kerberos heard was the rush of falling water. He ran, hoping that a running cloaked figure would be far less suspicious in the rain.

The rain meant that the streets were mostly empty; even people who lived in Ermoor didn't much like the weather. But soldiers were still patrolling, and most of them ignored him as he ran. Kerberos couldn't believe his luck. *If it even is luck,* he thought. He'd read all about the Gods and how they worked. Though Sithares hadn't spoken to him in years, the God of Fire could be responsible for gently nudging events in his favour. Either way, it was no time to question his luck. After a while running through the torrential rain, Kerberos finally approached the docks in Ivorstorm.

Despite his size, Kerberos' disguised Ermoori face meant that getting on a ship bound for Tarsium was easy. The Ermoori didn’t restrict their own, unless the Ermoori in question was wanted by the law. They were quick to judge every other race in Pandeia, but wouldn't so much as raise an eyebrow when it came to their own people. Nodding to the Ermoori captain, Kerberos strolled onto the ship and headed straight for the cabins below deck. During the long journey to Tarsium, he recited the prayers he'd remembered in his head, fixing the words in his mind until he could say them out loud in safety.

Aella

1780

Two years after naming herself queen, Aella sat in the throne room where the ancient rulers of Theara sat thousands of years before. The sun was low, the city peaceful, and the smell of fire, stone and ash filled the air. Aella hadn't felt as whole since waking on the banks of the Alpheus. *That was seven years ago,* she thought, *seven years, and I still don't remember much of my life before*.

Every few weeks, another tribe would show up at Theara's gates. They all wanted to pledge their allegiance to the Thearan queen and rejoin their ancient homeland. Spreading the news to Tarsius had worked wonders; now she could focus on ruling Theara, and more warriors for her army simply came to her. Occasionally, she would get challengers for the crown. They didn't last long. Even the ones who wielded Fire Magic were no match for Aella. She encouraged fighting among her people, to feed Sithares, but she made sure it was controlled enough that her army didn't diminish much in size.

Aella ordered raids on the western cities in Omas; Theara had almost no natural resources of its own, and she had a whole city to take care of. She also sent teams into the mountains south west of Theara, to search for anything they could use. It proved far more fruitful than she hoped. They returned with water, fruits and vegetables, and a huge assortment of kills ready to be skinned, gutted, and cooked. It didn't take her long to order a village be built in the mountains, and a more stable path built between the village and the city.

Her people adored her; she saw it in their eyes every day. But the only thing on Aella's mind was Kerberos. She formed a war council, demanding that any Thearan with years of experience and the intelligence to plan battles come forward. With them, she made plans for the attack on Omatus. Sithares still hadn't ordered an attack, but it couldn't be much longer, and Aella wanted to be prepared to march as soon as the order was given.

They sat together in the throne room. A large table stood in the centre of the room, designed specifically for the war council of the ancient Thearans. Using it for the same purpose now felt right. Her war council was discussing the different entrances into Omatus when a warrior opened the heavy doors and crept into the room. As quiet as he was trying to be, the door creaked and the entire war council stopped and stared.

"My queen," he said, "I'm sorry to interrupt, but a new tribe has appeared to join us."

"Very well," she said, "I'll begin the ceremony after my war council is done."

She gestured to Selene, one of her best strategists, to continue talking. The warrior at the door cleared his throat gently, staring at Aella as though expecting to be killed on the spot. Selene stopped talking and the council stared again at the man.

"I'm very sorry to interrupt again, my queen, it's just that, well... One of the tribe says she is your mother."

Aella stared. She was sure she misheard the man. A part of her mind lit up like Sitharkos erupting; *your mother is alive!* It said, *go to her, she came back for you!* But another part of her, the part that needed Sithares' voice, suspected a trap. Or simply a trick.

"My mother?"

"Yes, my queen."

She turned to the war council, and back to the warrior.

"Bring her to me."

"Your highness," one of her council said, "is our meeting done?"

"Yes. Leave me be, and we will meet again tomorrow."

After they left, the woman walked into the empty throne room. Aella watched her mother walk towards her, and a bright, powerful memory exploded in her mind. *Helene,* she suddenly knew, *my mother's name is Helene*. She remembered climbing the mountains with her mother, looking out over the desert from the top and talking. Laughing together. She remembered feeling loved, protected; as though nothing could hurt her while Helene was near. As they came close to each other, Aella felt her lip tremble. Her heart thumped in her chest, and tears spilled from her without warning. Helene ran towards her, arms outstretched.

"Aella! It's really you!"

Aella burst into shaking sobs. Her mother held her, and a fractured part of her mind became whole again. They stayed like that a while, holding each other, both crying silently. Aella couldn't believe it; *how did she survive? Where has she been?* She realised she hadn't actually seen her mother after Omatus. Or any of her previous tribe, for that matter.

"I thought you died," she said, her voice shaking as the sobs quieted.

"I thought you did!" her mother said, shaking her head.

They stared at each other, huge grins spread across their faces. Helene's grin faded as she glanced around the throne room.

"So," her mother said, "you're queen of Theara."

Aella nodded. It felt strange, almost as though she was a little girl again, pretending to be a queen.

"How did that happen?"

She didn't know what to say. Thinking about it, her becoming queen made no sense. Sithares had guided her every step of the way, so much so that she barely remembered any of it.

"I escaped Omatus, but only barely. I don't remember much."

The rushing, swirling chaos of the Alpheus came back to her then. Her Fire had almost gone out so many times as the river tried to take her into the ocean. She wasn't conscious, but reliving it with Sithares' help had been as traumatic as if she had been awake when it happened.

"Aella..."

Aella shook her head, pulled out of the Alpheus by her mother's words. Even the memory of it pulled like a strong current.

"After Omatus, I walked to Sitharkos. Then Sithares gave me my memories back, and I travelled to Theara. I gained so many followers, you wouldn't believe. When I got here, I was named queen."

"Your memories... Aella, did you die?"

Tears spilled from her eyes as she looked at her mother. Helene's eyes echoed her own, tears gently slipping down her cheeks. Aella nodded, and another surge of sobs erupted from her as her mother pulled her into a tight embrace.

"It's awful, isn't it?" her mother said, her voice barely a whisper, "like being tortured by Sithares itself."

Aella pulled back, staring into Helene's eyes in horror.

"You died too?"

"Yes. I don't remember much of it either, nor my life before it happened. But when I heard your name, a lot of it came back, and I left straight for Theara."

My mother died, she thought, *and I had no idea*. She wondered if she would have felt it if not for their immortality. Maybe she had felt it, but her mind was so fractured that she didn't know what the feeling meant. For the first time, Aella was glad their tribe had been made immortal; if her mother died somewhere in the Omasi deserts without her even knowing, it would have destroyed her. But Aella lived through death twice at least, and she wouldn't have wished it on anyone; except maybe Kerberos. The fact that her mother went through the same thing tore at her heart. She would put Kerberos through that, and much worse. It was just a matter of time.

Mara

1783

Eliza stood as tall as Mara's chest now. At ten years old, she had grown not just physically, but emotionally. She was mature and intelligent, and her control of the magic they shared was uncanny. Not just control, either; Eliza was truly powerful. Mara was beginning to feel her presence in the same way she felt Riffolk's. Except in Eliza's case, Mara felt a far deeper well of energy. She leaned down to Eliza's ear, as they both faced a tree.

"Focus on the tree, and on the magic inside you," she said. "Picture a bolt of lightning hitting the trunk. Make it as strong as you like."

Her daughter stared at the tree, took a few breaths, and unleashed a bolt of lightning. It streaked towards the trunk, hitting within a second. A huge chunk of the wood was obliterated; splinters and chunks of bark flew outwards, raining onto the grass around them. Eliza squealed and threw her hands around Mara, squeezing tightly.

"Thank you Mumma," she said.

She turned to Mathys, who stood further back.

"Did you see that?"

Mara didn't hear Mathys' response. As Eliza twirled on the grass, laughing and celebrating, she stared at the tree trunk. It was utterly destroyed. A strange feeling crept into her stomach, uncomfortable and cold; a feeling that somehow seemed to say *this power will be your death.* The tree trunk, scorched and scarred, changed in front of her eyes to the ruined stump of Pera's destroyed head.

Mara couldn't breathe. Her throat was hot and dry, her lungs burning. Eliza moved to her side again, and sent more lightning into the trees around them. It took everything Mara had to appear calm and happy for her daughter. After the last bolt struck another tree, Mathys guided them home again. She couldn't shake the feeling that came over her, no matter how hard she tried. Sleep eluded her that night, and for a few nights after.

When Eliza started combat training with Mathys, it left Mara alone to her thoughts. She tried sitting out in the garden, she tried practising magic, but nothing helped. All she could think of was the feeling that swept through her as she'd watched Eliza destroy trees. *This power will be your death.* It sat in her mind, as solid as the feel of the ground beneath her feet. It felt not like fear, but like knowledge. As though it were a fact and not just some scary thought that appeared from nowhere.

Lightning that she created couldn't hurt her, she knew that. But if an attack came from Riffolk, or an accident happened with Eliza... There was no escaping the danger that magic held. She didn't want it; she never had. She didn't want Eliza to have that burden either.

Mara couldn't bare to watch Mathys training Eliza. She remembered the early days of her own training all too well; as exhilarating and empowering as it was, every day left her battered and sore. So she left them to it. Mathys trained her in the morning, then he trained Mara, and then Mara trained Eliza in the use of magic. Every day passed like that, and finally Mara was so exhausted each night that she could sleep again.

It didn't take long for Eliza's power and control to overtake Mara's own. After a while, her daughter began practising magic on her own on top of their daily training. Her combat skills were brilliant as well, from what Mathys said.

"She has a natural instinct for combat," he said, "she picks things up faster than anyone I know."

Two equally strong feelings tore at her insides; pride for her daughter, but also an intense terror that her little girl was growing up as a warrior.

"That's good," she managed to say.

"I know you're not entirely comfortable with Eliza learning to fight," he said, "even if you're the one who asked me to train her. But learning to fight is not the same thing as fighting."

Mara nodded. She knew that; after all, she hadn't been in a fight herself, and Mathys trained her too. But ever since the odd certainty came over her that the lightning would end up being fatal, her daughter's safety had become less certain.

"I know. But Mathys, there's something about this magic, something that scares me. It's not just the fighting. I'm scared that this magic will end up putting her in too much danger."

"We're well hidden, Mara. No one has found us in ten years, we'll be okay."

She sat in silence for a moment, trying to control the fear that threatened to overwhelm her. Mathys talked as if he understood, but the fear she felt was something he couldn't understand.

"Besides," he said, "if anyone does find us, I'll protect you."

Mathys

1783

Eliza frowned, focusing on the tree in front of her. Mathys stood back, watching from a safe distance. Mara stood beside her, whispering something Mathys couldn't hear. She was ten years old now, and just as Mathys had feared, she was growing up too fast. It felt like she'd been a child for months instead of years, and at ten she was far more mature than Mara had been at sixteen. *At least she learns quickly,* he thought, *if she hadn't gotten the hang of magic so quickly, she would have been a danger to everyone.*

Eliza took a few deep breaths, then brought her hands up, pointed at the tree. An arc of pale yellow lightning leapt from her fingers to the thick wood, and bark exploded outwards in a shower of splinters. She squealed, hugged Mara, then glanced over at Mathys with a bright grin.

"Did you see that?"

"Yes, little one," he said, trying and failing to contain his own grin, "I saw it."

She jumped a few times, and twirled around on her toes. Her joy filled Mathys' heart with warmth, and he forgot about the danger of the magic she wielded as he watched her celebrate. After another few bolts of lightning that left scorched craters in the trees, they returned to their home.

A few hours later, the sun had set, and Mathys sat with Mara in the living room. Eliza was asleep in her room, and Mara looked as tired as he felt.

"I want you to train her to fight."

Mathys paused a moment, thinking about what Mara was asking. He had no doubt Eliza would learn everything well. And Mathys himself was getting older; he wouldn't be able to protect them forever. As much as he loved Mara, and as talented as she'd become in combat, she couldn't fight a battle against a real enemy. Eliza would have to protect them both when Mathys was gone.

"Alright," he finally said, "when should I start?"

"Tomorrow."

The next day, he stood facing Eliza in the forest north of their home, in a loose combat stance. As fast as she'd grown up, Eliza was still tiny, and he had to remind himself to be gentle during her training. But she was determined; though they'd started two hours ago, she was still focused and alert. Her stance was almost perfect. Whenever he showed her a new technique, she only needed a few minor corrections before she could do it well.

"Attack," he said, and she did.

He blocked her, moving slowly but precisely, and countered. She swiped his counter away just as he'd taught her. Mathys moved his arm with hers, letting her block push his attack away gently. Her strength would come with training, growth, and exercise; for now he focused on technique.

"Good. Again."

She attacked again, though with a different move this time without him asking. Her instincts were good; she didn’t attack the same way twice. He couldn't remember if he told her that and she remembered, or if she was just trying all the moves he'd taught her. Either way, he couldn't have been more pleased with her progress after just two hours.

"Okay. Now block my attack."

Slowly, he swept his leg towards her neck. She brought up both her arms together, her back foot planted and her front knee bent. Her form was uncanny, and when his shin connected gently with her forearms, there was almost no give. He expected her to get bored quickly. With the repetition of combat training, even most adults grew sick of drilling the same moves again and again. But no matter how many times he told her to repeat a move, she did so with the same enthusiasm and focus. It filled him with a fierce pride that made his eyes sting and his heart glow.

"Good. Again."

Lashek

1793

Outside the city, he felt safe and welcome, like the forest itself was simply a part of him. Running and leaping through the canopy, the entire forest now open to him, he knew a joy unlike any he'd felt before. He'd stopped staying in the bed chambers in the city less than a year after Amalus blessed him. The forest itself was his home now, the Zuzuk his family. Before, even the rumoured sighting of a Zuzuk would spread through the city and make certain no Shenza approached the area. Now, Lashek spotted them everywhere as he ran, their intense gaze watching him pass without contest.

For the first time, he truly belonged in Shanaken. There was no doubt in his mind any more that he'd spoken to Amalus; the real Amalus. The idea that Amalus was also Zanela still confused him, but he didn't presume to understand the way Gods worked. A fair distance outside of the city, Lashek stopped. Amalus had been talking with him often, and it was time to talk again. He could have stopped and sat down anywhere, but there was a certain spot which had become his favourite. A small clearing to the south, where thick beams of sunlight fell over the undergrowth and a family of Zuzuk slept together in piles.

Lashek leapt silently into the clearing, knowing before he landed that he wouldn't startle the Zuzuk. They lay in the wide pools of sunlight, warming themselves lazily and ignoring him. He sat between two large groups of them, more or less in the centre of the clearing.

Lashek.

"Yes, Amalus."

Are you ready for your first mission?

Finally! he thought, *twenty years go by, and I finally get a mission!*

"I'm ready."

A small Ermoori family have taken residence in Tarsium, in a small town east of Azar. I believe they are to play a pivotal role in the war to come. They are being hunted, but the Ermoori don't yet know where they are.

"What must I do?"

Hire an assassin to kill the girl and her child. Offer a very high price, and pay some in advance.

"Woah, hold on," he said, the Zuzuk around him stirring, "You want me to hire an assassin? What kind of God are you?"

You must trust me, Lashek. No harm will come to them, but the attempted assassination will put something else in motion.

He'd devoted himself to the service of Amalus, so there was no backing out; but the plan made absolutely no sense to him.

"I see. Well then I'll see what I can do. But if the girl and her child die, that's on you."

They won't.

"Okay, if you say so. One more thing," he added, "this very high price you speak of; where is that going to come from? I'm assuming you're not exactly paid much for being a God?"

I leave that to you, Lashek. This must be done as quickly as possible.

And then Amalus was gone. Lashek sighed, and headed towards the clearing where he kept his things; it was time to go back to Tarsium.

Two weeks after Amalus gave him the mission, he sat in the Shining Sceptre, hearing word that an attempted assassination had failed. The assassin had been killed by an unknown attacker and buried in the words north of the target's home. Lashek shook his head, marvelling at Amalus, and at the fact that he was a servant of the Shenza God. It was an odd mission, but a relatively easy one. The only tricky part had been organising the payment and hiring the assassin in a way that couldn't be traced back to him.

Both targets were innocent, so if the Tarsi found out he'd called a hit on them he'd be in breach of their no violence rule. Usually they knew everything, but a bonus of having worked for them for so long was that he knew how to cover his tracks. Amalus had also given him a detailed description of the woman and her daughter, and Lashek had commissioned a drawing for the contract. Seeing them drawn, even if he had no idea how accurate it was, made the whole thing feel real, and he'd been terrified as he looked for an assassin; what if Amalus was wrong, and the assassin succeeded?

In the end, he'd found a man named Amphidas, an Omati who'd made a name for himself as a mercenary in Tarsium. He had a natural skill for combat, apparently, and followed money wherever it led him, but rarely took on assassination jobs. *Perfect,* he'd thought, *someone who will take on the contract but who isn't too talented.* Lashek wasn't paid for the job; in fact he'd lost a huge chunk of his savings paying the now dead assassin. But if Amalus was right, he'd be playing a huge part in the most important battle in Pandeia. And he had no reason to doubt Amalus now.

"Can you believe it?" Koros was saying, "once whoever ordered the hit is found, they're going to pay with their life."

Lashek grunted, taking a long sip from his fortified wine.

"I can't imagine why anyone would order a hit on innocents in Tarsium," Koros said, "you'd have to be stupid."

"Well, the world is full of stupid people, Koros."

"True, I suppose. Still, it takes an exceptional level of stupid to cross the Tarsi."

Lashek grunted again. Amalus was still on his mind; he was wondering what exactly had been set into motion as a result of his mission. *Are the targets like me?* He thought, *Heroes chosen by Amalus? Or even chosen by some other God?*

"Lashek!"

"Huh? What?"

Koros chuckled and shook his head.

"You've been away twenty years and then you come back and just drink. Don't get me wrong, I'm happy to see you after all this time, but... Are you shopping for a job, or just getting drunk for no reason?"

He'd never been in the Sceptre without picking up a job; it would look suspicious if he didn't at least look through the menu again.

"What do you think, Koros?"

"Alright, alright, one menu coming up."

Amalus hadn't told him what to do after the mission was complete. For all he knew, there was nothing stopping him from taking a new job. After pretending to read the contracts for a moment, he started actually paying attention, and one caught his eye for real. *Kaizeluun wanted,* it said, *with strong Shadow Magic skills. Powerful Shenza warrior is threatening and attacking innocents in Azar. Reward: 8,000 gold pieces, 12,000 if alive. Preferably to be taken alive, can be handed to the Tarsi authorities in Azar.*

He tore the page out and handed it to Koros without a word. The reward alone was insane, but beyond that, this was a job perfectly suited to him. There weren't many *Kaizeluun* in Tarsium strong enough to take on a powerful Shenza warrior.

"I thought you'd like that one," Koros said, "if only to inflate your pride."

"I can't help being the best *Kaizeluun* in Tarsium."

"We'll see. Don't underestimate this one, Lashek. If they've put that big a bounty on him, he's dangerous."

"I know, I know," Lashek said, "I thought after so many years you'd stop worrying over me."

"I'm still not convinced you're actually the best, that's all."

"Thanks for the vote of confidence, old friend. Don't suppose you'd like to put a wager on it?"

"A gold piece says this Shenza kicks your ass."

"Done. Looks like I'll be making twelve thousand and one gold pieces."

Lashek left the bar with a smile on his face. Koros was as good a friend as he'd ever had; he was certainly the only person in Tarsium that Lashek trusted. One more job, and he'd have more than enough money to go without jobs until Amalus was done with him. Whenever that might be.

Amphidas

1793

Times were tough. Omatus, as lucrative as it could be for a mercenary, had changed since Thorinos Argyris died. Amphidas hadn't kept a decent job since the young master Atillus commissioned his training. He'd had to stoop to assassination; sneaking around in the darkness and taking lives from unaware victims. It paid well, and there was an art to it, but Amphidas wanted combat. Honourable and honest combat. A few big jobs had come in, but nothing big enough that he could stop searching for the next contract. His current job, a woman and her daughter, was a new low. The only reason he'd even considered it was the pay.

The whole thing had been unusual from the start. He'd been commissioned via letter, a mysterious parcel which showed up at the inn he lived in with his name on it. Inside the parcel was a life-like drawing of a woman and a girl, the letter explaining the job, and a pile of shiny gold coins. He always took half the payment before a job, and the other half after the target was dead. But the parcel he received contained more gold than he'd ever been paid for a full job before, and the letter promised far more after the woman and her daughter were dead. He couldn't help himself; the pay was simply too good. His instincts, which said anything that seemed too good to be true usually was, were buried under a mountain of gold.

So he was on his way to a small village east of Azar, his mind focused on the gold he'd get after he was done. He was getting older now, but not too old that he couldn't handle the job. But the fortune he'd get after the targets were dead would mean he could finally rest easy for a while. Tarsium had the self-drawn carriages used in Ermoor, and Amphidas sat covered by his cloak, his hood obscuring his face as the cart glided through the countryside. Underneath his cloak, a dagger hung from his belt, and a second sat in the side of his boot. Several throwing knives rested in sheaths under his armpits and at his ribs and chest, attached to a harness he wore like a vest. It was overkill for two women, but assassins and mercenaries didn't live long if they weren't ready for anything.

The trip took a while, and Amphidas busied himself by mentally preparing for the kill. Every kill took planning and preparation, and he knew almost nothing about the woman's situation. He'd need to find out where she lived, case the place out, and make a plan around that. Mara Hayne. Amphidas memorised her face and her name. Hair could be changed, and clothing, so Amphidas didn't pay attention to those. Height and weight were harder to fake, but not impossible. Tarsi magic could do amazing things, but this girl had no Tarsi connections he knew of; she would most likely look exactly like her drawing.

Targets could easily use fake names, but nothing could stop the instant reaction to hearing one's real name. Amphidas had once lost a target in a crowded market street; and found him again by shouting his name. The target had turned, then realised his mistake a second after one of Amphidas' throwing knives slammed into his neck. A little messy, and not very discreet, but Amphidas still got paid. The letter described her as naive and vulnerable. Naivety was a good trait in a target. Naive targets were more likely to take poisoned food or drink. They could be convinced to follow him somewhere more private. Trust easy, die easy.

A few hours later, Amphidas arrived in the small village where Mara Hayne apparently lived. The village contained two small inns, one pub, a blacksmith, some farms, and a few dozen houses. *The good news is I'll find her quickly,* he thought as he stepped off the cart, *the bad news is she'll see me coming.* There was simply no way to hide in such a tiny place. He shouldn't need to hide from a woman, but a surprise attack was always the best option. Exploiting her naivety was his best and only chance. If he identified the house she lived in before he was seen, he could pick a night to wander by. Knock on her door and claim to be lost or disadvantaged.

After he arrived, Amphidas spent a while walking aimlessly through the village. Now that he was here, there was no rush. He'd find her sooner rather than later, kill her when the chance presented itself, then disappear. Just like the hundreds of jobs he'd done before.

One house stood out to him. Off the main road, small and inconspicuous. Comfortable. Safe. The perfect place to hide. He walked right by it, careful not to pay it any extra attention. He looked at each house in the village evenly, as though he was simply admiring each one, or appraising them like a potential buyer might.

When the sun went down he circled around the village and approached from the woods nearby, silent and invisible. He climbed a tree as close as possible to the house, peering in through the windows. Mara Hayne, though in her mid thirties, was beautiful. Her face was flawless, like the Austris Arans from old legend; the beings created by the God of the Air, beautiful and ethereal, with golden wings and sculpted bodies. Amphidas had seen statues of them in Sarnia. He'd been as awestruck looking at them as he was now looking at Mara.

Her daughter clearly had her mother's beauty too. She was around twenty years of age, and a heart-stopping purity painted her features. For a brief moment, Amphidas forgot about the fortune he'd been promised. It had been easy to begin the journey to his target after holding all that gold in his hands. But now, with the gold stowed safely in the inn room and an innocent girl's face laughing in front of him... He thought about going back. Taking the gold he'd already received and disappearing. It was more than he'd ever been given for a single job since the Argyris boy. He could find somewhere new, somewhere his mysterious client couldn't find him.

Damn it, old man, he thought, *you're getting soft in your old age.* No. Whoever paid him for this job would be able to find him anywhere. He'd already accepted the contract. The targets were right in front of him. Steeling himself, staring at the girl and her mother, he hardened his heart for the violence to come. They were indoors; it was after dark. Two vulnerable targets, the firelight inside blocking most of their vision outside the windows and the deep night blocking the rest. No weapons could be seen in the room. No other people.

Amphidas leapt lightly to the ground, running his fingers over the hilts of his throwing knives. He'd kill them from a distance; too close and he'd have to hit them or hold them down, and he couldn't bring himself to do that. He approached from the side of the house;

there was only one small window, dark and silent. When he reached the wall, he circled around to the side he'd looked in on. Their voices carried softly through the window, both giggling. Warmth from the fire inside drifted out to touch his skin, even through the cloak he wore. Hesitating again, he bowed his head. He didn't believe in Gods, so he focused on the gold. The way it felt in his hands, the way it glinted in the sun.

He slid a throwing knife from its sheath. The windows in Tarsium were large, with sliding glass panels. The one in front of him was half open, which gave him enough space to sweep in before they could react. *Get in, kill the mother, then the girl,* he thought. He could try throwing two knives at once, but he always lost accuracy that way, and he needed them to die as quickly as possible. *No need for them to suffer.*

Carefree laughter rang out from the two girls. *Breathe,* he told himself, *they'll be dead in a moment.* The throwing knife felt cold and heavy in his hands. He'd killed hundreds before today, maybe even thousands; but never women or children. Hefting the blade in his hand, finding the perfect balance, he placed his other hand on the corner of the windowsill. He pictured the attack in his mind, clear and focused, and settled onto the balls of his feet.

Something smacked his wrist, hard. He heard a thump on the ground, and turned to see a demon behind him. It grabbed his throat with inhuman strength, and suddenly there was no ground beneath his feet. He tried to ask the thing what it was, what it was doing, but no words came. It sprinted from the house, Amphidas' neck still caught in its grip. He saw trees pass them, faster than they should. The darkness seemed to press against him, cold and violent. When the forest grew wilder and trees filled his vision, the thing dumped Amphidas to the ground.

Habit kicked in, and he reached for a throwing knife. Searing pain ripped through his wrist. He realised what had happened a second before he pulled his arm back out from under the cloak. The demon had cut his hand off outside the window. He'd felt it and heard his hand hit the ground. His thoughts blurred, suddenly numb, and the demon pulled a sword from the many folds of its black cloak. It spoke in a voice that couldn't be human.

"Tell me who hired you."

Amphidas shook his head, staring at the stump where his hand used to be. *How did this happen?* Surely only a few seconds ago he'd been preparing for the biggest job of his career. Now he was in a forest with his hand cut off, confronting some kind of monster.

"I don't know," he said, "I just got a letter. Anonymous. Lot of gold."

He felt himself slipping, his thoughts blurring more each second. Blood pumped out of his wrist, and the white of his bone shone through the red.

"Tell me where you're staying."

"The second inn. Further down. First room, upstairs."

The trees had disappeared, replaced by pure inky blackness. It was just Amphidas and the demon. He knew he was about to die; the gold didn't matter any more. He shouldn't have taken the job.

"Tell me your name."

At the edges of his vision, everything drained from the world; even the blackness. A terrifying, cold white seeped in instead, spreading over the demon, over the cold forest floor, over his bleeding wrist. *I'm about to die.* Had the demon spoken again? He couldn't think. The face of his wife appeared, young, smiling and gentle. She was dead, killed by a rival mercenary years ago. But here she was, beautiful as ever.

He didn't feel the forest floor smash into him as he fell. He didn't feel the demon shove him into a deep grave as he took his last shallow breaths. All he felt in the moments before he died was the smile on his lips, and the love that filled his failing heart as his wife kept smiling.

Mathys

1793

Mathys grabbed the assassin's severed hand from beneath the window and walked back to the grave. He knew it would come, eventually; Riffolk was far too vengeful to let Mara live. But after twenty years, his hopes that they might remain hidden forever had started growing. The man was still alive, but barely, as Mathys began shovelling dirt over him. He'd already stripped the man of his weapons and valuables, and would go to the inn after he was buried to claim whatever he might have left in his room.

He spotted the man earlier that day, walking slowly through the village and glancing at each house. The assassin was so busy trying to remain unnoticed that he didn't notice Mathys watching him. He might have been talented in combat, but he wasn't a natural when it came to stealth and assassination. Mathys hadn't bothered following him after he moved on from their house. As soon as the sun drew low on the horizon, he'd donned his Spectre gear and disappeared into the woods to wait for the killer.

The Spectre's mask allowed him not only to see through the darkness as though it was broad daylight, but also to see over great distances clearly. From the woods, he'd watched the would be assassin climb a nearby tree, stare into the house for a while, then make his way over. It was too easy. The man had no situational awareness, he was far too focused on his targets; not that Mathys was complaining. He was beginning to get too old, and wasn't training as often as he should. Mara and Eliza were both still improving a lot, and training them kept him fit, but he still felt his years.

Breathing heavy as he patted down the grave, he took a moment to calm his heart again. He returned the shovel to the basement as quietly as he could, then left for the inn. The village where they lived was small, quiet and sleepy. Things he'd taken for granted in Ermoor, things like door locks and paranoia, had no place in such a tiny village. Sneaking into the assassin's room was easier than getting into his own basement without Mara hearing. He'd travelled light; as most assassins did. But under a pile of clothes in the closet, Mathys found a bag of gold coins. A big bag. He must have planned on going straight from this job to a new city. Mathys made sure there were no important documents or items that might have helped him identify the assassin; nothing. Ignoring everything else, he grabbed the bag of gold and left the inn.

Later that night, he sat by the living room fire with a glass of mulled wine. Mara and Eliza were fast asleep. He wondered if it was worth moving; how many more assassins Riffolk would send their way. Moving often was the best way to keep ahead of assassins, but it also meant Mara and Eliza wouldn't have a stable home. If they stayed, he could protect them, but not forever. And though Eliza was twenty and becoming deadlier every day, he didn't feel comfortable leaving their safety in her hands just yet. They had no one to turn to, no one who could help protect them. They had a lot of gold, but hiring someone just opened them up to the wrong kind of attention.

Tarsium was famous for its zero tolerance for violence, so in theory they should have been safe. But the Tarsi weren't everywhere, and being in a tiny village meant being outside of their protection. Besides, Mathys had already killed the assassin, so whatever they might have done to punish him was moot, even if they'd been in one of the three districts. After he finished the mulled wine, he crept upstairs to his bedroom. Mara and Eliza slept in the bedroom furthest from the stairs, at the back of the house, but he was still always careful to avoid waking them. He fell asleep still worried, with no idea what the best course of action was.

Mathys brought the axe down, vicious but precise, and the thick block of wood flew into two parts either side of the tree stump. He paused, wiping the sweat from his brow, and saw a stranger approaching from the main road. Tall and draped in a mottled grey cloak with a hood that covered their face, the stranger strolled onto the grass in front of Mathys' modest home. Hefting the axe in his hand, he walked out to meet them.

"Greetings, stranger," he said, not bothering to feign friendliness, "what brings you here?"

"I see the Spectre in you," the woman said, "in the way you stand, and in the way you fight."

His blood ran cold. *How could she possibly know that?* he thought. She couldn't be bluffing; the Spectre was an Ermoori legend, nothing to do with Tarsium. He wasn't well known in this place even as Mathys Corby, let alone as the Spectre of Ermoor. Only Arthor Symond knew his secret identity, and Mara. It was likely that Arthor had told Riffolk after Mathys left Ermoor, but if this strange woman was working for Riffolk she would have simply attacked him.

"I don't know what you're talking about. What Spectre?"

"Don't bother trying to fool me, Ermoori," the stranger said, "I can see who you are inside as clearly as I see your face. What I need to know is what happened to the Spectre. Why have you abandoned your post?"

Lashek

1793

The Shining Sceptre was in Carmerth, the southernmost district of Tarsium. Travelling from Carmerth to Azar took about two weeks, and Lashek spent the entire time alone. No Amalus speaking in his head, no travel companions. He loved the Tarsi countryside, but he found himself wishing for either Koros or Amalus' company. Inns and taverns were scattered along the road between the two districts, and Lashek stayed overnight when he needed the rest. Ever since he'd been blessed by Amalus, he found he could go far longer without sleep when he needed to; he only stopped for the night twice on the journey.

After he arrived in Azar, he went straight to another tavern where he'd built up a few contacts. People in Azar working for the Tarsi might have heard something about his target. The Azar Tavern sat in a quieter part of the district, in a back alley. Its clientele was the same as the Shining Sceptre; anyone who worked for the Tarsi hunting down violent criminals spent their nights in the tavern. Lashek made his way to the bar; he knew the bartender, Lokar, though not quite as well as Koros.

"Lashek," he said, "it's been quite a while. What brings you to Azar?"

"Work," Lashek said, "what else?"

"Target in the city? That'll be interesting. Careful, you don't want to go starting a magical fight in the middle of the most populated city in Pandeia."

"I know. I've got it under control, Lokar. I just wanted to know if you'd heard anything about a violent Shenza somewhere in Azar."

Lokar pulled back slightly, shoulders dropping. He nodded his head slowly, looking at the wall. Lashek waited; Lokar's reactions sometimes didn't mean anything, it could be hard to tell what he was thinking.

"Yes, I've heard some things. He strikes at night. He doesn't steal anything, and so far hasn't killed. He seems to be focused on a few small areas, I'll show you on a city map."

Lashek pulled his own map from his bag; he didn't spend much time in Azar and had a map drawn before he left Carmerth. He watched Lokar draw three small circles in the city, fairly close together. He had a target, and a location. Now he just had to wait until sundown.

His target was *Kaizeluun*. Not well trained, but powerful. It was common for newly made *Kaizeluun* to branch out from Shanaken, usually without the blessing of the *Duulshen*; ego plagued most young warriors in Lashek's experience. For a while, he watched the Shenza. As Lokar had said, there was no murder and no theft; a motive had yet to present itself. Very occasionally, Shenza were born naturally aggressive. Most of the time, those rare few were identified before anything terrible happened, but sometimes, as with the traitor Dakesh, they snuck through the *Duulshen's* notice.

Lashek's target seemed to be one of those. He used violence simply for its own sake. As he watched, Lashek grew more and more sickened by the Shenza before him. A man who had taken the training and the generosity of the *Duulshen*, and completely disregarded the tenets and the oath he'd sworn to them. *Strength without aggression.* Lashek had lived outside of Shanaken for over ten years before Amalus spoke to him, but he always lived by the tenets. He let go of the anger building towards his target, and settled into the alert calm that came with the *Zuunshai*; he couldn't perform the dance right now, but he could control his mind enough to reach the same mental state.

Unsheathing his *Kaizuun*, Lashek leapt off the rooftop and landed silently on the smooth pavement. The Shenza was on the other side of the street, harassing and threatening a small group of Omati tourists.

"Fighting tourists, Shenza?" Lashek yelled over the rabble of the street, "you must be weak if you won't fight real warriors."

People had been walking through the street as normal, trying to ignore the dangerous Shenza. As soon as they heard Lashek's shouted challenge, and saw the Shenza's furious face turn up to him, they scattered. The street emptied in moments.

"You dare call me weak, *Kaizeluun*?" the man shouted back.

He said *Kaizeluun* with undisguised distaste, as though there could be nothing worse in Pandeia.

"I call you what you are; *Ladzuud*."

He screamed and launched himself at Lashek. *Ladzuud* was usually an insult for outsiders, but when aimed at a Shenza warrior, became one of the worst insults; it meant weak outsider. His target was dismissive enough of his home country to disregard the title of *Kaizeluun*, but his pride still blinded him.

The Shenza swept his blade in a tight horizontal arc, and a shadow leapt from it, razor sharp and faster than a person could move. *Kaizeluun* were no mere people, however, and Lashek brought his own blade up. Shadow attacks only lasted seconds, and it disappeared almost as soon as Lashek blocked it. By the time the magical blade was gone, his target appeared right in front of him, swinging his own *Kaizuun* savagely at Lashek's neck and sides. He was emotional; reckless. He wouldn't win against a real *Kaizeluun* in such a state.

Lashek blocked easily, breathing through the battle as the *Zuunshai* taught. His opponent's breaths were ragged, filled with emotion. Although he was powerful, he'd obviously neglected his training in favour of picking on the weak and helpless.

"I've been told the preference is to take you alive," Lashek said through the fighting, "but if you make me kill you I won't hesitate."

The man's reply was a wordless scream, and another wave of vicious attacks.

"Your choice, *Ladzuud*."

There. His target slipped, ego smothering clarity, and Lashek ducked underneath a too wide swing at his neck and countered by slicing the back of the man's hand. His blade fell to the ground. The Shenza continued attacking, beyond reason now, raining blows on Lashek with his left fist and feet. Lashek sheathed his own blade, blocking and dodging as he did. The fight was almost over; he could feel it. His target was already exhausted, wounded, and far too emotional to employ tactics.

He swiped the man's left fist away from his face and brought his heel down onto his ankle, forcing it to twist into the ground. The man stumbled, and Lashek grabbed his head, pulling it down as he threw his knee up. They connected with an audible crack, and his target slumped to the ground. Several of the shop owners within view applauded, and the people on the street followed suit. Lashek couldn't remember receiving applause for his work before; he waved, mumbled a quick thanks, hauled the Shenza over his shoulders and left.

Tarsi Peacekeepers had a base of operations in each district. Their base in Azar was the largest. Lashek had dealt with the Carmerth Peacekeepers many times; every completed contract had to be reported to them directly, with some form of proof. The authorities provided a card, which was then traded at one of the taverns for the final payment. A slightly complicated system, but it worked for the Tarsi. Lashek was willing to play by their rules if it meant being paid, and being in the Tarsi's good books.

He brought the Shenza into the base at Azar, getting stares in the street all the way there and up the marble steps into the building itself. The contracts office was always near the front of the building, and he saw the sign above the door to his left. The Tarsi officer in charge of contracts was silent and serious; his face didn't move when Lashek entered the room.

"I'm here for the contract on this one," Lashek said as he nodded to the unconscious man over his shoulders, "alive, though a little wounded. That's still twelve thousand, right?"

A careless grunt was his only answer, and the Tarsi behind the desk brought out a card, stamped it, and held it out to Lashek.

"Where do I put him?"

The Tarsi sighed.

"In the cell, through there," he said.

Behind Lashek, a doorway led out from the room. He walked through, careful to fit the Shenza through without smacking him into the door frame. Sure enough, in the long narrow room was a cell with several benches. A prisoner already lay on one of them, either sleeping or dead. Lashek was about to try to open the door when the Tarsi shouted after him.

"Hold on, hold on."

He entered the room carrying a giant ring of keys, filling the narrow space with clinking and rustling. Unlocking the cell door, he held it open for Lashek. Dumping the Shenza on the closest bench, Lashek left the cell as quickly as he could; the Tarsi's attitude was a little off, and he wouldn't have been surprised if the man had locked him in there with his target.

"Card's on the table," the Tarsi said, "don't touch anything else."

"Sure thing. Thanks for your hospitality," Lashek said as he grabbed the card and left.

Halfway through the building's lobby, he stopped. His stomach twisted, turning cold and heavy. Right in front of him, talking to an official-looking Tarsi, was the Ermoori woman and her daughter. They looked exactly like the drawing he'd commissioned. With them was an older Ermoori man. Though his hair was greying and his eyes looked tired, he radiated strength and authority. Lashek saw years of intense combat training in his posture and movements. He knew at a glance this was the man who'd killed the assassin.

Lashek was frozen in place, unable to move, when the older man saw him and narrowed his eyes. He couldn't have known Lashek by sight. *I'm acting too suspicious not to be noticed,* he thought, *especially by the likes of this man.* Turning away from the small family, he glanced around, looking for anything to do other than standing around like an idiot.

"How do you know us?"

The man's voice was quiet, casual and even friendly. Lashek had expected a deep, grating voice full of menace. He faced the Ermoori, his mind utterly blank.

"I-well, you... just look very familiar, I suppose," he said.

Well done, Lashek, he thought to himself, *very casual.*

"Don't lie to me, Shenza. I've had a rough few weeks."

His voice was still pleasant. Although he'd killed many Ermoori soldiers on the north shore before he'd left Shanaken, this man made him uneasy. It was the first time he'd ever felt genuinely intimidated by an Ermoori; and the man wasn't even armed or armoured.

"It's a long story, Ermoori," he said, "you wouldn't believe me if I told you."

"Try me."

The Tarsi who'd been speaking with the family appeared beside the older Ermoori man.

"I believe this is a conversation best held in private," she said, her voice barely above a whisper, "follow me, both of you."

Mathys

1793

They sat in the living room of Mathys' home, Mara hiding with Eliza in her bedroom. The stranger lowered her hood after she sat across from him, revealing the face of a Tarsi woman. Before she sat down, she'd been taller than Mathys; afterwards she couldn't have been taller than four feet.

"My name is Zeera Sol," she said, "I represent an organisation dedicated to the protection of all of Pandeia. The Circle of Shadows."

She stopped there, waiting for him to react; as though the name should have meant a great deal.

"I see. What does that have to do with the Spectre?"

"Everything."

"I don't understand. If this Circle of Shadows is so important to the Spectre, why haven't I heard of it?"

She blinked, her gigantic eyes fixed on his. For a moment, nothing happened, except the lazy crackling of the fire. He waited as patiently as he could, her large eyes unsettling as they stared.

"You've never heard of the Circle of Shadows."

"That's what I said."

"Tell me, Mathys, what exactly do you know about the Spectre of Ermoor?"

"The Spectre is a legend, a spirit who protects the people of Ermoor against crime and violence."

Zeera slumped back in the chair, shaking her head faintly.

"And that's all you think the Spectre is meant to be?"

"What do you mean, *that's all*? An entire city protected, what more do you expect of one man?"

"Tell me how you came to meet Krana Toor."

The name brought a cold flush of goose pimples to his skin; Mathys hadn't heard it in decades. Hadn't thought about him in decades.

"I was young," he began, "rising in the Ermoori military, and letting my ego take over. There were rumours of a ghost fighting against the Twelve Crowns, and I wanted to take it down."

She said nothing, simply nodding and staring.

"I tracked the Spectre as well as I could. I saw it a few times, but came up with nothing. I even put a team together of the few men I trusted-even back then, I knew how corrupt Ermoor was-and we hunted day and night. We didn't find it. Then one night it came to me."

The memory flooded his mind's eye as he spoke to Zeera, as vivid as the night it happened.

Thick fog blanketed the city outside his window, and Mathys rubbed his hands together in front of his fire. Despite the late hour, he'd only just gotten home; his house was almost as cold as the streets outside. But the fire was growing, and it wouldn't be long before its warmth spread through the room. They'd been searching for the Spectre for months, and were still no closer. It felt like they were simply chasing shadows.

He threw another log on the fire, watching it slowly catch as the flames washed over the dried wood. The things it could do made no sense. No human could move the way the Spectre did. Mathys knew that magic couldn't exist except for the miracles of God, and yet he'd seen the Spectre leap from the ground to the tops of buildings as easily as a man stepped into a carriage. It was unharmed by Ermoori guns, faster and stronger than any man Mathys had ever seen, and it could disappear into shadows without a trace.

One of his men had seen its face. He said it was a demon made of living metal, snarling and inhuman. One of the other men claimed it was one of the Twelve Crowns gone rogue, and said the Twelve were ancient demons cast out by God, who chose to rule over men instead. Another swore it was one of the tree people from Shanaken, a vicious savage that had somehow smuggled itself into the city. Of course, the Spectre of Ermoor had been an Ermoori legend long before it started appearing a couple of months ago. Whatever it was, it certainly wasn't from Shanaken.

Mathys stood to fix himself a drink, and almost fell back into the fire. In the corner of the room, standing in the doorway between Mathys and the kitchen, stood the Spectre of Ermoor. Mathys drew his gun, and the Spectre ignored it.

"Mathys Corby," it said in a grating, metallic voice, "we need to talk."

Mathys shook his head, returning his attention to Zeera. Even though he now knew the Spectre was simply a costume, a symbol, the memory still made Mathys shiver. The effect of the mask was jarring.

"He approached you. Revealed himself."

Again, she stated something instead of asking.

"He did. He told me what the Spectre was, and offered to train me."

"But he didn't tell you any more than you've told me."

"No."

Zeera sighed, shaking her head.

"What is the Spectre?" he asked, sick of waiting for answers.

She sighed again before speaking.

"Simply put, the Spectre is an agent of the Circle of Shadows. His mission is to keep a lookout for signs of magic. Signs that the Gods are returning, reawakening. If those signs appear, the Spectre is to report back to the Circle immediately."

"So the Spectre is just a lookout? A scout?"

"It's a little more complicated than that, but yes, that is the mission."

"Well," he said, "then I have something to report."

Mara

1793

Mara was sitting in the living room with Eliza when the stranger appeared. A cloaked figure, tall and menacing, approached Mathys. They spoke for a short time, but Mara had seen enough by then.

"Eliza, come to the bedroom with me."

"What's happening?"

"No questions, let's go!"

They swept up the stairs together, and when they were safely in the bedroom, Mara closed the door and sat on the bed next to Eliza.

"What's happening?" Eliza asked again.

"A stranger is talking with Mathys right now," she said, "someone who looks dangerous."

In the living room below, they heard the front door open and close, and two voices floated gently up the stairs. One was female. The other was Mathys, and his voice, though tense, brought her endless comfort. Mara glanced at Eliza. Her daughter's eyes burned with intense concentration; but no fear.

"I don't think we're in danger," Eliza said.

She was twenty years old now, and emanated a sense of calm confidence that echoed Mathys'. Mara had no idea how she did it; but she was grateful, and pride bloomed in her heart like a sudden sunrise. Her own fear never left, however. Mara was constantly scared, even before the stranger showed up. Her days were spent terrified of being found by Riffolk, or terrified that Eliza might cause too much damage with her magic. Her nights were filled with nightmares, vivid horrors that plagued her like a sickness.

Mara knew that Mathys could protect them. She knew that Eliza could too, if it came to that. But nothing stopped the fear, and her heart thudded so loud in her chest that she couldn't make out the conversation in the living room below. Eliza sat with her, as steady and calm as Mathys. Mara put an arm around her, resting her head on Eliza's shoulder.

Eventually, footsteps thumped up the stairs, and Mara's breathing turned instantly into ragged hitches. Eliza pulled her close, whispering comforts in her ear as the footsteps grew close. Pale yellow crackled in her daughters free hand as the door handle turned. Mathys peeked his head in, nodding at Eliza when he saw her magic at the ready.

"Mara, I'd like you to come and say hello to someone."

Zeera

1793

It is time.

Zeera jumped at the voice; Asheilos very rarely spoke to her any more. Fifteen years had passed since she stopped the Ermoori spies from stealing the book of Asheilos. Recovering from the battle took a while, but after that Zeera went straight back to travelling and searching for Heroes. Business as usual; she didn't find any. After her initial shock, the actual words finally took meaning.

"A Hero?" she asked.

Yes. Two are in Tarsium.

Two of them? she thought. After almost fifty years of searching for Heroes, two of them showed up in her own country, without her knowing. Something about it filled her with fury, but at the same time she was elated just to know they were finally out there.

You will need to approach one. The other will come to you.

"Where do I go?"

Saford. I will guide you when you are close.

After such a long time finding nothing, Zeera found herself almost overwhelmed. Doubt and fear crept into her mind, and all she could think was that she might have been the wrong choice as Hero. *What if I find them and they don't believe me?* She thought, *or they think I'm a threat and kill me instead of joining the Circle?* She knew it was illogical, but suddenly nothing else made sense.

You will be okay. The Heroes will join together.

Trying to calm herself, Zeera prepared for the trip to Saford. It wouldn't take long; she was already in Azar, between trips. Before she left, she had to speak with Zalla. The Speaker had to know everything Zeera did. Once the Heroes were all together, the Speaker would have to know everything all of them did. Even though Zeera was Asheilos' chosen Hero, Zalla was in charge. She walked into the Speaker's chamber in the above ground Circle headquarters. Zalla was speaking with a messenger, but dismissed them when she saw Zeera.

"Ah, Zeera," she said, "I was expecting you. Do you have anything to report from the Western cities?"

Zeera spent the last few years going from city to city along the western coast of Omas. It was dry, hot, and worst of all, uneventful.

"Nothing out of the ordinary," she said, "but I have news from Asheilos."

Zalla's eyes widened for just a second before she resumed her usual blank expression.

"Interesting. A possible Hero?"

"Two. Right here in Tarsium."

This time, real shock spread over Zalla's features. She stared for a moment, as speechless as Zeera had been moments ago.

"Asheilos told you this? My scouts didn't see anything... Well then, two Heroes. It's finally happening."

She sent Zeera on her way as quickly as possible, and Zeera was more than happy to go. Even with the good news, things between Zalla and Zeera were still a little cold. Zalla took their misunderstanding years ago personally, and hadn't let her guard down since. Zeera followed orders perfectly since then, and she would have thought saving the book of Asheilos would close the gap between them; but Zalla remained distant. *Maybe once the Heroes are gathered, she'll drop it,* Zeera thought.

The journey to Saford was peaceful. Zeera's favourite moments lately were the trips between cities and countries; she didn't have to focus on finding Heroes, or magic, or anything else. She could just relax, let her mind wander. She could just be herself, without expectations or orders. Trees slid past the cart's window as she watched, vibrant blurs of green breaking up the solid pale blue of the sky. In the cart, in this moment, she didn't have to be the Hero of Tarsium, searching for the other Heroes on a mission to save the world. She didn't have to be a servant of the Circle, following orders even when she didn't agree with them. She was just Zeera. When Saford appeared on the horizon, Asheilos spoke to her again. This time she was ready, and didn't jump.

The house is off the main road, on the north side of the village facing the forest.

She left the driver in the cart to wait for her; it was a Circle cart, and the driver would wait as long as she needed. Warm, still afternoon air caressed her skin as she approached the house. Smells of freshly blooming flowers surrounded the village, and Zeera found herself thinking of the gorgeous paintings hanging in the museums of Sarnia. She so rarely visited the Tarsi countryside, and its beauty always moved her.

An Ermoori man, with mostly grey hair and an immense tiredness behind his eyes, chopped wood in the yard. Despite his age, Zeera saw the strength and training of a disciplined military man in his movement. There was something odd about him, too; he had no magic, of that Zeera was certain. But there was somehow an imprint of magic on him, like an echo or a shadow. Barely there, but just strong enough to feel. Even more interesting was that she recognised the magic she felt; It felt like Krana Toor. *So,* she thought, *this is the last Spectre of Ermoor*.

Mathys

1793

Mara sat in front of Zeera, terrified and silent. Zeera watched her even more intently than she'd stared at Mathys. She must have known she was frightening the poor girl, but she stared regardless. When she spoke, her tone was gentle and encouraging. Mathys was grateful for that much.

"Hello, child," she said, "my name is Zeera Sol. I am Tarsi, and I represent an organisation called the Circle of Shadows."

Mara glanced at Mathys, questioning without words, and Mathys gave a smile and a nod. Her trust in him was as heart-warming as it was scary; he hadn't pictured himself with children before. Then it was thrust upon him, along with a newborn baby. At least Eliza was grown up now, and old enough to be a woman in her own right. But even now, whenever Mara gave him that fearful, questioning look, it made him feel as though he could take on the entire Shenza army alone to protect her.

"Hello Zeera Sol," Mara said, her voice barely a whisper, "my name is Mara Watson."

Zeera's smile warmed, and Mathys found himself trusting the Tarsi woman; for now at least.

"Mathys told me you've been given magic powers."

Another quick glance at Mathys, another nod from him to say *it's okay.*

"Yes, I can make lightning. And control it, sometimes."

Zeera nodded again, her warm smile still centred on Mara.

"That's called Power Magic, child. It's very strong magic, and if you're the person I think you are, you'll be very powerful indeed."

Mara's cheeks drained of colour and she huddled as deep into her chair as possible, wide-eyed and thin-lipped. Zeera turned to Mathys, then back to Mara, and then addressed them both.

"I'll stop dancing around the purpose of my visit. The Circle is interested in both of you. Mathys, the Spectre is an integral agent in our mission. Mara, your role will be more important than either of you realise. You are a Hero, chosen by Taranos."

Mara shook her head, pure terror shining in her eyes. She'd been through so much, and finally escaped the horror that was Riffolk. A sharp, cold pain lanced Mathys' chest as he looked at Mara. She deserved a peaceful life, with Mathys and Eliza. Mathys stopped believing in the God of Ermoor after they left; it took him far too long to see the corruption and decay seething underneath Ermoor's surface. It was beyond even the crime that plagued the poor districts; the Twelve Crowns were evil. He suspected the God worshipped by Ermoor was merely fabricated by the Twelve.

Now that Mathys and Mara had discovered more about Taranos through her ability to commune with it, Mathys and Mara both understood far more about the Gods than he'd ever learned in Ermoor. But knowing about them didn't quiet his anger at the Gods in the moment Zeera announced Mara's title of Hero. If anything, he was more angry; for knowing they'd stepped away from a false God's tyranny and into the games of a real God who cared just as little for them.

"Why was Mara chosen?" he asked.

"We cannot begin to question the decisions of the Gods, Mathys."

"Can I take her place?"

"A new Hero can only be named if the last one dies."

"Why should we join your Circle?" Mathys asked, "it seems to me that all you offer is danger and death."

Mara shrank bank. He regretted saying it in front of her, but his anger overrode his discretion.

"We offer quite the opposite, Mathys," Zeera said, "nowhere in Pandeia is safer than the Circle. We can train the Heroes to use their magic. Our guards patrol invisibly every hour of every day."

He thought about the assassin, and how they would always be on the run from Riffolk. They'd remained in hiding for so long, far longer than he thought they could. But they were still found, and now that they had been, it would only encourage Riffolk to step up his efforts. He didn't know much about the Tarsi, but then again no one really did other than the Tarsi themselves. He trusted his instincts, and Zeera seemed genuine. Mathys nodded, sighing as he glanced at Mara.

"Alright. Consider us a part of the Circle of Shadows."

Zeera nodded back, her eyes also on Mara.

"Perfect," she said, "now, if you don't mind... would you call your daughter in here please?"

Eliza sat between Mathys and Mara, looking even more nervous than her mother. Zeera studied her in silence, though not without a gentle kindness in her eyes. Mathys had no idea how the Tarsi woman knew Mara had a daughter, let alone how she knew Eliza was hiding in the bedroom. But if nothing else, the Tarsi were infamous for their vast knowledge and secrets; as long as no one but the Tarsi knew, Mathys could live with it. Especially if they were on the same side.

"You can use magic too," Zeera said, "can't you, child?"

Eliza looked just like her mother in that moment; pale, wide-eyed, and fragile. But after a pause, and a glance at Mathys, Eliza sat up straighter.

"Yes I can," she said, her voice only wavering slightly, "mother is teaching me."

Zeera nodded with a satisfied smile.

"That's good. We'll need as many people wielding magic as possible."

She explained the Circle once again, and Eliza's eyes lit up at the idea. By the time Zeera had finished talking, Eliza was looking between Mathys, Mara and Zeera with a huge grin.

"We're joining the Circle, aren't we Mathys?"

"Yes, we are. But you-"

He flinched at her sudden squeal, and motioned for her to calm down.

"But you need to do as I say, and stay close to your mother and I the entire time, do you understand?"

"Yes, yes, of course!"

Lashek

1793

I*s this what Amalus meant by setting things in motion?* Lashek thought as he followed the group through the building. The Ermoori man, the woman, and her daughter walked in front of him, and the Tarsi who'd been speaking to them led in front. She walked down several corridors where none of the doors were labelled and no signs adorned the walls above them. Every door looked the same. Despite working for Tarsium for so long, Lashek had never been so far inside any of these buildings.

As far as he could tell, meeting the people he'd hired someone to kill had been complete coincidence. But then again, Amalus had known the assassin wouldn't succeed. Lashek didn't remember hearing about Amalus seeing the future, but he supposed no one really knew exactly what Gods were capable of other than Gods themselves.

Finally, they were ushered into a room. The Tarsi woman closed the door behind them and locked it. Lashek's instincts forced a wave of cold down his spine as the lock clicked home. The room itself was utterly bare, other than a few benches along the walls. Its resemblance to the cell he'd just left his target in was striking, and only made the cold flush down his spine worse.

"What are we doing in here?" he asked the Tarsi woman.

She looked at each of them in turn, her giant eyes taking in everything. Curiously, she stared at the girl longer than anyone else.

"You're all here because you're going to be part of something unimaginably big. Mathys, Mara, I've already spoken with you."

She turned to him.

"Lashek, you have been working for Tarsium for quite a while. Your work has been invaluable, but the time has come to play a much bigger role in Pandeia's fate. You are to join the Circle of Shadows."

Mathys and Mara barely reacted, but Lashek's mind whirled as he blinked at the Tarsi woman. He hadn't heard of the Circle of Shadows; was this what Amalus wanted of him? No one had given him any useful information so far. Without context, his mind raced trying to put things together.

"Are you going to tell me what that actually means?"

"It's an ancient order dedicated to the protection of Pandeia and all its people," Mathys said, "made up of the best warriors and mages of each country; Heroes chosen by the Gods themselves."

Chosen by the Gods. His heart leapt into his throat. Twenty years ago, when he'd first been blessed, Amalus had said *you will wake tomorrow as Shanaken's Hero.* He shook his head, words escaping his mind like water slipping through cupped fingers.

"You were chosen, weren't you?" the Tarsi woman said, "by Amalus?"

"Yes, I... How did you know? How *could* you know?"

But she only smiled, nodding slightly to herself as though she'd won a wager.

"Mara was chosen too, weren't you?"

Mara, the woman who might have died because of his gold, nodded and blushed.

"Wait... her? Not Mathys?"

The name felt weird in his mouth; Ermoori was an ugly language.

"We cannot begin to understand how the Gods work, Lashek. She was chosen. Our role is not to doubt, but to fulfil the work set out for us by the Gods."

"And you're chosen for Tarsium's God? Does Tarsium even have a God?"

"Yes."

Her eyes twinkled with humour; considering their size, it was impossible to miss.

"Asheilos is the God of Water. I was chosen almost fifty years ago, but I've been part of the Circle for a very long time."

"So what does the Circle actually do?" Lashek asked.

The humour in the Tarsi woman's eyes slowly drained, replaced by a look as hard and cold as the ocean.

"We fight the war of the Gods in the mortal realm, to stop the destruction of all of Pandeia."

Amalus hadn't said it so bluntly. It suddenly felt too big, too momentous, to even think about.

"Have you found the chosen for Omas?" Mathys asked quietly.

"Yes," she said, "but he will be a challenge."

"And the fight over Pandeia's fate won't be a challenge?" Lashek said.

The Tarsi woman ignored him, keeping her eyes on Mathys as she spoke.

"The war of the Gods is fought between Sithares, God of Fire, and the other four Gods."

Amalus, he thought, *Asheilos, Sithares, the Ermoori God... I remember hearing that the Thearans worship Sithares along with the people of Omas...*

"What's the fifth God? And the people that worship it?" he said.

"One thing at a time, *Kaizeluun*," she said, "Sithares, as the God of Fire, is naturally destructive. Its purpose is to burn and spread until everything is destroyed."

Lashek knew that much; every Shenza was taught about the fire worshippers and the dangers they posed to Pandeia.

"For aeons, the Gods have been resisting Sithares' attempts to destroy Pandeia. But they can't interact with the physical world unless they are summoned or are able to take a physical form. So they must select heroes to fight on their behalf."

"But if we can get to Sithares' chosen," Mathys said, "we could convince him to fight for our side, instead of trying to destroy Pandeia?"

"That's the challenge," the Tarsi woman said, "Sithares also corrupts the minds of its followers. It preys on negative emotion. If we are to change this hero's mind, it may make the difference, but it will not be easy. The chosen Hero of Sithares is not only one of the most powerful mages in Pandeia, he is the most devoted worshipper of Sithares."

Lashek gasped. Something surfaced from the bottom of his mind, a connection he wouldn't have made.

"What exactly do you mean when you say Sithares corrupts minds?"

"Sithares turns doubt, fear and jealousy into rage. Anger and aggression become stronger. Sithares also feeds lies and deceptions to its followers."

When he'd found out that Elana was killed, he remembered thinking that it made no sense for Dakesh to be the murderer. By all accounts he'd been in love with Elana; everyone in Shanaken knew it.

Lashek remembered hearing that Dakesh had become a fire worshipper too. *A follower of Sithares.* What if he'd simply been corrupted and tricked into murdering the woman he loved?

He realised everyone in the room was staring at him.

"I think I've heard of someone who was corrupted," he said, "someone from Shanaken."

"What happened to him?" Mathys asked.

"He was... executed. For being a traitor."

The room went quiet for a moment. Dakesh being possibly innocent hadn't occurred to him, but now his death seemed so pointless, so much more horrible, than it had before. He wondered if any Shenza would find out, and whether they would change their opinion of Dakesh. He doubted it.

"Well, how can we change this man's mind?" Lashek said, trying to move past Dakesh's fate.

"We have a Tarsi spy in Omatus now, if he does his job correctly, Sithares' Hero will come to us."

"I couldn't help but notice that didn't answer my question," Lashek said.

"Once he's here, we can all talk with him together. If we can get him on our side, the war can be stopped before it begins. If not, well... he's powerful, but all of us together should be able to defeat him."

"And killing him ends the war? Wouldn't Sithares simply choose another hero?" Mathys asked.

"Choosing a hero is not merely naming someone Hero," the Tarsi said, "the Hero is blessed with powers beyond any normal mage. That takes its toll; Gods have limits, just like any other beings."

"So if we kill this one, the next one will be weaker?" Lashek asked.

"Theoretically, yes. But we would have to find them all over again."

"So how do we actually win this war?" Mathys asked.

"There is a physical manifestation of every God," she said, "in the form of a book bound in magic. We need to find the book of Sithares, and bind it in magic. Historically, that has kept the God of Fire trapped for thousands of years at a time. But if we really want to end the war for good, we have to destroy the book. If that's even possible."

Mathys

1793

Zeera had her own private cart, and they travelled back to Azar with her. It was the biggest cart Mathys had ever seen; it fit the four of them comfortably with an entire separate storage space for their belongings. The cart took them from Saford all the way to the headquarters of the Peacekeepers of Tarsi; a huge marble building with a wide staircase leading up to the entrance. Though he trusted Zeera—as much as he could trust a stranger—

Mathys found himself on high alert, his senses sharp and his heartbeat erratic. The way he always felt just before combat.

They walked up the stairs together, and a group of Tarsi carried their belongings into the building for them. Mathys was unarmed, his weapons and armour in one of the chests being carried for them. He was getting older now; in his mid sixties. Protecting Mara and Eliza without his Spectre gear would be difficult if something happened. If Zeera's promise of safety was legitimate, it shouldn't be an issue; but he still hated feeling like he couldn't protect them as well as he wanted to.

They entered the building, and Mathys found himself looking at everything at once. People were everywhere; some in restraints, some in uniforms, some looking inconspicuous. He had no idea who could be a danger, who might recognise him and send a message to Riffolk. But Zeera seemed at ease. They stopped in the middle of the lobby, and Zeera turned to them.

"I've been searching for the Heroes for decades now, and Mara is the first one to be found. Now, somehow, I find another one without even looking."

"What do you mean?" Mathys said.

"The Hero chosen by Amalus is in this lobby, right now. I feel his magic."

Mathys spotted him almost as soon as Zeera said something. A Shenza warrior stood in the lobby, facing the main entrance. He looked as guilty and conspicuous as it was possible to look without being covered in blood. He wore the shirtless tunic of the *Kaizeluun*, with the tattoos to match. Every instinct in Mathys' body screamed *fight, kill!* but he forced himself to approach without aggression. The *Kaizeluun* was so focused on looking everywhere but at him that he didn't see Mathys get close.

"How do you know us?" he said to the Shenza, keeping his voice as friendly and casual as he could.

The man stammered a response, and if not for Zeera telling Mathys he was chosen, Mathys would have assumed he was guilty of something serious. *He must just be nervous around Ermoori,* Mathys thought, *which is fair enough*. They exchanged a few words that didn't tell Mathys anything useful, and then Zeera showed up beside them. She told them to follow her, and they did. An uncomfortable, almost hostile silence stretched between Mathys and the *Kaizeluun* as they followed Zeera. She led them down corridors that all looked the same, until they reached a meeting room where she closed the door after them and locked it.

In the meeting room, Zeera spoke to them in more detail about the actual purpose of the Circle, and the role the Heroes would play. Mathys found himself wishing again that the Hero could be him instead of Mara; not out of ego or pride, but out of a desperate wish to keep her out of harm's way. Knowing there was no way to take her place made him feel utterly helpless; if she was forced to fight as Ermoor's Hero, what could he do to save her against the might of Sithares itself? The Hero of Sithares sounded like their biggest threat.

If they were to fight against him, they would need all the help they could get. Mathys, though not the Hero, could at least try to protect Mara in whatever battles were to come.

After the conversation with Zeera, which left Mathys feeling helpless, they were shown to their individual quarters. Mara and Eliza shared a room next to his. The *Kaizeluun* had a room closer to the corridor that led to the building's lobby. Several training rooms were set up along the corridor, and Mathys spent a lot of his time training Eliza and Mara. They were both skilled enough now that either one could have taken his place as the Spectre in Ermoor, if they still lived there. Mara wouldn't have been able to deal with real combat situations, but he'd started focusing her training on more stressful scenarios to try to help her deal with the anxiety she felt.

Eliza absolutely loved Azar, and the Circle. She kept training, even harder now that she had access to more trainers with different skills. It didn't take her long to pick up a lot of tips and tricks from the Tarsi trainers. She became friends with a few of them, and Mathys grew to love the Tarsi who befriended her; she'd never really had friends growing up because of Mathys' secrecy. Now he could finally relax a little knowing she was in a place where her safety was almost guaranteed. He took a while to let his guard down, and he didn't drop it entirely; but for the first time in over twenty years, Mathys was able to relax and focus on his own needs.

He kept training too, though his age meant he had to take it easier than he used to. The Tarsi trainers were immensely talented, and other than the Shenza, he'd fought against no other martial art before. Even then, most of his involvement on the north shore of Shanaken was long range; the Ermoori used guns far more often than swords, and Mathys was a Commander. He had to be alive to give orders, which meant remaining at the back of the battlefield, or at least behind a few lines of soldiers. He didn't particularly agree with staying back while his men died, but the men needed a Commander and he was a great strategist.

Besides, Mathys had been swapped from Battle Commander over to Commander of Security after a few years, which meant he stayed in Ermoor and kept the peace. It had allowed him more time to focus on the Spectre, but less time honing his combat skills. Still, he'd continued training, and he was glad now that he had. One of the Tarsi who trained with them, named Zalla, taught him more than he ever thought he would learn from another person since Krana had trained him to be the Spectre. After an intense round of sparring, they sat together and spoke.

"You are very talented, Mathys," she said.

"As are you."

"I can certainly see Krana's style in your technique. He was one of our best."

"He didn't train me for long before he disappeared," Mathys said, "but he taught me more than anyone else."

He missed the Tarsi man now, though he'd gone quite a while without ever thinking of him. It seemed wrong, and a heavy guilt settled into his stomach.

"He was a good man."

Zalla nodded in agreement. It didn't feel like enough, but at least it was true.

"Why do you think he didn't tell me what the Spectre really was?"

The question weighed heavily on him ever since Zeera first spoke to him about the Spectre's true role.

"We don't know. There's no more information about why or how he disappeared, either."

Mathys shook his head; it was certainly a mystery to him. Krana had always been quite secretive, even though he was eager to train and teach Mathys.

"Have any other Circle agents gone missing like that?"

"Never."

Mara

1793

Travelling back to Azar filled Mara with an overwhelming dread. All she could think of was the Ermoori soldiers they'd narrowly avoided when they first arrived, and then Riffolk's horrible face and cold laughter. But she was with Mathys and Eliza, and the Tarsi woman promised them safety. Mara didn't trust her, but Mathys seemed to, and she trusted Mathys. Eliza, on the other hand, couldn't have been more excited. They hadn't taken her to the districts, for fear of spies or Ermoori soldiers finding out that Mara had a daughter. She had no idea why anyone would be so excited to visit a big city; Mara loved Ermoor as a child, but ever since leaving, big cities had become evil and terrifying things.

Eliza did travel with Mathys to Berda every now and then, and whenever they returned she was always in a fantastic mood. Mara hated herself for taking away so much of Eliza's freedom; but at least she could go to Berda sometimes, and she was well taken care of at home. And now she would finally get to see Azar. As glad as she was that her daughter was seeing more of the world, she couldn't escape the fear grinding away at her insides.

When they arrived in Azar, Eliza leaped out of the cart, so excited she was close to jumping up and down on the building's stairs. Mara laughed, for the first time in a long time, and Eliza laughed too. For just a moment, Eliza looked like she was a child again. Her eyes were wide and bright, her mouth set in a huge grin, and she danced and twirled as she stared in every direction.

Mathys was the complete opposite; quiet, serious, and deadly. Sometimes he still intimidated Mara, but she found herself glad in that moment. She hoped others would be as intimidated by him as she was. Eliza finally calmed down when Mathys gestured to her to follow, and she saw the look on his face. They walked up the stairs together, and into the massive marble building.

Mara found herself withdrawing a lot in the Circle headquarters. Speaking to strangers terrified her, and Mathys and Eliza spent most of their time training. Mara trained as well, but not as often, and she returned to her room as quickly as possible afterwards. Azar felt strange and uncomfortable to her, as though she didn't belong.

Eliza, on the other hand, thrived in the Circle. She made friends with everyone she came across, and trained with as many people as she could. Mara forced herself to think about Eliza's happiness whenever she felt the need to leave. It helped; Eliza's happiness and safety were here biggest priority. Perhaps her *only* priority. Shortly after they all arrived, each member of the Circle was asked to show their abilities in front of the others. When Mara's turn came, she was terrified. She'd spent so long hiding that revealing her power felt wrong. She felt naked, more vulnerable than she'd ever been since Riffolk.

But after the targets in the room exploded into ash, Zeera smiled as warmly as anyone had ever smiled to her.

"Well done," the Tarsi woman said, "you're very powerful indeed."

For the first time since she first received the magic, Mara felt truly powerful. It always filled her with energy, but over the last twenty years it had become more a distraction from her nightmares than anything else. To have someone genuinely compliment her felt odd; but it filled her with giddy happiness. Eliza loved Zeera, and now Mara saw why.

One thing that kept her nervous and scared, however, was the Shenza man. Mara had spent her life terrified of the tree people of Shanaken. Reports and announcements on the teleradio condemned them every single day, and the priests spoke of their savagery in almost every sermon. Mara now knew how corrupt Ermoor truly was, but she still hadn't met one of them before joining the Circle. He made her hands shake and her heartbeat erratic. Mara found herself almost as terrified of him as she was of Riffolk.

Eventually, his gentle nature, and Eliza's enjoyment of his company, helped Mara relax a little around him. She still felt nervous, and she couldn't completely trust him; but with Mathys and Eliza both very capable warriors, she tried to let it go. Zeera and the other Tarsi went to great lengths to make everyone feel welcome in the Circle, and Mara tried her hardest to settle in. As long as Eliza was happy, Mara tried to be happy too.

Karak

1793

Almost twenty years passed, and other than Eirene Argyris passing away, they were uneventful and surprisingly peaceful. Kerberos had become a truly great leader, just as Karak always thought he would when he'd first trained Atillus Argyris. Omatus was thriving more than it had in centuries. The increased traffic from other countries and cities meant that Omatus was also becoming just as much a hub of multiculturalism as Tarsium.

A side effect of that was far more information coming in as well; Karak was beginning to hear rumours from the other countries, and even from within Omas. One such rumour was the newly self-titled queen of Theara; a warrior had apparently gathered most of the Thearan tribes who hadn't joined Kerberos, and had retaken their ancient home city. The large tribe, under the leadership of their new queen, had apparently started attacking the western cities, taking their supplies and bringing them back to Theara.

Karak had stopped visiting the arena entirely years ago, but he spent a lot of time roaming the city in disguise. He kept himself abreast of every rumour and story that passed through Omatus. No one suspected who he was, and when he disguised himself as Anamas, no one knew anything was out of the ordinary. He spent most days outside now, but in the mornings he would walk to the library as Anamas, and then sneak out again as someone else.

One night, as he returned to Anamas' chambers, he spotted a note on the small table where he ate his meals. In all the years he'd lived in Omatus, no one had ever written to him. A cold, prickling feeling spread through his stomach and into his chest as he approached the letter. As he read it, his throat tightened and his hands began shaking.

Karak

The Heroes are gathered.
Send Kerberos to Tarsium.
Tell him about the war.
If he can be convinced to
join us, he will be a powerful
ally. It could make all the
difference. When he comes
to us, take the book and bring it
here. It is unlikely he will join
us, and the book is our
biggest priority.

Zeera

The Circle had found him. *Why Zeera?* he thought, *and how could she possibly know where I am after so long?* Karak had more or less given up on Tarsium. Still, the letter was intriguing. *She must have been chosen as Hero.* Zeera made no promise about rejoining the Circle, but to give him such an important mission meant he may be accepted back into the organisation if he succeeded. Sithares couldn't be defeated without the book; all of the Circle's hopes were on Karak's shoulders.

If Zeera had asked him twenty years ago to send Kerberos to her, he would have written back to tell her he was a danger to all of Pandeia. But he'd turned Omatus into a thriving and powerful city, and he ruled better than any king or queen had in hundreds of years. *He's changed. He may still worship Sithares, and may still be the Hero of the God of Fire, but he is a great king.*

Appearing before Kerberos was risky; he had to make sure he didn't show up as a threat or the king would kill him without hesitation. He leapt down onto the rail of the king's balcony, then onto the balcony floor. Shifting was silent, and thankfully not painful, though it was uncomfortable. Karak was used to shifting silently, and took the shape of his own body behind the balcony door. When he was ready, he took a deep breath and stepped into the open doorway.

Kerberos sat on the foot of his bed, still and menacing. He didn't move when Karak stepped into view. Karak stayed where he was, waiting for Kerberos to speak or move first.

"Who are you?"

He approached Kerberos slowly, hands visible and open, and stopped several metres from him.

"I represent an organisation called the Circle of Shadows," Karak said, "and we need your help."

Zeera

1793

Zeera and Mathys spoke, at length, and her original feeling was correct; Mathys had spent time around Krana, was trained by him, and was now the Spectre of Ermoor. He clearly wasn't the Hero, but that only made the coincidence even more jarring. The Hero, she found out that night, was a woman named Mara. She was shy, quiet, and harmless; despite the powerful magic within her. But Asheilos confirmed that Mara was indeed the Hero of Taranos.

Mara and Mathys then introduced her to Mara's daughter, Eliza. The girl was even more powerful than Mara, as well as being far more confident; Zeera found herself wondering why Eliza wasn't the Hero. They spoke for a while and Mathys agreed that they would join the Circle. *Finally,* she thought, *I've found a Hero, and they're with us.* The relief she felt pushed her close to tears. Almost fifty years of searching endlessly; Mara wasn't exactly the Hero she would have chosen, but who was Zeera to question the decisions of the Gods? They travelled back to the headquarters at Azar. When they arrived, Asheilos spoke again.

He is here. The Hero of Amalus.

She was talking with Mathys, and stopped in the middle of the lobby; the Hero's magic pulsed from a *Kaizeluun* who stood awkwardly facing them across the room. Mathys approached first, and Zeera followed soon after. Mathys spoke to the man as though he'd been spying on them; he did have an unmistakably guilty expression, but Zeera diffused the situation and asked them to follow her. Leading the way to the back of the lobby, Zeera took them through the corridors into the actual headquarters of the Circle. The entire front half of the building was a public front, but even that was a mystery to most; the Peacekeepers of Tarsium, the organisation that enforced the zero violence policy in Tarsium.

They spoke as a group. Zeera explained the Circle to Lashek, and all of them seemed to understand the weight of the situation. She'd already spoken to Mathys, Mara, and Eliza, so it was only Lashek who had to be caught up. But they discussed Sithares and Heroes as well, things that the Ermoori didn't know. Once again, Zeera found herself feeling doubtful of her role as Hero; talking to the group didn't make her feel like a leader.

After the meeting, Zeera wrote a note to send to Omatus; it was time for Karak to prove himself to the Circle once again. He'd been exiled decades ago, but Zeera knew he was still in Omatus, and she didn't believe Tarat took his role seriously enough to be given the job she had in mind. Besides, she needed Karak to travel back to Azar, and Tarat was their scout in Omatus; he would have to stay there. If she knew Karak as well as she thought she did, he would be keen to help; if not for acceptance back in the Circle, at the very least for the chance to help save the world.

Folding the note, she gave it to a messenger; the Tarsi employed hundreds of messengers, whose sole job was to constantly travel between countries and cities, ferrying notes and information between Tarsi agents and scouts. She didn't envy them. They spent even less time settled in each place they visited than she did. Her favourite times were travelling between the cities she visited, but she would hate to move constantly as they did. Still, messengers were as important as scouts and agents, and Zeera was grateful for their work.

For the month or so after Zeera sent the note to Karak, the Circle members trained together, becoming closer to each other and to the Tarsi agents who trained with them as well. Zalla helped out a lot, training the Heroes to use their magic more effectively. Zeera had become very talented with Water Magic, but Zalla understood magic on a deeper level; she somehow understood the other types of magic well enough to teach the other Heroes the way she taught Zeera.

A month after her note, Kerberos showed up, and Zeera's hopes for her plan shot up; Karak followed her orders after all. Beyond that, Kerberos' appearance disturbed her more than she could say; when she looked at him, the magic within his body roiled and clashed like a horrendous storm. She saw Fire; but there was more, far more, and it terrified Zeera. It shouldn't have been possible. She tried to ignore it; asking him would be prying, and Zeera had a feeling Kerberos wouldn't have much patience for prying. They had a Hero from each country, with each type of magic; if the worse should happen, Zeera hoped it would be enough.

He settled in, and though a sense of tension built up between Kerberos and the others, he trained with them and spent time with them without causing trouble. Zeera had to admit, though; he made her nervous. Zeera decided to talk to him directly, as much as possible. If she could engage with him and create a connection, he might be more likely to turn and join the Circle. It was a desperate plan, but they had to try every single option; it was that or face certain destruction.

A few days after Kerberos arrived, Zeera invited him to the meeting room. She wanted to give him a little time to settle before she started talking with him properly. Kerberos didn’t seem fazed by anything. He was always in control, always reserved and perfectly calm. It unnerved Zeera.

"How are you finding it here, Kerberos?" she asked.

"I enjoy the training."

"Do you know why you're here?"

"Yes."

"How do you feel about the Circle?"

"I understand its purpose. Saving Pandeia, if necessary at all, is a noble pursuit."

"How do you feel about Sithares?"

He turned away for a moment, his eyes gazing at the wall. Underneath his stoicism, she saw a deep sadness. Somehow it chilled her spine.

"Sithares... My parents let me down," he said suddenly, "Sithares did not."

Her heart dropped into her stomach; he would remain loyal to his God. But she still saw some hope.

"If you had no intention of joining the Circle, why come here?"

"I cannot make a decision until I have considered every outcome. As devoted as I am to Sithares, my priority is Omatus. I am its king, and I will do whatever I deem is best for my city. If that means joining you and fighting Sithares, so be it. If it means destroying the Circle of Shadows... So be it."

They spoke a lot over the next two weeks. Zeera talked with him every chance she got; whenever he wasn't sparring with one of the other Heroes. Each conversation they had revealed a little more about Kerberos, and his past. He slowly opened up to her, and they even shared a few laughs. By the end of the two weeks, and despite his initial aggression, she felt as though Kerberos had swayed enough in favour of the Circle. Finally, she called a meeting with all of the Heroes, and asked Kerberos to choose between Sithares and the Circle.

He chose the Circle, and Zeera cheered inwardly, fighting to control her face enough to stop the grin that was trying to form. He left for Omatus, and Zeera felt that things might be okay after all. Zeera trained with Mathys again the next day. He'd improved drastically since fighting against Kerberos and Zalla; she would have thought an Ermoori man as old as him wouldn't learn new things well, but Mathys had a natural talent for combat.

Other than training, with Kerberos gone everyone settled into a quiet peace, and Zeera found it hard not to let the feeling overtake her too. Things were looking up for the Circle of Shadows. Even Zalla looked pleased with her; she said hello as they passed each other in the corridor, and offered to spar with her some time soon. It brought a warmth to her chest that she hadn't felt in a long time.

Lashek

1793

When he saw Mara's magical abilities for the first time, he couldn't think of a single thing to say. Zeera, the Tarsi woman who introduced them all, had set up training rooms full of people-shaped targets made of hay. They each took turns attacking targets in front of the others; Zeera said a good team had to know each other's strengths and weaknesses to understand how to fight a powerful enemy. His turn was first.

Lashek decapitated or dismembered every target in a few seconds, wrapping himself in Shadow and leaping across the room with each attack. He stepped back, and gestured for Mara to try. She stood in the centre of the room, blushing and looking intensely at the floor.

"Stay outside the doorway please," she whispered.

Then her eyes narrowed, her jaw clenched, and a flash of crackling yellow filled Lashek's vision, with a vicious, high pitched hum. When the room reappeared, there were no targets left. The room was empty but for Mara and some slowly drifting ashes in the air.

"Well done," Zeera said, her giant eyes twinkling almost as bright as the lightning they'd witnessed, "you're very powerful indeed."

She turned to Mathys, staring with a small smile as though he'd brought her attention to him.

"Mathys?" she gestured into the room.

"I'm not one of the chosen," he said, his voice just as pleasant as always, "is this not an exercise for members of the Circle?"

"But you are a member of the Circle, Mathys," she said, "the Circle has existed for thousands of years. In all that time, we've had but a few chosen Heroes in our ranks. You are as important as anyone here, and as powerful too."

Without responding, Mathys walked into the room, putting his hand on Mara's shoulder as she walked out.

"I don't use magic," he said, "so don't expect anything too amazing."

Zeera brought in new targets and set them up in the same places. Mathys stood in the centre of the room until she left again, still and calm. Lashek watched him carefully; every move, every second. He'd known from the start that Mathys was a dangerous man, and finding out he didn't even wield magic was intriguing. Zeera had even said he was as powerful as Mara and Lashek; in his mid sixties, and without magic, how could that be so?

Mathys stood still for a few seconds more, took a deep breath, and then began. Despite his age, he moved faster than most *Kaizeluun*. His style was vicious, deadly; each movement was precise and controlled, each attack designed to inflict maximum damage as quickly as possible. It was shockingly similar to the *Zuunshai*. Out of curiosity, Lashek drew his *Kaizuun*. As Mathys had said, there was no magic there. But his aura was vibrant and solid, radiating a strength of will Lashek could barely believe.

Mathys hit each of the targets hard enough to kill almost as quickly as Lashek had. If he hadn't seen it with his own eyes, he wouldn't have believed it. When he was done, Mathys resumed his calm, friendly demeanour as though nothing had happened.

"That was..." Lashek started to say, forgot the words, and then began again, "I've never seen any Ermoori fight like that."

Mathys chuckled, scratching his cheek absently.

"Well I've never seen another Ermoori fight like that either."

They trained together for a while, learning from each other. Mara and her daughter had been training with Mathys for quite a while already, and both of their skill in combat was frighteningly close to Mathys' own. Mara's daughter, Eliza, was a remarkable young woman. She was about twenty years old, and far more social than her mother. Where Mara seemed scared of everyone and everything, Eliza had no such fear. She even took a liking to Lashek.

Eliza hung around as the others trained, watching with her eyes almost as wide as Zeera's. She trained with Mathys and Mara, and very occasionally with Lashek and the Tarsi. She loved Lashek's *Katzuun*, and stared at the pitch black sword when he trained with it. Mara and Mathys were protective of her; he understood, but it still annoyed Lashek that they seemed constantly on guard whenever she was near him. They were supposed to be a team. Eliza was oblivious to Mathys' suspicion, however, and chatted happily to Lashek at every opportunity.

"Why is it black?" she asked one day, just after Lashek had finished an intense spar with Mathys.

"It's a long story," Lashek said, "but basically it's mixed with a black oil which gives it magical properties."

Though everyone in the Circle spoke Tarsi, Lashek was getting used to speaking Ermoori, and his vocabulary grew every day.

Strangely enough, he learned more by speaking with Eliza than Mathys and Mara combined. He trained with Mara several times. She was brilliant, but far too gentle, and terrified of actual battle. She was also too worried about hurting people, even during training. It infuriated Lashek, who like all Shenza, endured broken bones and countless other injuries as part of standard training.

Normally he wouldn't care if someone didn't want to be involved in battle. The Shenza, though among the deadliest warriors in Pandeia, were perhaps the most peaceful. They didn't seek battle, but were prepared to fight if needed. But what they were doing now was far more important than a wave of Ermoori soldiers on Shanaken's north shore; they were fighting for the entire world.

Mathys trained with him a few times as well, and they fought in almost complete silence. There was an intensity to those sparring sessions; a competitive edge that bordered on aggression. Lashek found it intoxicating. Mathys' style, technique, and strength more than made up for his lack of magic. His training with Mathys was by far the most useful to him, other than the Tarsi teaching him some secrets about the use of magic. His connection to Shadow Magic grew almost as much in the short time he trained with the Tarsi than it had in the years he'd lived in the forests of Shanaken.

Lashek spent any time he could dancing the *Zuunshai*; he hated people watching other than fellow Shenza, so he tried to find time to himself as much as possible. Other than that, the group trained together every day. The corridors and rooms at the back of the building in Azar were expansive, and organised into patterns based on the room's purpose; beds, kitchens, training rooms, and storage rooms. The room in which he'd first been introduced to the Circle of Shadows was technically a training room, though the others were better equipped. As such, it was used for meetings like the one they'd had when Lashek first arrived.

After a week, Zeera announced a visitor; another member of the Circle. Lashek went to the meeting room, expecting to find the hero chosen by Sithares. Instead, his heart stopped, and he dropped to a knee and lowered his head. He wouldn't have expected it in a hundred lifetimes; for the longest moment, the words wouldn't come. Finally, he was able to greet the visitor in the way he'd been taught since childhood.

"Welcome, oh great *Duulshen*," he said, "how may I serve?"

Karak

1793

Kerberos left almost immediately, after Karak told him about the Circle, packing only what he needed before striding from the room. Karak couldn't believe his luck; the son of Sithares had left the chest, with the book inside it, behind in his chambers. He ran to it, examining the lock. It was heavy; impossible to break. But any lock could be picked, and the Tarsi were the best in Pandeia when it came to picking locks. *But then what?* He thought as he stared at the lock, *I can't carry the book myself; I'll be burned to death.* The chest was far too heavy for him to carry as well.

Kerberos would be gone a while, if Zeera could fulfil her side of the mission. Even if she couldn't, the trip was long enough there and back that Karak had some time to plan and think. He stared at the chest, trying to think of some way he could move it or the book without drawing attention to himself. *And without burning myself to death with Sithares' fire,* he thought. Out of curiosity, he picked the lock. Inside the chest was solid black metal; Shenza steel.

The Shenza were famous blacksmiths, and the only people in Pandeia who could forge the black-bladed swords they wielded. But the metal itself was exported and used for other things; buildings in Tarsium, armour plating in Omas and Theara, as well as jewellery and keys. An idea sparked in Karak's mind, almost fully formed and startling in its clarity.

Blacksmiths weren't too common in Omatus; there were only three in the entire city. The biggest of them was dedicated to the royal guard and Omati military. The other two were far smaller, and struggled along by repairing any metal fixtures the citizens needed, and supplying mercenaries with armour and weapons.

The only problem was getting to the blacksmith; sneaking out of his chambers was just as difficult without Kerberos in the city. The king must have told the Argyris guards to keep a close eye on him, because they never left him alone. He could still sneak out, but there were a few times when the guards had randomly knocked on his door, and whenever he left the idea of them knocking and then entering his chambers while he was gone invaded his mind.

Karak entered one of the smaller businesses. Hammers beat against anvils in the next room, filling the entire shop with constant noise. Even one room over, the heat was intense, dry and suffocating. The master blacksmith walked in just after Karak did, wiping sweat off his forehead and muttering about one of the incompetent apprentices. He spotted Karak halfway through the room and gave a start, though it couldn't have been due to seeing a Tarsi; Karak had shifted to an Omati face and body. *He just wasn't expecting any customers,* Karak thought, *interesting.*

"Greetings, sir," the master blacksmith said, "What are you looking for today?"

"Do you have any Shenza steel?"

The master blacksmith's demeanour changed entirely. He stood straighter, his face serious, and properly looked at Karak for the first time.

"We may have a little," he said, "but that stuff's expensive."

"I'm willing to pay whatever you think is a fair price," Karak said, "to make what I need."

"And what is it that you need?"

Karak put a sheet of paper covered in drawings on the bench. The master blacksmith picked it up, glancing between Karak and the paper.

"I can make this. Five thousand, and I'll need at least a week."

Every day that passed with Kerberos gone added more weight to the writhing mass in Karak's stomach. Every day was another day Kerberos could reappear. Waiting for the blacksmith was the worst; he knew Kerberos wouldn't come back so early, but a small part of him expected to see the giant man show up at any moment. Each day, the guards outside his door knocked and checked in on him, always at random times. The day he spoke to the blacksmith, he returned to his chambers to aggressive knocking and shouts from behind the door.

"Master Anamas," a guard said, "Master Anamas, are you alright?"

Karak sprinted through the chambers to his bed and leapt under the covers, shifting from the cat body to Anamas'. He was still halfway through creating Anamas' face when the guards burst in. They approached the bed slowly. Karak knew without needing to poke his head above the sheet that their weapons were drawn.

"Master Anamas, why didn't you answer?"

He altered the spell just before attaching it to his face, turning his skin pale and sweaty. When he pulled the sheet down and looked at the guards, they pulled back in disgust, their weapons lowered.

"I'm not feeling very well," Karak said, "I need some rest and quiet, please."

They left immediately, resuming their post just outside his chambers. Karak breathed a sigh, scrubbing the spell off his face and shifting back into his own body. *That was too close.* He would feel much better on his way to Tarsium, with the book in his possession. Until then, avoiding trouble with the guards would take all of his concentration.

It would still be the better part of a week until the blacksmith would be finished, so Karak stayed in his chambers and continued pretending to be ill. The guards gave him a little space, but didn't stop knocking randomly each day. Every time he heard the booming thuds, his heart thundered in his chest until he yelled at them that he was still ill and still in his bed.

Eight days later, straight after the guards checked on him again, he shifted into a cat and leapt off the balcony. He hadn't left since he first spoke to the master blacksmith, and finally being outside again felt incredible. The cat body was nimble and fast, and he sprinted and jumped across the rooftops, free from the guards and unnoticed by the citizens below.

When he approached the blacksmith, he dropped into a side alley nearby and shifted into the same Omati form he'd originally used. This time, the master blacksmith was already at the bench and saw him enter.

"Hello again, stranger," he said with a warm smile, "your order is finished."

Relief flooded Karak's entire body with warmth. Some of the weight in his stomach lifted, and he returned the man's smile.

"Good to hear."

Karak put a bag of gold on the bench, noting the brief spark of greed and shock in the master blacksmith's eyes. *It really is a small business,* he thought as the man pulled a satchel from under the bench and placed it next to his gold. *But at least he didn't ask questions.* Karak took the satchel, opening it and peering in. It looked perfect. He wouldn't know for sure until he tried, but so far it met Karak's specifications perfectly.

"Thank you," he said, "this is exactly what I needed."

Mathys

1793

Lashek faced him, a look of fierce determination darkening his features. Mathys wore his Spectre gear, the armour more comforting than he'd expected. The *Kaizeluun* looked far younger than him, and his training and battle experience were far more recent; but the Spectre's armour added to Mathy's strength and agility. Lashek launched over Mathys' head, his blade dipping down at the height of his leap. Mathys dove away, throwing a small smoke pellet at the spot he knew Lashek would land.

He rolled to his feet and spun to face the *Kaizeluun*, pulling a gas-powered grappling hook from underneath his cloak and launching it at Lashek's right hand. It latched onto his blade and Mathys yanked it towards him, pulling Lashek forward several metres. Mathys used the momentum to leap towards Lashek, but the man was fast, and he turned his own momentum into a forward roll, slipping underneath Mathys.

They faced each other again, from the same positions they'd been in only moments before. The entire fight had been this way; they were perfectly matched, at least so far. Mathys knew Lashek hadn't used any Shadow Magic yet. Though he was a little tired already, Mathys was also holding back, and he hoped Lashek didn't notice. They fought on, and he saw sweat beading on Lashek's forehead just as it was on his own.

Finally, after another few exchanges, they called a stop to the session, and shook hands. He took off the Spectre mask as they sat on the bench and cooled off. Silence filled the room, but it was a comfortable silence, and Mathys let his mind wander.

"I've travelled Pandeia a bit," Lashek said eventually, "mostly Tarsium. I never once thought I'd end up training against an Ermoori without trying to kill him."

Mathys chuckled.

"I spent some time talking to other Shenza, in the countryside," he said, "and I've learned a lot about you. Your culture, I mean. I respect it."

"I wish I could say the same about the Ermoori."

They both laughed, and though a fierce competition still sat heavy between them, Mathys found himself enjoying Lashek's company.

The next day, Mathys trained with Zalla again. Before they started, she brought in a barrel of water, setting it against the wall. As she dragged it in slowly, he offered to help.

"No, it's easier than it looks for me," she said, "trust me."

Once the sparring started, he forgot about the barrel. Zalla moved so quickly, but there was always utter peace in her face as she fought. As though she was simply thinking about sparring, instead of actually fighting. She swiped at his neck, her fingers pointed straight like a spear head. He ducked, and she swung low with a kick at his ankles. He couldn't get out of the way fast enough, and his feet were swept out from under him. As he rolled to his feet, Mathys was suddenly washed with cold. He breathed in but water filled his lungs. Coughing, he tried to stand, but everything was moving; he felt as though he stood on the deck of a ship in the middle of a storm.

He couldn't see anything but a watery blur, couldn't hear anything but the water rushing around him and his own choking. The water pulled at him, and he felt himself go with it. Desperately, he drew a flash grenade from his belt with one hand and his grappling hook with the other. Throwing the grenade in the direction he was being pulled, Mathys pointed the grappling hook away and fired. It latched to something and he engaged the retraction control; he was yanked out of the water just as the grenade exploded behind him.

Mathys crashed against the wall, still blind and choking. He threw a smoke pellet nearby for cover and rubbed the water from his eyes.

"Very well done, Mathys," Zalla's voice carried softly through the ringing left by the flash grenade's explosion.

He stood, shaking and coughing, and settled into a combat stance again. Zalla laughed, her genuine good humour lightening the room.

"You really are tenacious. I've never seen a non-Tarsi your age fight like this."

Blinking the last of the water from his eyes, Mathys pulled another smoke pellet from the pouch on his belt, and readied the grappling hook again.

"As much as I enjoy your spirit, Mathys," Zalla said, "I think that's enough for now."

After the fight, they sat next to each other as Lashek and Mathys had done the day before. But where there was an unmistakeable tension between him and the *Kaizeluun*, Zalla emanated a sense of calm stillness. She stared at the wall as they sat quietly for a moment, her eyes unfocused. Her comment about his age came back to him, and he couldn't stop the question before it escaped him.

"How old are you, Zalla?"

She glanced at him and smiled, and the fear he'd felt for asking dissipated. In Ermoor, asking a woman her age was rude. It seemed the Tarsi didn't share the same attitude.

"I am two hundred and fifteen years old."

He was certain he misheard her. Frowning, he tried to work out what she'd said, but nothing matched in his mind.

"I'm sorry," he said, "you're *two hundred and fifteen years old*?"

She laughed again, and Mathys couldn't tell if she was joking.

"Yes, I am. Tarsi live for hundreds of years on average."

Hundreds of years. The idea was almost inconceivable. He couldn't imagine living so long, let alone still being as agile and strong as Zalla was at that age.

"Mathys..." Eliza peeked her head around the doorway of the training room.

"Eliza, what's wrong?" Mathys stood instantly, walking over to her.

"Nothing! Nothing." she giggled, shaking her head and blushing, "nothing is wrong, just mother and I are about to eat our midday meal with Zeera and Lashek, and she wanted to invite you too."

He glanced at Zalla, who nodded and gestured to the doorway.

"I have business to attend to," she said, "go and eat with the Heroes."

Lashek

1793

One of the *Duulshen* outside of Shanaken was almost unimaginable. Their name was well earned; they truly were the eldest warriors in Shanaken. The elder before Lashek looked to be well over a hundred years old. At this point, Lashek believed it was mostly magic keeping the man alive. He remained on his knee with his head bowed until the *Duulshen* returned his greeting and told him to stand.

"I am glad to see you, *Kaizeluun*," the *Duulshen* said, "we had not found the chosen of Amalus until word arrived from Tarsium."

They knew, all this time. Lashek only nodded.

"I'm glad to see you too, great *Duulshen*. With all due respect, though... why are you here?"

A dry, frail laugh escaped the old man in front of him.

"I am the *Duulshen* representative for the Circle of Shadows. I am here to help contain or destroy the book of Sithares."

The *Duulshen* were revered and obeyed without question in Shanaken, but Lashek hadn't seen them use much Shadow Magic directly. He'd heard stories of their immense power, however; and he hoped the stories were true.

"We will have the book here as quickly as we can, *Duulshen*," Zeera said, "in the meantime, you can make yourself comfortable in our private bed chambers and meditate in our garden rooms."

Garden rooms? Lashek thought, *why didn't they tell me about the garden rooms?* Zeera, as though reading his mind, glanced at him and gave him a wry smile.

"Yes, you can use our garden rooms too, Lashek, if you need somewhere private to practice your *Zuunshai*."

A few days after the *Duulshen* representative arrived, their visitor from Omatus finally appeared. Lashek walked to the meeting room, oddly anxious to see the person who might be corrupted by Sithares. He was a giant; at least seven feet tall, all muscle and silent fury. His bald head and bright white beard framed a pair of lethal golden eyes. Lashek had seen many Thearans when he lived in Tarsium, but Sithares' hero was something else. Something terrifying. He looked at each of them, weighing them, and then his eyes came to rest on Zeera as she finished introducing everyone. Tension filled the room; they were all ready for him to attack, and he knew it.

After they met, Zeera showed him the rest of the rooms, and they settled into another normal day of training. Lashek felt uncomfortable training in front of the man, whose name was Kerberos, but Zeera insisted, just as she had with the rest of them. After Kerberos watched everyone attack the hay targets, he stepped into the room. When he started moving, Lashek watched even more closely than he'd watched Mathys. Kerberos moved faster than should have been possible, especially for someone his size. He wielded Fire Magic with the ease and thoughtlessness of someone who'd done it his whole life.

But there was something off. It took all of Lashek's attention and focus to realise what it was. *He's holding back,* he thought, *he's moving insanely fast, but he can move even faster than this. He's hiding his true skill from the Circle.* As he had done with Mathys, Lashek drew his *Kaizuun*. Immediately, the room filled with an aura that terrified him; flame and magic thrashing and blending together in a controlled and conscious pulse. He'd never seen an aura so perfectly under the owner's control. And as well as Fire, Lashek clearly saw Shadows weaving through Kerberos' aura. A third energy, something as destructive and chaotic as Fire, crackled around him as well. Lashek couldn't breathe. Kerberos was already more powerful than all of the other Heroes combined. *I really hope Zeera's plan works,* he thought, *if this man attacks, I don't think we can win.*

A few more days passed, and Lashek became a little more used to Kerberos' presence. He always felt a little guarded around the giant man, but being in the same room stopped giving him a sense of immediate danger. They even talked a little bit. Kerberos' voice was oddly gentle, almost soothing. Lashek sat on one of the benches around the training room, resting after a sparring session with Mathys. The Ermoori man had left the room as soon as Kerberos entered, and Kerberos sat next to Lashek.

"I've known a few Shenza," he said, "but none who fight as well as you."

"I'm *Kaizeluun*," Lashek said, "we're a little different to the rest of the Shenza."

"More powerful with magic? You are far more powerful than the Shenza I knew."

"Yes, we have a strong connection to Shadow Magic," he said, "most Shenza don't use it. And we have the *Kaizuun*, which Shenza don't have."

He unsheathed his blade halfway, letting Kerberos see the runes carved into it. Kerberos' aura exploded around him; he still wasn't used to the perfect balance of brute power and total control.

"I knew one Shenza who carried a blade like this," Kerberos said.

"Dakesh." It wasn't a question; Lashek had suspected Kerberos might have known him.

The giant man raised his eyebrows, then brought them down again, narrowing his eyes.

"Yes. Did you know him?"

"I knew of him. Kerberos, the man Dakesh was wouldn't have done... what he did. Do you know what happened?"

He was silent for a long while, staring at the opposite wall. Lashek sheathed his blade, unable to stop a sigh of relief as the room settled down into calm quiet again.

"Sithares is a difficult God to serve. Fire needs to keep burning, and Sithares needs to keep destroying. All I ever wanted was to rule Omatus. My birthright. When I finally gained the crown, Sithares was not satisfied."

He paused, jaws clenched and eyes unfocused. Lashek waited as patiently as he could.

"With Omatus finally mine, I tried to create peace. Sithares was not happy. I realised after that that a lot of what I had done was terrible. At the time it felt justified, even necessary."

Kerberos finally looked directly at Lashek.

"Something happens when Sithares gets in your thoughts. It feels no different. You think all your ideas are your own, but they belong to Sithares. I think Dakesh went through what I did. Sithares was in his head."

Lashek hadn't expected much to come from the conversation, but the bare honesty Kerberos spoke with shocked him. Zeera had been having conversations with him in the meeting room, but they hadn't yet talked with him as a group. They were waiting for Zeera to call a group meeting; until then, things would go on as normal. They trained, and ate, and spoke together. Mathys wouldn't let Kerberos close to Mara or Eliza, and Lashek didn't blame them; even after the conversation they'd had, he still felt nervous around Kerberos.

After almost two weeks, Zeera finally stepped into the training room. Lashek and Kerberos were sparring. He was fighting harder than he'd ever fought in his life, and still he could see Kerberos was holding back.

"Lashek, Kerberos," Zeera said, her voice carrying over the sounds of combat filling the room, "could you please come into the meeting room?"

Kerberos stopped immediately, and Lashek sheathed his *Kaizuun*. They both followed Zeera into the meeting room. Mara, Mathys and Eliza were already waiting.

"Heroes of the circle," she said, "we are here to fulfil the purpose of the Circle of Shadows. The Circle has existed for thousands of years, but we are in new territory now. For the first time, we have a Hero chosen by Sithares in our ranks."

She gestured to Kerberos, who made no move to acknowledge her attention.

"The last time the war of the Gods ended, we locked Sithares away under Omatus. Magical defences were laid down, stronger than anything Pandeia had ever seen. But magic is not eternal, and gradually those defences weakened. Sithares is out again, intent on destroying Pandeia. We must destroy Sithares first."

"We're going to kill a God?" Lashek asked.

"If it's possible, yes."

"How exactly do we do that?"

"I told you already, Lashek. The book of Sithares must be destroyed."

She turned to Kerberos again, this time staring him straight in the eyes.

"To be made Hero, a person must read directly from a book of the Gods. You do have the book of Sithares, Kerberos?"

"I do. Not with me; it is still in Omatus."

"Wait a minute," Mara said, her voice barely a whisper, "I didn't see a book. Does that mean I'm not a Hero after all?"

She sounded almost hopeful, as though she desperately didn't want to be a Hero. He felt a stab of deep, aching pain within his chest as he looked at her in that moment. Zeera's brow furrowed; with such giant eyes, the look was comically exaggerated.

"You didn't read from the book of Taranos? Then you must have..."

Zeera trailed off. She glanced between Mara and Mathys, eyes widening until they took up half of her face.

"You saw the real Taranos. It touched you."

Mara squeaked, her cheeks flushing to a deep red as everyone in the room stared at her.

"How did you know that?" she whispered.

"It is the only other way someone can become a Hero," Zeera said, her voice breathless with wonder.

"But how did you know Kerberos has the book?" Lashek said, "I was given Amalus' book only long enough to read it. After that, it was taken back and hidden wherever Amalus keeps it."

"Because the book of Sithares was already in Omatus, and someone as intelligent as Kerberos wouldn't let the book go after realising its importance."

"So you have the book of Asheilos, then?" Kerberos asked.

"Of course," Zeera said, "hidden deep underneath this very building."

Kerberos nodded as though she'd simply told him where they kept the spare training targets. Zeera continued, steering the conversation back on track.

"Kerberos, we need the book of Sithares. We need it brought back here."

He nodded again. Silence filled the room, and Lashek began wondering what the next step would be when Zeera spoke again.

"Kerberos. You want to rule Omatus in peace. Sithares chose you to destroy. We have spoken at length over the past two weeks, and now it is time to make a decision. Will you fight for Sithares, or will you fight to save Pandeia?"

Kerberos

1793

His chambers were warm, and quiet, and Kerberos was enjoying the comfortable solitude after a morning spent in the arena. Late afternoon sun slanted into the room. Fifteen years had gone by since Kerberos visited Ermoor. Fifteen years of practising and training with the two new magic types he now wielded. He didn't have the benefit of the books to learn everything about Shadow Magic or Power Magic, so he had to teach himself. But he found he could apply a lot of what he'd learned about Fire Magic to them, at least enough to understand how magic was used generally.

The secret room in the royal library was still his, and he used it to train himself. He'd also kneeled in that room to recite the prayers out loud after returning from Ermoor. Each time, he was overcome by raw power and different sensations. Magic had a profound effect on the human body, and Kerberos was as fascinated as he was concerned; what if he was putting too much strain on his body? But he'd survived all three types of magic so far. He could even use more than one type simultaneously. Fire and lightning together were more powerful than the sum of their parts.

For the last fifteen years, as well as training himself to be as powerful as possible, Kerberos had focused on the Omati military. He used his Thearan warriors to train every able-bodied man and woman in Omatus, regardless of station. There had always been a royal guard and an army in Omatus, but for the first time in history, their soldiers outnumbered their civilians. They trained every day, and Kerberos had all three of the city's blacksmiths building armour and weapons for them. *If Riffolk wants Omatus,* he thought, *he will have to claim it over my dead body*. Riffolk was going to try to take all of Pandeia at some point. But all Kerberos had to do was stop him from taking Omatus. Eventually, Riffolk would die; magic itself didn't make a man immortal. Kerberos' immortality came from Sithares, a specific spell cast in return for the souls of his most loyal warriors.

In the two decades since he'd been made immortal, Kerberos hadn't aged at all. He never would. Kerberos and those of his tribe who were immortal couldn't die of natural causes. The only way they could possibly die was the Soul Blade gifted to Kerberos by Sithares; and Kerberos owned that himself. All he had to do was wait. Once Riffolk was dead, Kerberos could sweep in and take Riffolk's army, any cities he had by then, and all of Pandeia. He was a patient man, and he would wait.

As he sat alone in his chambers, ruminating on the coming war, a flicker caught his eye. A shadow, flitting across the floor in the pool of light streaming in from the open balcony door. It was brief, but enough to know someone was there.

"Who are you?" he said.

From behind the balcony door, a Tarsi approached slowly with his hands out. He stopped a respectful distance from Kerberos. *Is that the same Tarsi?* he thought, *the one who tried to attack me so long ago?* But it had been too long, and Kerberos hadn't paid much attention to the would-be assassin's face at the time.

"I represent an organisation called the Circle of Shadows," he said, "and we need your help."

"Why should I care what the Tarsi need?"

"The Circle isn't just Tarsi, it's made up of members from all over the world, and Pandeia is in danger."

"From Sithares."

"I... yes."

"So why should I betray my God for you?"

"I've watched you become a great king, Kerberos," he said, "you've turned Omatus into a beacon of civilisation. Sithares will see it burn to the ground, along with every city in Pandeia. If you don't do its bidding and destroy Omatus, it will find another way."

"How do you know? I have ruled Omatus for twenty years. Sithares has not asked me to destroy my city yet."

"It is Sithares' nature, and its purpose. Sooner or later, everything burns. I'm asking you as king, please protect your people."

"This Circle of yours," Kerberos said, "it knows about the history of the Gods? And magic?"

"Yes. Tarsium is the largest repository of knowledge in the world, and the Circle of Shadows knows even more than the rest of Pandeia ever will."

Kerberos only knew of Sithares what it wanted him to know. He hadn't heard its voice for a long time. *Maybe it has abandoned me entirely,* he thought, *to find someone else to destroy Omatus, and Pandeia.* The answer screamed in his mind before he'd even properly considered it; *Aella.* It made sense. She would want revenge, and she was powerful. Sithares could easily claw its way into her mind.

"If I join your Circle, would I have access to this knowledge?"

"I suppose so," the Tarsi said, "though that's not my decision to make."

"If I can find weaknesses, I could destroy Sithares myself."

"We already have a plan, Kerberos. If you join us, we can save Pandeia together."

"By destroying Sithares."

"If it's possible. Yes."

"And if it is not possible?"

"Then we trap Sithares, the way our ancestors did thousands of years ago."

"Surely that would take a huge amount of magic."

"Of course," the Tarsi nodded, "the Circle has brought together powerful Heroes from each country. The Gods are active again, and magic has returned in full."

"Including the Tarsi God?"

"Asheilos, yes."

If their book is in Tarsium, he thought, *I could gain another type of magic.*

"Tell me; what exactly is the Tarsi magic type?"

"Asheilos is the God of Water."

I wonder if Water Magic and Fire Magic together would be dangerous in the same person, he thought.

"And I assume the book is safely in Tarsium?"

"Yes. The Circle guards it every hour of the day and night."

"Good," he said, feigning a reassured smile, "the ruler of Ermoor is trying to steal the books. Spies have attempted to steal my book already, and no doubt more will come for yours."

"Well, there's no need to worry," the Tarsi said, "the book of Asheilos is safe with us."

For now, Kerberos thought.

A little while after their discussion, Kerberos arrived in Azar. The Tarsi told him where the Circle's headquarters were, and he headed straight there. *If I can destroy or trap Sithares,* he thought, *it might make Aella weaker*. Even if it took Fire Magic from him too, he still had Power Magic and Shadow Magic. It was a fair trade to eliminate Aella, and Sithares. Especially if his suspicion was correct, and Sithares had abandoned him.

If he could gain Water Magic as well, he'd still be as powerful as he was now; even more powerful if Sithares' magic stayed with him after the God's defeat. Riffolk was trying to do the same thing, but so far had only succeeded in obtaining two books. *If I can join this Circle,* he thought, *I may even be able to convince them to help me destroy Ermoor*. Ermoor posed a threat to all of Pandeia; it wouldn't be a stretch to convince the Circle, if they didn't already know.

He stayed in Azar for a little while, training with the Circle and pretending to be one of them. It wasn't difficult; to a certain extent, they shared several goals. Nomiki was left in charge of Omatus again. She handled everything perfectly the last time he left the city, and her loyalty was beyond question.

Zeera and Kerberos spoke many times while he was there. They spoke about Sithares, the history of the Gods, and the fate of Pandeia. She made a lot of good points, but the Circle had no plans beyond stopping Sithares; with all their power and influence, they could have led all of Pandeia into a new age of enlightenment. Instead, they chose to keep their hoarded knowledge for themselves. Other than possibly helping to stop Sithares, they presented no value to him whatsoever. It was clear to him that he would do far better in his journey without them.

Eventually, Zeera called a meeting between the Heroes. She presented an ultimatum; join in their efforts to destroy Sithares, or leave the Circle and remain loyal to Sithares. During the meeting, she let slip that the book of Asheilos was in an underground cave underneath the Circle's headquarters. *Time to take what I can,* he thought, *and leave the Circle to die.*

Karak

1793

He crouched in front of the chest, holding the black metal box like a fishing net ready to throw over a school of Luduk. Karak had never been fishing, but he'd watched the Shenza fishers enough to see the similarity in what he was doing. The padlock lay on the floor, and the chest's heavy lid was open. In the centre of the pitch black chest lay the book of Sithares, its fire burning in calm flickers of intense heat.

In one movement, he swept the box down into the chest, angled so it would collect the book without touching his skin. The box's edge caught on the corner of the book and nudged it against the back of the chest, flipping it up and almost touching his finger. Even without touching, it was so close that his skin seared. He fell back, dropping the box and crawling away. Sithares didn't punish him. The guards outside the royal chamber didn't hear anything.

Slowly, he crept back to the chest. He couldn't waste any time; he needed to leave Omatus with the book as soon as possible. Trying not to rush and burn himself again, Karak took the box and slid it carefully over the burning book. It fit, the book not quite as snug as he would have wanted; it rattled a little as he tipped the box up and closed the lid. He'd specified in his designs that the lid had to close and lock as securely as possible, and the blacksmith lived up to his promise.

Carrying the book would be impossible as a cat, so Karak threw it from the king's balcony up onto the palace roof. He shifted into the cat to leap up himself, then back into his own body to sprint over to the rear of the building. Behind the royal palace, on a rooftop, lay a basket full of hay and all of Karak's personal belongings in a large bag. As carefully as he could, he threw the satchel with the metal box down at the basket. It landed in the hay, but slid off and clattered to the rooftop.

Cursing, Karak shifted back into the cat and leapt down from balcony to balcony until he reached the ground. As fast as he could, he sprinted to the building and climbed onto the roof. No one was there yet, but he heard someone yelling about kids on the roof damaging his property. He shifted into the same generic Omati form he used to speak with the blacksmith and gathered his things, almost dropping the satchel again in his haste.

The person yelling scrambled onto the edge of the roof just as Karak climbed off the other side. They locked eyes for a moment and the man started screaming at him, red faced from fury and exertion. Karak dropped to the ground, landing in a heap and rushing to his feet again, his ankle screaming as he ran. He sprinted down half a dozen streets and alleys, then slowed to a walk; his ankle throbbed with every step.

Yelling continued behind him, but it grew distant as he walked. There weren't many citizens on this side of the city, but there were still plenty of streets and alleys. Karak changed his face again, into an old Omati man, and headed for the commoner's side of the city. Royal guards were everywhere, and Karak's heart sped up as they saw him; but he was an old, limping man carrying bags towards the commoner's side. They ignored him other than a gruff order to "move along, old man."

Royal guards were posted every twenty or thirty feet along the bridge that joined the two halves of the city. One stood on each side, facing in at the people crossing the bridge. Karak walked as slowly as he could bear down the bridge, his thudding heart demanding he get away from so many guards and his screaming ankle telling him to slow down even more.

"You there, old man," one of the guards said as Karak drew close, "what's in those bags?"

He stopped, breath trapped in his tightening lungs as the guard gestured for him to come close. He shuffled slowly towards the guard, stalling for time as his mind flooded with chaos.

"What would an old man be carrying all this stuff for?" the guard said, "don't you have a son to do this for you?"

Karak shook his head, keeping his eyes low. He stopped a couple of steps from the guard; if he absolutely had to run or fight, he wanted at least that minimal advantage.

"What's in the bags?"

Karak bowed his head, slumped his shoulders, and shook his head again. He needed to appear as pathetic and non threatening as possible.

"It's just some things I'm throwing away for master Cidoro," Karak said, "he said I could keep them if I wanted, just old clothes and things."

Cidoro Raptis was the eldest son of the most famous tailor in Omatus. The Raptis family was one of the noble families, and if Karak could convince the guards he was a slave, they might leave him alone.

"How do I know you didn't steal this stuff?" the guard said.

"If I'd stolen it, I would've been killed on the spot, sir," Karak said.

"True enough," the guard said with a careless chuckle, "but maybe I should go through the bags just to be sure you're not a thieving slave."

"Please, sir," Karak said, his voice wavering with not entirely pretend fear, "I just want to go home."

"Come here, old man."

"Please, I haven't done anything wrong."

The guard grabbed his shoulder roughly, pulling him close and laughing. He grabbed the large pack and yanked it hard, spinning Karak around until he toppled. His arm was still caught in the pack's shoulder strap, and he hung by his arm halfway off the floor of the bridge. A few more guards noticed and laughed at him. After a moment of unmoving humiliation, the guard finally let go of the pack. Karak slammed into the floor, scrambling back to his feet as quickly as he could.

"Alright, get out of here, slave," the guard said, still chuckling.

Karak continued shuffling down the bridge, his heart not slowing until well after he entered the street on the commoner's side.

Just outside of the northern entrance into Omatus was a stable full of camels. The animals were used to travel between Omatus and Tarsius for anyone too feeble to make the journey themselves, and anyone who couldn't afford the Ermoori self-drawn carriages that occasionally took on passengers. Karak hired a camel, and a guide, from the tavern on the other side of the wall to the stable where its business was conducted.

The Omati woman who was to be his guide was a little older than most of the other guides, but he immediately saw her experience on the road; she was weathered and strong, and had an easy confidence that spoke of years of travel.

"Let me have another drink before we head off," she said, "it's a long journey and the desert will make anyone thirsty."

Karak joined her, and they each had a mug of her favourite drink; a cold, golden Ermoori ale. Karak couldn’t remember feeling so refreshed in his life.

"Everyone around here loves the wine," she said, "and it isn't bad. But nothing soothes a parched tongue like a cold ale. My name's Tasia, by the way."

They spoke for a while, and ended up having another drink each before leaving the tavern. He smelled the ale on her breath even from a metre away as they talked in the stable; she'd obviously had quite a few drinks before Karak turned up.

"You'll take the one at the end," Tasia said, "I've got this one. You ever ridden a camel before?"

"No."

"Well, it isn't too hard. Mostly just sitting down and not falling off, really."

She showed Karak how to mount and ride, and they set off for Tarsius.

Mathys

1793

About a month after they arrived, the Hero of Sithares appeared before them. Mathys hadn't been as intimidated by another person in his life; not even Riffolk. Kerberos was gigantic, covered in muscle, exuding a palpable strength and power which made Mathys feel every minute of his sixty-seven years. On top of his considerable physical presence, a deep, terrifying intelligence lurked behind Kerberos' golden eyes.

Mathys felt old and frail standing next to such a man; never had the word Hero been so fitting. From everything Mathys had heard about Sithares and Fire Magic, he wouldn't trust the giant Thearan as far as he could throw him; but he trusted that Zeera and Zalla both knew what they were doing inviting him here. He pulled Mara and Eliza into their room shortly after Kerberos arrived, closing the door and speaking quietly.

"I don't trust Kerberos," he said, "I need you both to be very careful around him. Don't ever let him get too close, and don't stay in a room with him if no one else is there."

They both nodded, faces pale and eyes wide. Both of them looked on the verge of tears. Mathys hated scaring them like that, but he would see Kerberos as a threat until he proved his loyalty. He had to protect Mara and Eliza at any cost. If the Circle could convince Kerberos to join them and help them destroy Sithares, he would relax; but not before then.

In the days following Kerberos appearing, Mathys trained with him once. Though fighting against Lashek and Zalla was intense, sparring with Kerberos brought a whole new sense of danger. He felt like he was balanced on the edge of a cliff, and the slightest motion would mean the fall to his death. Fighting against Kerberos, even just for practice, he felt like a kitten fighting a lion. Mathys had been in deadly situations many times in his life, but Kerberos scared him more than anything else.

The worst part about their sparring was that even when Mathys pushed himself to his limits, he knew that Kerberos was barely trying. The man looked almost bored; a distance settled into his eyes as they fought, as though they'd rehearsed the same movements a thousand times and Kerberos was merely going through the motions. After the sparring session, Kerberos simply walked out of the room, leaving Mathys to catch his breath. *If we can't convince him to join us,* he thought, *we can't win. If we have to fight him, even all of us together, we'll lose*. Their only chance was possibly to find and destroy the book of Sithares before Kerberos could stop them, but Mathys had no idea how to do that. He decided to speak with Zeera about it.

"You don't think he'll join us?" she asked.

"No. You heard what Lashek said about the Shenza who was corrupted and became a traitor. Kerberos is far more dedicated to Sithares than a Shenza would be, he's the Hero after all. What's more, he's holding back. There's a lot he's not showing or telling us, and if he was really convinced to join us he wouldn't be so secretive."

She sat back, pondering. They were in her quarters, the door closed; they spoke in whispers.

"I understand, Mathys. But we need to give him space and privacy. If he feels like he's being pushed, he'll only push back. Manipulation is Sithares' tool, not ours."

"We need a more solid back-up plan," Mathys said. "We just can't leave it in Kerberos' hands like this. He's too dangerous."

"Our agent in Omatus is working on getting the book to us as we speak, Mathys. We don't leave things to chance."

Almost two weeks after Kerberos arrived, Zeera called a meeting. She asked Kerberos to choose between serving Sithares and saving the world; he picked the latter, but Mathys still couldn't relax. Something about the man just screamed danger in his mind. Kerberos left for Omatus shortly after, and as soon as he'd gone, the feeling of imminent threat almost disappeared.

For the next few days, things returned to normal, and they continued training together, waiting for Kerberos to return or for the agent to bring Sithares' book to them. Either one would take a while, so Mathys enjoyed the peace while he could; no matter how it turned out, when Kerberos returned, things would become difficult. They would either have to destroy the book, or fight the Hero of Sithares. He tried to remain hopeful, but he didn't think either option would end well.

Lashek

1793

I *choose Omatus,* Kerberos had said, *I choose Pandeia.* After the meeting he left, heading back to Omatus to retrieve the book. Mathys, Mara and Lashek filled their time by training, and things went back to normal while they waited. A sense of tension sat over the Circle for the next couple of days, however, and Lashek found himself spending most of his time thinking about Kerberos's return.

Halfway through a sparring session with Mara, an explosion rocked the training room. She squealed, toppling to the ground, and

Lashek stumbled and almost fell. Screams and shouts echoed down the corridors. A moment later, Mathys sprinted into the training room, straight to Mara's side. He wore a black cloak and armour, an array of weapons and gadgets holstered all over his body. Over his face was a terrifying, inhuman mask. Lashek still hadn't gotten used to the way Mathys looked in his combat gear.

"Are you okay?" he asked as he helped her to her feet.

She nodded, her lips trembling. Her hands shook violently, and her eyes glistened in the room's light.

"I'll see what's wrong," he said to her, "run to the garden rooms, they're private and much further back. Eliza is there already, she's safe."

He glanced over at Lashek as Mara ran from the room.

"Lashek, come with me."

He nodded and they ran towards the chaos together.

Fire and smoke smothered everything. A jagged hole was torn through the floor and roof, burnt and spewing thick smoke into the corridor. Tarsi guards and mercenaries from Theara and Shanaken fought the attacker, screaming as they died. In the middle of it all was Kerberos. Wreathed in flame, lightning, and shadow, he sliced effortlessly through everyone who attacked. Lashek could barely see through the fire and smoke, but there was no mistaking his giant frame. Lashek drew his *Kaizuun* and the battle changed. The blackness of the smoke opened to his eyes, the fire paled, and the auras of the people in the corridor leapt to life. It was still too chaotic to see clearly, but he at least could tell what was going on.

Mathys threw something at Kerberos and leapt in to meet him as he dodged. Lashek paused, terrified of battle for the first time in his life. With his armour and helmet on, Mathys somehow moved even faster than he had before. Exhaling in a sharp sigh, Lashek ran to engage Kerberos too. Out of nowhere a heavy spiked ball flew at his face, and he barely dodged in time. Mathys leapt over Kerberos, attacking from the other side of the corridor, but the giant man fought on.

The heat of the fire beat at Lashek's skin as he approached Kerberos. A spearhead swept at his face, and he blocked with his *Kaizuun* just in time. Another mercenary screamed and died. Lashek swept his blade up, sending a razor sharp shadow through the corridor at Kerberos' back, but it simply passed through Kerberos and sliced into one of the Tarsi guards on the other side. It was like trying to fight an actual raging fire.

The spear head streaked towards him again, and he ducked under it. Then barely a second later the spiked ball smashed his chest, throwing him against the wall. His *Kaizuun* flew from his hand, the smoke and fire taking over his vision once again. As the chaos around him continued, Lashek fought to get up off the ground. His chest felt heavy, as though he was trapped under a boulder. The air, already too full of smoke, didn't pull into his lungs when he tried to breathe.

Screaming and fighting faded into the background as Lashek tried desperately to breathe again. In the corner of his eye, he saw the blurred shape of his *Kaizuun*. He crawled towards it, reaching. Just before he touched the hilt, his mind faded into the smoke and the corridor disappeared.

Karak

1793

Tasia was great company, despite being a little grouchy when she sobered up. They rode down the wide, long path between Omatus and Tarsius and talked about everything Karak could think of. She told stories of her time as a mercenary, and the few years she lived in Azar. Karak pretended to be amazed by her descriptions, but other than that his reactions were all genuine; she was a very interesting woman.

The camels moved fairly slowly, but faster than Karak could have walked with his twisted ankle and heavy bags. It was the height of summer; the sun hung huge in the sky, burning everything in its sight, and black smoke drifted from the peak of Sitharkos in the distant west. Over a week after they left Omatus, Tarsius appeared on the horizon. A short while after that, they saw the distant faces of the Thearans camped outside Tarsius' walls. There was a lot of movement; they were packing up to head back into the deserts of Omas.

"Be careful," Tasia said, "the Thearans are most aggressive after visiting Tarsius. They've spent days or weeks cooped up without violence. When they finally leave, they're ready to fight or kill over nothing."

Karak didn't answer. There was nothing to say; nothing to do other than hope they didn't get in the way of any Thearan tribes. *If I was on my own*, he thought, *I could have shifted into a Thearan body, or even an animal*. But even as the idea occurred to him, he knew it wouldn't help; the Thearans killed their own as savagely as they killed outsiders, and they hunted and ate every kind of animal. Their culture was a true manifestation of the nature of Sithares; indiscriminate destruction and chaos.

As they rode, a group of travellers appeared on the road before them, heading towards Omatus. Karak cursed inwardly as soon as he saw them, and Tasia cursed out loud; it was a group of Thearan warriors. Not quite enough to make a full tribe, but more than enough to make him fear for his life. Tasia drew her sword as they approached.

Karak readied a defensive spell. He would only use it if absolutely necessary; but something told him it would be necessary very soon.

"Close enough, warriors," Tasia said.

Karak stayed as silent and inconspicuous as possible. He tried to convince himself Tasia had a handle on the situation; if she'd survived this long as a guide, she had to be able to get through gangs of Thearan warriors. They kept approaching, their weapons already drawn.

"I said close enough."

"The old one feels different," one of them said, ignoring Tasia, "you feel that magic?"

His heart stopped. Despite the heat of the road, his mouth flooded with cold, dry panic. *They can feel Sithares' presence,* he thought, *why didn't I realise that would happen?* There was no way out now; they would kill him for the book, and in the hands of the nomadic Thearans it wouldn't be seen by the Circle again. Tarsius was a fairly close ride by now. *I might make it if this camel can move*, he thought.

"The queen would give us anything we wanted if we gave her such magic," one of them said.

Without another moment of hesitation, he unleashed the defensive spell he'd been holding. A flash of blinding light exploded in the Thearans' faces, and a boom as loud as thunder filled their ears.

"Run!" he shouted at Tasia, and dug his heels into the camel's flanks.

With a grunt, it started sprinting down the road to Tarsius, picking up speed slowly at first. Tasia wasn't far behind; her instincts were good, her reflexes even better. Behind them, Karak heard the Thearans screaming and cursing at them. After a brief moment their footsteps thudded along the desert road; the effects of the defensive spell wore off quickly.

A spear slammed into the road beside Karak, and another flew just past Tasia's head. Tarsius was still too far away. He urged the camel on, his lungs burning. Tarsius' southern entrance appeared, and Karak saw the wall's details properly; thin cracks and ancient pockmarks in the Tarsi marble. They were getting close. He felt a thud vibrate through the camel's body and it toppled before he realised what happened. The desert road, bright and merciless, raced up to smash against his face.

The footsteps of the Thearan warriors pulled him back into consciousness. Pain exploded everywhere; his neck, ankle, back, arms, and head all throbbed in the heat of the desert sun. When they reached him, he could barely move. Laughing, they took the satchel, ignoring his larger bag. Then they roped up the now dead camel to drag it into the desert with them.

Tasia screamed, and Karak vaguely heard the clashing of metal on metal. A couple more screams, not Tasia but the Thearans she fought, echoed around him, and then the group ran off the road.

"For the queen!" they shouted, screaming and laughing as they faded into the bright desert sky. "For the queen!"

They headed west, towards the towering shape of Sitharkos in the distance. Tasia ran over to him, kneeling by his side.

"Are you alright?"

He tried to speak, and groaned instead.

"Good enough for now," she said, "Tarsius is close, and there's still a camel to carry you the rest of the way."

She hauled him up, ignoring his screams as agony ignited his entire body, and dumped him face down over the camel's back. He slipped into blackness as Tasia led the camel by foot into Tarsius.

Mathys

1793

A couple of days after Kerberos left, an explosion rocked Mathys' quarters, and he immediately pulled on his Spectre gear. He'd become used to putting the armour on within moments. He made sure Eliza was okay and told her to get to the garden rooms at the back of the building, then sprinted to the training room; he knew Mara was training with Lashek. She'd fallen, and he helped her up. Telling Mara to go to the garden rooms too, he rushed out into the corridor to see what had happened.

Mathys was so wary of Kerberos that he hadn't even considered threats from elsewhere. *I don't know the enemies of the Circle well enough to even begin to guess who's attacking,* he thought. The corridor ahead was torn open, as though one of the Gods themselves had smashed a giant fist through it. Smoke and fire whirled through the air, as chaotic as the battle itself. A lone figure stood just next to the jagged hole in the ground, surrounded by Tarsi guards and other Circle warriors; Kerberos.

Of course it's Kerberos, Mathys thought, *why did I doubt myself?* They trusted him so easily, as soon as he said he'd fight for Pandeia. Even Mathys relaxed after he left. But the man radiated danger like a wild animal, and Mathys was furious at himself for thinking they were safe. For believing Kerberos, even for a brief moment. As he watched, fear making him hesitate for the first time in his life, dozens of Circle warriors died. Mathys shouted wordless fury and forced himself to engage.

He threw a blade at Kerberos, and leapt at the giant man as he dodged. The Spectre's gloves were designed to inflict maximum damage; hardened, spiked knuckles made from the same black metal as the armour itself. His suit also increased his own strength significantly. Still, when he punched Kerberos as hard as he could, the man only grunted slightly and back-handed him into a wall. Mathys jumped to his feet again, and threw another knife; it hit home, in Kerberos' shoulder.

Mathys leapt over the giant man, attacking from the other side; he knew Lashek was behind him, as well as any other Circle members. A coordinated attack from every direction was their best chance. *If we even have a chance at all,* he thought. His throwing knife didn't seem to register with Kerberos. It didn't slow him down in the slightest. His body was entirely sheathed in flame, his movements unbelievably fast. *The fire must protect him.* He didn't know the first thing about Fire Magic, but it was clearly deadly.

A black blade streaked through the smoke of the corridor, and Mathys ducked; but it hit one of the Tarsi and disappeared. Mathys recognised it as a Shadow Magic attack. He thought Shadow Magic would be effective against fire, but the blade had passed through Kerberos with no apparent effect. Kerberos still faced Lashek, aiming a barrage of attacks at the *Kaizeluun*. Mathys kept throwing blades at him, but nothing stopped him.

On the other side of the corridor, Lashek caught an attack from Kerberos and slammed against the wall. His black sword fell to the ground and he fell after it, collapsing in a heap. Mathys pulled an explosive from his belt, pressed the button, and hurled it at the giant Thearan. It exploded on impact, forcing Kerberos to his knees, but the fire that resulted simply melted into his body harmlessly. The Tarsi near him focused their attacks on the kneeling giant, stabbing and cutting in a frenzy. Mathys leapt in as well, drawing a dagger from his boot sheath.

They kept their attacks up, and Mathys heard Kerberos grunt under the barrage of blades, boots and fists. For a moment, Mathys thought they had him. He stabbed the man's head, neck and shoulders over and over, hearing the grunts of pain as Kerberos faltered under them. But as he brought his dagger up for another attack, he saw the blade and faltered. It was melting. His gloves were fireproof, but he saw the warriors around him start to catch fire. They began screaming, and abandoned their attacks.

Kerberos roared, on his feet before Mathys realised. *He's so fast,* he thought, and didn't have time to think anything else. Kerberos grabbed his neck and lifted, still roaring, until Mathys dangled above the ground. Kerberos punched him viciously in the face, and even with the mask on, his vision burst into bright white explosions. It felt like being hit by a cart going full speed. He hit Mathys again and again, then tore the mask off his face.

"You think your pitiful little Circle can stop me?" he said.

He drew Mathys close, close enough that the fire covering Kerberos' face began burning Mathys' own.

"I'll burn you all to the ground. Nothing can stop the Fire."

He brought his fist back. Mathys couldn't move, could barely breathe. When Kerberos hit him again, the pain of the punch was lost under the pain of fire tearing through his skin. Another punch slammed into his head, and he tried to scream. Before he could make a sound, the fire rushed into his mouth, down his throat. He felt nothing after that. Nothing but fire reaching every part of him, spreading like a disease, eating him alive.

Mathys fought with everything he had, fought to stay alive. For Mara and Eliza. If he could get away, throw smoke pellets and grenades and get away somehow, he could survive. Mara and Eliza needed him. He would never let this monster near them, no matter what it took. He fought, but the fire spread quickly, burning everything it touched and touching everything. Even when he knew it was too late, Mathys fought it with every fibre of his being. He fought up until the second the fire took him.

Kerberos

1793

T*he tunnels are flooded.* Kerberos stared down into the entrance he'd found. *The Tarsi must be amphibious*. Faint, but powerful, he felt the book's magic calling to him. After agreeing to fight for the Circle, Kerberos laid low for a few days; they would lower their guard, thinking he really had gone back to Omatus. He had no idea how long he could hold his breath for; but he wasn't willing to find out if it wasn't long enough to get the book. Only one option made sense to him, and even that was a long shot. After a few deep breaths, Kerberos brought the Fire from his core to reach every part of him, spreading in seconds. The rush of energy and power still thrilled him. *I do not die in this form,* he thought, *nor receive any damage. Now to find out if I can go without breathing.*

Gritting his teeth, Kerberos jumped into the water. A rush of vicious bubbling and hissing surrounded him instantly. Through the boiling water, his Fire held. He felt no weaker, no closer to running out of magic than he would normally be. Smiling, he raced down the tunnel, grabbing at the walls and hauling himself forwards. The tunnels were mostly empty, but he did come across several Tarsi. He killed them quickly, sending slithers of razor sharp Shadow Magic through their heads and hearts simultaneously as he continued down the tunnels.

No alarms were raised. He reached the chamber where he knew the book was kept, and stared up at it. A sealed box sat in the very centre of the cave, chains stretching from each of its corners off into the black depths. Several Tarsi were posted around the cave, and all turned to look at him when he appeared. They held spears, and each had a dagger or two sheathed at their belts. Kerberos kicked off from the tunnel entrance, swimming as fast as he could towards the book. The guards sped towards him, their Tarsi bodies far better equipped to swim than Kerberos' bulk.

Kerberos launched a bubbling river of fire through the cave, which devoured two of the Tarsi as it snaked through the dark water. He stretched tendrils of Shadows Magic towards the book, hooking it and yanking himself forwards. As the last two Tarsi reached him, they stabbed with their spears. But the blades simply passed into his fiery flesh, ignored by Kerberos as he lashed out at them with Shadow and Fire. Razor sharp Shadow Magic blades severed the box from its chains, and Kerberos sped back down to the tunnel where he'd come from with the box under his arm.

Shadow Magic slipped through the water from his reaching hand, ripping into the tunnel walls and pulling him forwards faster than his hands alone could have. A large group of Tarsi appeared in the water before him. Instead of pausing, Kerberos merged a huge surge of lightning and fire together, angled upwards and unleashed it into the roof above him. A wide hole opened, through the top of the tunnel and the ceiling of the corridor above that. He reached above with Shadow Magic, hauling himself up into the corridor.

Another group of guards poured into the corridor seconds after he landed. Finally out of the water, he unfurled his Demon's Tail from his body. The corridor made it impossible to use the way he preferred, twirling it in deadly circles; but he could still throw the spiked ball and the spear head. And for such close quarters it would work wonders.

Lashek and Mathys both leapt out to meet him, and Kerberos grinned. He knew he would win, but they may give him at least some challenge. Mathys leapt over him to attack from behind, and Lashek stayed in front. For a moment, it looked to Kerberos as though they were coordinating their efforts; but after watching their movements it was clear they were fighting desperately without a plan. Mathys was the only one who presented a real threat, and he was the only one of the actual Circle with no magic. The broader organisation was full of non magic wielders, but the inner Circle, made up of Zeera and the Heroes, were the only ones worth fighting.

Kerberos killed everything that came near him. Fire, lightning and Shadow flew from him in deadly, unstoppable waves. Even holding the book under his arm, the fight was too easy. He caught Lashek with the spiked ball, smashing him against the wall, then turned his attention on Mathys. By then, most of the guards were dead or too injured to fight. Screams filled the corridor, feeding Kerberos' rage and blood-lust.

An explosion hit Kerberos high on the back, forcing him to his knees. He didn't feel any damage, but instead a surge of energy and strength. The surviving Tarsi guards ran in and attacked. A constant wave of blades stabbed into his head, neck and back. Though it didn't hurt, and wasn't wounding him, the discomfort was enough that for a moment he was overwhelmed. Cold metal jammed into his flesh, cutting and tearing. His body, covered by and filled with Fire, healed instantly in bursts of bright flame.

At least a full minute passed, until his attackers caught fire. He rose, facing Mathys again and grabbing him by the neck. To the man's credit, no fear brightened his eyes as he stared back at Kerberos. Only an unbending will shined from the greying Ermoori man. It didn't save him, however. Nothing would have. He watched Mathys struggle and fight against his fate, up until the moment Kerberos' Fire took his life.

He threw the corpse to the ground, reached up to the hole in the ceiling, and pulled himself out from the corridor. *Shadow Magic is even more useful than I realised,* he thought, *no wonder I was not impressed with Dakesh.* He'd discovered that Dakesh was merely a *Daishen*, not one of the Shadow Magicians called the *Kaizeluun*. When the Shenza hunter found Dakesh outside of Omatus all those years ago, Kerberos watched them fight. But the battle was short and anticlimactic, and Kerberos still hadn't been very impressed with Shadow Magic at the time.

On the roof of the huge building, Kerberos saw Azar stretch into the distance. Though smaller than Ermoor, it was still one of the largest cities in Pandeia; and he had to get out as quickly as possible. He smashed the box with his fist, imbuing it with all three Magic types; the box stood no chance. Inside it sat a large book bound in pure, shimmering water. He wrapped it in leather, tied it shut and tucked it into his belt under his cloak. Leaping off the roof, he brought the hood of his cloak up and ran through the streets of Azar.

Zeera

1793

Zeera was in the garden rooms with the *Duulshen* visitor when an explosion rocked the building. Eliza sprinted into the room shortly after, and Mara a few minutes after that.

Stay in this room. Do not leave for any reason until I say it is safe.

Asheilos' voice filled her mind, gentle but powerful. Zeera watched Mara rush to her daughter.

"What's happening?" Zeera asked.

"I don't know, Mathys just told me to get back here." Mara said.

"It's not Kerberos, is it?" Eliza said. "He scares me."

Zeera shook her head.

"I don't think so," she said, though deep down she knew it likely was him, "he joined the Circle. That means something."

They huddled together in the garden rooms, trying to focus on the sound of the water fountains as screams and fire raged outside the door. The Duulshen sat as still and expressionless as he'd been before the explosion; his eyes were closed, his breathing controlled and even. He was utterly unaffected. The attack didn't last long; but the chaos outside the garden rooms still felt like it went on for hours. Once the screams settled and the fountains again became the only sound in the garden rooms, Zeera stood, shaking.

It is safe now. Go, a Hero needs your help.

She ran, fearing the worst; Lashek and Mathys had both joined the fight. Losing either one would be a horrible blow to the Circle. In the corridor, thick black smoke filled the top third of the room. A few scattered screams pierced the silence. Further down, the corridor itself had been utterly destroyed.

Burned and burning corpses littered the floor everywhere, so many that she almost couldn't see the floor. Zeera had to step carefully to avoid them, her stomach churning. Despite the fact that she was too short to reach it, the smoke scratched against her throat as she breathed. A cloak and armour she recognised clung to a mass of scorched flesh. Zeera turned her head away and kept walking; forcing the well of sadness and fury that threatened to overtake her down deeper. Asheilos said a Hero needed her help, and she had to help Lashek first.

Tears ran down her cheeks, and she barely felt them through the smoke and heat and fear. Finally, on the other side of the huge hole in the corridor, she found Lashek. He lay crumpled against the wall, broken and semi-conscious. She cried his name out when she saw him, desperately hoping he wasn't too far gone already. Trying to comfort him with words that felt empty, she hauled him off the ground. Tarsi were stronger than they looked; but it was still an effort. Lashek tried to say something, mumbling incoherently as she carried him down the corridor. The only word she understood was Kerberos.

"Don't try to talk, Lashek. Just relax," she said.

Most of the quarters were undamaged. She brought Lashek to his own room, and placed him on the bed as gently as she could. Once he was settled, she rushed out and searched desperately for healers. Lashek was alive, but barely, and she didn't know how long he might survive without the attention of a healer. As she ran towards the lobby, a group of Tarsi appeared in the corridor ahead. They split up immediately, each rushing to the guards and mercenaries who still lived.

"Help!" Zeera screamed, and several heads turned in her direction, "one of the chosen is injured!"

Two of them ran to her without a moment's hesitation, and Zeera ran back to Lashek's quarters as they followed. Once she was sure they were doing all they could, she went back to the garden rooms. Every step was a terrible effort; the two people who loved Mathys most were in those rooms, and she would have to tell them he was dead. A crushing weight bore down on her as she approached the closed door. Mara and Eliza had no idea what they were about to hear, and it broke Zeera's heart all the more.

Her hand paused above the door handle. *How do I even tell them?* she thought. She remembered the pain she'd felt when Talas died; she still felt it even now. Making Mara and Eliza feel that same pain would hurt her just as much. *I can't. I can't do it.*

You are the Hero I chose. You will do it, even if it hurts.

The voice was tiny, barely there. Zeera gasped as the situation became clear all at once. *Kerberos stole the book of Asheilos.*

Yes.

Her heart thudded in her chest, painful and fast. In a moment, a single horrible moment, they'd lost so much. How could the Circle recover enough to win the war against Sithares now? What if Kerberos destroyed Asheilos? Zeera's mind raced, trying to plan around it, to come up with a way to win. *Kerberos attacked us at the place we were supposed to be safest,* she thought, *and fought Lashek, Mathys and the guards as though they were nothing.* Mathys' name brought her back to the moment, and she stared at the door handle. Forcing herself to open the door was one of the hardest things Zeera had ever done. When she entered the garden rooms, Eliza and Mara were holding each other, sitting on one of the wooden benches lining the soft grass walkway. The *Duulshen* still sat cross-legged on the ground, unmoving.

"What happened?" Eliza said.

Zeera sat next to them, staring at the nearest fountain as she tried to form the words. After a moment passed and she couldn't say it out loud, she started with the easier part.

"Kerberos attacked. He stole the book of Asheilos."

"He got away?" Eliza said, "What about Mathys? I bet he could've stopped Kerberos if they fought for real."

"Eliza... Mara. I'm so sorry, but..."

"No," Mara said, "no, no. No. He's not, don't say it, please don't say it."

"What?" Eliza said. "What are you talking about, Zeera?"

It's too late, she thought, *I have to tell them now. Mara already knows, she just needs to hear it.*

"I'm so, so sorry," Zeera said, "Mathys is dead."

She watched the healers care for Lashek, and she visited his quarters every day as he slowly recovered. Mara and Eliza withdrew to their own company, and Mara stopped talking altogether. Zeera had no idea what to do. It felt as though the Circle had shattered, broken into mangled shards that would never fit together again. Every day that passed felt like another failure, another missed chance to win the war against Sithares. Their hopes were pinned on Karak now, far more than they had been before. If he could bring the book of Sithares to the Circle, they may still be able to destroy it. All the Heroes were alive, they just had to wait for Lashek to recover.

A little while after the attack, a messenger ran into her quarters, not bothering to knock.

"Zeera," he said, "Karak is in Azar. At the docks now."

She dashed out of her quarters without hesitating. With the book, they had a chance. A good chance. Zeera sprinted out of the headquarters, shifting to a form that let her run as quickly as possible. Azar was a huge district, but Tarsi were adept at moving quickly through crowded places. She saw him heading towards the Circle headquarters, still close to the docks. *He's walking slowly,* she thought, *as though he's avoiding the conversation with me.* As soon as she thought it, a cold twisting wrenched her stomach; it hadn't even occurred to her that he may not have the book.

Zeera caught up with him, moving so fast she almost bowled him over. He gasped, and for a second he looked as though he was about to run from her. She grabbed his arm, and pulled him into the nearest tavern. Shoving him into a seat, she sat down opposite him and stared into his eyes. *There is something different about him*, she thought. It unsettled her; there was a sense of power, brutal and dangerous. *It must just be a side effect of his carrying the book of Sithares*.

"Do you have it?" She asked.

He sighed, his lips turned down in an almost child-like display of infuriated sadness.

"No. I was on the way to Tarsius with it, but we were intercepted by a gang of Thearans. They sensed its magic, and beat me close to death to steal it. They took it into the desert, saying it was for their queen."

Karak

1793

He woke up in a comfortable bed, but the pain took him immediately. Groaning, he tried to open his eyes; the light was soft and warm, but his vision still blurred.

"Alive, I knew it."

Tasia. She waited around to make sure I'm okay. The thought made the pain bearable for just a moment, and he tried to focus on her blurry form.

"So, you're a Tarsi. Didn't expect that, to be honest."

Shock brought the room into sharp focus, his pain utterly forgotten as he looked down at his body and hands; his shifted body must have dissolved while he was asleep. Most Tarsi could hold a new form through unconsciousness, even if they couldn't hold active magic spells. Usually Karak could too, but his body must have shifted back to his natural form so that it could put all its energy into healing.

"I... I'm sorry for deceiving you," he said, "I can't trust anyone right now."

She gave a dry smile, but genuine humour twinkled in her eyes.

"I don't care either way," she said, "I guess it was just too good a disguise."

Chuckling, she turned to leave.

"Wait, where are you going?"

"You paid to get to Tarsius. You're in Tarsius." She shrugged, looking over her shoulder at him as she reached the doorway. "As long as you aren't dead when you get here, I've done my job."

She left without another word, and Karak settled into an uncomfortable and painful wait; he had to heal as soon as possible.

He stayed in Tarsius for far longer than he wanted to. His body was damaged; his bones broken, his muscles bruised and torn. It was only a week, but every day was a day closer to Pandeia's destruction. He was in a Tarsi doctor's room, being given potions and spells at even intervals. He used his own magic too, and he healed much faster than a non Tarsi person would have. By the time he was well enough to walk, he knew he wouldn't find the book of Sithares again.

How can I fix this? he thought, trying to imagine what he could say to Zeera if he returned without the book. *At least I know where the Circle can start their search.* It wasn't much, and he knew Zeera wouldn't be happy to see him, but it was all he could do to try to make things right. Omatus wasn't an option for him any more, and he couldn't imagine living anywhere else.

He'd bet everything he had on the book, only to have it stolen by savage desert warriors. If only he could have fought properly; his ankle and his disguise meant that fighting would have achieved nothing but a quick death. Then again, Tasia wasn't very disturbed by his true form; if he'd used an offensive spell instead of the flash, and dropped his disguise to kill the Thearans... But wondering what could have been was a waste of time, and Karak had already wasted too much.

When he was finally healed enough to travel, he paid the doctors for their time, hauled his bags onto his back with a grunt, and walked to the docks. Ships travelled between Tarsius and Azar constantly, and Karak bought a small room on a passenger barge within an hour of arriving at the docks. Luckily, he didn't have to hide being Tarsi any more, so he could save his energy for carrying his bags. Once he was on the barge, he dumped them next to the bed and lay down, waiting for the journey to be over.

"You let Thearans take the book of Sithares."

It wasn't a question; Zeera's voice wasn't even raised. She'd come straight to him when he arrived, dragging him into a small tavern and staring at him until he confessed what happened. After he told her, she displayed no emotion whatsoever, and Karak couldn't stop his heartbeat from speeding up under her intense gaze.

"Yes. It was unavoidable."

"Don't give me that. It means nothing. You could have done something, anything. By Asheilos, that book is the difference between salvation and destruction for all of Pandeia."

Her voice remained even, but there was no mistaking the fury in her eyes; cold, hard, and pointed straight at Karak.

"We have lost, Karak."

His heart sped up even more; tingling swept across his skin and grew cold.

"Lost? Surely we can find the book again with more Circle members. If we can-"

"It's more than that. The book of Asheilos was stolen as well. Our base was attacked. Half of it is destroyed, and a lot of our agents are dead."

Kerberos. He knew without asking; he shouldn't have sent Sithares' Hero to the Circle.

"What can we do?"

"I don't know," she said, and the bright fury in her eyes softened enough to break his heart, "I don't think there's anything we can do."

"Are the Heroes still alive?"

"Yes. But one of them is a terrified woman who relied on her guardian, and he was killed."

"Well, at least we have them," he said, "and we know where to start looking for the book of Sithares."

"Karak, we can't win. Kerberos is simply too powerful, and with the book of Asheilos..."

She didn't say it out loud. She didn't need to. With another book, he would become immensely more powerful than he already was.

"Karak, I have reason to believe Kerberos already wields more than just Fire Magic."

"*What?*"

"I felt the magic within him when he showed up in Azar. There is more than Fire there."

Karak felt himself growing sick. Kerberos terrified him. He knew there was something more to the king than there seemed. He'd felt something more as well, though he hadn't truly thought about what it meant. All Tarsi could sense magic, but Karak wasn’t very sensitive to it other than its mere presence.

"What about the Guardians?" he said.

Zeera stared at him, her eyes open as wide as they could go. He couldn't remember the last time he'd thought of the Guardians of Austris Ara, but his mind was reaching for anything that might help.

"Is this a joke to you, Karak?"

"You know it's not."

"The Guardians haven't been seen since Sithares was last defeated. They may not even still exist."

"Isn't it worth trying?"

She threw her hands in the air, glancing up at the ceiling and shaking her head.

"Trying how? They've disappeared, Karak. How do we reach them? How do we even know they're not all dead?"

"There's only one way, Zeera. You should know it too. How were the Heroes gathered in ancient times, when all of Pandeia knew what it meant to be a Hero of the Gods?"

There was no trace of fury in Zeera's eyes as they settled on his again; only fear, and a spark of hope that made his spirits soar.

"The summoning spell..." Zeera looked away again, talking quietly as though Karak was no longer in the room, "that can only be done in Aethos. And we'll need the other Heroes with us."

"But we can do it, can't we?"

A faint smile pulled at her lips, and for the first time in decades she looked at him with real happiness.

"Yes, I believe we can."

Lashek

1793

He woke slowly, pain screaming from every part of his body. Smoke still covered the corridor's ceiling, though it streamed out through the hole above. The sound of fire crackling, and wounded warriors screaming or groaning, was all he could hear. He tried to stand, but the pain blinded him. His strength was gone.

"Lashek!" a voice cried from somewhere.

He felt hands on him, but his vision was as blurry as his mind, and he slipped into blackness again. Pain burned through him as whoever it was struggled to lift him off the ground. Not quite conscious, but aware enough to feel everything, all Lashek could do was wait for the pain to go down.

"I've got you, Lashek. You're safe now. Try to rest."

The voice drifted to him from another place, far away but still so clear. Pain made the words almost meaningless, and the voice unfamiliar. He might have screamed as they carried him, he wasn't sure. *Broken,* he thought, the word floating in his mind like the echoes of flashing lightning. *I'm broken.* Kerberos had thrown him away like a training dummy, effortlessly. He couldn't be stopped.

"Kerberos isn't dead, is he?" he said, but the words turned to mush in his mouth.

"Don't try to talk, Lashek. Just relax."

He could taste blood. Breathing hurt; everything hurt. Where was he? *I wish he'd killed me,* he thought, *or at least knocked me out for longer.* Unconsciousness wouldn't come, however, and Lashek found himself fighting the pain until he was placed onto a soft bed and given some bitter liquid. It burned his throat, all the way down to his stomach, and the burning washed everything else away until he finally stopped hurting.

The next time he woke, the pain wasn't quite as bad. He remembered where he was; there were no windows in the Circle's headquarters. Instead, the brightness of the lights could be controlled with switches on the wall. In the room where he lay, which he recognised as his own quarters, the lights were turned to a gentle, dim glow. Underneath him, the bed was soft and comfortable; though not enough to soften any of the pain.

"How are you feeling?"

Lashek jumped, then groaned as a fresh bolt of pain shot through him. Glancing in the voice's direction, he saw Zeera sitting in a small chair against the wall.

"I don't think I've ever been in this much pain before," he said, wincing as he spoke.

Zeera nodded, her giant eyes full of sympathy.

"If not for the extra strength your *Kaizuun* grants you, I think you would be dead."

"I feel like I *am* dead."

A small, sad smile pulled her mouth, and Lashek remembered the damage in the corridor, the chaos of the attack.

"How many people did he kill?" he asked, desperately not wanting to know but helpless to ask.

"He killed thirty four Circle members, and a considerable number of citizens in his escape afterwards."

Cold, lurching grief twisted his entire body, and his eyes stung as tears welled and fell. Even a few would have been too many. *Thirty four?* he thought, his tears falling freely, *and for what?*

"Why? Why did he attack?"

Zeera's eyes fell to the floor.

"He stole the book of Asheilos."

"What... what does that mean for us?"

She paused, staring hard at the floor. The silence pressed against him, and his heartbeat sped. Every moment that passed without her answer, his mind offered another worst case scenario. *We've lost,* he thought, *that's it. Sithares has won, and the Circle will be destroyed. Pandeia wil be destroyed.*

"It means Kerberos will be much more powerful. It means we need to destroy the book of Sithares as soon as possible, at any cost, or we all die."

Aella

1793

Over ten years after her mother appeared, Aella still ruled Theara as queen. Despite the resources they pulled in from the mountains, Aella ordered raids and attacks on the western cities as often as she could. Once a year, she took her entire army south to Sitharkos, to worship Sithares in the fire festival. From there, smaller groups of her warriors raided south of the mountains and travelled to Tarsius for more supplies, before returning to the festival. Aella stood near the edge of the plateau, looking southeast towards Omatus.

The smell of smoke and dust filled the air. Aella loved it; it filled her with a sense of power and strength. Being on Sitharkos boosted her Fire Magic more than anything else, and the fire festival was her favourite thing. Her mother stayed in Theara. Aella had named her second in command in her absence, and though Helene was far more gentle and kind than Aella, she trusted her to run the city well during the festival.

Two weeks after the festival began, one of the groups who travelled to Tarsius returned. Aella felt something when she saw them approach; she couldn't describe it, but their presence felt important somehow.

"My queen," one of them said, "we found something outside Tarsius. We thought you would want it."

Kneeling at her feet, he pulled a black metal box from his carry bag. He opened the lid, and held it for her to see. A large book lay inside, almost perfectly fitted to the size of the box. The book was bound in fire, burning constantly without need for fuel. Aella's breath caught, and for a moment she simply stared. Then she grasped the book, pulled it out of the box, and held it as carefully as she would have held a newborn baby.

I am home.

Sithares. She flipped the cover, and on the first page saw the words that lit her heart on fire:

Sithares: God of Fire

Yes. It is almost time. After the festival, you will march on Omatus.

The festival still had another two weeks at least. After that, Aella would finally see her wish fulfilled; the destruction of Kerberos. Omatus would be free of a tyrant, Aella would be free of her nightmares, and she could focus on serving Sithares properly. *It's so close,* she thought. Twenty years had passed since she died in the Alpheus. It felt like an eternity; but it also felt like a month. Time had blurred for her, in the same way that her memories blurred. Knowing that she could attack Kerberos as soon as the festival finished brought a whole new excitement for it; she always loved the festival, but now it felt like a real milestone.

Smiling, Aella turned to her army. Many of them stood watching the exchange, curious about what the warriors had brought their queen. She lifted the book above her head for all to see, and they cheered.

"Our time has finally come," she said, "after the festival, we march on Omatus!"

The cheers grew even louder, exploding from the entire army. Fights and contests were paused as all of her warriors joined their voices to the crowd. After the shouting died down, combat resumed with even more enthusiasm, and Aella watched the violence with a wide smile.

Two weeks later, Aella fought against three of her warriors in a contest. Battle was an integral part of the fire festival, and a tribe's leader was not excluded from taking part. To make things interesting, she always fought multiple opponents. It also meant more death for Sithares. Her warriors were devout followers and willingly fought their queen, though they knew it meant their death. Many died at the fire festival each year. But Theara also drew in new warriors so often that her army still grew. Almost every Thearan must have joined her by now. She wasn't sure about the mountain tribes, but the desert tribes were surely almost non existent now.

Aella leapt over a low sweep and kicked a warrior in the head before she landed. She rolled to her feet and swayed out of the way of a sword that would have opened her from neck to stomach. In moments like these, Aella missed her Fire Blades desperately. Her mother mentioned them shortly after appearing in Theara all those years ago, and Aella realised she hadn't remembered ever owning them until then. They must have been left behind in Omatus, picked up by one of Kerberos' warriors no doubt. He might even have taken them for his own weapons. The thought ignited Aella's fury, and she couldn't stop a wave of fire bursting from her.

It slammed into all three warriors, hurling them back into the grey sand and setting fire to their armour. They jumped to their feet, ignoring the fire; what was fire to a Thearan warrior? Snatching their weapons from the dirt, they sidestepped Aella until she was surrounded. Fire still coursed over her skin, and they watched her, taking slow, cautious steps as they circled.

All three moved in at once, attacking and screaming as they rushed in at her. Aella twirled around, a sword in each hand, blocking and evading everything they threw at her. She could have ended the fight in seconds, but it was the final battle of the festival, and Aella wanted to put on a show for her warriors. Sithares' favour would work wonders for morale, and that favour could only come with a violent and entertaining fight.

Aella continued twirling around the warriors, leaping and rolling. Occasionally, she sliced shallow cuts into their legs, arms, or torso. The screams and chants of her army echoed through her mind. She couldn't remember a single moment more powerful and vivid than fighting in front of her warriors, covered in Fire and filled with power. *Sithares has been good to me,* she thought. One of her opponents overextended their attack and Aella cut his arm off at the elbow. The other two pushed their attacks further, giving the third a chance to back away.

My army works together so well. One thing she remembered clearly about her life before Kerberos was that most Thearans fought without cooperation. They were brilliant and ruthless warriors, but they hadn't been great strategists since ancient times. The ancient Thearans were known across the world for being unbeatable. After they abandoned their city and wandered into the Omasi deserts, their fighting style became more aggressive and less organised. Aella had been working to reverse that from the day she'd taken Theara; and it worked.

The two uninjured warriors attacked from opposite sides, aiming for different areas to put her off balance. She couldn't be beaten so easily; leaping over one of them, she landed next to the dismembered warrior and cut his throat. Diving into a roll that brought her to the other side of the two surviving opponents, she cut through the calf of one and sliced into the other's back. They turned to face her, but by then she was back on her feet and ready.

Fire roared all over her, filling her with endless energy. The two warriors in front of her were sweating, injuries forcing their posture down. It would be an easy fight to win even for an unskilled warrior; there was no more fun to be had here. She killed them in a succession of blindingly fast cuts, hitting every weak point within her reach. When she finally stopped moving, they stood still for a moment. Then their cuts opened, and though they both tried to attack, they stumbled and fell as blood slid from them in waves of quiet red.

Cheers erupted from the crowd again, and a surge of Fire roared within her. The festival was done. As the two men died at her feet, she looked around at the rest of her army. They were ready. She was ready. Sithares wanted a war, and Aella wanted it too.

"It is time," she said.

Another cheer went up, and Aella let them enjoy it. When it quietened, she spoke again.

"The festival is over. At dawn, we march for Omatus!"

Epilogue

1793

In the secret room of the royal library, Kerberos finally took the book out of its leather wrapping. Unlike the books of Sithares and Taranos, this one didn't hurt him when he held it; though it felt strange in his hands, as if it was struggling to get away from him. The same way the Shadow Magic book had felt. In all his years of reading and researching the Gods, he'd never once read about someone wielding conflicting types of magic. Then again, Kerberos himself had done many things no one else could have achieved. He already wielded three magic types.

Breathing as evenly as he could, Kerberos flipped the cover over, his hands tingling where they touched the water that bound the book. He read as quickly as he could, stopping only when he reached the prayer. As he had three times before, he read the prayer over and over, committing it to memory. When he was sure he knew it, he sat cross-legged on the floor and repeated it aloud.

As he knew it would, magic and power flooded through his body the second he finished the prayer. For a terrifying moment, he felt the Fire that had coursed through his veins for almost fifty years leave him. He fell back, and water filled his lungs, spilling from his mouth and splashing over the floor of his chamber.

Just like the book of Sithares, when Fire Magic overwhelmed him for the first time, for a moment he thought he was about to die. Eventually he calmed down when he realised he could breathe through the water. When he stood, his knees shook a little, and his throat burned from the sudden rush of water. The floor was covered, as though someone had tipped an entire bath tub of water over. Warmth returned to his body, and he realised it was his Fire burning again.

A new kind of strength flowed through his body, as powerful as the Fire but much more calm. He'd been using Fire Magic for a long time now, and though Water Magic was new to him, he understood how it should work. Looking down at the spilled water on the floor, he raised his hand to it. At first, nothing happened. He focused, reaching out to the water and feeling its presence. Slowly, it began pooling towards him, drop by drop.

Holding out his hands, he focused once again. His body was attuned to magic now, perhaps more than anyone in the history of Pandeia. He pictured each element under his control, all the magic at his disposal, and focused them all to his hands. A small flame, flickering but powerful, sparked into life on his palm. Next to it, a tiny bolt of yellow lightning shuddered and crackled. A formless swath of pure darkness appeared next to that, roiling like smoke. Last of all, a perfect sphere of water formed, calm and quiet.

Kerberos stared at the magic, willing it to merge into one larger sphere that rotated just above his palm. *Pandeia,* he thought, as the world turned in his hand, *is mine*.

THE END

If you loved this book (or even if you didn’t), please leave a review on Amazon, Goodreads, or anywhere else that hosts reviews.

It really makes a huge difference to me being able to share my books with the world.

www.ingramcontent.com/pod-product-compliance
Lightning Source LLC
Chambersburg PA
CBHW020718310726
48979CB00004B/969

* 9 7 8 0 6 4 8 4 2 9 4 5 6 *